I0601411

KENNETH KAPPELMANN

The DEATH *of the* DRAGON

HIDDEN MAGIC VOLUME III

BLACK ROSE writing™

© 2017 by Kenneth Kappelmann
All rights reserved. No part of this book may be reproduced, stored in a retrieval system or transmitted in any form or by any means without the prior written permission of the publishers, except by a reviewer who may quote brief passages in a review to be printed in a newspaper, magazine or journal.

The final approval for this literary material is granted by the author.

Second printing

This is a work of fiction. Names, characters, businesses, places, events and incidents are either the products of the author's imagination or used in a fictitious manner. Any resemblance to actual persons, living or dead, or actual events is purely coincidental.

ISBN: 978-1-61296-846-9
PUBLISHED BY BLACK ROSE WRITING
www.blackrosewriting.com

Printed in the United States of America
Suggested retail price $19.95

The Death of the Dragon is printed in Adobe Caslon Pro

For Margaret Weis and Tracy Hickman,
Without whom this series would never have been written
For Katherine Sawyer,
A woman I never met,
But helped change the world from Topeka, Kansas.
"Do what's right. If you see something, go for it.
Don't let someone push you to the side.
Do what's right" (In reference to the
Brown versus Board of Education ruling;
May 17, 1954)

The DEATH of the DRAGON

The Return

"Schram, where do you think you are going?"

"I am just checking in with the scouting party that left this morning, Stepha. They are late, and I want to be certain the trouble they ran into several days back does not repeat itself."

"Madeiris can do that. He is already on his way as well." Stepha looked agitated that her husband of so many years was still resistant to allow anyone else to take the lead. "We have to prepare to head to the maneth homeland. Maldor is eager to see us, as well as Geoff, I am sure."

Schram smiled back at his wife. "I know, Stepha, but they will still be there if we leave a few moments later. I feel compelled to check."

Stepha shook her head, but inside she smiled at her husband. As she watched him dart through the trees with the grace of the most accomplished elf, she could not believe how much he had changed over the years. There were not as many elves now who remembered those days when he was in their wondrous tree city, captive as a kidnapped baby in an attempt to prevent a war. Stepha looked away. She felt the tears form as they did every time she had these thoughts—the thoughts of her father, King Hoangis, who died nearly two decades ago during the Slayne-driven dragon wars. She lifted her eyes just in time to see Schram vanish into the trees.

Stepha opened her large wings and stretched them out to the morning air. *He will be much more than a few moments*, she said to herself as she lifted in the air to head back to their home.

Schram used a simple spell to break the limbs from his path. He was able to move with a speed like no other with the benefit of his inner magic, which he had now fully come to understand. Over the last eighteen years, he had spent countless days and nights mastering that which he knew was within him. And now, in many ways as easy as taking a step, he could manipulate the world around him with just thought. Schram still held the same powerful build. Though below that of a maneth, he was probably the most developed human and easily the largest elf in all of Troyf. When one looked upon him, they usually saw what they wanted to see. When Stepha stared into his eyes, she saw nothing but elven being. When in Toopek, his people saw him as their human king. His hair remained long; something in him refused to have it cut. He kept it in a tight tail most of the time, but today it hung down in what Stepha called "warrior drag."

As Schram burst through the trees, his mind went to his last trek to find his human mother. Since the end of the dragon wars, he had traveled nearly all of Troyf with no sign of her presence. He did not even know if she was still alive, but he also knew he would not quit looking until he was certain, one way or the other. And even with the time that had passed, still buried deep within him were Slayne's—the evil black dragon that had plotted to take over all of Troyf by using the unborn young dragons as his puppets—final words: "My plans have not as yet turned full circle, and your destiny is not complete." What had the dragon meant, and how, with his death, was the dragon oppression not over? Those were the two questions Schram never let fade from his thoughts.

He reached a clearing, and in the distance, his elven ears heard a faint sound. He could not place it, but he instantly recognized that it should not be there. He was just at the edge of the Elvinott Forest enchantment, and based on the distance away, this sound was coming from outside its barrier. He stopped where he stood and listened. The sound was gone. In fact, all sound was gone. No birds, no animal's crackling steps along the leaf-covered forest bed—nothing. Schram twitched his long ears, drawing on any movement or break.

Just then, pain tightened along his lips as a hand reached around and gripped his head, placing its fingers across the human's mouth. The grip was tight, and Schram could not break it physically.

However, calmly, he began to incant a short spell that would easily render his attacker helpless.

"Relax, my brother," whispered a soft but still strong voice. "I only needed to ensure our meeting would create no sound."

The fingers loosened, and Schram turned to face the voice he already recognized. "Madeiris, damn you," he whispered. "There are only two beings on all of Troyf that can do that, but only one seems to take such great pleasure in it."

Madeiris was smiling but still motioning to keep all voices low. "I assume the other one is my sister."

He nodded appropriately. Madeiris leaned in. "I have already scouted ahead. There are five elven guards down. I cannot tell if they are alive or not, but there is a creature standing above them, a very large black creature, one the likes of which I have never seen before. Because of that, I was coming to get you."

Schram's jaw dropped. "What do you mean, 'creature'?"

"I mean something out of elven folklore. Two heads, scales like a dragon, but a body with characteristics similar to a canok or tigon. Its teeth are long and sharp, and its eyes are large and sit high on each head able to look all directions. I lived with my father's stories for my entire life until he passed, and never did he describe this creature." He paused, shaking his head softly, adding, "Do you know it?"

Schram turned his head, showing a lack of understanding no longer common to him. "I believe if there was one being on Troyf that knew every creature, it was your father, but the creature you describe, I carry no knowledge of its existence."

"Then please come with me. We must hurry should we have any chance to save our brothers. However, please run like an elf and not like a human. I would prefer to have our advance remain undetected." He was smiling broadly as he broke through the trees without even causing a leaf to rustle.

"Damn you, Madeiris," was all he heard in his wake. They arrived at the site to find the creature with both heads down, almost touching one of the elven guards' motionless face as he lay on his back in the clearing. Saliva dripped from one mouth as the other head seemed to be locked into some sort of bond with the elf, though it appeared this was not a joint bond but simply the creature drawing something from his subconscious.

Schram leaned forward and whispered to the elf king, "The guards are alive but unconscious. Magic holds them in that state, strong magic the source of which I cannot place. The creature is connected to the one guard. I do not know what for, but—"

Schram's voice ended, and the human magician grabbed both his ears and his eyes burned shut in pain. He fought to avoid making sounds to give away their presence, but he also knew it did not matter. The creature knew they were there. The pain in his head erupted, and the powerful magician doubled over on bent knees with both hands grabbing his head, as if trying to prevent it from exploding. Madeiris knelt down by his longtime friend, yelling his name above Schram's torturing screams of agony.

"Schram, what is it? What can I do?" Schram fell flat on his stomach, and then his cries of pain stopped, and all fell silent. Madeiris, still with his arms around the fallen human, looked up to see the creature had moved to stand only feet from their position. Schram did not move, but Madeiris saw he was breathing strongly.

The creature angled one head toward the elf king. "He and you live because I choose you to live. Now step away from him, or I shall choose that you do not live."

The elf did not step away and moved to stand between the creature and his fallen friend. The creature's eyes narrowed on Madeiris, sending a shiver down his back. Without a movement of its eyes, wings, or either head, the elf was thrown nearly twenty feet in the air to crash against the base of a large oak. "Do not test me, Madeiris. It would mean nothing to me to kill you."

The creature took a step toward Schram's body, and Madeiris gingerly pulled himself up, knocking an arrow as he moved. Pain erupted through his spine, and he felt and heard his back break, dropping him to the ground. The elf king was paralyzed, motionless on the ground, only able to move his head and eyes. To his anguish, he had fallen, so he could watch what took place before him but was powerless to do anything. The creature turned back to Schram and moved only inches from his head. Moments later, there was a flash of light, and the creature was gone.

Madeiris looked toward where Schram lay, and as his eyes

readjusted following the flash of light, he realized two things: his back was no longer broken, and Schram was no longer breathing. He leaped to his feet and ran to the motionless body of the magician. He turned him over and yelled his name. There was no response. Schram wore little armor, which made exposing his chest easy, and the elf king began to pound his chest directly across the human's heart. He did not know if the elven techniques would work on a human, but he also did not know for sure if Schram was still human on the inside. As he fought with what to do, Schram gasped hard and coughed.

"For all the gods, you are alive," shouted Madeiris.

"Aye," replied Schram with a long pause as he tried to regain his position. Softly he added, "And that was the most powerful creature I have ever encountered." Madeiris nodded and could see Schram was completely exhausted but did not speak as he raised his hand. In broken breath, Schram pointed and said, "Go to your guards. I am in no danger. See to them now before it is too late."

Without hesitation, Madeiris leaped to his feet and darted to the fallen guards. Two were moving slightly, and the rest remained motionless, but all were breathing.

Schram had made it to his feet and walked gingerly over to the group. "Are they all okay?"

"They are," replied Madeiris. "But they could have been killed. They were allowed to live."

"The creature was not after them. They were a necessary interaction, a means to an end, so to speak."

There was a pause. Most of the guards were stirring and trying to sit up. The elf king guided all of them to a small circle in the glade. When the commotion had subsided for what he deemed was enough time, Madeiris stared toward the group ending on the human. "I want to know everything that happened, including anything any of you know about that creature, starting with you, Schram."

He smiled but did not answer immediately, causing one of the guards, the one whom the creature stood directly over when they arrived, to break in with a comment, "All I know, my king, is that the creature could have killed me, but instead kept telling me to 'let

Schram know I am here.' He must have said it one hundred times."

Schram nodded inquisitively. "Interesting. The creature told me that today was not my day to die, but I would die by his hand, as the prophecy has said I would. He told me he could not kill me now because it would be too easy, and his mother swore that I must know the truth before I died."

Madeiris asked. "Who is his mother and what truth?"

"I do not know," Schram replied.

"Do you think it has something to do with your human mother?"

"I do not know. My bigger concern is why it was directed to me and why now and here? Also, who is the creature's father who swore this prophecy?"

"All good questions," added Madeiris. "Did anyone even learn what this creature is?"

All shook their heads except Schram. "I do not know what it is called, but I can tell you what it is." All eyes fell toward the human king. "It is a creature that wields powers stronger than any on Troyf, possibly even stronger than mine harnessed with the staff. My staff did not defend me or protect me from this creature's magic. This creature entered my mind and knows that which I know."

Schram's response dropped an ominous silence across the glade. None knew what to say or even if anything should be said. It was as if they had just been asked a question to which there was no answer. Schram was the one being each of them believed to be the strongest creature on Troyf, yet he was brought down as if he carried no powers. Each of them felt fear, and Schram could see it in their eyes. Schram, however, saw things more clearly than the others. What he saw was a powerful creature that did not wish him dead, or possibly more accurately, a creature that did not wish him dead *yet*. He did not believe any words of the prophecy. If the creature wanted him dead, he would be. That creature wanted Schram to know he was out there, and now the next play was his.

"We should continue to the maneth camp," stated Schram, breaking the silence. "You two guards, please return and notify Stepha of our intentions. Madeiris, you, I, and the remaining guards should meet with Geoff. We may need his help."

Madeiris nodded approval, though the guards followed Schram's words as easily as their king's. Madeiris did have some additional questions for Schram but held his tongue for now. He could see the human was deep in thought working through what took place. He had learned over the last twenty years that these were the times you did not interrupt him.

The two warrior kings did not delay their leave, and together they led the way through the trees. Schram remained in his elven form, though part of him longed to walk or fly as a dragon. He rarely had a desire to be one form or another, and he questioned why now he felt as such. Although he felt he had come to some level of understanding of the powers used against him previously, he still questioned how a creature so powerful had gone unknown for so long. He knew he would have to consult with Cameron and his dragon brothers in the near future, and that most likely meant another trip to the Black Pool.

"Are you able to speak now, my brother?" asked Madeiris, the calmness in his voice clearly showing he would be fine with whatever Schram answered.

"I am, but I fear I do not hold the answers you seek."

"I am sure you do not, but sometimes, just speaking out loud brings about some clarity previously not realized." The elven king had a natural ability to remain calm in all situations, a trait Schram admired of his longtime friend.

Schram nodded agreement and smiled. "My friend, I can only provide theories, and those theories are not based on any truths."

"Why don't we first talk about what we know?"

"Okay." Schram stopped his walk and faced the elf. "First, a creature we have never seen before with immense power completely disabled some of the strongest elven guard units without question, and used them as some sort of bait to lure me to this area to give me a message. A message that appears to only be—hey, look at me, I am a powerful creature you did not know existed, and I will, in time, bring about your death."

Madeiris smiled. "You always have a way with words, my friend. Do not be too broad with your summation. The creature told my elven guard to inform you of its existence. The creature then spoke directly to you. Nobody was in danger here. This was all simply a display, much like a male tigon gaining the attention of a female pride. It was simply a show." Madeiris leaned closer and his voice softened. "Now, the question is, think hard about what was said and what our next step should be."

Schram looked up with his eyes widening. "As with any potential conflict, the first step is to learn everything you can about your opposition."

"Right!" stated Madeiris, now seeming to like the direction the conversation was going. "Who might know this creature?"

"I only know of few who still live that may provide some knowledge. My dragon brothers at the Black Pool and possibly Khaled, the great physeter of the Toopekian Sea."

"What about the canoks?" asked Madeiris.

"Yes, they may hold some knowledge, but I believe they would have mentioned this creature to me before. Remember, I was essentially one of them for twenty years as I traveled with my friend." He paused and smiled a bit as he thought about Kirven. Madeiris saw that turn and gave him the time. Then, before Madeiris could interject, Schram continued, "Let's get to the maneth camp. We have some travel to plan."

Madeiris motioned to the elven guard who had now spread a great range across the forest on ground and air. They communicated instantly with their entire team, and in moments, the group was again moving forward.

Schram slapped Madeiris on the back. "Thank you, my brother. You can always keep me focused."

"You are the most powerful creature on all of Troyf, no matter what doubt you may carry. I do not keep you focused. Your mind is stronger than any who has ever lived. All I do is provide a venue for you to show it."

The two split hands and truly made an impressive site as they broke through the trees, tearing a path without making a sound. Schram stood taller than his elven counterpart, but the elf king was broad, as if the strongest oak had built his legs and arms. He carried armor fit for a king and wore it proud, as if every day he was showing his father, Hoangis, what he had become in his absence. Schram carried some armor, but little in comparison to any other warrior.

The thing he held most tightly was his staff. Although it was no longer the absolute source for his power, it still carried many secrets beneath its wooden shell.

"What? You thought you would leave without me?" shot a woman's voice from behind.

Instantly Schram's mind soothed. "Stepha, despite your ability to approach without warning, I am unbelievably glad to see you."

The two embraced, and Stepha shook out her wings with a smile that could stop the wind. "I heard what happened. I am sure your mind is troubled. I also am sure you are continuing to the maneth camp, which is why I opted to join. I have brought another flyer guard team to see to our safe travel."

Madeiris motioned to the flyers, and they joined in the field ahead. He turned back to Stepha. "Was Elvinott at all penetrated by this creature?"

"No," she replied. "Until the guards returned, we had no knowledge of the strange visitor."

Madeiris motioned to his sister with his eyes sending a message that Schram was well, but he still carried concern for him. She understood and broke the momentary silence. "I assume we should continue. We do not want to lose the light we have remaining. I brought some food as well. We can eat as we walk." Both men seemed to approve of the notion, and soon they were on their way.

Schram felt much calmer now, either by the additional time to absorb the situation or the presence of the one he loved like no other. Either way, he felt confident that although this new creature was an unknown and unexpected force potentially against them, he knew they were strong and united. Not like in the past. Since the days of Slayne's tyranny when all the creatures were divided, they were now as one.

MANETH

"But, Father, to lift that would be impossible without holding my club. You can't expect me to complete this task." The young maneth paused and then mumbled, "*You* could not even do it."

Maldor stared hard at his son. His eyes narrowed beneath his shiny maneth helm depicting him as the lead of the Batt Line. He pushed his arm out, placed it on his son's chest, and then effortlessly slid him aside. Maldor removed his giant maneth club with one hand and then knelt down with the other and slid his arm around the fallen tree. His muscles bulged large, even causing his shoulder armor to rub hard against the upper plate, creating a high-pitched sound of scraping steel. Maldor groaned slightly as the tree began to move. He lifted the trunk over toward the side of the glade, and using his club as leverage, tossed the tree to the side. He turned back to his son. "Lars, I did not want you to lift the tree. I wanted you to find a way to lift the tree. There is a difference."

Lars, his given name Ry-Larson Wayward, smiled. "Father, it looks to me like I did find a way to lift the tree." He paused then added, "It does not take much to get you to show off. Just a mumbled 'it is impossible' comment usually fires you right up. You told me I had to get that tree out of the glade." He paused, and his lips grew into a large smile. "I got the tree out of the glade without even using my club." The young maneth seemed overly pleased with himself by this point.

Maldor looked on with fire in his eyes. "You are definitely your mother's son, and I am now going to show you what I can do to you while holding my club in my hand."

He lunged at his son, and both took off at a full run. Despite their size, their speed was incredible. Maldor was starting to realize his son was catching up to him in ability, and chasing him now, he could only shake his head knowing he was not going to catch his boy, now eighteen years old and taller than his father. Although Lars had a human mother, other than his eyes, you would never know it—until you met him, that is.

16

Despite never knowing Krirtie, who gave her life during his birth, Lars's actions spoke that he had been around her his entire life. Maldor truly believed he was somehow connected to her because the similarities could not be naturally driven, the least of which was his ability to communicate and understand animals, in particular, bandicoots. He had seven of them that were with him nearly all the time. Even Fehr, when he came to visit, thought it was too many. In Fehr's words, "Always talking and telling stories. Annoying."

Maldor stopped near the center of the village, placed his hands on his knees and took some deep breaths.

"He got you again, didn't he, my friend?"

"Yes, Geoff, he did."

"The kid has spirit, that's for sure." Geoff, the king of the maneth, placed his hand on his friend's shoulder.

"That is one word for it," replied Maldor between breaths.

"Hey, Dad!" shouted a voice from the trees. "Thanks for moving that tree for me."

"Damn kid," Maldor mumbled under his repeated breaths.

The maneth king did not hold back his smile as he watched Maldor's emotions battle: love for his son intermixed with a father's frustrations. "Come, Maldor, I believe some of the elves will be here in the next few days. I would like to prepare a nice reception. Denisi just headed toward Elvinott to see to their timing and will attend their travel in support. Though the forests have not shown dangers of late, we have both seen some changes in the animals. I have always believed that changes do not happen without a cause. We should be cautious."

Maldor raised his head and saw Geoff's smile turn serious as he spoke, "I agree. Should we call the lines to order for a short conference? Perhaps others have felt and seen the signs."

"A good idea, my friend. Make it so as soon as you can get everyone together."

"I will." The two broke just as Lars came back into the glade, hoping he had given his father enough time to accept all that had occurred. Maldor motioned to him. "My son, I will get even, but now is not the time. I need your support. Come with me."

He recognized that his father was serious, and with that, he fell right in line at full attention to his father's direction, and the leader on the Batt Line.

"Please, send notice to all that we will be holding lines in one hour. Everyone is required to be present. Please, move in haste as it is on the king's order."

His son nodded, and without further comment, disappeared to deliver the message in person to all line elders.

Lines had not changed much in more than four hundred years for the maneth. Two rows sat facing each other with the highest-ranking individuals sitting closest to the head table near the king. In one row was the Dimat Line, which were the diplomats. Although they had shown over the years that they would support war, they always sided with avoidance. The other line, the Batt Line, where Maldor sat at the head and previously where Geoff had sat, were those prepared and ready for battle.

Horns signaled the start of the lines, and each of the two respected groups slowly made their way to their seats. Once a new batch of horns sounded, the king would enter walking between the lines. He would shake hands with everyone, speak to some, but greet everybody. He always stopped longest at Maldor. Their special relationship from the past still bonded them in ways beyond the reach of most.

Today was no different. Geoff and Maldor locked hands in a curled grip. Each of their arms was bent upward, and when they locked their hands tight, almost making a fist in front of each of their faces, it appeared as one of the most powerful sights imaginable. It always brought a hush to the lines.

Geoff proceeded to his seat, and when he raised his hands, the maneth along the lines and in the respective grounds nearby all roared as they sat. Geoff remained standing. "My friends, I know it is not customary to have lines this day, and usually these would only be required in great times of need, but I feel it is important we do not ignore the signs we have seen. As with any situation, to be prepared is the key. Therefore, I thank each of you for being here on such short notice."

With that, he took his seat, and all in the line became much more attentive. Although they had assumed there was a reason for calling lines out of turn, none of them had thought the subject would be tied to anything serious. Although Geoff was vague, the message in his tone was clear. Something was amiss.

Darse stood. He was an older maneth who had moved into the head of the Dimat Line following the death of Alhize, Maldor's father, during the dragon wars about twenty years ago. "King Geoff, I sense some tension in your voice. Are not the times better now than they have been since the Slayne-driven dragon wars? Our crops grow well. We have been party to no attacks. We have completed the rebuild of the human city of Toopek, and our relationships have never been stronger with the humans, elves, and dwarves. What has happened that brings this fear to you?"

Geoff nodded and looked across the lines following the question. Many of the maneth before him on both sides showed they held the same beliefs. "My friends, it is not fear that brings me before you today. Nor do I feel that, at this moment, we are in any danger. But nearly all of you were part of the line twenty years ago. For months before, we saw signs that we ignored. We did not speak about them until it was almost too late. At that time, one of our own highest elders had been turned to evil. I will never allow that to happen again. Therefore, these lines are called for one reason and one reason only: I want to know everything any of you have seen that is not as it should be, no matter how insignificant you believe it to be."

Several maneth shifted uncomfortably in their seats. Referencing the tragic situation where one of their highest elders, Selbee, joined with Slayne and murdered their king in an attempt to take over the leadership of the maneth, was simply a subject not discussed.

There was a long silence then, with a stir from those around. Maldor rose. "The animals have left the forests between here and Toopek. There are some, but for the most part, you will not see their presence."

"Good information, Maldor," replied the king. "Can anyone else confirm this or add additional information?"

With the ice broken, many in the group were able to add different things. All would be cast off as nothing by themselves, but it was clear in Geoff's eyes that, together, they had meaning. After he had asked several times for anything additional and there was no answer, signaling everyone with ideas had spoken, Darse again stood. "My fellow maneth, you have heard these words from everyone—and yes, some of them seem odd—but is there anything that is truly of concern? Animals migrate all the time for many reasons. Trees dying and extended times without rain also occur every year at some level. Everything I have heard today happens because they happen, not because of any evil force. Nobody has even seen any of those forces in twenty years. They have all fled to other parts of Troyf and will never return."

His words did bring about some smiles as much because it was what everyone wanted to hear and it was also the truth, if you chose to take that point of view.

Geoff began to reply but stopped when he heard a voice from the back. "What was that?" he asked. "Please, I said this was an open forum, so do not hold your voice. Please step forward and speak."

Maldor's eyes opened wide, and his mane seemed to twinge as Lars stepped forward. "I said I have heard of one of those evil forces in our woods as recently as three moons back."

Maldor now stood. "What! Why have you not spoken to me about this?"

Geoff raised his hand to his friend. "My friend, it is not so long ago you were the voice standing at the end of the line. Let's hear what your son has to say. Perhaps it is not as defined as his first words appear."

"It is not, my king. I have not personally seen them. However, one of my bandicoots was shot by one of their arrows. Only wounded, and he claims it was a very lucky shot, but he also stated it was a goblin that fired the shot. He was certain. I did not speak it because the source is the source. Bandicoots are not typically where you want to base your information. As I listen to everyone here though, I do think it is worth noting."

Geoff lifted his eyebrow. He stared at the young maneth who seemed to be sinking back into the woods as their eyes met. "Lars, you know these creatures better than any of us. This one, do you believe him?"

The young maneth smiled and removed an arrow from inside his armor. "I was not sure at first, but a short while ago, he gave me the arrow because it seemed like it was very important to him for me to believe him. I have never seen an arrow such as this, but if it were goblin, I assume some of you would recognize it."

All their eyes locked on the arrow he held before them. Maldor rose and walked toward his son. Taking the arrow in his hand, he carried it to his king. "Geoff, you know as well as I do that this arrow is goblin. There is no mistaking that."

Just then, shouts were heard from the maneth grouped well to the back of the lines. "Flyers returning in haste. It is Denisi."

Geoff lifted his head. "She should not be back yet," he stated softly. "What is going on here?"

The flyer elf dropped in the center of the camp with two additional guards at her back. Denisi was beautiful. Many said she rivaled Princess Stepha's beauty. Though Denisi was the most cunning female warrior ever to walk or fly on Troyf, she was one of the most gifted archers, and no man, woman, maneth, human, or elf would ever wish to take arms against her. She and Madeiris won the bow contests every year, and both could hit a spot the size of a small fruit from one thousand yards, but even Madeiris would admit she was better. Above all else, however, she was the queen of the maneth, joined with Geoff for the last seventeen years.

Geoff rose and hurried to her side. "Denisi, what is it that has brought you here so soon since your leave? Is there trouble?"

"There is," she said with deep breaths, providing evidence that she had been flying hard and fast to return so quickly. "We must speak, but what is going on here? Did you call lines?"

"Yes. As you know, I have had fears of some strange occurrences. I wanted to discuss these among all, and much have we learned. Is your information also for this audience?"

"I had not planned it as such, but it is probably the right decision."

Geoff took her arm in his as she continued to work to relax her wings after such a hard flight. Together, they walked back toward the group assembled before them. Maldor rose and hugged the queen as she approached. She had a special place in the large maneth's heart as, with Krirtie's death, she had filled a void for Lars, almost becoming his adopted mother, a title she did not seem to mind holding.

Geoff spoke, "Denisi has returned early and has flown with Shriak's grace to get here quickly. As most of you know, she had left to return to Elvinott to learn the timing of the elven leaders' visit, and to aid in their travels if warranted. She says she has critical information for the lines."

Geoff motioned to Denisi, who rose and stood before the maneths. She was a powerful and breathtaking sight with well-toned muscles and long flowing hair, which danced over her wings. She often found herself having to repeat comments because those with her became entranced with her beauty. However, this time, her voice was strong, and everyone heard her words. She described in detail that she had met with the elven party that was already on its way and then replayed the troubles they had experienced, ending on the creature they met in the forest. Stepha had suggested that Denisi return ahead of them to prepare for their arrival and speak to the king about the situation. When she finished, the silence that ensued was deafening.

Geoff turned back to the group. "I believe we now can all agree that there is more than droughts and animal migrations at hand. I am not suggesting any action at this time, for we are only now beginning to learn that there is something amiss. I want each of you to think about all we have discussed here this day and provide feedback to your elders. They will, in turn, speak to me when the elven party arrives. King Schram and King Madeiris will meet with my heads, and we will decide our plans. Are there any that do not agree?" The large king of the maneth turned his eyes briefly to Darse and, seeing no response, nodded slightly before continuing, "Very well, let it be so. Now return to your homes and let's be sure to welcome the elven party to our village. The times indeed grow grave, and we will not stand by and let evil grow."

DIRECTION

"You all look well," stated Geoff as he greeted his longtime friends. He shook hands with each but gave Stepha the customary deep hug. Madeiris and Geoff wrapped their arms a certain way, which spoke of the indescribable bond between warriors.

Schram stepped forward. "You look well also, my friend. I am sorry we must meet under such circumstances, and I am pleased to see Denisi made it to you safely. So, I assume you have more questions."

"That I do," replied the maneth king. "But let's hold these questions until you have gotten settled. We have arranged for meals to be set in my private chambers, but please take a moment to rest and strengthen your tired legs and wings."

The group each moved to their respective tents, which were actually magnificent structures made completely of materials from the forests. Yet, even as their size was great, they blended to the land as if they grew directly from it. Schram and Stepha were pleased to have a few moments of quiet between them. The elf princess was concerned for her husband, who had been lost deep in thought almost since their trek from the creature to the maneth camp had commenced.

She placed her soft hand on his shoulder. "Schram, will it help to speak to me and bring your thoughts together?"

"I don't know, Stepha. Each time I roll the events over in my mind, I still come back to what that creature was, why it wanted me to know it existed, why I never felt its presence before, and what is significant about today that brought it from its hiding?"

Stepha ran her hands through her husband's long hair, which now hung free from his traditional ponytail. "These are all good questions. Should seeking their answers be your first goal, or do you simply try to find the creature again?"

The warrior looked stunned. "I did not consider going after the creature. Since I do not know where it lives or even where it went, that trek would prove difficult to justify. Further, I am still more concerned with the *why* versus the *where*. Why did it seek me out? Why does it claim a prophecy that includes my death, and why would it act as such when clearly it is more powerful than I?"

Stepha frowned slightly at his talk of death, a subject very sacred to elves. However, she could see the struggle within him and let it pass. Softly she said, "Even more questions? It has been a long time since I have seen you this troubled. Perhaps there is something I can share with you that will make you feel better."

The human looked up to his beautiful princess and felt sorry for burdening her with his confused feelings. "Just being next to you is my antidote. Your presence makes me better."

Stepha smiled and whispered, "But I have something that will eclipse even that, my husband."

Schram returned her smile and asked, "What secret do you keep this day?"

She reached for his hands and took them in hers. In a soft voice that carried a tone he had never heard from her lips before, she said, "Soon there will be more than just me to keep you company." Schram's eyes grew wide, and a tear formed in one as he stared deep into her large green elven eyes. Her head was shaking slowly up and down to confirm that he was understanding her message.

"A child? We are having a child?"

"We are, my love. I wanted to tell you when we woke up, but you were already gone. Then, with the creature and everything else, the time never provided itself. Now, however, I could wait no longer."

He grabbed his wife and held her tight. "For so long, I have dreamed of this. For so long, I have believed it could not happen. We were from two different lives, and it simply would not work. I love you, Stephanatilantilis. I love you with all my heart."

"And I you, Schramilis. And I you," she whispered as they held their embrace.

***

Geoff stared at the human magician as he approached. "What in all of Troyf is that stare for? You look like you just sat on a dragon's tail, spines up."

Schram's glossy stare did not even flinch or change with the reference. He simply smiled at the maneth, who stood about eight inches taller than him and replied, "Ask me again sometime. Today is not the day for it. Just know I have a great reason to fight for our world again, a great reason."

The maneth tilted his head a bit but did not pursue the conversation further. Since Schram and Stepha were the last two to join the gathering of leaders, it was time to organize everyone and begin their discussion. The proceedings were not nearly as formal as the lines, and the group simply sat around the table, each with food before them if they desired, but taking some was not expected or required.

Geoff rose and spoke to the small group, "Friends, we are here today because once again, fate has brought us together. I do not know if the troubles of the past are back to again greet us with their evil ways, or some new force will bring its wrath upon us. Whichever, the purpose today is to decide what steps we should take to defend ourselves and our country. The table is open. There are no rules or formal proceedings to follow, so please, simply speak your thoughts."

Eyes darted around with each person not knowing who would speak first. In the room sat all the leaders of the maneth—Geoff, Maldor, Darse—and Denisi sat next to her husband. Across the table were the elves, Madeiris and Stepha, and with them was Schram. The human was the first to speak as most eyes ended on him.

"I am struggling with what might occur. This creature brings with it several mysteries. Further, this creature was strong, very strong with magic. I do not know if it was acting on its own, or if it was sent, but regardless, finding that answer must be paramount for us."

They all nodded, and Maldor added, "We must also get word to the dwarves and humans. They must be prepared as well."

"Very good point," added Geoff. "Toopek, Antaag, and Feldschlosschen must be warned."

Going back to Schram's comment, Denisi asked, "Schram, how will you discover the answer to the origin of the creature? Who would know, or where would you go?"

The human's eyes sank. "I am not sure. I believe the dragons at the Black Pool—my brothers—would be able to provide some insight. Also, possibly the physeter, as they seem to know more about Troyf than any creature." He paused then added, "And maybe the canoks."

Maldor leaned toward his longtime friend. "Have things gotten better with your old friends? We have seen none in more time than we could easily measure."

Schram shook his head and replied, "For that, I have no answer. I too have been unable to contact our old friends."

"Perhaps that in itself is another sign," added Madeiris. "The canok owe you everything in their eyes. You brought them back together. You gave them their sun, their color. They swore allegiance during the oppression and to simply end that without word…something is amiss. We should attempt to contact them, under the same guidance as the dwarves and humans, but we need to know if they are with us. Their powers are significant when on our side but potentially insurmountable if not."

Schram did not like the discussion about canoks and references to being part of whatever was happening. He trusted them as much as he trusted any creatures on Troyf. They have been treated worse than nearly any race, yet they never relented; and in the end, they were a significant factor in the defeat of Slayne. Maldor caught his friend's discomfort but let his words stand as spoken.

After a short pause, Schram added, "Then we really have several fronts to take action. We must notify the dwarves and humans. They are opposite directions, so that is two separate parties. We have also offered possible options such as the Black Pool, the canok homeland, and reaching out to the physeter in the oceans. Well, the Black Pool and the canok homeland are limited to me. They are different directions, so we must choose which would bring the most critical information, and that should be my first goal. As for the dwarves, my path could go directly through Feldschlosschen should I head to the Black Pool. I could make that my requirement also. Whoever goes to Toopek would be able to reach out to the physeter. It is no guarantee they will come, but my gut tells me they will."

Stepha replied, "Schram, only you know which would be more valuable, the canoks or the dragons. The creature was for you. The message was for you. What do you feel about that?"

"My gut tells me the dragons will know more about this creature, but finding out what has happened to the canoks may be more pertinent in the immediate future."

Geoff rose and held his club high, bringing all eyes to him and silence to the room. "I propose this. Maldor, Denisi, and I will head to Toopek. We were due a visit with Alan anyway, so we will use this as that duty. While there, we will speak to his army about what they have seen. I know he has regular patrols in the forests surrounding Toopek, so maybe he has seen signs of the old dragon armies or this creature. Then, you"—motioning to Schram—"take a team to Feldschlosschen. Once there, you can let the dwarves pass word to Antaag, or your team may go there, but regardless, they will be informed. Jermys will most likely want to join you or head this direction. Then, Schram, you can decide what direction to go next. As a dragon, you could get to either location in equal time. Whether you go alone or with others is also your call. However, you are the only one that should travel in numbers less than three. Is that understood by all?"

Schram now also stood. "I agree, and I will add that I must seek my dragon brothers first. They may be able to provide not only insight into the creature but into the canoks as well. Perhaps I find both answers in one location."

Stepha stood. "I will go with you, my husband. But who could be our third? Madeiris must return to Elvinott should support from the elves be needed."

Maldor looked upward at the two standing. "Although young, I feel Lars would do well to spend time with you. He asks so many questions about Kri—" He stopped in midsentence then continued, "His mother. Being with you may provide some of those answers. Plus, he is a cunning warrior for his age, and support you well he could, should hand-to-hand combat commence."

The elf princess smiled because she knew Schram had wanted to spend some time with the young maneth, the son of his closest human friend. One of his main reasons for wanting to visit the maneths even before the issues with this creature was to see Lars again. She was confident Schram would accept this offer without question.

As expected, his smile started almost as the name was said. "Yes, that would be fine. It would most likely do us both some good and get him out of your hair for a while. I hear he is running circles around you most days."

Maldor just grumbled but accepted the answer as such.

Geoff was also smiling. He remembered so long ago when young Maldor joined a trek he had no business leading but proved to be a powerful asset.

He had watched Lars his entire life. He had guided him where he could but left him to learn on his own as well. He was not only maneth but also half human. Although Geoff was his king, he could not help him with his human half. Lars was the only maneth-human in the history of Troyf, and with that, much he would have to learn on his own. However, when you looked at the young man, although you saw some slight human attributes, he was all maneth. But when you truly watched him, he was all Krirtie. Geoff had no idea how this journey would go for Schram and his new companion, but he knew it was something that was long overdue for the two of them.

The maneth king turned back to the group and left his momentary thoughts. "Then it is decided. The night is before us. We will rest well in the safety of the maneth camp and then head out in the morning. I believe we should set a time or place to meet in thirty days. Because Madeiris is headed out alone, I suggest we all meet in Elvinott. Its boundaries are safe, and we will be able to plan our next strategy should one exist. Does anyone disagree?"

The group all nodded, and Stepha seemed even more pleased that although this journey was taking her away from her home, it would be short-lived before she returned. She looked toward her husband, who seemed lost in thought. She was going to inquire but held off to ask the question when they were alone.

Geoff raised his club again. "Then let it be said. We will meet at first light. Please rest well, my friends, for we do not know what waits before us. I know there are still some unanswered questions from our past,"—a few eyes fell to Schram and thoughts of his human mother—"but we also have some new evils trying to make their way upon us. If they are related, we do not know, but smother them, as we have in the past, I am confident we will."

The group all placed their hands together in a display of power that was felt, not just seen. Madeiris pulled his hand back and raised his glass of ale that had been set before him. "Sleep well tonight, my friends, and travel safe. Should you need Elvinott, we will not be far."

Everyone slowly broke up, and then disappeared to their respective tents. Each was refreshed with the knowledge that they had a plan. Although fear was still in their minds, they rested easier knowing they were once again as one. The next day would be a new chapter in their lives, one with only unknowns before them, but this was not twenty years earlier. They held a power about them that all creatures on Troyf knew existed. They were no longer a band of renegades. They were the union defending the land, and they were very strong.

***

"Lars," shouted Schram across the glade.

The maneth turned from his passel of bandicoots and waved to the approaching human. Schram was the only human Lars ever associated with except on short visits to Toopek. He felt very close to his mom's best friend, and when Schram looked at the boy, who already stood taller than him, it was clear he felt the same.

"What do you need, Schram?" shouted the maneth back. The human arrived at the area and was astounded at what he saw. Lars had about twelve bandicoots organized in building a fort for them to live in. He shook his head in disbelief. "I am not even going to ask, but I can tell you that your mother would be very proud." He paused then added, "But she would be the only creature on Troyf that would feel that way."

Lars smiled and put his arm around Schram the way he always did when they saw each other. "Nah, Mom would say I was taking too much time with them, from what Dad tells me."

"Never underestimate your mother," he replied sadly.

"What do you need, Big Ears?" the maneth asked, smiling. It was a name Schram not only disliked, but it actually caused him the same immediate and negative reaction each time he heard it.

"First, I need to ask if you would do something for me. Then secondly, I want to stress again, I am a king. I am half your king. You do not refer to kings as 'Big Ears,' especially when the king is still not used to having..." his voice trailed off.

"Big ears?" finished Lars.

Schram smiled. "I want to ask if you would join me on a mission."

Lars nearly knocked over the bandicoot's work as he jumped back away from his friend. "Seriously? You want me to go with you on a mission? Just name the time. I can get things together quickly. When do we leave?"

"I take that as, 'Yes, Big Ears, I would love to join you,'" Schram stated, mocking the maneth's voice.

Lars looked down, slightly embarrassed. "Yes, sir. I would very much like to join you wherever your travel takes you."

The king placed his hand on the maneth's shoulder. "I am pleased to hear it. Go spend some time with your father. He will not be joining us, and I am sure he would like this evening with you. He will fill you in on the details." He paused then added as he turned to head to his tent to join Stepha, "Lars, I too am very pleased to have this time with you. If you have any questions about your mother, I would be pleased to answer them. However, this is a mission that could be filled with danger, so please hold it at the highest level."

"I will, sir. And thank you." The young maneth ran and threw his arms around the elf magician, which was returned with a tight grip.

Lars mumbled a few words to the bandicoots. Schram only picked up some of the meaning, and then he disappeared back toward the camp. Schram looked down at the passel of rats, and they all stared up at him. "I know that you know I hate you guys, so what are we trying to do here, have a stare-off?"

The largest bandicoot, without a pause, hacked a large yellow sludge from its throat, which landed on Schram's nose. The magician turned and walked away without wiping it away, only remembering that Fehr was one of those creatures he hated so much.

MISSION

"Well, at least it is not raining," Stepha said as she approached the group.

"Yes, but it will be soon," added Geoff. "It has not rained in days, but it chooses today to bring its wrath."

"We will be fine," added Schram. He mumbled a few words then winked at the maneth king.

"You crazy fool. I have never liked your winks."

Schram replied, "Let me put it this way. Your mane will not need Denisi to fix it tonight. You will be well protected from any drops from the sky." Schram turned and saw Maldor. "Hello, my friend. Did Lars speak to you last night?"

"Yes, we had a wonderful night. We probably stayed up too long, but well worth it." Maldor turned and stood right in front of Schram. "I have never seen him more excited. I know he loves me, but he has always just had me. He is seeing this time with you as getting a piece of his mother. Thank you for letting him join you. I know it makes no sense in the level of the lines."

"This has nothing to do with lines, my friend. I need this as much as he does. When she died, part of me passed with her. In him, I want to bring that out. Only he knows its value."

Maldor smiled, then his smile turned more serious. He placed his hand on Schram's shoulder. "That being said, please protect him well. He is still young, and I can't..."

"I know, my friend. I know. We will be safe." Maldor smiled. "There is nobody in this world I would ever trust those words from more than you."

Geoff, hearing the comment, added, "I will remember that, Maldor. Picking Big Ears over your king, eh?"

Maldor looked embarrassed and started to answer but could not by the redness in Schram's face and raised hand from the magician. "All right, friends. I have accepted it from Lars for a short time, but I do believe that

31

enough is enough with the—"

Stepha smiled and placed a single finger across Schram's lips, silencing the magician. Softly she said, "Really, Schram, I think the ears are delicious, and besides, everyone knows what big ears means on a man."

Schram smiled with an actual look of pride on his face and did not speak any longer. Lars leaned over to his father and whispered just loud enough for everyone to hear, "Big earmuffs."

Scattered laughter ensued as Schram's smile was only slightly wiped away.

Geoff raised his club again as he had last night. "Friends, brothers, family, please know that on this day, we are embarking on a new journey, a journey that, if history repeats itself, could be filled with danger. Our lives may be threatened, and with that, I want each of you to know I cannot allow any harm to come to you. Therefore, you must travel with utmost caution. If the situation is too grave, retreat is an answer. We must live to fight another day. Do not forget that. Only together can we save this world. The weapons several of you carry show that more than anything else. Individually they are strong, but together, as one, their strength brings fear into every creature that dares challenge us. Trust in yourselves, trust in each other, and we will be successful."

There were cheers from those around, and although both Schram and Madeiris thought about saying more to the group and the other maneth and elves in the area, they both held their tongues, thinking Geoff had said it well. Maldor and Lars stood to the side with Maldor facing his young son with one hand on each shoulder. Nobody could hear what they were saying, but as Stepha looked closely, she saw a tear run down each of their faces. As she thought about the two, she realized that in the last twenty years, they had never been apart. Each time Maldor went to Toopek or Elvinott, Lars came with him. This was possibly the hardest moment of Maldor's life, even exceeding the time he spent captured in Draag and tortured by Slayne. The big maneth was truly humbled.

Schram pulled Stepha to his side, and with a soft holler to Lars, they all headed down the forest path toward the dwarven city. Maldor stood next to Geoff and watched his son disappear in the trees, and the maneth king placed his arm around his longtime friend. "Don't worry, Maldor. I agree with you. If there is anyone on Troyf I would trust my son with, it is Schram."

There was no reply as the two maneths simply turned and headed the other direction toward Toopek with Denisi in tow, her long blonde hair flowing behind her in the gentle breeze and her bow already nocked with an arrow.

Stepha started some polite conversation with the two men and then realized they would waste no time finding conversation among themselves. When her questions repeatedly were answered with silence, she said, "I guess I will just fly up and keep an eye from above."

Again, no reply. She then said, "I guess I will set fire to my wings, and hopefully it will catch the trees on fire and burn all the way to Elvinott."

Schram lifted his head slightly, tilted it a bit, and then replied, "Yes, I am sure Madeiris will make it to Elvinott."

She smiled, leaned forward, gave him a quick kiss on the cheek, and then took to the air.

Lars watched Stepha take off and asked, "Did they get along?" "Your mother and Stepha?"

"Yes," the maneth replied.

"Did they like each other?"

"Why do you ask?"

"Dad said Mom liked you a lot. More than him sometimes."

Schram smiled. "Your mother and I knew each other for twenty-five years before we ever met Maldor. We were very close, but never more than friends. But we were the type of friends that you only come across once or twice in a lifetime, a bond you never can replace or duplicate just because you want to. It just has to happen." He smiled as he thought about his old friend. "I had another friend I walked with for all my life. I was lucky to have two such friends."

"Stepha?"

"Stepha, I knew for a long time, but we were always more than friends, at least in my heart."

"Who was your other friend? A friend like my mom?" Lars was very intrigued.

Schram stopped and looked at him. "I am sure I have told you stories of the white canok with a black diamond patch."

"Oh yes, you, Dad, and King Geoff have told stories. He sounded extremely powerful."

Schram smiled broadly. "That does not even begin to describe it."

Lars shuffled forward to get slightly ahead of the human magician and added, "Now back to Stepha and Mom. Were they friends?"

"Yes, Stepha and your mother were very close. They went through a lot together. Don't forget, they traveled across most of Troyf together to save your father. With the help of Jermys, they were able to do it. That whole time, she carried you in her belly. Stepha was there when you were born. They held a special bond."

"What about at first? Before they spent all that time together? Did they get along from the start?"

Schram stopped walking. He turned to the maneth and smiled. "We have a long journey with plenty of time for questions. But I am surprised your first questions are about Stepha." He paused, smiled, and then added, "To be honest, neither trusted or liked the other one in the beginning. In fact, I remember the very first day we left Toopek for Elvinott so many years ago, and I told your mother where we were going. She was, shall we say, not happy."

Lars smiled. "I am glad they were friends. I like Stepha."

"You know, Lars, I thought this trip would be good for you and me to talk. I can tell you a great deal about your mother, but do not be afraid to ask Stepha as well. She knew a different woman than I did. She can give you even a different perspective."

He smiled. "I will, Schram. I will."

The two walked in silence for the next several hours before making a small camp in a clearing. Stepha surveyed the area from the air and saw no signs of any life that should not be there, so they felt they could eat in peace and then continue until they made camp for the night. It was going to take two solid days to reach Feldschlosschen, and with any delays, a second overnight and reaching on the third day could happen. They also never wanted to miss an opportunity to sit and enjoy a meal without the stress of being in dangerous lands. Although these forests should always be free of danger, after the creature outside Elvinott, nobody was sure of anything anymore.

As they sat with idle chatter, Stepha asked, "How long will it take the others to reach Toopek? I have not done that trek in some time."

"If all goes well, they will be there by tomorrow evening, about the same time as us to Feldschlosschen. Although they are closer, the terrain is more difficult."

She smiled and let the questions end there. Each seemed fine to sit in silence for the rest of the break.

"Denisi, what do you see?" shouted Maldor.

"About ten. All walking directly across our path."

"Do you think they know we are here?"

"I do not think they have seen us, but yes, they know we are here. There is a much clearer way to travel than their current direction. They are coming to intercept us."

Geoff replied. "Hostile?"

Denisi stopped shouting from the air and landed by the two large men. "If you consider seven black canoks, a troll, and a hooded figure hostile, then yes, I would consider them hostile."

Maldor and Geoff stared at each other in horror. "A dragon lord and black canoks? How can that be?" stated the king.

Maldor replied, "All the dragon lords were killed, and the canoks returned to their homeland of old with their black fur turned back to red, united as one."

Denisi appeared concerned. "I am confident in my sight."

"Do we head around?" asked Maldor.

Geoff looked toward Denisi. "Can we get around them?"

"I don't think so," she replied. "As I said, I am sure by their direction they know of our presence. They intend to meet us. What their intent is from there, I do not know."

"Geoff," Maldor stated, "you just told everyone retreat is always an option. Live to fight another day, you said. We can retreat to our camp or continue all the way to Feldschlosschen. But right here, we are no match for seven canoks and a dragon lord."

Do not flee. I have but only a message for your leader.

The three looked at each other, and each knew they had all heard the telepathic message. In a blunt voice, Maldor said, "I guess that confirms Denisi is correct. They know we are here."

Geoff added, "To flee would be self-defeating. We cannot escape, and we would only lead them to our camp."

"I could fly and provide warning. They are too far to catch me." Denisi said.

Geoff thought a moment. "No, this is not a typical advance. I do not sense this as an attack. I believe this to be similar to the creature. They want us to know they are here. Let's approach them to meet in the glade. Should we take to arms, I don't want to be hindered in the trees."

A brave decision, young Geoff. Our master did not underestimate you.

They all shrugged and then began to draw a path toward the group. Each had their weapons drawn—Denisi with her bow, Geoff with his maneth club, and Maldor still carrying the weapon of the ring, the Anbarian Hammer. The two groups remained in silence as they met. Geoff studied each of the canoks and the hooded figure intently, trying to put into memory everything he could to relay it back to Schram at his first opportunity. The hooded figure was not like the dragon lords of the past. This figure appeared only human. Though not much of its physical attributes were visible, there was definitely no dragon tail, and the face was white and even soft in texture. The troll was just a troll and appeared to be there only for weapon value. However, the canoks were different. Taller legs but young, only pups. Possibly as young as Lars. All were black, but it was not the jet-black of the past; it was more deep gray. To Geoff, this only left questions.

The large maneth stepped in front of Maldor and Denisi and dropped his club to his side. "Well, sirs, this is your meeting. What can we do for you?"

The hooded figure looked down to the canoks, and it was clear they were in conversation. Then their eyes all turned back to the group. The hooded figure spoke, and to their surprise, the voice was female.

"The dragon oppression is upon you. The failures of the past are now complete. In thirty moons, we will move on Elvinott, Toopek, Feldschlosschen, and the maneth camp. All will be destroyed unless you provide Schram Starland to us, along with all the weapons of the Ring of Ku within that time. Any resistance to our presence will be met with the immediate destruction of those cities. There are no negotiations, no further discussions, and no war. This is that which it is. Nothing more. Follow these rules completely, and your race will be allowed to live under our rule. Any resistance or failure as stated, and your entire race will be destroyed. We have demonstrated only a small piece of our power."

Geoff was completely caught by the words but responded with force, even taking a step closer as he spoke, "Do not intimidate me with your words. You may have hidden your forces and built some power that you feel is worthy of aggression. Do not forget the dragons have been defeated twice. The dragons that remain are loyal to nobody, but if pushed, you know as well as I do they will side with Schram. Your black dragon leader is dead. We are too strong for you to simply wipe us away. We will never kneel to your leadership, whoever you are. You hide behind your robes with a handful of young canoks who would be a minor threat if not for the race of canoks on our side. I hope you have all the trolls with you as they smell too nasty to be mixed in our lands. Go back to wherever you came from and find a very large rock to hide behind, because not only will we refuse to hand over my friend Schram, we will stand by his side as we destroy you."

The hooded woman walked right in front of Geoff's face. "Schram will never destroy me. It is not possible for him to do so."

The canoks turned their eyes all on Denisi, and in only a moment, she was on the ground, screaming in pain. Geoff raised his club to strike the woman, and his hand was thrown back by some magical force, lifting his whole body in the air and slamming it against a tree. He was pinned by magical fingers holding both arms at bay. Denisi writhed in pain, and it looked like both her legs and arms were broken, and her head was being held down by her hair. She could not move.

Maldor raised his hammer, and it began to hum at a never-before-heard level. The gray canoks and the hooded woman all turned toward the maneth and sent a magical explosion of fire his direction. Maldor stood unmoved, the hammer creating a ring around him, out of his control. Although he was protected, he sensed he was still vulnerable as he did not know how this protection was generated. Just then, he felt a hand over his.

The human woman had reached out to take the hammer from him. Although the protection from the fire remained, it seemed impervious to stopping the woman's touch. This was not magic but rather a physical pull to free the hammer from the large maneth.

"Maldor," hollered Geoff, "do not let go. This whole setup was to get the hammer. It can't be taken..." Geoff's voice trailed off as a bolt from the largest canok struck him unconscious.

Maldor stared into the woman's eyes. "Who are you?" he whispered as he pulled his other hand up to grip his hammer with both hands. "What are you?"

The woman smiled. "I am everything you need to fear. Release the hammer, or your friends will die. You have but only a moment to decide." She paused, smiled, and then added, "And trust that I am not bluffing."

"I will not release the hammer. Should you destroy my friends, then that is their destiny. The fight for freedom is more important."

She turned to the canoks but did not remove her grip on the hammer. "Kill them."

Maldor used the moment to pull with all his might to free her grip. The moment did catch the woman by surprise, and in one sweep, he struck her hard with every measure of physical strength he could muster. Somehow the woman was not protected from a physical assault. The strike was hard and sent her to the ground. Red blood spewed from her nose, and she appeared to be momentarily unconscious.

The canoks appeared extremely disturbed by the turn of events. They moved between the maneth and the fallen woman.

Do not take another step forward, or the elf woman dies.

Maldor looked toward Geoff, who, though slightly conscious now, had fallen to his knees when released from the magical grip but had still remained connected to the events before him. Although he could not speak, he shook his head no to his longtime maneth friend. The woman began to move slightly but still appeared momentarily disoriented. As her eyes returned their color, she whispered a few words, and the entire band vanished, leaving Maldor, Geoff, and Denisi alone in the glade.

Geoff, in a broken voice hardly his own, mustered, "Denisi, are you all right?"

She gasped for breath. "I am going to destroy that woman...," her statement broke off as she writhed in pain.

Maldor looked down to the beautiful flyer in agony on the ground. He leaned to his king and whispered, "I believe both her legs are broken in multiple places, along with her arms."

"You do not have to whisper, Maldor. I can confirm that my arms and legs are broken, and it hurts as if they had been cut from my body altogether."

As she spoke, Maldor's hammer began to hum softly. Geoff's eyes widened, and he pointed toward her and said, "Now place your hammer across her body."

Maldor laid the hammer across the woman's chest, and the humming grew deafening. In only moments, Denisi's eyes calmed, and her color returned. The woman sat up. "I have got to get me one of those," she stated softly. "Thank you, my friend. Thank you very much."

"What the hell was that?" asked Maldor. "What did they want with us, and who was that woman?"

Geoff reached his hand out to Denisi and helped her up before replying, "The woman, I do not know, but what they wanted from us was the hammer. They want the weapons of the ring."

"That means the others are in danger as well," added Denisi.

"It does."

"What do you want to do, Geoff? Turn back or continue to Toopek?" asked Maldor.

The king thought only a moment before answering, "We will continue to Toopek. They have to be prepared. There is clearly danger growing again, and they have given only thirty days before they strike. They spoke with a confidence that makes me uncomfortable. In thirty days, we were to be back in Elvinott to discuss what to do. If they hold to their timeline, there will be no Elvinott to go to."

Denisi appeared extremely concerned with the last statement as she stood gingerly on her freshly healed legs and stretched her arms. "They cannot have the power to destroy all that they claim. My homeland is protected with a magic that is unmatched on this world."

Geoff reached to add support to the woman, who moved away to avoid his touch. The king shook his head. "I too believed that to be the case. However, I have never heard the forces against us speak with such confidence. She did not consider us a threat. She did not consider any discussions or negotiations. She stated as it would be. That confidence leads me to believe she has something with her of which we are not aware."

"We should proceed with caution," added Maldor. Denisi and Geoff both nodded in agreement. As they started walking, Denisi did move closer to her husband, who relished the contact. All could see the worry in each other's eyes, and with that, their pace quickened, though no words were spoken the rest of the day.

Schram looked at his friends sleeping in the small clearing. The fact that they could sleep so deeply was refreshing to the human. He was deep in thought when a knife was placed to his throat. A voice whispered, "Do not move, Schram. Your magic will not work on me as I am protected. Should you try, I will slit your throat."

Schram did not turn but gripped his staff tightly. There was no reaction. It did not hum. It did not create a protective force around him. He felt no power from it. It appeared to be neutralized. He still felt his power was strong, but not through the staff. He was puzzled by this change but more puzzled as his eyes looked around, and he was no longer in the clearing with his friends. He was someplace different. It was not clear or familiar. There were trees in the distance, but they appeared different, like a part of Troyf he had never seen before.

The knife at his throat was released, and the voice again whispered, "You cannot defeat me. Should you try, it will be your day to die. I do not wish to kill you, but if that is your destiny, then so it shall be."

Schram turned to the source of the voice, and when his eyes met its source, it was gone. The environment was back as it had been before. The staff felt as it should be, and as his eyes quickly turned back to his sleeping friends, Schram knelt down and just concentrated. His mind went to his friends on their trek to Toopek. He could see they were well and walking at a quick pace toward his kingdom. He concentrated on the elf king and could see him leading his warriors at the Great Oak. He thought about his friend Jermys and saw the dwarf and Fehr eating and smoking in their chambers. He shook his head. *What is happening?* he thought to himself. He thought about Werner and felt nothing. That is not surprising. They protect themselves from my thoughts. They are still fine.

With that, Schram went back to his post on watch, wanting morning to come quickly so they could continue to the dwarven city.

THE EVIL AMONG US

Archers from the wall pelted arrows across the fields providing cover for the three as they ran toward Toopek's boundaries. Where are all these trolls coming from, and what is their goal? A red dragon soared over the wall, and Geoff and Maldor dove to the ground as fire shot across their backs. Maldor roared as the heat burned his fur and skin. The large band of trolls that had entered pursuit scattered as the flames struck across their main front. More than twenty fell to the ground with their flesh in flames. The remaining scattered, and the pursuit was over.

Geoff jumped to his feet. "I am still not used to having them on our side."

"You can say that again," added Maldor, "but that was too close for comfort."

Denisi landed by their side. "That was amazing. Where did all those trolls come from? How did they appear so quickly? We were just in the forests, and then out of nowhere, the forests were filled with trolls."

Geoff began to answer but stopped as the large young red dragon landed directly adjacent to him. The dragon stared down at them. The site from the Toopekian wall was something that could not be described in words. The large maneth king stepped toward the dragon and placed his hand on its neck. Although one of the larger creatures on Troyf, a maneth is still dwarfed by dragons. "Thank you, my friend. I do not know where you came from or how you knew to be here, but I do not know how to properly thank you other than to simply say it."

The dragon nodded. "I was asked to come." It lifted its wings in a truly ominous sight, shaking out the muscles, as it was clear it had flown with tremendous speed to arrive in time.

"Could I ask you who asked you to be here?" asked Geoff.

"Your and my friend, Schram. He felt there would be an issue."

Maldor shook his head. "An 'issue,' huh? Damn human magician. I hate owing him." Maldor was still shaking his head in disbelief when he asked,

41

"Could we know your name?"

"I am Rosstim. I hold no love for the evil forces. I understand the past and will continue to spread the word. The dragons are still divided and not as one. You cannot trust any, but please know that you may always trust me."

Geoff removed his hands from the dragon's neck. "Thank you, Rosstim, for we are in your debt. Although we may have made it with support from Toopek, one hundred trolls is still a daunting number, and you answered that without question. We are in your debt."

The dragon nodded and lifted its wings, and in moments, had disappeared across the Toopekian city and then the bay. The three nodded in agreement that it was time to go, and they took the final steps toward Toopek with Alan Grove, the human leader of the city, waiting at the gate to greet them.

After traditional greetings and respects, they made their way to the city center and the chambers of the council. Alan shook his head. "I had no idea you were coming. What a great surprise, but what is going on that so many trolls were in your wake?"

Geoff nodded. "We are pleased to see you again, my friend, but we hold no answers. The forests were clear when we passed. Then when we reached the tree line and had only steps to get to Toopek, it erupted with trolls. They seemed to come out of nowhere in numbers I have never seen. We have much to discuss. Although we initially believed the trip would be free of issue, it was clearly a different story."

The two maneths and Denisi replayed their saga to Alan and his team of leaders, much to their surprise. The humans seemed completely puzzled by the occurrences. Angus Reid, Alan's second-in-command, nodded to his leader before Alan started to speak, "We have seen nothing of evil. Our city has been prospering. Trade between the human cities of Lawren and Empor has never been stronger. Until today, we had not even seen a troll in years. Now you say forces will destroy our city if we do not hand over our king? That is tough to believe."

"That is exactly what I said," replied Geoff.

"If I did not know you better, I would call you crazy." Alan paused, thought about his next words, and added, "But I have known you too long not to trust you."

Angus then broke in and asked, "So are you saying this force has the power to destroy Toopek and the other cities?"

The maneth nodded. "I have no way of knowing that, but I can tell you this force is powerful and claims as much—"

Alan cut off Geoff before he could speak further. "What is our next move?"

To everyone's surprise, Geoff answered with confidence, "We protect this city, and the four of us get to Elvinott immediately."

"Four?" inquired Alan.

"If I could take more, I would. However, traveling with three is a huge risk. Four is only slightly better. But Angus here has not taken his hand from his sword even in our presence. He has a knife sticking from his back armor and a small dagger tied to his calf. My gut tells me he will be good in a fight."

Alan smiled while Angus removed his hand from his sword and placed it in its scabbard. "Yes, Captain Reid will serve you well in your efforts." Alan turned to the leader of his forces, and the two exchanged nods of understanding. To Angus, Alan added, "Follow King Geoff as you would me. He saved our city once before, and his actions continue to be for our entire land. Make Toopek proud."

"I will, sir." To Geoff, he explained, "I meant no disrespect by holding my sword. It is simply what I feel I do when I do not understand the situation."

Geoff smiled. "No disrespect was taken. Your actions answered my question for me. Instead of asking for Alan's best man to join us, I saw who I knew would be up for the task. Please understand, I believe we will face grave hardships. Do not believe for one minute this is an adventure. For today, my fear for this world exceeds any I have felt in the past. Something is not right, and we are about to find out what it is. We have to get word to Elvinott and then meet with Schram in Feldschlosschen if he is still there. If not, we must reach the dwarves in time. All our allies must be warned should we have any chance of mounting a defense."

Alan nodded. "We will solidify the boundaries. There are about eight dragons that have stayed on the old castle island. If you add in the one who just cleared your path, we have nine dragons loyal to Toopek. Although they will not fight for me, I also believe they will not allow Toopek to be destroyed without a fight. I do wish Schram could speak to them, but I will make haste to the island to ensure they understand. Do you believe there will be dragons with these forces?"

Geoff shook his head. "The powers with this group were strong, but not that of the dragons, though I am only guessing. I really have no way of knowing." He paused and turned to Angus. "We leave at first light. Will you be ready?"

"Aye, sir, I will." Geoff nodded.

"Great, and don't call me *sir*. My name is Geoff, and as of today, we are brothers."

Angus smiled but did not respond. Just then, the innkeeper from across the street brought in a tray of about ten dwarven ales. "We just got them in a few hours ago. I thought you might like the first few taps."

Collectively, the room let out a sigh, but none as loud as Denisi. When all eyes fell on her, she shook them off, adding, "Hey, I broke both my arms and both my legs today. I can't have an ale after that?"

Despite the times, there were five very large smiles as the pungent dwarven ale crossed each of their lips. Geoff turned a small frown when Denisi snuck half of his last mug as her own, but in the long run, he knew a happy Denisi made for a happier Geoff.

Schram woke the others, causing a range of various motions and comments. The human magician had not slept the rest of the night as he'd been consumed in thought about his vision. He had learned a long time ago that all his dreams did mean something, that there was a message in them, and he needed to heed that warning. He concentrated on what he had seen. The location, the person, the words she used, and the fact that his staff was powerless. He was left with only questions and a sleepless night.

"What troubles you, Schram?" echoed Stepha's soft voice. "Did something happen during the night?"

His entire body dropped. "How do you always know what I am feeling?"

She smiled. "You have to ask? I am an elf, as are you. We feel all that is around us. The forest, the trees, and the spirits. Yours is troubled today."

"I had a vision. It was one that leaves me many questions and concerns. My life was in peril, and the staff was without power. The hand that held my life under its control was powerful, possibly more powerful that any on Troyf, but I am not sure of its meaning."

"Do not trouble your mind. I know you hold value in your dreams, but remember they are dreams. They are molded through thoughts and energy. Perhaps there is a power out there that is great, but realize where there is a great power, there is recklessness. You are balanced. You are not reckless.

You do not crave power.

"You wish to diminish it. You never use it for expanding your will, only for the good of Troyf. There is a difference, a very big difference. Please don't forget it."

"Thank you, my love," he replied as he pulled her close.

Lars came bounding through the trees, interrupting their exchange. "There are a large number of trolls approaching from the north."

"What?" replied Schram, lifting his staff. "I have felt nothing."

"I assure you they are there, and in the hundreds."

Schram looked toward Stepha, who immediately took to the air. He then motioned Lars over. "Did they see you?"

"No. I was gathering wood for a morning fire, and I saw them across a glade. However, their path is toward us. There is no doubt. It is as if they know we are here."

Stepha as quickly returned, landing beside them, shaking out her wings at first touch. "Lars is correct. A mass I have not seen in twenty years. They are headed directly this way and appear to have drawn a path from the maneth homeland. If their direction is true, they will be here very quickly."

Lars drew his weapon. "I must return." The anger in his voice was clear. "Forgive my leave, but I have no choice."

Stepha's eyes grew fearful before Schram placed his hand on his young friend's shoulder. "Lars, to do so would mean your own death. You know this to be true. No human, maneth, elf, or magician could defeat this number of trolls. You will be overtaken at first meet. Your village is strong. They will defend themselves well. Further, I do not feel these trolls came through your camp. There is magic here with their presence. We must go at once."

Lars pushed Schram's hand away and began to reply, but as he thought about his words, he knew them to be sound. He reluctantly nodded, and they hastily packed their weapons and other provisions while Stepha erased all signs of their presence. Schram pointed their direction, and without speech, they continued toward the dwarven city.

Schram believed they only needed to move at their pace for about an hour before they should have enough distance between them and the mass of trolls, and then they could slow their steps and calm their fears. He still held many questions as to the strange presence and numbers of these trolls. He could see the faces of those with him start to show the tiredness of their quick pace when he raised his hand, motioning to slow. Between staggered breaths, he said, "We should be well ahead of that force by now. We can slow our pace. Stepha, please provide a quick scan from above to verify our course is clear ahead and behind."

Stepha immediately took to the air, and although Schram thought she should be gone for quite some time to verify the land ahead of them, she was back in only seconds. "Schram, the trolls are right behind us, even closer than when we first saw them."

"How is that possible? There is no way a group of that size could keep such a pace."

The elf shook her head. "I cannot explain it, but I tell you they are there, and they will be on us in moments."

Schram appeared in a trance as he closed his eyes. Lars had only seen this a few times, so he did not recognize what was happening, but Stepha knew it all too well. Suddenly Schram spread his huge dragon wings and blew fire into the air. In a deep voice that was different but still his own, he said, "Go. I will take care of the trolls. You make a straight path to Feldschlosschen."

Lars raised his club and replied sternly, "No! We were told to stay together. I will not leave you to fight alone."

Lars appeared instantly concerned, and Stepha stood by Lars' side, clearly carrying the same feelings. "This is not a request," Schram stated. "These may appear to be trolls, but there is magic at work here. We must get word to Jermys and the dwarves. They must be warned and..." Schram's voice trailed off.

Stepha stepped forward. "Schram, what is it?"

"Maldor is in trouble. I can feel it through the hammer." He closed his eyes. *Khaled, do you hear me. Toopek is threatened. Can you assist?*

Stepha did not speak, but she knew her husband was trying to learn more about what was occurring, though he was not speaking. She knew he was connected somewhere. Then she saw his eyes soften. The elf grabbed his hand. "Schram, are you all right?"

The magician turned to face her with the color back to his eyes and the sense of urgency restored. "Yes, Khaled will find help for our friends at Toopek. Now we can talk no further. Please go. I will face the trolls." Scuffling could be heard through the trees a short distance away. "Now, before it is too late."

Stepha and Lars looked toward each other, and both agreed without speaking. The maneth was very large, but Stepha believed their best chance to create some distance was to fly. Without a word, she grabbed the maneth under both arms from behind and took to the sky. Lars gave a quick roar at the surprise and then closed his eyes. Stepha could feel his body tremble. The elf leaned forward and whispered, "Don't tell me a big guy like you is afraid of heights?"

There was no answer as the two quickly vanished through the trees.

Schram walked slowly toward the approaching noise. He was not sure what was about to happen. Would it be a fight? Would it be a meeting? Would some source of the magic behind these movements make their presence known? Whatever the answer, he was about to find out. As he broke through the trees to enter a large clearing, all noise ahead of him vanished. His large dragon eyes stared across the open field to a wall of motionless trolls. He estimated their numbers to be greater than three hundred. He stared across the vast line in a sort of stalemate. Neither side seemed to know why they were there but knew they had to be there nonetheless.

Schram took one step closer, causing a small shuffle in the center of the line of trolls. An area of trolls divided, allowing another creature to walk between them. A young black canok took three steps out in front of the troll line and then stopped and stared at the human. His look appeared to be one of surprise, as if he did not anticipate a dragon before his path.

Schram felt the canok try to enter his mind, but it was easily blocked. Schram tried the same to the canok, and to his surprise, was able to enter before being pushed out. He saw a woman, a large black canok, and then nothing.

What do you want here? Schram asked telepathically. *I was to track and kill a human and elf. I hold no issue with you, dragon.*

Schram's eyes narrowed, and he telepathically replied, *That human and elf are with me, so with that, your issue with me is clear.* He spread his wings and took to the air, driving an aggressive direction directly toward the canok. He let out sheets of fire across the glade, sending the trolls scattering, but the canok remained stoic and without fear. Schram turned his fire toward the canok directly, and as the rolling flames arrived just short of his nose, all life except Schram vanished. Schram felt a tremor through his mind the likes of which he had not felt before. His mind went blank, and he nearly crashed to the ground, fighting his disorientation. When he stumbled back to his feet and tried to gain his bearings, he confirmed he was alone. There was no sign of the troll army or canok remaining, and no sign they had even been there.

The large dragon walked slowly to where the canok had previously stood only moments before. He used all his senses to try to find how such magic had been performed but he could feel nothing. Schram looked around for a short while more and then took to the skies to follow in Stepha's and Lars's wake.

"I can go no farther by air," Stepha stated. "My wings are too tired to continue to carry your weight and mine."

Lars instantly smiled. "It's about time. Let's get back to the ground."

The elf joined the smile as she softly set the big maneth down inside some deep tree cover. "We should be well protected here. I will take back to the air after a short rest and see if there is any pursuit."

"What about Schram? Shouldn't we help him?" The elf's smile turned serious. "Though I would like to, I will honor his wishes. He has proven wise beyond any I have known. If he believes he will be safe, then I believe in him enough to let him show it." There was a pause, then she added. "Still, if you will be all right here, I might accidently make my way farther back than he would feel is necessary, if you know what I am saying."

The maneth smiled broadly. "I do know what you are saying, and you should accidently get back there now."

Just then, the tree rustled loudly, and a few branches fell as Schram barreled through landing with a thump and a slew of leaves and shrubbery cracking under his feet.

"What in Shriak's name are you doing crashing through like that? Is everything all right?" The elf was angered but also worried at the abrupt entrance.

Schram shrugged. "Could you have picked a thicker area to hide?"

Lars smiled as he saw the two starting to push each other. "Really, Schram, when you think about the two things, thick cover and hide, they seem to go together, don't they?"

Schram was about to respond then shook his head as well. "Needless to say, for a dragon, I am still not the best flyer."

Lars held his smile but was still concerned about the trolls. "What happened with the trolls?"

"Yes, Schram," added the elf, "why are you back so quickly? I can see the concern on your face."

Schram motioned for the group to begin walking as he knew they still needed to make good time if they were going to reach the dwarven city before nightfall. "I actually have two concerns. First, how come when I landed, it appeared you were about to take off back in my direction."

"You could see that?" asked Stepha.

"And secondly, how is it that more than three hundred trolls and a black canok can appear and disappear in seconds?"

Stepha heard only one thing. "A black canok? How can that be?"

"I don't know, Stepha. But he was present, and he was different."

Lars now stepped forward. "Different? How?"

"He was reckless. I should never have been able to enter his mind, but I did, just for a moment. It was as if he did not know I would try."

Stepha stopped her husband, who had changed back into his elf-human self after landing. Grabbing his hand, she said, "Like a child. Like he was still learning?"

He turned to face her. "Yes, exactly like that. He was inexperienced."

"Then maybe he was just a pup. You said he was different. How?"

Schram now turned and started walking again. "His fur was more dark gray than black. He was smaller. My original thought was a different breed or race. However, young makes sense. Canoks live hundreds of years. Perhaps these were only fifteen- or twenty-year-old pups."

The elf added, "And if they never lived in the canok homeland, their training would be limited, so they may not have known about entering their mind and defending against it."

Schram stopped. "You mean they were born of parents outside of the homeland? How can that be?"

Stepha smiled, though the smile was tied to her next statement. "It only takes two."

"But which two would remain out of the homeland to continue the division, and how did they prevent the joining back to the combined race of canoks? All went back to the proud red fur of the past."

"I don't know, Schram, but when you go to the canok homeland, you have to find those answers."

Lars had remained out of the conversations as he was not as knowledgeable about canoks and their ways. He just listened intently. There was a much longer break in the silence than had been for some time when he finally broke in, changing the subject, "We increased our time by going to flight. When do you think we will arrive in Feldschlosschen?"

Schram seemed to break from a trance, showing he was deep in thought. He slapped Lars on the back to try to show he was in good spirits and not completely enveloped in their world's current situation. "Before sunfall, we should reach the outermost mines." That statement seemed to bring a sigh of relief to both his companions. Their steps increased, and Schram refrained from concentrating on the canoks and trolls and remained present to his friends for the rest of the walk. He felt there would be plenty of time for reflection later, and right now his friends needed him with them.

**

Geoff, Denisi, Maldor, and Angus left Toopek at first light and headed a straight path toward Elvinott. It was truly a unique sight as two maneths, a flyer elf, and human were definitely not the typical quartet. They talked only for short periods of time, the three learning as much as they could about their new friend but not prying too deeply. He was an orphan. His parents were killed twenty years ago in the dragon attacks defended so bravely by Schram and his friends. Angus listened intently to those stories as if they answered some questions about his past that he never knew. He was only six years old at the time, and although the family that raised him told him about the dragon wars, never had he heard so much detail.

Angus was motionless when they came to a great tigon in the forest. His sword was drawn, and he was ready to attack when Geoff motioned him down and walked directly to the large beast. Geoff ran his hand down its thick mane and along the stripes on his back. The tigon bowed slightly, clearly respecting Geoff, although in seconds it could have torn him in two. They growled toward each other, which sounded like nothing to everyone except Maldor. The tigon looked at both Denisi and Angus and seemed to smile before turning to Maldor and issuing a small bow that he returned. With that, there was one more brief exchange between Geoff and the beast, then he bounded into the trees.

Geoff turned back to the others and said, "We now have a plan."

Denisi shook her head, and Maldor added, "Should we follow his direction? Going to Lawren will take us well out of our way."

Geoff nodded in return. "We would be foolish not to heed the warning of our friend. The path between us and Elvinott is lined with trolls. Huge numbers similar to what we saw as we approached Toopek. He said they just appeared there and now wait. A path to Lawren will take us around them, plus give us a town to rest for the night. Both seem like good choices to me."

"I agree," added Denisi. "Do you want me to fly ahead and verify our path to Lawren?"

"Exactly what I was thinking. Angus, take the left, and Maldor, to my right. Let's make a nice, clean path to Lawren and arrive before nightfall."

Maldor made a small face but then fell in line. Geoff turned back to the maneth. "What is it, Maldor? Please speak if you disagree."

"No, I agree. I just think it is odd that in these times, Lawren, a place where all crime can flourish at unhealthy levels, a place where not so long ago one of our most trusted leaders sold our race to the evil forces, is now our place of refuge. Evil takes many forms and pushes individuals in strange directions."

Angus answered the comment, though it was directed at Geoff, "Perhaps because as it is it will make a party of two maneths, an elf, and human less noticeable when we arrive."

They all seemed satisfied with the answer. In short order, Denisi returned and said there were no signs of any presence ahead, exactly as the tigon had stated; and with that, the four began their path perpendicular to Elvinott toward Lawren.

THΣ RΣUNION

"There it is, Lars. The outskirts of Feldschlosschen. The largest series of mines in all of Troyf. All carved by hand over an unknown number of years."

The maneth was taken by Schram's words, but from where they stood, there was really nothing to see. It was not like walking into Elvinott where Lars had been several times and was always amazed at the intricate world cut into the forest trees. No, here they stood a short distance outside a cave. A cave that appeared dark and without life.

"So what do we do now?" the maneth asked.

"Why don't you come in and greet everyone properly?" issued a small voice from the side.

"Fehr," cried Stepha, "is it really you?"

"Aye," answered the bandicoot moving toward the elf princess, who nearly knocked him over grabbing his large body.

Lars looked on in amazement. "Fehr, you get larger every time I see you."

Fehr issued a small frown. "I am not sure that is the greeting I was hoping for, but it is a pleasure to see you as well. How have all my brethren been treating you?" he asked, referring to the large number of bandicoots Lars considered his family back in the maneth homeland.

"Very well," he replied. "But they miss you coming to train them."

Fehr only half heard the response as he broke from Stepha and stared at Schram. "It has been a while, my brother."

Schram reached his arm out to shake like he always did with Maldor, Geoff, and the rest of his close friends. However, Fehr simply jumped in the air and right into his arms. With a quick lick across the face, even Schram felt the need to hug the rodent. "It is good to see you, my friend."

Although the words were few, since Krirtie's passing, the two had become very close, though Schram would never admit it. Krirtie had brought them together. She had constantly defended Fehr to Schram, and over several years of fighting together for the good of their world and learning that Fehr had been very close with Schram's birth mother, Hawthorne, their bond had grown to beyond measureable levels.

Schram dropped his friend to the ground and said, "Fehr, can you please lead us in? We have had a trip filled with danger and concern, and we must speak with your king about what is happening."

"Aye, sir, let's go."

The group started moving, and Fehr then jumped in front of Schram and Lars, pushing them back to ensure Stepha could go first. The elf scratched the rat's head as she passed, causing a large smile to move across his face. He leaned over to the human magician and whispered, "You better be careful, old man, or I might just steal her away from you. I think she is starting to see the way of the bandicoot may not be that bad of a direction to go." Schram just smiled, along with Lars, who heard the comment but added nothing more. Stepha reached back and scratched him again as her elven ears had heard everything.

"Four ales please," stated Maldor as he nodded to the others at the far table in the bar.

"So far, so good," stated Denisi. "I do not know about this bar, the Minok Café. Pretty dirty and looks to be a place people go to hide rather than enjoy their evening in peace."

"Maybe this is perfect for us then." Angus paused then added, "A place to hide, I mean. There are a good number of humans, but as far as elves and maneth, you are definitely the minority."

Maldor sat back down. "Interesting bartender. A bit free with the comments, to say the least."

"And the cleavage," added Denisi. "Eyes over here, big guy." She was now directing her speech toward Geoff.

The big maneth smiled. "Really, I had not even noticed."

They all smiled and enjoyed their dwarven ales for several minutes before Geoff broke in with a very serious tone, "You know, I think this is the same bar Schram told me about when he first saw the one who betrayed us. I had just met him in the woods and guided him to Lawren while I took his injured friend to Mi-Kevan, the sorcerer who saved him. Schram came here with Lars's mom, and this was his first run-in with Almok, the black canok with the white diamond patch. It is amazing when you think about how much has happened since then."

Denisi grabbed his hand and added sadly, "So many in that bar that day have passed."

"I remember them," echoed a female voice from behind. All jumped, and Angus even drew a dagger in the process. The girl stepped back. "I meant no disrespect. I just was saying I remember your friends. It is not so often that a delicious human like Schram comes to these parts. He was truly amazing."

"What else do you remember?" asked Geoff.

"Nothing much. They came, they drank, and they talked to the old man and canok, then left. It was a long time ago. I remember him more than the whole day. Make sure you tell Schram I am still here if he wants to talk again."

Denisi smiled and answered sarcastically, "I will be sure to mention it to him and Stepha."

She began to walk away when Angus added, "Excuse me, one more thing. Have you seen that canok or any other maneth, canok, or odd humans in here recently?"

She smiled at still being included in the conversation. "Well, odd humans is relative, but to answer the other questions, no—until you four, that is." She motioned out the doors. "But your presence seems to be causing a small stir outside. Don't forget about the back door if you need it."

They all swung their heads to the windows and saw a fairly large gathering of humans wearing whatever homemade weapon, shank, or the like on their person, ready for battle.

Geoff turned back to the others. "These are just thieves interested in our armor and weapons. Let's not risk a confrontation." Turning back to the bartender, he nodded. "Thank you for the warning, and we will be leaving out the back as you suggest."

"Very well, and remember, tell Schram I am here." The group vanished through the back and quickly made their way to the inn for the night, leaving the band of renegade humans to do nothing but sip ales and talk about the ones that got away.

"Greetings, King Jermys. It is a pleasure to see you again. And let me say how sorry I was to hear about your former king." Schram gripped Jermys's hand tightly.

"Yes, Krystof is dearly missed." He grimaced when he had spoken the king's name and nodded apologetically to both Schram and Stepha. Both nodded in return, showing no true offense. "I was very surprised when I was chosen to be his successor. I do not know that I am qualified."

"Trust by the dwarves makes you qualified," stated Schram. "A true leader must be trusted and believed. They know you will fight for the dwarves until the bitter end."

"Thank you, my friend, as I know that I have learned much from you and continue to learn every day." He turned to the group. "What brings you here in such haste?" His eyes turned and finally caught sight of Lars. The dwarf king walked up to the maneth and gave him a huge hug. The sight was quite comical as the dwarf stood only to the maneth's thigh. "Lars, I think about you all the time. I miss your mother every day. Thank you for coming to our land."

The maneth was caught off guard by the greeting. He had met Jermys several times in the maneth camp and Elvinott, but in his memory, he had never been to Feldschlosschen; though, as a very young maneth, his father did bring him here several times. Although uncomfortable, he returned the hug deeply.

Schram leaned over and whispered, "Your mother affected everyone very deeply in many different ways. As you travel more and those realize who you are, you will continue to be received well. Do not fight it. Simply honor her with acceptance of the love."

Lars nodded. "I am very pleased to be here, and I should also say that I should have come long ago."

Schram smiled at hearing his response and said nothing more. Jermys took a step back and reached out his hand, and the two locked wrists, with Jermys cupping his second hand over the maneth's hand in his own.

Jermys turned to the group, breaking hands. "Now let's get back to my previous question. What brings you here in such haste? Historically, this has not been a good sign."

Schram motioned to walk before responding. The group made it to the king's chambers, where they had sat so many times in the past in front of Krystof, not knowing if the dwarves where there to help or hinder. Today, however, they knew where they stood. Schram replayed the occurrences of the past several days, ending with the strange occurrence in the clearing on their way to Feldschlosschen. Jermys motioned to some dwarven guards, and quickly they left, returning with a double round of ales and a large map.

Jermys laid out the map. Schram's eyes grew wide, and the human magician asked, "Is this what I think it is?"

"Yes, Schram," Jermys replied proudly. "It is everywhere we traveled on

Troyf. I figured we are the best at mapping our caverns and mines, why can't I map Troyf? If it will help you, it is yours."

All the companions were in awe of the parchment. It stretched across the entire table and had such great detail. Draag caverns were drawn specifically, even including the secret mirror passage. Icly, Cindif, Anbari's Dominion, and the Black Sea were all drawn to scale with detail down to the water's depth and mountain's height.

Schram shook his head. "I will study this in great detail, but I cannot take it from you."

Jermys smiled and walked over to a wall where a delicately carved wooden frame had been affixed. He slid the boards aside, revealing an even larger version of the same map. "This one is mine. You get the copy." He was smiling broadly.

Schram smiled in return. "Thank you, my friend."

The dwarf replied, "My goal was it may be used to save us the way you saved us in the past. Saying that, do you have a plan?"

Schram flattened the map across the table. "Well, I have been thinking about this for some time, and with everyone's agreement, I think we need to split up. If we assume the others have realized that the times are indeed grave, then I believe they will make a straight path to Elvinott to try to meet with us earlier than originally intended. With that, I believe a party should head directly there."

The others nodded in agreement, but Stepha had a slightly worried look. "Because you said 'a party' should head there, does that mean you are not in that party?"

Schram glanced to her but held a serious expression. "I must go to the Black Pool to have discussions with my brothers and then to the canok homeland. I fear something with the canoks is at the heart of these troubled times."

Jermys motioned to his guards to leave and for everyone to sit down as food was being prepared. The dwarf raised his hand, interrupting Stepha, who was about to protest. "Stepha, I know your feelings before you speak them. You know as well as I do that Schram, no matter how powerful he feels he is, should not travel alone during these times. We followed those rules in the past, and they served us well." He turned to face Schram. "My friend, you know that which you will face more than any other. You must not travel alone, and I know each of us would gladly follow you into Sakton's lair, but for us to choose would be wrong. What support do you need? Who should accompany you?"

"Although my desire would be to have Stepha and Lars continue with me, Stepha is needed in Elvinott, and Lars would not be welcome in the canok homeland. There is only one other who may be able to make that trip with me." He turned to the small rodent who had already dug into the food that had been delivered and was only half listening to his longtime friend. "Fehr, I need your insight into the Black Pool and great oak. Are you willing to join me?"

Fehr coughed up some food, which shot across Stepha's plate. "Seriously, you want me?" He paused and looked for a smile or some signal that he was joking. When he saw none, the rat stood on his hind legs and proudly said, "Groovy. I will get packed. I have so many more stories to tell you. You won't be disappointed. We will need a lot of provisions. I have so many pouches I can carry everything. You can keep your staff, though. That thing scares me. When will we leave? What can I get set up? I think—"

Schram cut him off. "On second thought, maybe Stepha is not necessary in Elvinott, and she should join me in..." Schram tried not to smile, but even he could not keep the sides of his lips from turning slightly upward. Fehr looked stung but then saw Schram's smile. Schram then asked, "Who can travel with Stepha and Lars to Elvinott?"

Jermys rose, lifted his hatchet of the ring, and while scratching Fehr across the brow, said, "I will, of course, join my friends—as we have in the past and will again for all eternity. We will defend our world from any evil, and we will do it together."

Schram smiled. "Jermys, you are the king now. You cannot just leave. You must protect Feldschlosschen first."

"Did that matter to you or Geoff so many years ago? My city will be well protected. We have learned many new ways to prevent invasion. I have several that will stand in my place with honor."

"Very well, if you are certain," replied Schram. "Then, at first light tomorrow, Fehr and I will head to the Black Pool, and Jermys, you will lead Stepha and Lars back to Elvinott. From there, you will speak to Madeiris and determine our next steps. I hope Geoff has made the same decision and will be there waiting for you."

All nodded agreement before Jermys rose his glass. "Travel safe, my friends. I cannot believe after so long we are seeing each other again, and it is under these circumstances. I do not believe this new evil has returned, but I know, as we did last time, we will fight this evil and win."

All lifted their glasses, but then Schram added, "Please know, my friends, I fear this is not a new evil but the same evil. It may have taken a new form, but the source is the same as it has always been. It has waited until now for a reason only it knows to be true—to show itself. It is confident and powerful, much different than in the past. It does not appear to be motivated by power, but some other force drives it for spreading its rule. For us, finding that reason is the key."

Lars looked on slightly confused. "Are you saying this is the same evil that is responsible for all the stories I heard from the past?" He paused then continued softly, "For the death of my mother?"

Schram stared at his young friend. "I am."

Nobody spoke the rest of the evening except for small side conversations. To Schram's surprise, until his words, none of them considered that this was all related to the past. Their assumption was that this was some new evil—some new presence wanting to assert its way. Schram thought deeply about what had occurred. Yes, the types of things happening were different than in the past, but they also were planned. The first magical creature they met was there to meet Schram. It was there to show how powerful it was. Whatever force was behind the events, if it did not have anything to do with the wars over twenty years ago, was still connected with Schram. It was not random. It was personal. Schram was sure of it.

As everyone disbanded for the night, Schram motioned to Lars. "Please walk with me."

The maneth bid farewell to those for the night and began a short walk with Schram.

"I have something for you. It was your mother's."

Lars looked on anxiously. "What do you have? Something to help me remember her by?"

Schram smiled. "Not quite, but it should help you feel her."

"What do you mean?" answered the maneth questionably.

Schram pulled the long silver scimitar from his pack. "This was her sword. It is a weapon of the ring, guarded by Aizlan, the great blue dragon, son of Anbari. Save you it can, as it did her so long ago. She chose your life over her own with this scimitar providing the power to save you. At that time, it carried the spirit of my dragon brother, but today it is a sword of mystery. Use it wisely. Draw on its power, its spirit. Feel your mother within it. Never let it be apart from you. I cannot tell you how important it was to her, and to Troyf."

Lars lifted the sword and scabbard to the air and then removed the sword with a grinding sound that bit the air like music to Schram's ears. He lifted the scimitar, and suddenly a distant peace grew across the maneth's face. Then Schram saw it—faint at first then stronger and clearer. Surrounding the large maneth was Krirtie. It was the first time the sword had been drawn in twenty years, and the woman, his closest human friend, was around her now large half-maneth牛half-human son. The peace in his eyes was something Schram had never witnessed before. Schram looked at the maneth's eyes and saw two tears streaming down his face. Without a word, he left the young boy to be by himself.

Geoff removed his club from the head of the troll and let the body fall motionless to the ground. "This is ridiculous. Even if we could get through them all, who's to say there are not more behind? Angus, what do you think?"

"I think trolls smell awful, but if you are asking if we retreat or plow through, everything in my gut tells me these trolls are here to prevent us from making it to Elvinott. Therefore, I take it personally that we need to continue."

Maldor kicked one troll directly into another, causing both to fall back unconscious. "I too have had just about enough. Let's punch a hole through and go."

Geoff nodded. "Very well, I concur." He hollered up to Denisi, who hovered completely unnoticed in the air with an arrow notched. "Clear us a path, Denisi. We are going straight though."

Although not all trolls could normally communicate as such, several seemed to understand and clearly displayed their surprise in the decision. The front line buckled down, but the onslaught of precision archery, two great maneths, and what proved to be an extremely skilled human quickly divided the large force of trolls until a path large enough for a fleet could go through. The divided trolls became confused, and quickly, many simply scattered into the woods. The few that remained engaged in combat but were quickly left incapacitated.

The three on the ground headed at a swift pace toward Elvinott's protective forests while the flyer elf scouted ahead for any additional unplanned visitors. They all knew that making it to the Elvinott forests was key as no evil had been able to penetrate its protective barrier. It was possibly the strongest magical barrier ever created.

ELVINOTT

"Do not defy me, young Schram."

"How do you know who I am?" he replied, looking around the area. It was cold, much cooler than most of Troyf for this time of year. The ground was soft, much like the caverns of Draag, but it was not the dragon homeland he was in. He did not know when he arrived here or how he came to be, but he was here, and he was facing a power never felt before. He turned his head back to the creature before him. It was dark, but he could still make out its shape. A large dragon, a soft blue-green color. Large, but not like a full-grown male, most likely female. Its eyes were hard, beating on the human like swords. Schram wanted to say more but was cut off.

"If you truly think you can defeat me, you will have to take the form of a dragon. That is where all your power flows. You were dragon before you were anything. Face me now, or you will die."

He took a small step back, trying to gain his perception. "Why would I wish to defeat you? I do not know who you are."

"Because if you do not defend yourself, you will die." Just then, bolts of energy shot from the dragon directly into Schram's chest. He felt the pain erupt from his body and was helpless to defend himself. He gripped his staff hard, but like last time, it proved to be of no use. Pain bit through him as if a knife had cut his flesh without any defense. He fell to his knees and saw his human blood spilling across the ground.

"Who are you?" "Today is your day to die."

He spoke a few words and instantly appeared as a dragon, standing much larger than the blue-green beast in front of him. "You believe you can defeat your own, then please do it."

The dragon before him took a step forward. "You are still a fool, boy. I cannot believe you are so weak-minded."

The area exploded in light, and the pain Schram felt had never been matched in his life. It was as if every part of his body had been ignited into fire and then quickly extinguished. Schram was dead.

"Wow, Schram, you can really fly fast. This is great. We have to do this more often."

Schram's large dragon wings pounded the air as he moved at the fastest pace he had ever flown. The rat sat poised on his back as if he was sitting on a rock, not the back of what was one of the largest dragons on all of Troyf. "Why so quiet today?"

Schram did not want to answer, but he knew the rat would pummel him with questions until he at least gave him something. "I had dreams last light. Dreams about my death. Dreams about the future. Dreams about something."

"Really?" said Fehr. "You know, dragons can see their own death."

Schram smiled. "Yes, I have heard that before."

Fehr shook his head. "I wouldn't worry about it. You had several ales last night. It is probably just the ale talking."

"I am sure it is, my friend." Schram blew a little fire in front of him to heat the air and increase his speed. "Any other questions before I hit the high winds ahead?" Changing the subject with a bandicoot was always easy if you positioned questions back to him correctly.

"How long until we reach the pool?"

"Less than a day. We will not run into any trouble on our way. I feel our path is clear. We just need to get there."

Fehr nestled in a little tighter as the wind started to blow harder across Schram's back. "Are you nervous?"

Schram had not thought about it, but he was feeling some anxiety about returning to this place, which had been so important so many years ago. He had not seen his brothers since they left his side outside Elvinott forests. It had been since he learned about his true heritage and Hawthorne's death. He wondered if he had avoided coming or simply because knowing they were there was enough. He would soon find out.

"Madeiris, my friend, thank you so much for offering your home as our refuge one more time." Geoff and Madeiris locked hands, each with their free hand on the other's shoulder.

"My home is your home, my friend." He turned to the others. "And that goes for all of you." His eyes caught the human who was locked in a stare around the whole area. "Yes, my new friend, welcome to Elvinott. Our city is cut from the trees and is well protected. Since you are a friend of my friends, then you are a friend of ours."

Denisi smiled as the human did not seem able to answer and only remained locked in a stare at the large fountain they stood below. "This is Angus Reid. He joined us in Toopek with Alan's support. Although I am sure he is a bit tired from our journey, I know he is very pleased to be here."

Angus seemed to snap out of his trance. "Yes, Your Majesty. Your city is truly amazing. I have heard stories, but the words do not do it justice. I am very pleased to be here."

Madeiris, Denisi, and the other elves in the area seemed pleased with this response, but it was the elf king who replied, "Please, my name is Madeiris. I am your brother and not your king." Angus nodded as Madeiris turned back to Geoff. "Now, tell me, my friend, I did not expect you for some time. What has brought you here in such haste? We have seen more trolls coming into the area, but I can't believe that is behind your sudden return. Is Toopek in danger?"

Geoff motioned with his eyes, which clearly told Madeiris they would need to continue this in the Great Hall. The elf took the message and motioned to the group. "Come, my friends, let's speak in my chambers. The chill in the air has begun to bite at my fingers, and I am sure you are all tired. I will have food and drink brought in." He motioned to the group to follow and whispered to a nearby elf, who then hustled away. He did not speak again as they made their way to the great oak at the center of their city. Madeiris stood at the table after all had sat and began filling their plates with food. "Now, tell me, my friends, the floor is yours. What has happened since we last spoke only days ago?"

Geoff replayed the events to the best of his ability, and they all seemed extremely interested in what the elf king's feelings may be. The main question they held was if he would think they were possibly overreacting, or would he see validation in their fears? Madeiris let the large maneth finish before he again took the floor.

"Thank you for the very thorough overview. What I would like to do is something our good friend Schram taught me to do so long ago. Let's look at those things we know for sure. Let's not worry today about what we think but only what we know." He took a short breath, and as he looked around the room, he knew he definitely had everyone's attention. "Before we met last time, there was a very powerful magical presence outside Elvinott that clearly had a purpose involving Schram. Although he believes it was a message to him, I do not think we know that yet, but I will agree whatever its purpose, it was directed at our powerful friend. Then we know there are canoks involved. They may not be as directly involved as in the past, but they are present.

"Further, whatever power is behind this, be it canoks or other, they definitely have some powers over controlling large bands of trolls. Interestingly, however, there are no dark dwarves or goblins.

In the past, all three parties were used together, but now, as far as what we know today, only trolls. Finally, although we are divided, we should be relatively certain that Schram, Stepha, and Lars have seen the same thing, as Schram was able to lend support through his dragon ways when you were in need. I do not want to venture a guess as to how he does this, but regardless, he was able to do it, so we will hold it as fact. From there, we only know you faced troll interference multiple times, but nothing that was truly designed to destroy, just to simply remind you they are there. Does that cover everything?"

Maldor rose. "We also know we were given a deadline to fall in line and provide Schram."

Madeiris nodded. "Yes, that is correct. But I would add, provide him where?"

There was silence as all shook their heads, not realizing until that moment they had no idea where to go to provide Schram even if they intended to do so. The elf king paced the floor a bit before speaking again, "Because of this, we can also hold as fact that there will be more contact before that deadline is reached."

Maldor was still standing when he said, "So are you saying that knowing we will again, at some point, meet the one who claims to hold so much power to destroy our cities is a benefit to us?"

Madeiris smiled. "Would you rather be met by surprise or be prepared?"

There was no response, but everyone knew that answer. After a long silence, the elf king added, "So those are the facts. What do you think they all mean?"

A dead silence engulfed the room. None of them either had an answer or wanted to answer. Geoff surveyed the area, read each of their eyes, and then stood next to Maldor. "I believe Schram is correct."

Madeiris walked to his longtime friend. "Correct about what?"

"This is centered on him. I believe taking over our world is the end result, but he is a necessary step in the process."

Denisi asked, "Do you mean they cannot take over our world with him in the way?"

Geoff stepped forward. "No, I mean they believe they can take over the world regardless, but they want Schram. It is personal." Madeiris looked on, a bit surprised by the leap.

"You have no basis for that."

The large maneth's tone got stronger. "I am telling you everything that has occurred involves him. The creature outside Elvinott, the group we met directly stating it, his ability to get assistance to us from afar—I am telling you Schram is the key. Answer that question, and we will have our answer."

"How about his human mother?" asked a voice from the doorway.

"Stepha," said Madeiris with a newfound pleasure in his voice. "How are you here?"

Stepha ignored the question. "His heritage has been the key to this from the beginning. His canok friend saw it so long ago. He devised this deal that set this whole process in motion. His birth mother turns out to be a dragon, he learns secrets about an elven ring, and then finds his true self in a dragon. He has powers he still has only begun to understand, and now some force is seeking him out. Who is the only person or creature we have not seen since this all started twenty years ago?"

Maldor turned to her. "His human mother."

"And the one person he has continued to seek to find," added Geoff.

Madeiris asked, "Are you all suggesting his mother is behind all this?"

The elf princess turned to her brother. "I do not know what I am saying other than my husband is obsessed with finding his human mother, and I fear when he finds her, it will be his undoing."

Madeiris appeared extremely concerned as this had gone a completely different direction than he anticipated. "Stepha, please do not hide your words regardless of your feelings for Schram. Do you feel she is behind this evil?"

"I believe only she is alive and aware of his presence. I have no reason to believe she is behind it or even involved. She is only human, nothing else. From what Schram says, she was easily coerced away when his birth mother took her place. However, I do believe finding her will provide some answers, but those answers scare me. They scare me greatly."

Maldor was very surprised at the elf's response. "Have you told Schram of your feelings?"

"My husband wishes only to find her, which I have supported. I have never mentioned that he may not like what he finds. As I said, I have no reason to believe one thing or the other. I am an elf. I learned a long time ago to trust my feelings, even when they do not make sense." She shook her head, and a tear began to fall across her cheek.

Geoff moved to stand next to Madeiris. "We are doing exactly what you asked us not to do. We are dealing in conjecture. What is our next step? Where is Schram now?"

There was a commotion at the door, and Jermys broke through with two elven guards in his wake trying to remove his tobac. "Listen, elves, I have not burned down a tree yet, but I am going to have my smoke, or you will find yourself behind the blade of my hatchet trying to take it from me."

Madeiris raised his hand. "It is okay. King Jermys would never let his smoke bring down our city."

The elves were taken by the title of king used for Jermys, and they looked at each other in embarrassment, bowed to the small dwarf, and quickly departed. All looked upon the dwarf with complete pleasure seeing their longtime friend. He only stood half the height of the elves and less than that for the maneths. His long beard reached the ground and actually was brown and crusty from the dirt it had attracted on his walk. His face was hard, beaten down over time. But his smile still brought with it a feeling of calm and safety. He was pleased to be with his friends again; that much was certain.

Jermys took a deep suck from his pipe and then looked to Stepha. "In a hurry?"

She blushed a little under her smile. "I am sorry, my friend. I assumed you would be free to enter and join me here."

"Oh yeah, free to join you here. With six arrows nocked toward my backside as I entered. Maybe next time, you'll go ahead and let them know I am coming."

Lars smiled. "They did not seem to give me any problems."

The dwarf glared at the young maneth. "You really think that is helping?"

He shrugged, and they all seemed to like the humor in the dwarf's situation. Jermys moved toward the table and still had not extinguished his pipe. "Well, I sure am glad everyone can eat, drink, and have a great old time while I am being arrested and thrown out of my friend's city because I just want to have a quick suck of tobac."

Madeiris walked over and slapped Jermys on the back. "My friend, you are always welcome in our home. There is nothing more I can say, but it is good to have you back again."

Geoff and Maldor also approached the dwarf. Maldor spoke first and picked him up. "You are the toughest dwarf I have ever known. Having you here only solidifies my belief that we cannot be defeated. Thank you, my friend."

As he picked him up, a soft humming started from each of the four weapons—Jermys's hatchet, Maldor's hammer, Stepha's bow, and Lars's scimitar.

"They are together. The weapons of the ring are all together," Stepha said as she put her hands over her ears from the pitch of the sound.

"Look at the map," stated Madeiris. "This is where Schram said my father first located the weapons of the ring. Now they are all here, together again. What does it mean?"

The Great Hall was the room where Madeiris's father, Hoangis, had first shown Schram the location of all the weapons of the Ring of Ku. The map cut from the roots of the great oak identified each key location. Now there was a new message.

Stepha pointed. "Where is that?"

Madeiris's tone was cold and lost. "It is beyond the Realm of Darkness. I do not know if anyone has ever traveled there."

The room became silent as all looked around for any feedback. Maldor rose. "They pulled me to them when they left the Realm. I was in Draag. They used the hammer and found me, and then I was with them. But I was never in the Realm myself."

Stepha asked, "Who was there? Who was with you?"

"The big whale Khaled. Schram, his dragon mother, and the canok Werner."

Stepha did not like hearing the canok's name, and it was clear her trust of the four-legged creatures was very low. She believed Schram was blind to their true heritage because of his history with Kirven. The elf showed her displeasure. "That leaves us nothing. Only Schram, his dragon mother, and Werner ever summoned Khaled. We have nothing."

Nobody noticed Lars, who had fallen to his knees gripping his sword. They all were looking at each other when the maneth uttered a small, soft roar. All heads swung to him and noticed he was holding his sword as if it was on fire, but he could not let go.

Maldor moved to his son. "Lars, what is it?" The maneth gritted his teeth in pain but did not let go. "Place the weapons on the table. Do not let go, but place them on the map and have them all touch. Do it now."

Without question, the three others took their weapons to the map table and laid their weapons across its face. Stepha was first, then Maldor, Jermys; and then Lars, with his sword he had only received a day earlier, laid his across the faces, connecting them all. The room lit up as if the sun was rising right there inside the oak. Everyone turned away in pain, and nobody could look anywhere near the map.

Jermys thought he was blind but knew the answer was there. The smallest one in the room took a step toward the map and placed his second hand on the table still contacting his weapon. At first touch, a scream echoed off the walls. He turned his head toward the weapons, and his face went blank. "I know," he screamed.

The room went dark, and then everyone's eyes adjusted, and the four companions all fell to their knees.

Stepha climbed to her feet. "What was that?" she said, her voice slightly broken.

"The weapons," added Maldor, "they are back to normal." Each grabbed their weapons, except Jermys, who remained motionless kneeling at the side of the table.

Madeiris, who was closest to the dwarf, grabbed his shoulder. "Jermys, are you well? I heard you scream."

The dwarf turned to look upon the elf king with a look of amazement across his face. "I saw things. Things so beautiful. Dragons, elves, magic. It was amazing."

"Did you learn anything?" asked Stepha. "You shouted, 'I know.' Do you know what to do?"

The dwarf shook his head. "I do not know what it means, but I saw Maldor handing his hammer to those who called themselves the guardians. That is all I know."

Maldor jumped forward. "I know the guardians. I was told before. They are those who guard the Realm. They believe the hammer to be theirs."

All eyes suddenly went to Madeiris. The elf king was caught a bit off guard, but as was his place, he let no insecurity show. "This is out of my area of knowledge, but I learned a long time ago that this room holds special powers. In speaking with my sister and those who carry the weapons, there are many secrets carried within them as well. My friend, I would never ask you to give up your weapon, but the gods seem to be asking for it. What do you each think?"

Stepha brushed back her long hair and replaced her bow. "The map told us to go beyond the Realm. The weapons told us to go to the Realm. I believe we should go there, with the weapons, and in exchange for returning the hammer, we can learn how to go beyond."

"What if the guardians simply want to use the hammer for evil? Giving it up could be our undoing." Maldor gripped his hammer tightly. Although tied to its power and existence, it was not part of him as it had been at one time. He did not know if being tied to it was his destiny or the guardians'.

Geoff placed his hand on his young maneth's shoulder, much like Maldor would do to his son. "I believe the signs are clear. I remember Schram saying the promise was made. The hammer was to be returned to the guardians. I have never understood why Schram went to recover the Rift Amulet, as it was said it did not exist. However, on that journey, this agreement was made. Everything happens for a reason, just as you were meant to grab that hammer from its magical case and you were to become one with it. It now must be returned to its home."

Maldor stared into his leader's eyes. Geoff was not only his king but also his friend and his father when his birth father had been killed. When Alhize died, so did a piece of Maldor. But Geoff did not let the warrior die. He was there with him today, and he knew what his answer must be. "We must find our passage to the Realm of Darkness. I will hand-deliver the hammer. The way it was meant to be."

Madeiris nodded, as did Jermys and Stepha. Madeiris was the first to speak, "Who can get us there? Maldor mentioned Khaled of the physeter who helped them in the past. Who can summon such a passage?"

Stepha shook her head. "The only one on Troyf I know for sure is Schram."

Madeiris turned to his sister but still spoke to the group, "There is no way to summon his help at this time, so is there any other way?" He pointed to the map. "It is across the sea. Can we go by boat?"

Jermys looked at the map, then back to Madeiris, then back to the map. "We could not traverse it in time, even with Pete traveling at his best pace."

"What about dragons?" added Maldor. "There were several that Alan said were loyal to Toopek."

Geoff cautioned, "Alan said they would not allow Toopek to be destroyed. Willing to help us may be another story altogether."

"Aye, but do we have any other options?" The group looked at one another without speaking and then to the elf king.

Stepha stepped forward. "For the first time in nearly twenty years, we are all together. We have assembled the weapons of the ring in one place. Schram told me many times to trust in the weapons. I say we put our trust in the weapons. The four of us go to Toopek, we bring the weapons before the dragons, and if they do not accept it, the weapons will show us a way. We will get to the Realm of Darkness because our weapons will not allow it to not be the result."

Geoff nodded. "You are putting our world in the hands of fate?"

"Fate has been with us since the beginning. Fate brought us together. Fate dictated our actions. Fate brought us the weapons. Fate defeated the black dragon." She paused when she realized she had taken the room from her brother, but a quick nod from him that only she saw gave her the strength to continue. "It is time we take fate by the fists and drive it forward. We have to get to the Realm. We have Khaled, the dragons, or a boat. All three of these require travel back to Toopek. We do not have time to waste, and we cannot count on Schram to save us this time. We are strong, and with the weapons together, we are one."

She stepped back, awaiting a response, and the silence that ensued caused a quiver down her spine. However, the minute Maldor slammed his hammer to the table with a roar, she knew all were in agreement.

Geoff raised his giant hand and said, "I will return to the maneth homeland. We will move our entire camp to Toopek. It will take several days, but we will support Schram's homeland also as one. Lars and Denisi, continue with the group to Toopek now. They can use your support. Madeiris, if you feel your city is still strong, then any support for Toopek would be appreciated. I also believe this is personal toward Schram, and with that, I feel the humans will be hit first."

Denisi stared like daggers toward her husband. She began to speak, then when she saw his eyes, she knew his answer was final. To ask to go with him would be futile. Her place was in support of what her husband thought was the most dangerous: the trip to Toopek.

Madeiris drew his sword from its sheath, making a high-pitched scratch as the blade caught the sides. Raising the sword above his head, the elf king stated, "We will hold Elvinott and support Toopek as well. The elves will also guard your passage between our great cities."

Geoff then continued, "I would wish this night we could enjoy a feast and be with our friends, but I feel time is too critical. I will leave as soon as I can be packed and ready." To Madeiris, he added, "I would appreciate a scout or two along my path, but am comfortable alone even through the night if you cannot spare them."

Madeiris did not answer but quickly motioned for two guards to join his maneth friend. The rest of the group was surprised at the insistence on leaving immediately, but as they thought about it, they too came to the same conclusion. It was time to take this evil on directly and not wait for it to attack them.

Before Geoff left the room, he turned back to the group and said, "Travel safe, my friends, and be prepared for anything. This evil is different than in the past, and we are older and slower. This evil already believes it has won. It has given us an ultimatum, a timeline. Once that timeline is breached, it will try to destroy us. We have to believe it is powerful enough to do it, or it would not have made the threat. I will be in Toopek in no more than four days. Use that time to locate passage to the Realm. If you can leave without me, then do so. Otherwise, I will join you on this mission. If you cannot find passage, then we have to hope Schram will be close behind. I believe he is coming. I believe he is aware. I believe he knows."

The Dominion

"Greetings, Aizlan. It has been a long time."

"It has, Schram, too long." The large blue dragon with golden wings knelt slightly at Schram's presence, as did Schram in return. "And, Fehr, it is good to see you again, and welcome home."

"Thank you, big bluey. What has been going on here? Any new stories?"

"No, my friends. It seems we feel all the stories are with you these days. We felt you would be coming to join us. We felt it needed to be soon."

Schram nodded. "Yes, I seek council with my brothers. I fear something has changed in this world, and it has some newfound power behind it. Power I do not understand. Power that is strong, very strong."

The large blue dragon heard his words but did not respond. Instead, he closed his eyes and started through the long chamber beneath the silver oak in the center of the Black Pool. Fehr and Schram fell in behind. Both knew these passages from their time there in the past but relished in Aizlan's lead. They did not speak as Fehr seemed content to contemplate how much and when he was going to eat next, and Schram was simply absorbing all the power and strength carried in these walls. It appeared that although Aizlan resided here, he too was drawing on the spirits beneath the tree.

They entered a large room Schram knew all too well. His battles of the past were now thrust to the forefront of his mind. The place where his closest friend and his worst enemy were defeated. As the prophecy had dictated, so had it happened. The chamber was huge, and large side chambers broke from its delicately carved marble walls in multiple directions. In three of these chambers were three large dragons, all sitting poised and attentive.

"Cameron, my half-brother and guardian of the Hatched of Claude. Kylscot, guardian of the bow, and Kolkmeier, protector of the hammer. It is truly a dream to see you again. Thank you for allowing my presence."

All the large dragons nodded, but it was Cameron, a green dragon with extremely large silver wings, who rose to speak, "My brother, we had felt your presence and path. It is very good to see you. Welcome back to your home."

"Thank you, Cameron. I feel so much warmth and power here. Strength I have not felt in so long seems to flow from these walls through my blood."

All the dragons were now on their feet, and all smiled, clearly understanding his feelings. Schram had remained in dragon form, not because he felt he needed to but because it was becoming his most comfortable form when magic was involved. Cameron nodded to Fehr as well, who simply smiled between bites of fruit he had found at the small center table, which was probably there just for him.

The large green dragon continued, "We have many questions for you, as I am sure you have for us. The times appear to us to be very volatile."

There was a tension in Cameron's voice Schram had never heard before. He paused a moment to choose his words carefully. "I too have felt and seen this volatility. I cannot explain much of it. There is magic behind it. It is a powerful magic that I do not understand, and I was hoping my brothers, those who are the strongest with magic on all of Troyf, would be able to provide me direction."

Kylscot, the bright-yellow dragon with orange wings, the only one with these colorings on all of Troyf, had been silent since Schram had entered but added a simple comment in response, "You must always choose your own direction, as it has always been. We can provide you any knowledge we believe to be true, but most of all, we will simply bring out what you already know."

"I understand," Schram replied. "I value your knowledge and hope that it helps me see our world more clearly." Schram replayed the little information and experiences he had seen over the last several days, ending with the decision to come directly to the Black Pool.

Cameron knelt back down on the ground, letting out a sigh as he sat. A small look of worry crossed Schram's face as he could see and feel the pain in the dragon's movement. "Worry not, my friend. Age just wears at my bones each day. I am in fine health and will not be leaving this world just yet."

His face softened as the green dragon continued, "If you would be more comfortable in your human form, please do not remain dragon for us. We see your spirit, not your body." Schram nodded but did not change his appearance. Cameron smiled and then continued, "Very well, my brother. What conversation do you have for us?"

Schram was caught by the word "conversation," but let it go without comment. "I would like to ask what you feel about the world today."

"Too broad a question. We feel many things." Cameron was not annoyed with the question but seemed to want to push Schram a certain direction.

The human magician smiled. "Very well, the canoks. What has happened to them since they were returned to their proud race?"

Aizlan lowered his head. "In that, you answered your own question. They have not been returned to their proud race from the distant past. They are creatures of honor. They were at the source of the evil. Half of their race actually used their powers to try to take over our world. Although you were able to return them their heritage, you could not return their honor. They remain in their homeland disgraced. How they repair that damage, we cannot say. However, we do feel their lives will continue to fall before they climb."

Schram nodded, understanding. "Who is the new young canok I have seen?"

Cameron now replied, "We do not know. Until you told us, we had not felt this presence."

"Then why do you feel the canoks will still face dishonor before they return?"

The four dragons looked at each other questionably, but again, it was Cameron who answered, "Schram, my brother, to answer that question, I need you to answer the real question."

Schram did not know where this was going. Sometimes he just wanted the information fed to him. He did not want to solve every riddle. "What is the real question?"

"What is the one question you really want answered?" spouted the rat from the side with food again spewing from his mouth as he spoke.

Schram was startled by the comment from Fehr but did hear the words. There was a long period of silence before he answered, "Who is really behind this evil?"

"Even I knew that one," chattered the rat again.

Cameron nodded. "So answer your question."

Schram shook his head. "I don't know that answer."

"Yes, you do. Think about all you know."

He continued to shake his head. "If I knew, I would tell you. But I don't."

The dragons again fell silent and let the silence engulf the group.

Kolkmeier lifted his large head to stare directly toward his confused pupil and asked, "Who has been part of this from the beginning, but they were not part of the last ending?"

"I do not know." Schram's tone carried a slight frustration in it.

Cameron smiled. "When you do, then you will have your answer." He paused again as he watched Schram's face. The human in dragon form clearly did not like this line of questions and wanted answers, answers he was not getting. "What else do you wish to know?" The statement seemed to imply Schram had gained much thus far, but he felt he had gained nothing.

Schram simply replied, "I need to know what to do, where to go. Who and what is this magical creature that had so much power, whose sole purpose seemed to be to send a message to me?"

"All good questions," replied Cameron. "Let me start with the creature."

Without a word, the same creature appeared in the room. It was large and powerful and stood only inches from Schram's face. Schram leaped to his feet and roared before the beast. This time, however, the beast reached out with magical hands, grabbed Schram, lifted him in the air, and slammed him against the wall. Its grab held his entire body pinched so tightly he could not move. Schram quickly incanted a spell, but it was useless. He drew on his staff with no effect. Schram could not believe that in Anbari's dominion, the Staff of Anbari still was magically held powerless. With a flash, the creature vanished and Schram's body fell to the floor.

"Wow," stated Fehr, "you were able to defeat it this time. It came out of nowhere, and how did it get in here?"

Schram's face was devoid of any pleasure of defeating it. "I did nothing. Again, I was helpless. It must have been my brothers who saved me."

Their eyes turned to the dragon. "My young brother, we did not defeat the creature. We created it."

Schram looked on in disbelief. "What do you mean you created it?"

Cameron narrowed his stare on his younger half-brother. "Magic transition."

The other dragons nodded, but Schram still showed no knowledge of the subject. "What is magic transition?" he asked, his tone showing his interest but still lack of confidence on where this was going.

The large green dragon stretched his silver wings and then nestled back down into a more comfortable position. "It is possible for some, not many, to harness their magic and place it somewhere they are not. They are able to appear as real entities. They are able to continue to work their magic, but their body remains somewhere else. All they need is to have been in that place at some time in the past and have a passage there again."

"A passage there again?" asked Schram.

Cameron appeared slightly taken by the interruption but continued without comment, "It means there has to be a source to grab onto."

"So if a creature with this ability had been to a place before and there was some level of magic in that area again, they could use that magic as the source and place some level of their magic there as well."

Cameron smiled. "Correct."

Schram thought hard about his previous meeting. He then broke the silence still with a questioning tone. "How does it render my staff powerless?"

"Your staff needed no power here because there was no threat. Our magic and the staff's magic are the same. We could no longer use magic against the staff as it could against us."

"How about in the glade outside Toopek? Why was I powerless there?"

The four dragons looked at each other, and Schram knew they were in a telepathic conversation. Aizlan lifted his eyebrow as he turned to Schram. "We cannot answer that. The only logical answer is this magic is simply significantly more powerful than the staff, and that is an answer we cannot believe is possible."

The group sat in silence. The only noise heard was Fehr's soft chewing to the side, which he even stopped as it proved too uncomfortable against the ominous silence in the room. Schram had met that magic directly, and he felt how strong it was. Although he knew the others did not want to believe it, he knew it could be true. He also knew that if it was true, then he did not have any answers as to how to defeat it. If this enemy's power was strong enough to render Anbari helpless, then nothing he had seen on Troyf could defeat it. He could see in his brothers' eyes that they were thinking the same thing.

Schram's eyes lit up slightly. "Cameron," he began, breaking the silence and actually causing the four large dragons to jump slightly.

"Yes, Schram?"

"You said it was possible for some, not many, to harness power in this fashion. You can obviously perform a magic transition as you just proved it before me. But who else?"

The dragons again looked at each other without speaking before the large green one answered, "Before today, there was only our father, our mother, and the four of us." He paused then added, "I believe in time that you will be able to without question." His voice faded slightly. "It was not only dragons with this ability, but as I said, very few dragons."

"What does that mean?" Cameron did not shy from the question.

"That means, very simply, either another has harnessed the power to perform such a powerful task, or one of the four of us did it."

Schram smiled. "It was not one of you, so I ask you four again because you know the level of magic able to be harnessed by every dragon on Troyf. Do you know of any dragon that could have gained that power?"

"We do not."

Schram entered one final question because he had to ask. "Canok?"

Kolkmeier moved to answer as Cameron began to cough slightly, causing fire to shoot across Fehr's table of food. He seemed pleased as some of his breads were lightly toasted. Once eyes had fallen back away from the rat, the dragon replied, "Canok magic is different. They are talented magic fighters, but not skilled with a magic outside of their world. No canok can master a transition."

Schram rose and walked over to the center of the group of four, now taking his elven form to draw closer. His voice had softened slightly. "So is it your belief that a dragon is behind this?"

"It is," Kolkmeier replied.

All five of them became lost in thought for an unknown length of time. Schram could not believe there was another dragon out there. It had taken everything he had to defeat Slayne. What if Slayne was not even the master behind the original oppression? His last statement when he died stated that very thing: My plans have not as yet turned full circle, and your destiny is not complete. Schram had only questions, and that included one more he had to ask.

"My friends, I was going to return to the canok homeland to learn anything I could about what they knew and where they stood. I want to speak to Werner and Almok. Werner is now one of the strongest with magic, and my trust with him is unmatched. Almok was with the black dragon the longest. He will know more than any other as to what or who might be behind this. Do you agree with this direction?"

Cameron nodded. "We agree with your direction and believe that Almok is the key." He paused for a short moment, wanting the reinforcement to sink in, which gave Schram a new confidence and strength. "You then need to move as quickly as you can to Toopek. We feel turbulence there, and the city is in danger."

Schram had already felt the same tremors from Toopek, most likely because it was his kingdom, and he felt things about it that he did not for any other place. He already had planned that as his next stop and hoped his friends were already headed in that direction. He bowed his head. "I am sorry, my friends, but I must go. Time is critical for all of us."

"We understand. Please make the time before your next visit shorter. We too feel the destruction of the land in motion. We will use the time to focus our energy on identifying who is behind it and what their plans are. Knowing those things will help us."

The group exchanged many telepathic messages, which made all included feel very strong. Schram had only been to this place a couple of times, and each time it had been very difficult while there. This time, however, it was proving difficult to leave. He was starting to become more a dragon and less of anything else. He smiled as he wondered what Stepha would think about that thought. He closed his eyes and imagined her. He could see her flying over the forests. He could see through her eyes. Her bow was drawn, but she was not fighting, just providing support to those below. He hoped they were heading to Toopek, but his thoughts were broken as his wings hit the outskirts of the storm around the Black Pool, and Fehr's claws bit into his back.

The rat gritted his teeth. "Okay, big ugly, let's make up some time. My belly is full, and I am ready for anything."

They broke through the back side of the storm into clear sky as the rat got struck by a wall of fire and was sent flailing toward the ocean's surface in a ball of flames and profanity.

Hope Is Fading

The group sat nestled in the brush. Their trip to Toopek had been halted by choice, not interference. Stepha and Denisi had both seen masses building outside Elvinott, and rather than continue to Toopek immediately, the elves wanted to evaluate the extent of the troops and get word back to Madeiris.

"What are they all doing here?" asked Denisi.

Stepha replied, pointing, "First, there were trolls outside Toopek, and now goblins outside Elvinott in these numbers. What can their purpose be? They can never get through our magical barrier. My father made sure of that."

Maldor and Lars were surveying the numbers and types of weaponry but did hear the comments. Maldor replied to the unasked question, "From what has been told, magic attacked Schram, making him somewhat helpless. Perhaps this power can defeat your protection. These goblins are armed very clearly for hand-to-hand combat. They have heavier armor, and each carries at least three weapons. A good portion are lined with bows while others carry multiple swords and daggers. We all know a goblin cannot plan, but it appears someone or something is planning for them." He paused then added, "And yes, Madeiris must be prepared for this. I believe they mean to attack the village."

Stepha replied, "I will go back. I will stand with my brother and lead the flyers, and should our barrier be breeched, we will destroy all who enter. We will not lose and flee our city again."

Maldor turned to the dwarf. "Jermys, Toopek was surrounded by huge numbers of trolls. Elvinott we now see being compromised by goblins. I know you have said the dark dwarves and mining dwarves were at peace. Are you absolutely sure you can trust them? It seems the evil of the past is organized, and the dark brothers and dragons are the only ones we have not yet seen. Feldschlosschen has to be on the list as well."

Maldor expected the dwarf to simply reply that they were indeed one and was clearly concerned when he saw the look in his eyes. The dwarf's tone was strong. "I hold no belief that the dark brothers will raise arms against us. However, to say we are at peace and act as one would not be accurate. Though there are groups that think as I do and openly want to become one with our brethren, there are more that do not. Could they bring evil before us? Possibly."

Maldor leaned closer to the group. "Stepha, you may return and speak with your brother, but I believe you were to be with us. Madeiris will learn of these goblins, whether you return or not. However, I will not stop you if you feel you must go. I understand the draw to protect your city." He turned to the dwarf. "Jermys, that holds for you as well. If you wish to return to your home, I will bid you no ill will. The rest of us will push forward. I believe as I did in the past that Toopek is the key. We must hold Toopek."

Each nodded understanding, but the dwarf was compelled to answer, "I will return to my home, but only after we have won our war. I believe my kindred will do what they need to, whether I am present or not, and I believe that being with you again, as we were in the past, is the path to bring peace across our land once and for all. Together, we are strong."

Stepha placed her hand on the dwarf. "I agree with Jermys. I am with you here, as we were meant to be."

"Then let it be so," answered Maldor. "Now we can focus on getting through this army."

"What do you think we should do?" asked Denisi. "I don't think we can just break right through them and assume it will work."

Jermys leaned closer to the group. "I say we wait until nightfall. Their numbers will drop in more than half as most will sleep. Those that don't sleep will fill their bellies with ale." He paused, pointing to two large barrels on the far side of the glade ahead of them. "We will be able to pass."

"I have a better idea," stated Maldor, lifting his hammer. "We drive through them like fire. These are goblins, not dragons."

Denisi placed her hand on his shoulder, surprised at actually having to hold him back and that he was serious in his direction. "Maldor, why risk fighting hundreds when in a few short hours we can walk right by five or six?"

Stepha leaned closer and whispered, "Look at it this way, my friend. There are but five of us and most likely two hundred of them. That is forty goblins each. What do you think that means should we try to get through now?"

The maneth stared at the woman; then his body softened. "I think it means they better go find some more goblins."

He smiled but knew the correct answer. "Very well, but if they don't do as the dwarf says and they remain in full numbers, we will be at even more a disadvantage at night."

"Understood," answered Denisi as she removed her hand and nestled back into the tree line for cover.

Maldor could not believe Denisi and Stepha had such precision with a bow. It was pitch-black out, and as the dwarf had predicted, the goblin numbers had fallen to minimal levels. In fact, nearly the entire battalion was at the ale barrels, almost completely out of sight. The handful that did remain had already been at the barrels for some time, and with that, they did not even feel the arrows as each pierced their armor. Stepha still took time to prepare each for their afterlife, but in the time it took Maldor to stand, survey, and carefully move forward into the goblin-controlled area, the two girls had cleared a path large enough to bring all of Elvinott through if they desired.

The maneth shook his head. "This time, my friends, you were right."

The dwarf did not pause to entertain the conversation and simply motioned with his arm. "Let's go while we can. Time is not our friend in these forests. Goblins will notice, and with these numbers, some could easily pursue."

Denisi and Stepha burst into the air ahead of the dwarf and two maneths. Lars had remained quiet throughout the entire time for several reasons, the heaviest of which was that he was traveling with his father. He still felt he had something to live up to. His father was a hero to all maneths. Besides Geoff, there was none more respected. Tie that to being the son of a human woman and hero. He had a tough image to fulfill. Although he loved his dad more than words could describe, when they were together, he ceased being Lars and often became Maldor's son.

"Come on, Lars, we must take the lead to ensure the others' safety."

Jermys glared at Maldor. "Maneths need to see to my safety?" he mumbled under his breath.

Maldor did not hear nor care as he and Lars darted ahead with a grace completely against all that their body size would say was possible. In very short order, they were well beyond the goblin barrier, and the two flyers dropped to walk beside them.

"How far do you wish to go?" asked Stepha.

"Another hour will put enough distance between us. If we do not see any trouble between now and then, I say we set down for the rest of the night." Maldor paused then realized he was the lowest-ranking individual there other than his son. "If you all agree," he added softly, having it sound somewhat forced.

Stepha smiled. "Do not worry, Maldor. We all trust your judgment." Turning to the others, she said, "I think that makes sense. Does anyone disagree?"

All nodded, and they proceeded on the plan as described. Within moments of arriving in a very small clearing, which would provide the perfect protection during the very still and almost hauntingly silent night, the four were asleep with Maldor taking first watch.

"Fehr!" roared Schram as he turned his head and dove toward the water's surface.

Cursing answered his roar just before the small rodent with his fur still aflame hit the water with the force equal to a dragon landing in mud. Schram's eyes stared down toward where his friend had hit, hoping to see him burst back through the water's surface. Within moments, his high-pitched curses carried in about five languages, of which only two or three Schram recognized, filled the air.

Schram soared down across the face of the water leading to the bobbing rat but did not pick him up.

"Schram! What the hell are you doing? Get me out of here now!" hollered his cold and soaked friend.

Fire blew across the water's surface, causing the rat to dive again but resurface immediately following. Schram turned his head back at the rat. "Sit tight, Fehr. I need to take care of our friends first. Just be thankful that water does not burn. I will be back in a minute."

"Yeah! Thankful! That is what I am right now." Schram heard the comment but could not react as two smaller blue dragons were trying to corner him against the storm. *Why do you attack me?* he said telepathically. *I mean you no harm.*

The dragons clearly heard his word but opted to speak so all could hear. The smaller of the two blues answered first, "No harm. You have destroyed our homeland. Draag as we know it is gone. Only you have the power to do such a thing. For twenty years, you tricked us into believing a black dragon was behind this evil. For twenty years, we have fought amongst ourselves to determine what was true. Had I not seen it with my own eyes, I would not have believed it. I believed in you, and you destroyed us. Our only saving grace is that we were allowed to leave. Now, there is not a dragon alive that will not try to kill you. Your time bringing harm to us is over. You are our enemy, Schram. We are just glad we found you first."

The other blue shot a ball of fire at Schram, which was easily extinguished prior to contact. Schram stopped his flight and hovered directly between the two blues, who also stopped, still trying to corner him against the storm.

Schram spoke loud to ensure they could both hear him clearly. "My friends, I have no knowledge of what you say. I have not been to Draag since the days after the final battles took place twenty years ago when I spoke to every dragon about what had occurred. My heart aches to learn that Draag is destroyed. It aches for every dragon."

The other blue moved slightly closer. "You lie. We saw you. Many of us saw you. You were in dragon form, but you carried the staff. You used your power to destroy our home." He flew all the way in to stop only inches from Schram's face. "I saw you with my own two eyes."

"I believe you, but I am telling you it was not me."

"Then who? Another dragon that looks just like you and carries that magical staff? Stop with your lies. To us, you are dead. We will try to make you physically that way as well."

Just then, a rope flew around Schram's neck, and in seconds, more. Fehr was on his back. Schram smiled. "Glad to see you still keep a full survival kit in your pouches."

"Aye," answered Fehr. "We can talk more later. Let's get the—"

One blue moved in front of him.

"Do not ask us to fight. Show us you are who you say you are and come with us freely to Draag. We cannot allow you to leave. More dragons are coming, and we will take you back to Draag to face your fate one way or the other."

Schram smiled at the young dragons. "My young friends, you cannot defeat me. I will come to Draag, but I cannot come now. There are dangers in our world today, and I feel what has happened at Draag is only part of it. You must trust me. I will come, but not today."

The blue shot another ball across Schram's brow, intentionally missing but sending a message. "You may see us as young, but we are strong. You will come."

Fehr pointed across the distant horizon of the water where several small dots hovered in the air. "More dragons are coming, Schram. Looks to be about ten."

"Will you take arms against us here as you did at Draag and further prove your guilt?" asked one of the blues, now speaking with more confidence knowing the small group of dragons was so close in their wake.

Schram was about to answer when he noticed the two blues' eyes grow wide. Then a soft touch from behind kept his voice silent.

"My young friends, I am Cameron, and Schram is my brother. With me are my other brothers, all sons to Anbari. If Schram had brought any harm to Draag, I personally would deliver him to you, but he has not." Cameron's voice was deep, almost mystical, carrying so much power.

One of the blues moved slightly forward. "Cameron, I never truly believed you to be real." He nodded to the huge dragon and then to the three dragons along his sides. "But we saw Schram. We saw him with our own eyes."

Cameron's lips were devoid of any smile, and his eyes narrowed on the young blues. "But did you feel him? Your eyes can deceive you. That is what this evil was counting on."

The large dragon closed his eyes, and suddenly his image skewed. Even Schram was caught off guard, but he could also feel the magical power that had just grown immensely in the area. With Cameron's form cleared, before the two blue dragons flew two large identical dragons, both with staff in hand. One was Schram, and the other was Cameron, changed to be exactly that of Schram.

Cameron still showed no emotion in his stare or voice. "Maybe it was me who destroyed your homeland. Would you have known it was me, or would you blame Schram, the one who gave so much to save all of you so long ago?"

The blues looked down but still did not back down. "You have great magic within you, Cameron, and you are the most powerful. There is no other being on Troyf that could do that. It was Schram. His final words were, 'Tell all your kind that in less than thirty moons, my plan will be complete. The dragons, just like every other creature on Troyf, will honor me or die. I am Schram, king of Toopek and all of Troyf, including Draag.'"

Schram and Cameron looked at each other but did not speak. Schram then turned back to the blue dragons. "Your friends are drawing closer. I cannot go to Draag right now. You are not allowing me to leave. I"—he motioned to his brothers—"we will not fight you. Therefore, the call is yours. How do you want to proceed?"

The two dragons looked at each other, and Schram could tell they were questioning what they knew. Then Aizlan moved next to Cameron, who had returned to his normal form. "I will go to Draag in Schram's place. When his business is done, he will come to join me. This way, you will know he will come, and I can see what has happened to our old home."

Cameron then added, "No, we will all go. Schram will continue on his mission with Fehr, and we will all accompany you back to Draag."

One of the blues began to object, but the other cut off his speech. "Very well." Turning to Schram, he said, "Do not delay your return and know that you will not have assistance from the dragons. Word of your betrayal has spread. You may very well meet with a new destiny should your path cross others." He turned his head back to Cameron. "Do not betray us as well, Cameron. I do not understand all that is occurring, but you and Schram have earned your chance. We will trust your direction for now."

Cameron now smiled as he knew even the combined power of the two blues and the other ten coming was no match for them had they decided not to let them pass. However, he too wanted to see what had happened at Draag. He also had great concerns with the power that could do what was being described—shape-shift into Schram and then still have enough power to destroy one of the most heavily protected areas of Troyf. Indeed, this was a powerful enemy, and it was a powerful enemy that was clearly still targeting Schram.

The large dragon motioned to his brothers, and they all fell in line next to the blues. With a nod to Schram, they turned and headed back toward the approaching ten. Schram nodded back while Fehr leaned forward and whispered, "What the hell is going on here, Schram?"

"I don't know, my friend. I don't know."

Death Is Before Us

"Well, I did not expect to see that."

Denisi stared at Maldor, both holding the same expression. The flyer elf leaned in to respond to the maneth's statement but then held quiet. Stepha saw her confusion and then turned her stare back to the clearing that led to the walls of Toopek. "Okay, what do you think it means? Schram said dragons could be with us, or with the dragons, but not against us."

"What does that mean?" replied Maldor. "If they are with the dragons, does that not mean they are against us?"

"No, it means they won't interfere." Denisi now chimed in, "Those nine dragons are not attacking Toopek, but they are also not with us. They look on the verge of exploding."

"No, they look like they are looking for someone." Lars pointed to the largest, a red dragon in the center. "His eyes are always scanning the tree line. They are on a mission to find someone, or something." Just then, the eyes of the red froze on their location.

"Oops," added the young maneth, "found someone they did."

The group all looked at each other, and as Denisi and Stepha adjusted to take to the air, Maldor grabbed both elves on the shoulder. "We will not run until it is time to run. Right now, let's walk toward them as they approach us. Show no fear. Show no attack. If they are looking for someone, I do not believe it is us."

The elves glanced at each other and then at the same time said, "We were not running."

Stepha continued alone, "We were taking to the air for added protection. Staying in a group like this could get us all cooked in one breath."

Maldor smiled. "We have nothing to worry about," he said with confidence, though he moved his hand to his hammer and issued a short silent prayer. Jermys did the same with his hatchet. *You do not need to pray for your safety, Maldor*, the large red said telepathically but allowed all to hear. *You are not whom we seek, but I believe you know the whereabouts of the one we want*. The other dragons fell in behind the red and made a fairly ominous sight as they approached.

Archers filled the wall with what appeared to Maldor to be the entire city poised to attack on foot. The maneth smiled, though he knew nine dragons against a city was, at worst, a fair fight, and most likely they needed to get some more cities. "What do you want, red? We are friends to the dragons. You have to know that."

The red's eyes narrowed. "Don't patronize me. The lies between you and your leader have now come full circle. We witnessed your friendship firsthand as we fled our land seconds before he destroyed it. We want only one thing. Tell us the location of Schram, or his home will face our vengeance. We are the ones with honor. We will not destroy Toopek if he is returned to us immediately."

"Schram? Destroyed your home?" Maldor began to grip his hammer tighter. "What are you talking about? Schram is working to protect this world from evil, not spread its wrath. I say with certainty you are mistaken."

"We are not, for we saw him with our own eyes. He was in dragon form and still carried the staff. He is a liar, a murderer, and most of all, our enemy, and we will bring him home. Now, I ask you again, and for the last time, where is he?"

Stepha stepped forward. "This does not make sense. Schram is a dragon, or at least half dragon. He would not harm another dragon. He was not even near Draag."

"Ah, Stepha, I am so glad we found you. If we cannot find your husband, I am sure he will come to find you." The dragon gave a short roar of pleasure, knowing he had the bait that would ensure their eventual success. He paused then realized what the elf had said. "How do you know he was not anywhere near Draag?"

"Because up until a few days ago, we were together. His path was not to Draag."

"And when he split from the others, he came to Feldschlosschen before heading to the Black Pool," added the dwarf.

"So you split up? You all split up. How do you know where he went after you left? Has he ever gone somewhere on his own? Has he ever told you one thing and then done another?" Again, a pause, then he added, "Face it, Stepha. You don't know where he went, what he did, or what his true path is. Schram did go to my home, he did destroy it, and he will pay."

"No!" stated the elf sternly. "There is evil in the land. It has taken refuge around every race. It has issued a threat and timeline. And it has vowed to destroy us all. Schram is not your enemy, but this evil wants you to think he is. If you should destroy Schram, you will be doing the one thing it cannot do. It is using you like puppets, like the black dragon did so long ago."

The red roared, and fire shot between its lips as the anger boiled within him. "Listen to me, you fool elf. Never bear reference to the black dragon again in my presence, or it shall be the last word you offer."

The elf leaned back, surprised by the violent and immediate response, and all the companions drew their weapons as they too witnessed the fierce change in demeanor. The red ignored this movement and stared hard at Stepha. Its voice was still stern but softened just a bit. "I sense you believe your words. I believe that deception is not your intent. I will consider this as we continue our search. My question for you remains, where is Schram?"

Maldor held his hand to the elf princess, motioning her not to speak. "What is your intention should you locate Schram? We hold no secrets, nor do we believe he will hold any in return. When you locate him, you will learn he did not do as you believe. Therefore, I must know, when you find him, do you intend to kill him or speak to him about what you believe?"

The red's eyes turned to Maldor. "I cannot lie. Should he resist or run, we will fight. Our intent, however, is clear. We are to bring him back to Draag, the site of his wrath, and put him before our elders. Should he be found guilty, his fate will be in their hands."

Stepha leaned forward. "Schram is innocent, but Maldor, do not tell them a thing. They have shown they act without care. They are not looking for justice. They are looking for revenge. Much of our chance to save this world relies on Schram being successful. He cannot go to Draag to take part in this charade. He must complete his mission."

The red frowned. "He is guilty, and you just want to hide him." He turned and said something telepathically to the other dragons, who then moved into a formation where they could create a full assault against the small group. The companions stood firm but also adjusted their position to best protect against an attack should one commence.

"No, my friends," interrupted Maldor, drawing all eyes back on him. "Schram is innocent, and we have nothing to hide. He should have already arrived at the Black Pool and left. His next destination is the canok homeland, though I cannot even tell you where that is for sure. After that, he was to return to Elvinott, although I believe he will not make that trek and instead will come back here." He turned to Stepha. "Schram would want them to know. The dragons are a part of him. He is a part of them. He already knows of this evil and will address it without fear."

The elf nodded. "I understand." The dragons appeared to have another conversation, and then two groups of three each took off in different directions, the wind from their wings knocking the dwarf off his feet, and the ghostly white that had engulfed Angus's face slowly began to return to normal. The red arched its head back and spoke to the group, "We will find Schram. We will listen to him. Our fight is not with you unless we learn something different. We will remain near until we know."

Maldor smiled and replaced his hammer. "My friends, do not just remain near. Join us in the city. Learn what we learned. Evaluate what we are facing, and you may begin to understand our plight."

"We cannot. We will wait to see for ourselves what we learn from Schram. When we know for sure, we will return to Toopek." The three remaining dragons all spread their wings and fell into formation behind the large red. In moments, they were gone.

Angus let out a long sigh. "I have to be honest. You are all the bravest individuals I have ever seen. You all stood tall and without fear. I believe I have to change my bottom armor for fear of what I did inside it."

The dwarf smiled. "First, you say it, then you do it, huh?"

They all smiled, but it was Stepha's soft voice that answered, "Let's get to the city. We can rest and relax with friends and determine our next plan."

They were all content with that response, and without another word, headed to the largest human city on all of Troyf: Toopek.

***

Schram landed in the field and immediately shook out his wings. Fehr hustled about stretching his legs in a long yawn. Schram had immediately turned back into elf form and took his place next to the bandicoot. "You know, if you lost some weight, you would—"

"Not you too? You know, I don't say anything about your thinning hair or huge ears, do I? Why does everyone want to talk about my weight? So I eat. So does everyone."

Schram smiled. "Maybe it is a way we keep our old human friend and warrior alive in our hearts. You know what she would be saying to you right now."

With that, a large smile grew across the rat's face as he thought about Krirtie. "Yes, she would be very disappointed. I'll bet she wouldn't even carry me anymore. Remember how much I made her carry me before?"

Schram scratched his head. "I do, my friend. She carried you across all of Troyf, day and night."

The two thought a moment longer, then Schram motioned ahead. "That is the doorway."

"Do you want me to go with you?"

Schram nodded. "Yes, I do. Canoks do not typically like other visitors, but you, they will not mind. You have gained their respect through my brothers and my dragon mother, and whether I want to always admit it or not, you have a stronger history with them than I do in that perspective."

Fehr now smiled, but his tone was completely serious. "Yes, I suppose they hold me high in their hearts, but really, who wouldn't?"

Schram picked up the large rat and began walking toward the boulders marking the center of the field. "I need you close to me as we pass through."

Fehr had been to the canok homeland only once before, and he was not conscious when he had passed through its magical gate. Schram had taken him there after Krirtie had passed away, hoping to find some peace with his friends who were separated from all other races on Troyf. Fehr thought then Schram just needed to escape. Their visit was short, and when they left, it was the last time either had set foot in their world, not that Fehr could ever go on his own if he wanted to.

The canoks were a broken race. They were trying to rebuild their combined two nations but also live with the knowledge that members of their race were a significant force of evil against those on Troyf. The pride they carried was broken, and for the canoks to find peace was not possible so soon after the combining. The loss of the canoks' support only added to Schram's confusion at the time. Now it was twenty years later, and they were coming back. Fehr did not know what to expect.

The world melted around them as they passed the rock opening. As quickly as it vanished, the new world arrived. They were in. The rat looked around. "Where is everyone?"

Schram looked hesitantly nearby. "I don't know, my friend, but it is only a short walk to the main area. Perhaps we will find our friends there."

Fehr swung his eyes to his longtime companion to see if he really meant to say "friends," and with the smile carried in his eyes, he knew the human was living on hope for the world he once knew. Fehr only wished he would find what he was looking for.

Just then, Schram's pace picked up, and a smile grew across his face. "Werner, it has been a long time."

The red fur of the canok shined in the sun's light. "Indeed, it has, my friend. Too long." Werner stepped around some trees where he had not been seen until they were right on top of him. "And greetings to you as well, Fehr. Welcome back to our home."

"Thank you. I did not think you would remember my last visit."

"When you can count all your visitors on one paw, remembering them is not difficult." His tone changed and stared at Schram. "We felt you would be coming."

Schram shrugged slightly as he began a slow walk beside the canok. "If you felt I was coming, why did you not greet me at the gate or contact me as I passed? Is there something I should know?"

Werner did not look up or change expression. He carried a sad and drawn-out tone that even Fehr, who was captivated by his surroundings, picked up. "Schram, you did give us back so much. You know we could never repay the debt in all of our lives combined, but we are not the same race we once were. We may hold the same color, but we are changed inside. We were the cause of great harm to many on Troyf. We almost caused the conquering of every race. When our lives were split, we left our destined timeline and began a new destiny. A destiny not for one but for our entire race. Once we left our path, our former path can never be met again."

Schram reached down and patted the back of his friend, who had crossed the black reign and helped them so long ago. "You, as much as anyone, know you cannot deal in absolutes. It is because of the canoks we are where we are. It is because of the canoks I am who I am. Your insight and those of many of your race provided the avenue that we could defeat the black dragon and the oppression. You may feel you cannot recover your past direction, but I say you already have."

The canok stopped outside a cave where Schram had remembered sitting so long ago. It was the first place he had met Hawthorne, a woman and dragon whom he learned later was his birth mother.

Ignoring Schram's last comments, Werner motioned to the opening. "I have gathered a few of us to meet and talk. It is all we can offer you this time. We will be of little help, I fear, but we will tell you what we know."

The three entered, and Schram was taken by what he saw. Although he did not think he would be given a hero's welcome, he did believe it would be more than this. Across the opening sat two other canoks, both of which Schram recognized. He had seen them before but just in passing while in the homeland.

He had remained in his elf-human form and had to bend down to fit below the cavern ceiling. He turned to Werner. "Is there more you need to tell me? I am surprised that Almok is not here."

Werner and the other two canoks leaned back in disbelief, and then Schram believed they were having a conversation with each other. But as they often do, none was at any level to be heard by him. When he sat down, Schram felt the rat lifting his front paws to gain leverage so he could whisper in Schram's ear, "What are they hiding? Something is not right here. It is more than their shame or whatever he was implying."

Schram nodded but did not speak as Werner took his place by his side and the other canoks moved around beside him. Werner stared hard at Schram and then began to speak, "Schram, it is good to see you again, know this to be true, but we feel you should leave soon. You will always be our friend, but the disgrace we have shown this world is too much for us to bear. We will not allow ourselves to be caught again."

"What are you talking about, Werner? You don't make any sense."

One of the other canoks leaned forward a bit. "Schram, I am Wesling. Perhaps I can help explain as Werner is too close to say what needs to be said." He paused and had another brief telepathic conversation with Werner then continued, "We believed we could come to accept that which occurred in the past and even began to stray out of our protected world to try to mend our relationships with those other races affected by our failures. However, upon doing that, those that did venture out were destroyed. There is no reason to rejoin the world if it does not want us back. And then, with your question now and the rumors we have received and felt. We know our pain is not through."

"Wesling, I understand you feel beaten and betrayed by your own, but I know nothing of canoks being killed, nor what question you say I have asked, or the rumors you have heard." He stopped and got on his knees, to get closer to the heights of the canoks who were standing. "Listen, I can tell you this. The humans, elves, dwarves, and maneth will all welcome you back whenever you are ready to come."

"And the bandicoot nation as well," added Fehr.

"And the bandicoots," repeated Schram.

The canoks seemed confused for only a second before their tone remained as it was. "No, Schram," stated Werner. "Our pain and exile remains, as does the pain we have and will again cause."

"What do you mean?" asked Schram. "What question? What pain? What rumors?"

Wesling again spoke, "You stated you were surprised Almok was not here."

"I did. When he left me so long ago, he was finally in a place of peace. He was returning to this place to help with recovery."

Werner lifted a paw to Schram's arm. Shaking his head, he said, "Almok lied to you. There is no good in him. We thought he was killed in that final battle so long ago. He never returned here."

"We would not have taken him back," added Wesling. Werner shifted his eyes back to his counterpart quickly then back to Schram. "We would have tried him and most likely not taken him back. It would take much for us to wish for a death, but believing him killed in your battle was our best result."

Schram was caught by the statements. When Almok left him after the battle in Anbari's Dominion, he was broken free of the hold of evil. He was canok, and the canoks were again one. He could not have been pretending. Schram would have felt it.

Werner saw his thoughts and answered the unasked question, "He is strong with power, along with his twin brother and mother, probably the strongest canok in the history of Troyf. He blocked his true feelings from you so he could escape. He knew he was not going to win."

"Are you saying Almok is alive and behind the evil we are seeing today?"

Werner narrowed his stare on the human. In a cold voice, he issued the words that brought Schram almost to his knees in disbelief. "No. I am saying Almok has been behind this the entire time. The black dragon did not develop this plan and the deal, Almok did. Almok ruled Slayne. Slayne did not rule Almok. Almok, not Slayne, bested Kirven. Your enemy of so long ago was not beaten. He simply walked away."

Schram, as with the way of the elves, did not like hearing the names spoken of those passed but did not comment as the words he did hear were too much. "How can that be? I let him leave. I trusted him." He paused and looked blindly at the small fire in the center. "He used magic on me. Somehow in the Dominion, he was able to harness power and use it against me. I should not have trusted him. Why would I ever have trusted him?"

Werner and Wesling both nodded, but it was Werner who again spoke, "To use magic against you is one thing, but to use magic against you in the Dominion where all magic is blocked is quite another. He is truly powerful, and we believe he is the source of those who were killed when they left our protected barrier. He needs the canoks to remain here, and he knows his actions will demand just that.

"Then where did he go?" asked Schram. "I must face him again, and this time his path will be different."

"We do not know," Werner replied. "And we have not dared leave to find him."

Schram stared at the canok and realized just by saying that statement he was admitting something that cut him so deeply: to pursue his fears would only further break the canoks' pride. He paced back to the cavern opening then turned to face the group. "I feel your pain, Werner, but I have to know where to start. Do you have any idea where Almok lives?"

The two canoks appeared to have a brief conversation before Werner answered, "We do not know for sure, but we believe Almok has mastered the art of inner-space movements."

"What does that mean?" asked Fehr, who had been quiet since entering.

"It means if he has been to a place before, he can go there again with magic. He may not be physically there, which has its limitations, but he can be present." He paused then added, "He could be with us right now, and we would never know it."

"But where does he reside?" Schram asked again. "If I were to guess, I would say in the Realm of Darkness. Perhaps the elves of Eltak would know more. If he has mastered inner space, then distance is not an issue for him."

Schram lifted his head. "The Realm? I have been there." He turned to Werner. "We have been there, with my birth mother. Why the Realm?"

Werner now stepped forward. "Because nobody would follow him there."

"The guardians would not let him stay. That makes no sense."

Werner was now inches from his old friend's face. "They would if he promised them the hammer would eventually come to find him. Remember, the Anbarian Hammer is what they have always wanted. They would have traded anything for it."

Schram thought hard, trying to remember their exchange with the guardians. He stepped back from the canok, who had remained locked inches from him. "Maldor carries the hammer," he whispered. Closing his eyes, he gripped his staff and tried to feel the maneth through his weapon. He saw Stepha, Jermys, and Denisi crouched in the trees, which he recognized so well from his childhood. "They are outside Toopek right now."

Fehr stood on his hind legs. "Then we should go immediately. By dragon flight, we could be there tomorrow."

Schram did not even answer and only turned to leave. Wesling and Werner nodded but said nothing. With a quick turn back, Schram said, "Do not be ashamed, my friends. You are a proud race. Evil can take over even the strongest races. Do not let it define you now. We need you." He paused. "I need you."

The canoks did not answer.

START TO THE END

"**Y**ou have never flown like this," stated the bandicoot as he gripped his claws into Schram's back. The human turned elf and dragon did not answer. His mind was focused on his friends and Toopek. Their path was direct. He knew the line between the canok homeland and Toopek was a full three days on foot, but by air, possibly before nightfall, he could arrive. He longed for his friends. He longed for Stepha. However, despite his drive, he feared what the dragons had told him outside the Black Pool. He knew word would travel fast. If they believe he had destroyed their home, they would quickly turn. Should he run into a dragon party on his flight, there was no telling what direction it would take. He then thought about Almok. How could he have been so naive? How could he have missed it?

"What is up, Schram? No reply to my comment? What, you think I am wrong and flying like an exploding ball of dragon fire breath is a healthy way to travel?"

Schram blinked his eyes as if breaking from a trance. "No, my friend, I simply do not wish to fail in this endeavor. Should we meet with dragon resistance, I may have to go with them to Draag. In honor, I must."

Fehr gripped tighter and then added, "Then land in that clearing below for a brief rest. Then I will be good for the rest of the journey without break. A quick bite of food will do us both well."

Schram nodded. "You mean if I do this, you will require no further stops for the rest of the trip."

"Yes, that is what I am suggesting."

"Done," replied Schram as he turned downward. The two landed, and Schram shook out his wings as Fehr went immediately to digging through his pouches for food. Without warning, however, a group of branches divided, and through them stepped a creature Schram had not seen in longer than he chose to remember.

"Good afternoon, Schram. I have been waiting for this day." The voice was deep and strong.

"What day would that be?" asked Schram, now in human form. "The day you told me you betrayed me and all we fought for?"

"Young boy, I betrayed nobody. I needed a way out. Only your human desire for everyone to be good allowed me to leave." His voice faded a bit then got stronger. "Remember, you let me leave without question."

Schram turned his eyes to the floor as he remembered the battle. "Almok, you are pure evil. You chose to leave. You chose to ignore your heritage. You have chosen to be against what is right and good."

"Right and good?" offered the canok. "You think about this, my young friend. What if you are the one who is not on the good side? What if you are the one in the wrong? How would you ever know? You are the one who is brainwashed. You." The canok paced back and forth several times before the two. Fehr had moved beside his friend, but it was clear on his face, as well as Schram's, neither knew what direction this was going.

"I do not know what to make of you, Almok. However, I can tell you that, as of right now, I do not have time to figure it out. You are old news. Now leave before you get hurt."

Almok actually looked as if he was going to cringe and fall to the ground. "You are the fool, Schram," he stated blankly. "Fly directly to Draag. Anything short of that will result in your friends' deaths as well as your own. The entire dragon armies are united against you."

"You are crazy, Almok. We may fight here, or you may leave. Either way, our direction is not to Draag, and the dragons know that. I believe it is your direction that is in question."

Almok leaned closer. "I feel you, Schram. Everything you want, I feel. Everything you feel, I am in control. Most importantly, however, everything you know is about to come to an end. Your friends will not live through the night. Your kingdom is about to be destroyed. All of Troyf will follow my lead because you, your friends, and the weapons of the ring will be mine."

The last comment caught Schram, and his eyes showed it. "Yes," replied Almok, smiling, "the weapons you cherish so closely will be under my control. Then no power of Anbari will be able to touch us, or more appropriately, no one will ever be able to defy us."

Schram's hand shook, and he began to quickly recite a spell. Then he stopped. His mind cleared as if a power from the outside was providing him clarity. He did not need a spell. He did not need to fight. He needed answers. His goal needed to be only one thing—to keep the canok talking.

"Almok," he started abruptly. "How did you not change back to the red coats of the past? Why are you not again a true canok?" He smiled, reminding Schram for a second of Kirven, Almok's twin brother and Schram's strongest longtime companion.

"I am not a red coat because I am not a true-bred canok. My father was not canok."

"But is not the heritage with your mother of some value to you?" He paused and added with empathy, "She was your mother."

Almok realized what Schram was doing and began to try to pry into his mind. It was easily blocked by Schram, but this did not dissuade the canok from continuing to respond, "I hold no value in my mother. My allegiance is with another, one that is the most powerful on all of Troyf. A power you will very shortly experience personally."

Schram was stunned at the freedom of the response, but he started to believe the information he was hearing was as planned and calculated as the creature outside Elvinott. Schram had learned a long time ago that things do not happen by chance in war. Everything is scheduled. The human tried to appear almost uninterested. "Almok," he added nonchalantly, "what is your business here today? You are not here to fight. Are you simply trying to threaten or scare me into changing my direction?"

"On the contrary, my boy. I am here to tell you one thing." The canok moved closer. "I am alive, and your surrender is imminent. Save the lives of your friends and those cities you claim loyalty to. Come with me today. This will be your last warning. If you do not come today, Toopek, Elvinott, Feldschlosschen, and the maneth homeland will all be destroyed. This will happen."

Fehr looked on but still did not speak. Schram remained extremely calm, leaving his mind blank to prevent Almok from getting any insight into what he was about to do. "My friend, you will never want peace. You have been seduced by evil. Because of that, I cannot come with you any more than you can surrender to me."

He spoke no other words but raised his staff and fired a magical assault on the canok. Flashes of light and fire exploded across the small glade. Schram summoned all the power he could, calling on the staff and his own innate abilities. Fehr was nearly blinded and believed that although he had been present for many of Schram's one-on-one battles, this was the strongest and deadliest he had ever seen.

The rat covered his eyes slightly but then saw something. He looked closer and slowly began to nudge his human friend's feet. "Leave it, Schram. He is gone."

Schram stopped his assault then heard a message in his mind as clear as if it was being said by the canok previously directly in front of him. *I feel you, Schram. Everything you know is about to come to an end. Your friends are as good as dead. The weapons will be mine, and then no power of Anbari's will be able to touch us as no power of Anbari's may be used against the weapons of the ring.*

Fehr had not heard the message but responded to the exchange with Almok, "They truly just want you, don't they, my friend?"

"No Fehr, not just me. They want the weapons of the ring. With those, they know I would be powerless to defend against them at all. Why they want me is the real question."

The rat shrugged. "It is personal, Schram."

***

Stepha and Alan hugged. "Your team is back so soon. This cannot be good news." He nodded to Angus. "Are you well?"

Angus shook his head. "I am well, but I have seen things I would never have believed. The last few days, I have lived a full life."

Alan appeared even more concerned and turned back to the two flyer elves. "Stepha, Denisi, or Jermys, will one of you please tell me what has happened? What can Toopek do to support you?"

With the comment, he motioned to everyone to follow, and they began heading down the main street of Toopek. There was much activity on the street, which did occur to Stepha to be a good sign. The people seemed to be oblivious that if the prophecy were to come true, in less than thirty days, this city would not exist. Alan saw the strain on her face and asked again, in a whispered tone so only Stepha could hear, "Is Geoff okay?"

Instantly she pulled from her thoughts, and her face softened. "Yes, my friend, Geoff is well. He will be with us shortly here in Toopek. However, his entire maneth camp will be with him."

The statement brought out two emotions in the human leader. He was relieved to hear he was well, but as quickly, he felt concern when he learned the entire maneth camp would be coming to support Toopek. His only thought was war; he whispered mostly to himself.

The elf placed her hand on his shoulder. "We have much to discuss. So many things have happened in the last few days."

They sat around a large table, and each was given sizable portions of food and drink. Although they all seemed to be able to go extreme lengths of time without nourishment, when it did come, it was very well received. It actually worked to improve their view of the situation, even though nothing had really changed for them. Stepha explained the occurrences of late with both Denisi and Angus, adding pieces of support to fill in some blanks. Lars and Maldor had been quiet for most of the story, and once completed, Maldor motioned to Lars to join him.

Alan rose. "Maldor, do you need something?"

The large maneth appeared stoic, almost as a general leaving for a mission. "No, my friend. Geoff will be here shortly. He will want a summary of where the maneth support will be most effective. Lars and I will scout the city and prepare a detailed map for him."

"My officers can do that as well—"

The maneth raised a hand, cutting him off. "Trust when I say I mean no disrespect. I am 100 % sure you could provide more detailed information than we will be able to achieve. However, my king will ask me directly if I did my work to support this effort, and without scouting myself, I cannot answer him truly. It would be my wish that once we are complete, we join with you and your senior officers and put together a summary to ensure all areas of support are met."

Alan smiled. "Very well. Go perform your investigation and come find me when you are ready. I will assemble my men and start the same process. Can I ask, however, do we even know what type of destruction will be upon us? Is it from dragon or something else?"

Stepha thought the question was interesting as she had not truly thought about the mode of destruction. She was about to reply when Alan then added, "It is one thing to plan against a dragon assault, but should it be something else, we may be unprepared if the attack is not what is expected, if you follow my thoughts."

"I do follow," replied the elf. The others nodded as well. "I believe this evil is trying to pit the dragons against us. That is why they have tried to turn the dragons against Schram. However, Schram has told me with confidence he does not believe the dragons will ever again be made to attack our cities. They are no longer susceptible to the brainwashing of the past. The younger dragons have matured." She paused. "If what Schram says is true, then the work against the dragons is not to bring them to attack Toopek, it is to prevent them from defending it."

The others looked on in surprise. "Then who?"

Geoff looked on in disbelief. He was only a short way from the outskirts of his homeland, but his immediate path had become somewhat clouded. "How can I help you, my friends?"

The extremely dark-blue, almost black dragon looked on with a questioning gaze, but the large green narrowed his stare and he replied, "Where is he, Geoff?"

"Where is who?" asked the maneth.

"You know who we seek. To say his name only will sour my mind further."

"Tell me why you seek Schram. You cannot believe the lies that have been said."

The green dragon grimaced at the use of his name. "Then why does he run? Why does he flee? Why does he not come to us to explain his innocence? Explain how it was not him outside our home, staff in hand, destroying our heritage, destroying the last thing we had left."

Geoff took a step closer, and his voice softened. "Dragons are wise. We all know and accept that. Tell me one thing and search your feelings. What is the motive? If you can answer that, then I will help you find Schram. There is no play for Schram to attack Draag out of the blue. He has no motive. Let you forget not that he is dragon. His mother was dragon."

The blue seemed to be fighting the question, as if not completely in agreement with this plan, but the green did not relent. "It is not my place to be jury. We have been given one task: bring the human to face his crime."

Geoff thought it was interesting that the dragon used "human" to describe Schram when he had just stated his friend was a dragon. "My dragon friends, Schram will come to you. Spread word to those with you that seeking him is not needed. On my honor, I will ensure Schram does not run from the issues you believe to be true. However, the needs of our world require his presence first. Ask your brethren to accept he will come to you in time."

The green lowered his eyes. "He will come to us now, or we will begin taking action to bring him to us." His voice stopped abruptly, and the blue seemed to be in some sort of conversation with him, the likes of which was not within Geoff's ability to hear.

The blue then spoke for the first time, "Geoff, you may not remember me, but many years ago, I was one of seven dragons that nearly ended the maneth's place on Troyf." Immediately, the maneth placed his hand on his great maneth club. The blue's eye's narrowed. "So you do remember?"

"Yes, over two hundred years ago, you and six other dragons destroyed my village. I was but a pup. If not for the strength of the canok, we would have left this world for good." His eyes turned from the calm, controlled leader to a burnt fire of the memory. "Do I remember? Yes, and I swore should I ever meet those that waged that wrath, I would make them feel the same."

The blue stepped forward, and for the first time, Geoff could see the dragon's age taking shape—much older than the green, but a wiseness in his action and speech, not driven on emotion or hatred but on a need to find the truth. "I cannot speak to the past. I told you this so you would understand my place in our discussion. I am the last of that seven. Should I be destined to die by your hand because of my past actions, I will accept it. I feel nothing but shame, but it was a time of war. Our direction was not that of faith and pride but delusion."

Geoff's hand softened on the hilt of his hammer, but he did not remove it altogether. "Why do you tell me this?"

"Because for more than two hundred years, I have run from my past. I am ready to face it, the same way in which Schram should face his. If he is truly innocent, then bring him to us."

He shook his head. "As I said, I do not need to bring him to you, for he will come on his own."

"I know that is what you said. I am offering something to ensure that."

The blue shook his head. "Yes, me for him. I will come to face the maneth, and Schram comes to the dragon. Do you agree?"

Geoff nodded. "I am not here to make deals with others' lives. What I am telling you is this: I will ensure Schram comes to Draag as soon as our world is safe from this current evil. I will do that whether you come to face the maneth or not."

"Very well, my friend. I am not here to make a deal either." The dragon knelt down to where his mouth was only a short distance from Geoff's, and their eyes were at equal levels. "I am here to tell you that I am sorry, and I too will face that which I deserve."

Geoff nodded but did not address the last statement. "What is your name?"

"I am Bjork."

"Well, Bjork, we will be seeing each other again."

"I will be seeing some of you again. That much is certain."

TOOPEK'S SEPARATION

"It will be dark soon, Schram. Are we going to make it to Toopek?" "We will." He pointed his arm forward. "There, in the distance, you can see the light over the horizon."

The rat smiled. "Indeed. Nice job, and no dragon interference."

Schram returned the smile. "Not yet anyway, but should they be in our path, it would be right before Toopek. They would know that is my destination."

"You have to ruin every good thing with a bad. You need some bandicoot blood in you. You would be a much more pleasant person."

Schram smiled and only arched his wings to cut the wind faster. *We are so close*, he thought to himself. He focused his mind, trying to feel if there were dragons in their path. Though all dragons had some abilities with magic and power, not all were developed or had even begun to truly learn their inner strengths. He hoped that should there be any in their path, their presence would not be blocked and he could feel his way around them. He did sense something.

"Why are you turning? You said a straight line would be the quickest," Fehr inquired.

"I feel there is something ahead. I do not know what it is, but it is purposely trying to block our path, which means..." his voice trailed off as Fehr interrupted.

"We go around."

"Yes," Schram continued. "We go around."

He veered to the north, which would eventually take his path over the water. He knew there was an equal chance he would alert dragons that had remained on Castle Island, the small island off the Toopekian Coast where his parents' castle had originally stood, but that seemed preferable to what he was feeling. Fehr bit his claws into Schram's back as the dragon turned so sharply as to be perpendicular to the ground. The rat let out a huff before he turned back level to the ground. "Perhaps you warn me before making a turn like that."

Schram too let out a deep breath, only his was due to a sharp pain in his back, where a touch of blood flowed from below the rat's claws. "Perhaps I will."

The two relaxed and continued on their path. Schram could see the sea's edge a short distance ahead and knew if something was going to happen, it would be after he breached the water's surface. At that point, he would be close enough to Toopek that the spotters would be able to see him from the city. He also knew his presence as a dragon would cause quite a stir onshore. If he did not alert the dragons, he was certain the activity on land would.

He lowered his flight to right above the tree line and remained there as he crossed the water's surface. The smell of salt air bit both their noses, and all four eyes scanned the area in front of them. Night had fallen completely now, but the light from the full moon lit a path to the Toopekian shore. As their eyes followed that trail, they did see some movement commencing in the city harbor, but the thing that truly caught their eyes was the three shadows directly in their path.

"Dragons?" asked Fehr.

"Yes," Schram replied.

"Do we go around?"

The magician nodded negatively. "There is no way to go, my friend. We knew this was a possibility. We will do what we can to pass, but if they offer to fight or worse, bring a wrath upon Toopek should I resist, then I will go to Draag with them."

Fehr lifted an eyebrow. "Should that be the result, would you wish me to go with you or remain? I will gladly do either."

"I am sure you would, my friend. This day, I believe your place is with our friends and to support Toopek as best you can. Draag, I must face on my own."

"Very well, Schram." He paused. "Then let's do this thing and go greet our three friends."

"Yes, let's go say hello."

Their path did not alter, and in only moments, they were before the three—a large red and two slightly smaller but still full-grown adult blue dragons. Schram stopped and hovered in the air before them. Quickly the three encircled him in a formation to ensure compliance. The red remained in front, staring hard into Schram's eyes. If he was trying to read his thoughts, Schram could not feel it. However, he also did not try to block it as he had nothing to hide.

The red started the conversation abruptly, "Schram Starland, you are to come with us. Leave your friend in Toopek and do not deviate from a course to Draag. You must face trial for your actions."

"I cannot come with you at this time. Search my feelings, you know what we are up against. You know what this world—*our* world—is facing."

The red narrowed on the Toopekian king. "I do feel your thoughts but also know you are powerful. I believe you can make me feel what you want me to feel. You have to come where we can control your ability to control our minds." He paused then added, "Do not resist us, Schram. We do not want to use force."

Schram knew he could continue this effort but also knew that, in the end, it would come to a fight. He could win and most likely further the dragons' search for him. The only answer that made sense was to go with them, with one stipulation. "My friends, we can all see where this is going, and I will not be responsible for more dragons' or, for that matter, any more creatures' deaths. With that, I will go with you."

Fehr stood up on his back. "Schram, you can't!"

He swung his eyes to the rat, who quickly quieted. "I will go with you, but on one condition."

The red arched his head and replied, "What is the condition?"

"We will continue to Toopek. I will meet with my leaders there and hopefully my friends. We will discuss our actions to come and agree on a plan." He turned to the others and motioned them to come to one side as they did not need to surround him any longer. "You see, my friends, there is great evil among us, evil that has already struck several times, including at Draag, evil that is designed to bring about the end of the world as we know it. The problem is, for some reason, I am a part of it. This evil wants me, and having me go to Draag now will be a risk. That being said, I will not run from this. I will not allow the dragons to believe I have done that which is suggested. I will go to Draag of my own free will, and I will meet with those there and show them I am not who they think I am."

The three dragons had a brief conversation between only them before the red turned back. "You may continue to Toopek, but we will remain with you at all times. Do not try to flee, Schram, or before tracking you, we will take out our wrath on your home."

He nodded understanding and opened his wings without further comment. He knew more discussion would go nowhere, and he also knew that they had very little time.

Fehr leaned close to his ears. "So are you really going? I am confident we can control these three if you say so."

Schram smiled. "I agree, Fehr, but yes, I am going. I know the timing is bad, but if all goes as I hope, this will not take long, and it may bring the dragons back to our side for support. I do not understand the ploy to bring me to Draag. I am sure things happen for a reason, but this is a move I question, and it may work out to be a huge error by whatever evil is behind this."

Fehr returned his smile. "Now I understand."

Fehr and Schram reached the shoreline with the three dragons in tow. Archers lined the outside walls, and all eyes softened when they saw it was their king in the lead. Schram landed at the city center, and almost the moment his feet touched, he was back in his combined human-elf form, and Fehr crashed to the ground.

"Nice," spouted the rat. Schram paid no heed as quickly in his arms was Stepha.

"Thank Shriak you are here." She paused as she watched the three dragons land in his wake, the red being one she recognized from their entrance to the city. "Schram, what is going on?"

He pushed her back slightly and stared into her large green eyes. "I have missed you, Stepha, but time is of the essence. There is much to discuss, and I need everyone together. I will only be here a short while before I must return to Draag."

She now pushed him away, slightly angered. "No! They wish to kill you. The dragons will not listen to you. They have made that clear to us."

Schram was surprised at this response. "What do you mean they have made it clear to us? What has happened since we parted?" He paused then added, "Forget the question. We must meet. We all must know everything to make the best decision. These dragons will accompany everywhere I go, so know that what we know, they will know."

Everyone met at the city center to accommodate the dragons, who remained within earshot of all conversations. They exchanged every detail of their recent activities from what Schram learned at the Black Pool and the canok homeland to the new trek planned to the Realm of Darkness to return the hammer. Schram was taken by this direction, though he knew in his heart it was correct. The idea of splitting with one of the weapons of the ring was concerning nonetheless. Schram spoke at length with Angus and Alan and was pleased with their effort to protect the city. Knowing Geoff was coming with his maneth support made his fears almost nonexistent—almost. The only question that remained was, how could the companions make passage to the Realm of Darkness?

"Do you think you can call on Khaled?" asked Stepha, with all eyes falling to Schram.

"I can try, but I make no promises. The physeter existence by itself is somewhat unknown. They come only when they feel the situation is worthy. I believe they already know what is transpiring here but feel they are free from its touch."

Alan stepped forward. "Surely they see their existence is a symbiotic relationship with those on land. Should something destroy the world here, the seas would be affected."

"Wise, they are," added Schram, "but if they see beyond their own immediate lives, I cannot say."

The three dragons had been quiet the entire time, taking each statement in as it was said. They appeared to be in some sort of silent conversation when Schram turned toward the red. "I will be ready to go shortly. First, I must try to contact Khaled of the physeter."

One of the blues stepped forward. "Pardon my interruption, but we have an alternative option for you."

All heads turned to the dragons, but it was Schram who replied, "What do you mean?"

"Schram may return to Draag as has been stated, and with him will travel Kleinton, the red. We"—he motioned to the other blue—"will carry your group across the sea."

Schram asked, "Does this mean you believe us, and you know it was not I who struck against Draag?"

The red known as Kleinton replied, "No, this simply means we want to keep an eye on what is happening. Our trust for you has diminished, and if there is truth to what you say now, see it ourselves we must."

"Very well," stated Schram. "It is set. What do you need to prepare?"

The blue who had spoken before replied, "Simply time. It is a long trek, and one which will not have a refuge to rest. Therefore, we will leave at first light."

"And we shall do the same," added Schram toward the red, who nodded in reply.

With only idle chatter, the group disbanded and went to their respective rooms, or in the companion's case, the alehouse, where Jermys, although rarely in Toopek, was well-known.

***

They met the next morning in the town square. Schram and Stepha were busy most the morning greeting many throughout the city as he was still their king and Stepha their queen. Schram then took a great deal of time meeting with Alan and planning their defense should an attack occur. Knowing the maneths were coming was a comfort, but Schram also explained that the level of magic, the fact that dragons may or may not be involved, and the warnings had been straight ultimatums. This meant the force behind them was so confident it did not believe there was anything they could do to defend themselves. Total Armageddon. As each party appeared at the city center, it was clear that times were indeed serious. The citizens of the town began scampering to their homes, building supports for their windows as rumors of the activity coming was spreading like fire. The group made an ominous sight: their king and queen, three dragons, two maneth, another flyer elf, a dwarf, several human warriors, and what had to be the largest bandicoot on all of Troyf.

Jermys was the first to speak, "Schram, please travel safe. Should you need us, we will be too far to lend support. I can send a message to the dwarves to help, but they will be many days behind you should trouble arise."

The human placed his hand on the small dwarf's shoulder. "My time is not your concern. I did not do the evil claimed, and that will be seen. Do not worry about me. Please take care of those with you." He paused and turned to the group. "That brings me to my next question. Who, besides you"—nodding to Jermys—"is going on this venture to the Realm?"

Maldor spoke, "Because I must deliver the hammer, I will be going. Lars and Angus have offered to go in support." They both nodded.

"Denisi and I will be going as well," added Stepha. Schram appeared concerned at this, but he was already aware his wife would be going. Her duty as the leader of the elven guard was too deep to be avoided. Still, it was not just her she flew for now. He remembered the fate Krirtie had realized when fighting while pregnant. He looked to Lars, and as he stood there so proud, holding Krirtie's scimitar, he knew her decision was just.

Schram was about to speak when Fehr chimed in, "I will be joining you, Schram. Brothers stick together."

"Not this time, my friend." He scratched the rat on the head. "Although I would like you by my side as you have been so many times, this is something I must do alone." Kleinton shook his head in agreement.

Fehr was about to protest when he heard Jermys in the background. "Come with us, Fehr. I will need you to hold my tobac." He paused and motioned to Lars. "I am sure the giant fur ball can carry you. He seems to like your kind just like his mom did."

Many smiled at the comparison, but Fehr seemed especially pleased. "Yes, that sounds great. I will tell Lars so many stories. This will be perfect for him."

All smiled, including Lars, whose main goal originally had been to learn about his mother. Who better than Fehr to tell him? At least that was what he thought now.

Just then, two other dragons, one green and one a yellow-and-brown, arrived next to the blues. They were smaller and clearly younger but remained in order just the same. The two blues came forward with the larger of the two speaking first, "Because of the length of the voyage, we asked for two others to join us. Should we run into trouble, it will only improve our odds. It will also allow us to split the weight further. This should allow for faster travel as well as a reduced need to rest."

Everyone seemed pleased with this idea, though nobody really knew why they were putting so much trust in dragons. Just as Schram was about to reply, another dragon appeared over the horizon and landed with perfect agility next to the others. The sight was becoming more spectacular with each moment.

The dragons appeared to be in a conversation when Denisi spoke, "I know you," she said to the red dragon. "You helped us outside Toopek. You are Rosstim."

Maldor shook his head. "Yes, I remember. When the trolls appeared behind us."

The dragon nodded as Schram walked up to him. "You allowed me to connect to you." He patted his hand on the creature's neck. "Thank you, my friend." He paused and then turned to stare directly into his eyes. "What brings you here now in such haste?"

The dragon smiled to each of those who had recognized him. He then turned to Schram. "I will be accompanying you and Kleinton to Draag. There have been many more issues than just the attack on Draag to be considered, and I am going to make sure each one is taken into account."

Kleinton appeared taken by the change of events, giving the impression that he did not like his direction questioned. However, it also appeared to Schram that Rosstim was his senior, and to question him was not something that would be done. Kleinton had no choice but to accept the company. Schram did not know what this meant, but he thought it must be a step in his favor.

Everyone seemed satisfied with the direction, and after some long embraces and softly spoken words between parties, they each took off in almost exactly opposite directions. Schram had taken the form of a dragon to keep pace with the other reds for travel to Draag, and even after they had made a great distance, Schram thought he could still hear Fehr talking away, giving Lars no chance for a break.

***

The canok's voice was strong but did show a slight concern. "My queen, the troops are assembled, and their training is complete. We can attack anytime."

The woman moved over and rubbed the canok's white diamond patch. "Everything is proceeding exactly as I have foreseen it. Soon all of our enemies will be in one location. We will destroy Toopek, and with its destruction, have nothing left on Troyf to defend against us. We will assert our rule across the land."

"And if they present Schram before the deadline?"

"They will not. He may not even leave Draag, though I cannot see that future as clearly." She removed her hand and turned her stare across the huge frozen glacier below her castle. "How are the Dragoks?"

"They are performing better than we could have hoped. They are strong with magic, beyond that of any dragon. Further, they possess the power of the canok, a combination previously never before witnessed in the land."

She smiled. "Yes, when I saw Kirven as a pup, I knew, if channeled correctly, I could create the ultimate power. With your help, I have done it."

The canok smiled as well. "You have done it. That much is certain. What about the weapons of the ring? Why do you not seek them out now, as was our goal so long ago?"

"In time, we will seek them out, but we will take them off the dead bodies of those who wield them. I personally want to take the bow from her cold green fingers."

He shook his head. "I will see that you get your chance. And the group we know to be traveling across the sea? Do you wish them eliminated?"

"Not yet. There are dragons among them. One could escape and get word back. I need them to remain uninvolved. Schram has brought in only a fraction. As long as the rest remain uncommitted, by the time they realize their mistake, it will be too late."

"Then we let them pass?"

She smiled a crooked smile. "Let them find the elves destroyed. Perhaps that will stir the elves in Elvinott to leave their protected forest to help. Should they go to Toopek as well, only the dwarves would be left."

The canok nodded. "The dwarves would not even be a test for us."

"This may be working better than I had ever anticipated."

DRAAG

The three dragons landed outside Draag. Schram could not believe his eyes. "Don't look so surprised, Schram," stated Kleinton. "You did this. Several of us saw you, including me."

"Is that why you have refused to see anything else? To think that you could be made to believe something even if it was not there?"

"Nice try, but you could not be more mistaken. There was no magic used against us here. Draag has always been protected from magic used against it."

"If magic cannot be used against you here, then how did this attack occur?"

"That is our point exactly. There is only one with the power to appear in our caverns without warning, wage the most powerful attack we have seen in our memory, destroy everything, and then leave as if nothing happened." He leaned only inches from his face. "Only you."

Schram shook out his wings but remained in dragon form. "Soon you will see you are mistaken. I hope I can show that to you now before it is too late."

The sky was filled with spots as numerous dragons were arriving by flight. There also stood at least fifty in the fields around them. Schram remembered these fields from his travels in the past. Always before, he traveled here in fear, always on the ready. Today, however, outside the dragons dotting the horizon, life did not seem to exist. The area had been converted to almost desert, devoid of life, seemingly burned to the root.

Kleinton motioned to Schram and Rosstim. "He is to be placed at the cavern entrance, or what is left of it. The council is organizing there as well. We may begin the proceedings almost immediately."

"Great," replied Schram. "The sooner we can begin the discussions, the sooner we can get to the real truth."

"Truth seems to be a word you throw around lightly," added Kleinton. "I trust you will learn its true meaning."

He stopped, causing both reds to turn their eyes directly to him. Softly he spoke, "Kleinton, the irony with which you speak is astounding. Do you not remember who fought to save the dragons? When all the younglings were brainwashed by one evil dragon—yes, again by a dragon—it was my group of companions that fought to save them. I stood up for the dragons, knowing there was some other evil behind it. Why can't you believe that of me?"

"This was all part of your plan, Schram—twenty years ago, and before you, two hundred years ago—all part of a plan of which we have all been pawns. Now, as the plan comes to a close, only you remain on top. When determining guilt, it is easiest to simply look for who is benefitting. That answer is clear. With the dragons gone, there would be nobody to stop you."

Rosstim interrupted, "Both of you, stop. Save your comments for the council. That is the only chance we have to actually find the truth." Turning to Kleinton, he added, "To truly find whom we can trust."

With that comment, Schram's eyes turned to the area where the council was stated to be. He saw about ten dragons, most of which appeared young, gathering in a line. Schram walked slowly to stand before them with his head held high, Kleinton and Rosstim closely behind in his wake. "I am very proud to be here before you, for I feel—"

He was cut off by one of the dragons on the council. "Speak not, Schram Starland of Toopek. A decision has been reached on your guilt."

"What does that mean?" asked Schram.

"This is not one of your human courts. While we searched for your being, we held our court. The fact you went immediately into hiding, the fact that so many dragons saw you perform this fate, and the fact that you alone can wield this level of magic answered all the questions we had."

Schram began to respond again but was cut off this time by a larger brown-and-orange dragon. "You were told not to speak. We do not need to hear your pleas and excuses. Your fate has been decided."

"What fate has been decided?" asked Rosstim. The dragons on the council swung their heads up at the interruption and quickly silenced their words when they saw who spoke. Schram immediately realized Rosstim was respected. He assumed he was not present when this disaster took place, but at least he would be heard.

The original dragon that had spoken replied, "Rosstim, you are not on this council, though we respect your question and will answer. Schram is too powerful for us to believe we can destroy him by our usual sentencing. With that, he is to be tied to the Well-of-Antigraf deep within the caverns. After six nights, his powers will no longer be a concern for any on Troyf."

Schram had heard about many places, many things, but never had he heard the name Well-of-Antigraf. It did not sound good, but he needed to know what it was.

He wanted to ask but swung his eyes to Rosstim. The large dragon did not return the gaze but stared hard at the council. "My friends, Draag has been destroyed. The well may no longer even exist, and if it does, do you think it is still so starved for magic that it would drain Schram of his? Further, let me protest that Schram is not the only one on Troyf who could wield this magic. Your fear for the unknown over two hundred years ago decided our fate, and only now is it coming full circle."

Schram was intrigued by the idea that there was a place that drained individuals of magic. Not that he was thrilled with the idea of meeting said place, but its existence alone brought up new possibilities. What if those that were bringing this evil could be lured to this place? Did they know about it? If so, was that their whole plan for Schram? Had he walked into a trap?

"Rosstim, first let me tell you that with the destruction, the well has been exposed to the surface. Schram will be bound with our magical hands and tossed into the pit. As the well absorbs our magic, it too will render him helpless to defend against it. Therefore, I have but one question for you. Are you standing before Schram? Should you fail in this stance, his punishment would be yours as well. Do you understand the choice?"

The large red dragon glanced at Kleinton, who appeared completely taken by the discussion. Then he moved to stand beside the king of Toopek. "My friends, I cannot say whether Schram is guilty or not guilty. All I can say is that we do not know. Your decision did not take into account all the facts. It did not truly consider who else could be behind it. It did not truly investigate where Schram was when the attack happened. It did not ever ask Schram why he would have performed such an unprovoked attack."

There seemed to be some deliberation between the dragons for some time. Although no words were spoken, Schram believed they were in conversation. Schram could not hear anything, and he wondered if Rosstim was part of the conversation. Regardless, when the lead dragon on the council turned back to them, it was clear the discussion was over.

"We have heard your words and considered their meaning. However, we do not agree. The evidence is clear. Had we not seen him, the answer may be different. As is our rule, you will both now face the well. May your gods be with you, and your punishment is to commence immediately."

Schram was not prepared for the answer and quickly began to incant a spell only to have it ended before he could begin. It felt as if hundreds of magical arms gripped his body and were bringing him to his knees. He glanced to Rosstim and saw his fate was the same, though he was not struggling. He seemed content to be wrapped in their arms. Telepathically, he heard Rosstim's voice, *Do not struggle, my friend. Your strength you will need when the time is right.*

Schram released his mind and no longer fought the magic around him. Instantly he felt a peace begin to engulf him. The conversations the dragons were in were not discussing his fate; they were simply organizing those around to hold him. They had decided his fate long before he arrived. That much was now clear to the human-turned-dragon. Again, his eyes went to his friend. The dragons of Draag had begun moving their magically locked bodies toward the east side of the cavern face. Schram assumed that was where the hole exposing this well was located. Rosstim showed no fear or concern. Schram wanted to test the magical hold again but decided to wait until the absolute last moment, heeding the dragon's message. The dragon was ahead of him in line and would face whatever fate was bestowed on them first. Schram believed he would have his opportunity, though the combined magic of fifty or more dragons may not even be within his power to break.

As they approached what appeared to be an area where the ground had simply collapsed beneath itself, opening a giant narrow cavern to the center of Troyf, Schram began to feel concern creep into his mind. He did not know if he could count on support from Rosstim as the dragon appeared to be confident in his action. Because of this, all he wanted was to do anything to save his new companion. "Dragons of Draag, Rosstim has done nothing to you. He only asked that you look harder at me. Do not punish him for this choice. Release Rosstim, and I will, without fight, take my place above the Well-of-Antigraf. Do this with honor."

The second dragon from the council spoke for all to hear, "Schram, we have asked you not to speak. We have repeated that request. Should you speak another word, we will follow this action with an attack on Toopek. Rosstim made his choice with honor, and with honor he will experience the same fate as you." He turned to Rosstim. "My friend, do you wish to say anything before your sentencing is carried out?"

The dragon was released from the magical hold and allowed to stand before the dragons. The council of ten stood in front with nearly two hundred dragons in the area behind. Much of the area was desolate as all trees and shrubs had been scorched to the surface. Rosstim turned with raised head and spoke these words: "To all the dragons of Draag, please do not fear the world today. When fear guides your choices, then forever will it control your future. We are living in a time where the known is the unknown, and the unknown is not believable. Schram was born human, but clearly he is dragon. He is also elf and has deep friendships with both maneth and dwarves. His companions have fought for this world, and even when he thought the dragons were behind it, he did not hold us accountable. Today you will destroy me, for that is my fate, but do not destroy Schram."

The dragons stirred just a bit before the lead dragon on the council stood to face the crowd. "Please, guards, push Rosstim to the pit."

Several dragons focused their energy toward their large friend, and his feet slowly began to move toward the pit. Schram closed his eyes and focused his magic. The minute he did so, he felt incredibly strong, magical hands grip across his face and tear into his flesh. He was not able to think or speak. The dragons were blocking his use of magic. Somehow he was helpless, which meant he could not help his friend. He opened his eyes to see the large beast breach the plane of the opening and begin to descend.

Explosions followed, blinding him and sending him to the ground. Instantly he recognized he was free and sent a magical hand to the pit to try to grab Rosstim. He felt something and squeezed hard, but his size was immense. More explosions around, and the dragons on the ground had sent a wave back at whatever caused the disturbance. Schram did not care about the bolts being shot at him. He only had one goal: save the dragon.

Let me go, Schram. My fate was to bring you the time needed. My destiny is today. I have foreseen it.

Schram continued to grip tight but was beginning to be pulled forward. He was taking an intense punishment of magic from behind, and protecting against it was taking more power than he was prepared to use. More fighting was taking place around him as he continued to be pulled to the center. *Schram, let him go. It is okay.*

Schram recognized the voice immediately. *Cameron, I can save him.*

No, my brother. He has saved you, and with that, honor his action. Schram released the hold, and Rosstim was gone. No sound was heard but a burst of fire shot upward through the hole, igniting the sky before it was extinguished. Just then, Schram realized the fighting was over.

He turned his eyes back toward the council, who were all kneeling at a site behind him. Schram turned his head back and saw his four brothers hovering in the air above the pit. Schram pushed himself to his feet, but it was the council leader who spoke. "Cameron, why have you come here? This does not concern you."

Cameron swung his eyes along the council dragons and then back to the hundreds of dragons behind. "If you are going to perform such an injustice as to bring harm to my brother, then it does concern me. If you destroy that which made the dragons great by hiding behind rules without care for honesty, then it does concern me. If you use your fear to govern your decisions, then it does concern me. Dragons are the greatest creature on all of Troyf. I suggest you act like it." His last statement was directed toward the dragon council leader.

There was a hush across the entire area. All eyes went to the council leader. "You and your brothers come here, attack us, and tell us we are not acting with honor. Who has made you judge and juror?" Instantly other dragons on the council slowly moved away from him, knowing his words against what all would call the greatest dragons in the history of Troyf would not be met with silence. No sane dragon would take a stand against the four brothers, but the leader continued unfazed, "You and your brothers are in the wrong and should suffer the same fate if you are truly with honor."

Another on the council, a brilliant yellow female, interrupted the comments toward the leader. "Do not insult us as well as yourself. We believe you have acted with honor—until this moment, that is. If the four brothers believe there is more here, then before any more steps are taken, we owe them the honor of discussion."

Cameron was taken by the aggressive stance by the council leader, not that he was against having someone speak against him, which he wasn't, but more that this dragon was taking such a strong stance in this situation. Kolkmeier leaned forward and whispered something to Cameron. Schram saw this and knew they could easily speak telepathically, but the action to whisper was more important than the words said. Cameron was still the dragon who spoke, "Thank you, Linnea, but your words are not needed at this time. I am struggling to determine why Dyrkstra"— who was the leader—"feels so strongly, almost forcing Schram through this process as other dragons forced us through things in the past."

He turned to Dyrkstra to speak directly to him. "You have no power to challenge us. We will not forbid the dragons from taking action, but it will not be this day, and it will not be the Well-of-Antigraf. Tell me, young dragon, what is your motive, and do not answer that you wish to do right of our process."

"Cameron, I respect you and your brothers at the highest level, but the things that made us vulnerable in the past are not going to repeat themselves. We abandoned our principles and allowed ourselves to become tricked into believing that our world was in jeopardy. We do not feel that now. We saw it." He motioned to Schram. "The attacks on the dragons two hundred years ago were from within. They were from a self-fulfilling quest for power. This council met. We believe Schram holds those same traits. He sits back and pretends to be for this world, but slowly, over time, he has taken over more and more of it. His quest for power started with his first taste when he walked with the canok. Coincidentally, that canok was removed, and only he remains. We saw him put that plan into final motion. His failure was he did not destroy the dragons. He only destroyed Draag."

Schram still had not spoken for himself, and he did not think this was yet the time, but he looked to Cameron to confirm. The dragon did not even entertain his stare. "You are all making decisions out of fear. For over two hundred years, the dragons have made decisions out of fear." Cameron shook his head and began to turn away.

"Wait," stated Linnea, "perhaps we are making decisions out of fear, but why then did Schram destroy our world? Or are you saying, as has been implied, that there is another force out there so great that they can make us believe it was Schram? If that is the case, should we not fear it?"

"Fear it!" exclaimed Cameron. "The dragons are the strongest creatures on all of Troyf. Sure, Schram might have special powers, but look, is it not dragon? Even the black dragon of the past had special powers, but was he not dragon? I am standing beside my four brothers"—he nodded to Schram, including him in that count—"and in front of us are more than 250 dragons with more falling in behind. Who should we fear? They should fear us."

There was a hush across the clearing, and even Schram had become somewhat energized by the speech. Linnea looked toward Dyrkstra, hoping he would take the lead, which, upon her gaze, he slowly did.

"I hear your words and see their impression upon the council. I will not defend our decision further but ask only that we tread lightly forward. Something does not feel right, and it seems to be centered on Schram. However, your word is worth much, and I will respect it. If the council agrees with the decision, I will offer the release of Schram to continue his current quest. Should we find that, indeed, he is behind its source in any way, then his punishment will as justly be carried out."

There was no vote necessary, and the group quickly disbanded and brought Schram into their midst. Schram did not know what this meant, but he hoped it meant the dragons would be in his support. He also knew that word would spread quickly, but probably not quickly enough to cover all areas. Should he return to Toopek or farther, there was a good chance he would run into dragons that did not know of this direction, and in turn could lead to battles he did not wish or even need to fight. He prayed for the best.

He turned to greet his brothers and quickly realized they were gone. *We have business elsewhere, and time is too critical to ignore. We will be with you when the time is right.*

He turned to Kleinton, who was still by his side. "What about Rosstim?"

The dragon's head hung low. "I believe it was his time. I believe he knew. His destiny was to save you, to give you enough time." He paused then added softly, "And he did." His voice lifted slightly. "Do not be sad for him. Be proud for the life he lived. He was a force with you for a long time."

Schram shook his head and began to walk away. Kleinton reached out to grab his shoulder. "Where are you headed now?"

"I must go to help my friends. They are on their way to the Realm of Darkness. I must go there as well."

"Safe travels, Schram. I am not sure how I feel about the decisions made here, but I will honor them. Please don't make fools of us."

He stopped, not realizing the dragon was looking for some sort of closure that they were not making a huge mistake. "Kleinton, I have seen terrible tragedies from today all the way back to when I was a baby. The decisions we make every day can be right or wrong. What I can tell you is this: I have never meant any harm to dragons, but not all dragons are good, plain and simple. All we can do is take the information we have at our disposal and make the best decisions we can. I have killed dragons. Dragons have tried to kill me. I hope, as you do, those times are over."

Kleinton did not reply but watched as Schram took to the air. *Fly north, my brother. Go over the Arctic Circle to reach Cindif and the Realm. Your path will take you where you need to go.*

North? Not back through Toopek? questioned Schram telepathically back to Cameron. *I have never traveled there. Are you sure?*

There was no reply. Schram puffed a deep breath and turned his course straight north to travel over the top of his world instead of around it.

The Travel

The dragons flew hard across the sea. The flight was long, but they met with no delays in weather or injury. They met with what Stepha felt was surprisingly no interference. Though she was pleased with the clear path they traveled, something inside her twitched in discomfort, almost as if they were being invited in. She had decided during the long flight and in discussions with her companions that they could find refuge in Eltak. The elves had been forced to flee their home so long ago and found a new home on the other side of the world. Several had met these elves on their first visit to the Realm. Although they were not as free to greet strangers as the elves of Elvinott, Stepha was certain they would greet them as friends. They would have no love for the evil passing across this land, and having an elven princess in the group would only help matters.

She had also spent some time speaking with the dragons. The four dragons on which they flew were inquisitive about their travels as well, so it proved to be beneficial for both parties, seeming to evaluate the authenticity of the other's plight. Stepha spoke with all the dragons, but most of her conversation was with the smaller green known as Magdalene, who preferred to be called Maggie. With her traveled the two blues, Stellanta and Phredder, and the largest of the dragons, Lorinca, the yellow-and-brown. Phredder was the only male and seemed to question the group the most. Maggie simply was consumed with Stepha and Denisi.

Once they landed, she had convinced the group they should make a straight course to the hidden elf city. The four dragons opted not to join them at this time. They would remain on the coast for a while but made no promises to be there. Stepha looked toward Maggie, and when she saw her wink in her direction, she was confident they would remain. She did not know how far Eltak was or even what direction for sure. However, she had learned in Toopek that the Realm of Darkness was deep into the easternmost part of Cindif. Assuming they landed where her companions had previously, their path to the Realm should take them straight through to Eltak, as

Schram had told her it had before.

She thought about her husband and prayed for his safety in Draag. She had an empty feeling, almost like death, starting to come over her. By her expression, she knew Denisi felt it too. She did not know what it meant, but it was very strong here. Perhaps just being on the land that shared its home with the area where all passage to the afterlife was given was the source of this feeling. Perhaps it was something else. She did not know.

Suddenly all were pulled from their respective thoughts as a large explosion bit through the air. Both Stepha and Denisi immediately lifted into the air while the others all drew weapons. The dragons turned their attention to the disturbance, and fire even flew from Lorinca's mouth. The elves quickly dropped back to land and raced to the shore where the disturbance had occurred.

"Khaled, you are here," stated Stepha. His voice was deep and slow.

"I am here, young Stepha. When I learned of your travel, your safe passage I felt compelled to ensure."

All looked on in amazement, but none were as completely taken by the sight as Angus and Lars. Neither had ever seen this creature, and even the few stories from those that had could not do it justice. With only a slight pause but a flowing movement much surprising from such a large creature, the huge physeter lifted itself farther through the surface of the water. Its huge body spanned more than all four dragons, and its tail would break the water behind him and smash down like a dragon being pulled from flight crashing into the sea. Its large eyes rolled on its head like balls as a second blow of air shot from on top of its body, causing another explosion and rustling the trees well offshore. Its mouth did not move as telepathy was its chosen form of communication.

Nobody knew how many physeter there were. Nobody knew exactly how powerful they were. They tried to remain neutral in every affair regarding those on land, but twenty years ago, they had blurred the lines of neutrality and assisted Schram in the oppression. Khaled was the only physeter anyone had ever seen and the only one who had helped the companions in the past. Seeing him was a comfort to Stepha, and it showed in her face and tone.

"My friend," started the elf, "I cannot tell you how pleased I am to see you here, for we have a mission, but without Schram or the canoks with us, our direction has been left to chance. Can you assist us?"

"Is it true you seek the Realm?"

"It is, but if our path is true, then Eltak would also be a direction and possibly a place of refuge for the night."

The large whale immediately looked away, causing a stir in the group. It appeared he was going to say something, stopped, and then continued, "You must travel directly toward the mountain across the eastern horizon. Keep that path the entire way, and you will find what you seek." He paused again and seemed to be fighting for the right words. His eyes went mainly to the two elves. "Be mindful of your feelings. There is much evil around us this day—evil the likes of which we have not seen before, evil that will strike you deeper than you have ever felt."

There was a stir, but it was unclear what the message meant and why it was directed toward the two flyers. Stepha waded in a short distance and reached her hand out to the creature that had come just about to shore as he spoke. Softly she touched the area Lars thought must be a nose, but he saw nothing there. The elf's voice was very soft, "We will be mindful, my friend. Your words are sitting with me like knives in my chest. I fear for the safety of those I know to be my friends. I fear for the safety of the world we know. Is there any more you can say?"

He did not reply. His eyes closed, he slowly pulled his way back to the deeper water and then quickly vanished.

Angus came forward. "That was one of the most amazing things I have ever seen."

The elf smiled, but both Maldor and Jermys recognized the look she was covering. The words spoken put a fear in Stepha. Maldor thought about Schram. Had something happened to him? Fehr climbed up on the maneth's shoulder and whispered, "This is not good. I have seen this look before, and we need to watch her close. I don't know what has happened, but that whale does and simply did not want to tell her."

"Do you think it is Schram?" whispered Maldor. The rat grimaced. "Scary, that was my first question also."

The elf seemed to break from her stupor. She waved to the group and shouted, "Come, let's head the direction we have been given. Let's get to Eltak. We can find safety there, and with that, perhaps some answers. We will need their guidance to ensure a safe passage to the Realm of Darkness."

The others fell in behind, and although the males in the group did not hold Stepha as their leader, they also did not mind the direction. They all knew that in a fight, each possessed strengths that made their group extremely powerful. Taking the weapons of the ring aside, this was a band of warriors, plus one rat, who was, of course, busy eating as Lars carried him across his shoulders.

***

"What is that?" Schram said to himself, though he was not certain if he said it out loud or in his head. "Maybe I should quit talking to myself," he then added, smiling. Schram did laugh at his own jokes more than anyone else, but he also thought that fact alone was funny, which again made him laugh. He broke from his momentary escape when he looked across the snow- and ice-covered terrain and saw something. He could not make out what it was, but as his wings were tired and he was needing rest, he decided it would be worth investigation. As he drew near, it appeared to be some sort of a long-forgotten outpost or city. All he could see at this distance were numerous dark masses against the white base, but that was enough to provide shelter. He shifted his flight and began a slow descent.

The small black dots turned larger and larger as he approached. His senses did not feel danger. If his eyes did not see it, he would not know it existed. He slowed his flight a bit more as he saw that much of this expanse across the ice caps had motion. It was alive. He focused his feelings and powers on the site below but gained nothing.

Good or evil, I should feel something, he thought, not knowing if he actually spoke the words or not. He then whispered to himself, "Unless they are intentionally blocking my search." He contemplated, not continuing his descent, but then realized this could be part of it. He needed to know what was here.

He broke in closer, and if the cold bite of the air had not already done so, the sight before him almost froze the blood in his veins. Layered across the ice in some sort of training formation were hundreds and maybe thousands of the same creature he had met in the forest outside Elvinott: two-headed dragon bodies with canok-like features. Surrounding them were almost two dozen small black canoks, not the traditional canoks Schram knew from the past but canok-born nonetheless. He was completely outnumbered and would be completely outclassed. He had no escape. Nothing he could do. His poor decision had just cost him everything.

Greetings, dragon, stated a voice telepathically. *What brings you to this place so far north?*

Schram looked down to see one of the canoks had definitely engaged him. The others, though interested, held their attention on the two-headed dragon creatures. Schram did not know what this meant or what to do. He considered turning and flying with his greatest speed away, but with that many winged creatures behind him, he would not escape. He considered some sort of magical barrier, but he simply did not know what he was up against. He looked across the unending field of beasts and then suddenly realized—they did not know who he was. His eyes shot to the canoks. They had to be pups, only a few years old, which, in a canok's life, was a fraction of their full span. He then studied the two-headed dragon creatures. Yes, they were the same creature but smaller in size and seemed to be more like a class than an army. His lips turned slightly upward.

I am just a dragon flying by, he thought. *I recently left Draag on a course to Cindif. I am looking for the one who betrayed our dragon home. Word was sent he went across the sea from Toopek. The shortest path for me is across the circle.* He did not know how much to say or how little, so he stopped and waited for a response.

We do not know of this betrayal. We are simply here in training for the final oppression. You are welcome to seek refuge here should you need it, but know we have little food or cover. Our team does not require it.

He did not know what to make of this, but the words that struck him deeply stood out like a bandicoot at a dark dwarf party—final oppression. He was very close to the canoks now and could see they were waiting for a response. *I will join you briefly, if only for a rest. I would love to learn what your team can do. They look truly amazing.*

Please, join us. The canok who had been communicating turned to the others, and Schram knew they were speaking without his knowledge. That being said, he still sensed no deception and actually felt this was a break he could never have anticipated.

As Schram reached the ground, the canok motioned with his head and directed Schram to follow two of the others. Schram was captivated by the sight before him: thousands of dragon creatures standing in formation, being trained to use various acts of magic and to defend against such magic. Strategies for attacking cities were displayed in the sky as if projected on a wall. Schram watched briefly one of the trainings and saw that Toopek was the focus of their training. Toopek was to be destroyed.

I sense some concern in you. Is there something you question?

Schram quickly blinked from his trance. *No, it is not concern. It is amazement. I have never seen creatures such as this.*

The canok stopped and began speaking out loud. The reason for the change was not clear to Schram as he stood before them. "This is the queen's army. As you know, we are training, and as you can see, they are still young. They can barely wield and control their own magic, much less defend themselves from attack. But she has created many. The numbers will simply be too much. Plus, we are told magic cannot be used against them. With some basic training and the support of the others, we will be ready."

"Remind me what others you are referring to?" Schram was inquisitive but did not want to let on that he was not aware of the plans. When the canok added the "as you know," it was clear he was already in the circle of trust for the events to come.

The canok looked on with a brief questioning gaze, but it quickly vanished. "The queen has built this dragok force, and she has also assembled all the trolls and goblins from the past into an organized ground assault. She is so powerful that she is able to move groups directly into the areas of attack with her magic. All she has to do is ensure they have been there before. Therefore, over the last twenty years, she has sent them on missions not to do any attacks or even get noticed, but to just get close. When the day is right, the attack may begin without warning. They will not even know what hit them, and they will be powerless to defend, even with whatever powers they have on their side. The plan cannot fail."

His heart sunk a bit in his chest. If everything the canok said was true, he actually believed that last line. "The plan cannot fail," he repeated softly.

The canok smiled and even drooled a bit. "Yes. We will rule Troyf."

There was a brief pause, but Schram knew he needed all the information he could get. Even risking alerting the canok to who he was did not exceed the need for knowledge. "I have not met the queen. Can you tell me where I can find her?"

The canok did not miss a beat. "She is where she has always been. Beyond the Circle. Beyond the Realm."

"Aye, yes," he replied, trying to cover. "That is correct." The two continued walking, and then Schram motioned to the huge force of creatures on the ice plain before them. "You know, I have never heard much about the dragoks. What is their history?"

"They are a dream of the queen's. She combined with the canoks, and the result was a very powerful creature never seen before. She molded that creature with her magic into the two-headed beasts you see before us. She actually was able to create an army from nothing."

"Are you saying they are not living?"

"They are living, but I do not know how. First there were ten, then one hundred, then a thousand. They did not stop coming. I don't know how. I just know we, the new pups, were asked to train them on a very specific regiment. The training is limited but precise."

Schram pondered that a minute until he noticed they were approaching a break in the ice and what appeared to be the opening to some sort of underground ice city. Changing the subject to their arrival location, he asked, "What is this place?"

The canok smiled with what could only be called pride showing through, as if he himself had built this cavern. "Well, the dragons have Draag, and we have Dragoon."

The canok continued, "Yes, we fashioned it from magic, but it is large enough to hold our entire force. We use it for protection during some of the fierce storms that break across this area from time to time. It also serves to hide us should any of the rebellion come this direction, which we know won't happen but is enjoyable to consider."

Schram shook his head in agreement as they entered the frozen doorway. Immediately upon entering, he was consumed by the evil magic that had created it. It was as if a noise so loud was playing that it dropped him to his knees. Schram was weakened by the momentary engulfment, but he did not think the canok noticed. When they entered the first room, Schram could see a long corridor with two other black canoks walking down its length. They appeared larger, and his immediate fear was that they would not be so inviting to his presence, or even more, they would recognize him. He filled his thoughts with thoughts of joining the fight to destroy Toopek just in case his mind was compromised. Before they arrived, he had one more question he had to pose to his new "friend."

"You know, I do not even know your name."

"My name is Arston. I have been here since the beginning about nineteen years ago."

Schram looked on in amazement. "Wow, nineteen years," he replied, catching the time frame as very shortly after his defeat of Slayne at the Black

Pool. "I heard rumors that the canoks were all returned to their lives of the past. I am pleased to see that was not the case. How were you able to defeat the red coat magic?"

"Simple, my friend. We are not fully canok. My father was canok, but my mother was not." He paused and then added, "And I did not catch your name?"

Schram noticed a slight change in Arston's voice, a change that suddenly had begun to question whom he had led to this place. He looked down at the creature, who now appeared to be in communication with the others approaching. He did not want to delay too long so he replied simply, "I am Rodeisen, and I am pleased to have met you."

The two other blacks arrived, and Schram could feel them prying into his mind. He let them in exactly as far as he wished them to be. These canoks were older, but also young and inexperienced, and controlling their magical hands was easy for him. Schram turned to them. "Greetings, friends. Arston here was kind enough to give me refuge on my trek north."

These two appeared to want to show their superiority and rolled their eyes at the dragon. "We know why you are here, Rodeisen, and we are truly not interested." They turned to Arston and began a conversation that was void to Schram's ears. They quickly left, and Schram and Arston continued to what appeared to be a large room designed for eating and other activities. The canok explained that Schram would be welcome to stay as long as he needed but that he had to return to the training. Schram bid him well and actually used the time to eat and rest, a very ironic picture as he drifted to sleep—the leader of the group against the evil invading the land resting peacefully in their training stronghold.

***

"Alan," shouted a guard from the top of the Toopekian wall. "In the distance, a huge army approaches."

A stir commenced among all within earshot as archers ran to position, and guards fell into lines behind the wall gates. "How many?" shouted Alan in return as he ran to where the guard stood.

"Too many to count, sir, and they appear to be huge."

"Huge?" Alan whispered to himself. *What does that mean?* he thought.

Just then, the guard's face turned white. "What in all the gods? Alan, they are all maneth and all heavily armed."

Alan stopped his run and then turned to the guards at the gate. "Guards, pull open the gates, both rows. Archers, look sharp for any pursuit. Give the maneth cover to make it through."

Quickly, all heeded the general's direction, and commotion along the wall picked up tremendously. The large wooden doors swung slowly open on both lines of the wall, and the archers held their position. "All clear behind them to the west, General," shouted the original guard who had first seen them.

"All clear south," added an elven archer who stood at the ready should anything change.

"Very well," replied Alan. "Guide them in." Within several minutes, the first of maneths reached the gates. Geoff led the way but then remained in the glade, ensuring each and every maneth made it through safely. When the final maneth passed the entrance, Geoff walked through, still with club drawn. His eyes hit Alan, and the two locked arms.

"It is good to see you, my friend."

"And you," replied Alan.

"Did you meet with any trouble?"

The big maneth cleared his throat as if they had pushed hard the last bit to reach the human city. "We met with no interference, but I felt as if we were under surveillance for the last day. I pushed us hard, not knowing what it meant. I am very glad to have made it safely."

"As are we," Alan replied. "I have my guards seeing to your entire village's comfort. Our inns will not hold all, but we have places ready. You will all be welcome. Come, let's discuss our plans."

"Yes," Geoff added, "we have much to discuss."

***

"The maneth have arrived, my queen," stated the canok.

"Yes, I have felt it, but I am pleased to hear your sources confirm the movement."

"How will you get the elves to go there as well? If we can't get them out of Elvinott, it will be tough to break their magical protection."

The queen looked down toward her companion. "Did they take care of

Eltak as I stated they must?"

"They did," the canok replied.

"Then the elves will go. That fool Stepha will see to it. She will fear the destruction of Toopek and Elvinott and forget the strength of the magic of Hoangis. That old fool will simply fail again. Her feelings for Schram will drive her decision. She will make sure the message is sent."

The canok smiled. "Then we do nothing else." She thought a minute and added, "The troops in Dragoon. Are they ready?"

"I believe they can be, though more time would prove useful."

"Then more time they will receive, but only days." She stopped and reached down to the canok's head. "Almok, we are close. We are so close to bringing Schram here and destroying before his eyes everything he knows."

Almok tilted his head. "Are you saying this is about Schram?"

She caught his questioning gaze and smiled. "No, this is not about Schram. This is about everything he has done to try to destroy our world. His quest for power is gross. He plays this role of being hero, but what is his mission?"

The canok thought a minute but did not think she wanted an answer, so he remained quiet.

She continued, not taking notice to his indecision, "His desire to have Toopek rule the land and have every other nation fall under their rule and direction is so clear to those on the outside. We want equality. Sure, we will rule the land, but only to keep order. All races will be free to do as they please, and we will answer any questions that arise."

"Aye," added Almok. "Schram is worse than a dictator because he pretends he is not."

"Exactly," she said. "Exactly."

THE ELVES

Stepha led the companions toward Eltak. Her mind was consumed by the words from Khaled, but she did not speak of them. Several walked beside the elf princess, but none offered any conversation. They were there if she wanted to talk but did not force the issue either way. Stepha simply walked with a passion. Her thoughts were also tied to her husband. She tried to "feel" him but received nothing back. She feared the worst. She rubbed her belly as tears fell across her cheek.

Jermys broke the silence across the group. "This is a good glade for a rest. Should we stop and eat? Nightfall is still well ahead of us. Although we don't know how far our destination is, we will require some nourishment, and by stopping now, it will prevent us from running into the night and potentially resting in an area that is not safe."

The elf turned to the dwarf, and although her initial irritation did show through, she quickly changed her expression to one of understanding. "Yes, my friend, let's stop. Tell the others. Denisi and I will scout a short distance ahead and verify we are safe." She motioned to Denisi, who immediately took to the air without even a word exchanged.

There was something about elves and their ability to communicate. They did not use telepathy, but there was simply something understood by warriors. Stepha and Denisi were special. Both were incredibly talented with a bow and skilled in flight. Although Stepha was the princess, it was widely believed that Denisi possibly exceeded her in bow sight, a trait they both knew deep down inside but rarely, if ever, mentioned. They both simply knew that one of them would someday defeat Madeiris when they tested. That day, regardless of who was victor, would be a day they both celebrated.

The two elves returned to where the others had all found comfortable places to sit in the shade. Both had a strange look on their faces. Maldor was first to speak, "What is it? What did you see?"

They looked at each other, but Stepha was the one who replied, "We don't know. There is no danger ahead of us that we can see, but something is not right."

Jermys now stood, his lit pipe in hand, pulling his axe as he stood. "What do you mean, not right?"

"I mean, I think we found where the elves lived. There are changes in the trees and other things that looked like that of Eltak, but they were not there."

"How far?" asked the dwarf, lifting his hatchet as a pointer to the direction they were to travel.

Maldor and Angus also stood. Maldor pointed to the others and said, "The three of us will scout ahead. You remain here."

Denisi immediately cut Stepha from speaking, "Forget it. We are together now as we will be moving forward. Everyone, whatever the situation is ahead of us, it will not change with a few more moments of rest. Stepha and I will eat, and then we will gather our things and proceed together."

Maldor was about to protest when he saw Stepha nod. The two of them had been through more together than any two people ever should. Jermys caught the gaze and offered the same. The dwarf uttered one word, which brought silence to the glade. "Together."

Everyone understood. It was not long, however, when Stepha stood. "I am ready. Denisi?"

"I am as well," she replied, grabbing her bow, which she had laid by her side.

The others immediately began to stir, and they were off. Maldor, however, now took the lead, and although Stepha felt an elf should lead the way into Eltak, there was something not right with what she and Denisi had seen, and Maldor's presence seemed appropriate.

The maneth cut a clear path for the others as the vine and vegetation cover had become extremely thick. With a few long swings of his sword, which he rarely used, they came to a clearing. However, this was not a normal clearing. Cut into the trees were homes, rooms, and tunnels. It looked like a small version of Elvinott. Not anywhere close to the intricate, almost magical carvings that spoke to you as you passed, but still beautiful. There were buildings and different structures and a strong presence of magic, as if each of these buildings may have hidden passages or doors that could be called upon as needed. It was a magical view, except for one thing.

"Oh my," cried Stepha. "Help them! Help them now." Maldor grabbed the elf as she started to run toward what appeared to be the center of the city.

"Don't look at it, Stepha. Look away."

But it was too late. The elf could see the smoke. She could smell the flesh. She could feel the pain. In front of them, stacked in the city, were the elves of Eltak. All of them. All dead. It appeared they had been killed by dragon fire or something close to it. She instantly recognized the one tied to the center.

"The king," she whispered as a tear drained across her face. Her body was limp, and she swung her head to Denisi, who was on the ground in prayer, unable to move.

Maldor motioned to Lars to take Stepha to Denisi and stay with them while he, Jermys, and Fehr moved forward with weapons drawn. Even Fehr pulled a small blade from his pouch while Angus was directed to stay back with the others at full attention.

The three moved forward slowly. Although they carried some level of fear, their strongest emotion was raw anger. "Do you think whoever did this remains?" asked the rat.

"I don't know," replied Maldor. "But if they do and they could bring this level of wrath, I do not know what we can do to stop them."

His words sat with the other two a bit before Jermys added, "If this was Feldschlosschen, I know you would do everything to find the source behind it and destroy it. We will do the same for the elves."

"Aye, my friend," Maldor replied. "This is but one step in the world of evil we are now in. It is a big step, however, possibly the biggest step we have ever seen. This evil is not afraid to kill and maim. It is different than in the past."

"What do you mean?" asked Fehr.

"I mean that in the past, yes, there was fighting and death, but it was limited to those who were defending. The goal was to take over. The elves of Eltak may not be the marksmen that Elvinott is, but they are strong and able to defend themselves. Further, I was told about strong magic protecting their home. It even disabled Schram's dragon mother and separated Schram from the party. Had he not known the king's name, they could have defeated Schram and his party so long ago."

They were directly in front of the elven remains that had been carelessly tossed aside and left to rot in the sun. The smell was extreme, but by looking, this had only happened in the last few days. No birds or rodents or other scavengers had moved in, most likely due to the magic that protected them, but it clearly was not strong enough.

Maldor turned back to the group with a lost look. "This is not about taking over the land. This is about exterminating every creature on the land."

The words hit hard, but none could argue the point. They had all seen death before, but not like this. This was the type of thing that would not just take the wind out of you, but would simply destroy you. They did not know if the two elves with them would survive it.

"We will take care of this," said a soft voice behind him. "Please leave us to be with them."

Maldor turned when a gentle hand touched his shoulder. Her voice cracked a bit and was far from strong, but he could see the determination in her eyes. He looked to Denisi, who held the same stare, and then to Lars, who simply shrugged. Maldor knew there was nothing he could have done to keep them back. This was something they had to do. The large maneth pulled both girls, whose frame was so much smaller than his they almost vanished in his grip, into a deep embrace. "We are here for you," he whispered.

They pushed back, and each placed a hand on his chest on both sides of his heart.

"We know," Denisi whispered. "Now, please, take the others and leave us for a short time. We have to assist in passage."

Maldor had seen this many times in the past but never at this level. He motioned to all the others, and they continued into the city. He had begun to feel more confident that whatever had done this was long since gone, but that did not mean they should not investigate. They needed to ensure their current safety but also see if they could find any clues to who was behind this. He did not know how long the elves would be, but he was going to give them all the time they needed no matter how long it took. He knew both Stepha and Denisi needed this to have any chance of remaining with them.

It was deep into the night when the two elves rejoined their friends. They had set up a camp on the outskirts of the elven city and built a large fire for warmth and food preparation. It was a somber night with little discussion, and when the girls arrived, the others really did not know what to say or how to say it. Several exchanged hugs or placed their hands on their shoulders, but the pain they were feeling was deeper than what others felt. Elves were different from any other creature on Troyf, and life was something held at the highest level. The pain they were feeling could not be put into words.

Stepha took a place next to Maldor and Lars in front of the fire. "Denisi and I have spoken, and I must go back to Elvinott." Maldor instantly began to interject, but the elf raised her hand to stop him. "Please, hear me, my friends. This is not an evil like the past. This is a major destruction. We cannot defeat this alone, and who knows if we can defeat this together? The prophecy was given. We had thirty days to produce Schram, or this evil would destroy every creature on Troyf. None of us truly believed they could. We have heard these threats in the past. However, I believe this evil can. I believe they showed it here. I believe we have to fight as one if we have any chance to defeat them. Someone has to get word to my brother to move all the elves to Toopek. We have to help defend that city. If Geoff was successful, the maneth are already there."

Maldor placed his hand on her shoulder. "What about Elvinott and its magical barrier? Wouldn't the elves be safer there?"

"We"—Stepha motioned to Denisi—"don't believe so. There was strong magic here protecting them. It was not the same as that in Elvinott, but it was present and was strong. We fear that if we do not build our numbers, we will be exposed. Elvinott is not large enough to hold everyone, so Toopek is the logical choice, and perhaps Schram can add some protection as he did in the past. We do not want to see Elvinott find the same fate as Eltak. I must go."

Maldor looked into her eyes and then glanced to Jermys and Fehr to see their thoughts. Although there were others with them on this journey, the trust between those four was unmatched. Both Jermys and Fehr nodded appropriately, and Maldor looked back to the elf princess. "Very well, but how will you get there?"

"I felt a bond with the dragon Magdalene. She will fly me. Alone, she will be able to make good time."

"Lars will go with you." He waved his son over to him, and the maneth quickly was by their side. He was about to give some direction when the elf interrupted.

"No, my friend. The danger you will face here is great. We do not even know what it will be. You need him with you, not just for his ability with a weapon, but this is a time when a father and son should be together. I will be with a dragon, a powerful dragon. She will protect me."

Maldor did not like it, but when he saw the determination in the elf's eyes and the tone in her voice, he knew the discussion was over.

Lars knelt down and took Stepha's hand. "I hear your words and will respect them, princess, but please know I am here for you. There is no reason to face these things alone. You are among friends."

Her face softened, and a tear again ran down her cheek. "I know," was all she could whisper before standing and walking away.

***

Maldor took the lead the next morning. Stepha had risen early and headed directly back to the shore where hopefully she would find the dragons they had ridden still waiting for them. She felt pretty confident that Maggie would be there. Once everyone had bid her farewell, they began packing up their camp. The elves had assisted all those in their passage, and now the city center stood empty.

A hollow feeling engulfed the large maneth as he stood looking at the site of this tragedy. It was so wrong he did not believe it could be true. Something changed for all the companions that night. Although they all knew they were fighting a great power, none of them really thought they could lose. Much different from the last time they were together, and they spent years fighting every moment for their lives. They were confident now. The world was stable. There was no true evil, and with that, nothing to fear. One night, one event, one tragedy changed all that. Maldor looked at the empty city and then back to his friends. They were busy packing and getting set to leave. Denisi was even covering their signs of being there.

All this changed in one night, he thought. For the first time since he was tortured in the Draag caverns, Maldor was scared, truly scared. "Let's go," he shouted. "If Denisi is done covering our trail, then we should be on foot at once. We still do not know how far we have to travel, and who knows if we will run into resistance. Jermys, please take the rear. Be conscious of everything around you. Anything out of place, warn us at once. Whatever attacked this city will not give us much warning. We most likely cannot fight it, so a quick retreat must be our only answer. Denisi, I hate to ask, but if you can take to the air and keep watch on us, I would appreciate it. I know the tree cover is too thick to see the ground, but just knowing we have eyes against any dragon attack is a comfort."

She nodded acceptance, and the others finished packing and fell in behind. They traveled as fast as the thick trees and woods would allow.

Denisi's flight was easy, but as Maldor had predicted, she had trouble even knowing where her friends were, much less providing any support. She flew with an arrow notched and at the ready, and her eyes scanned the horizon. The sun had come up bright and clear without a cloud to break the view. The temperature was cooler as they were farther north and not far from the ice caps of the Arctic Circle, but to Denisi, it was very refreshing and an easier flight.

They traveled throughout much of the day without knowing if they headed the right direction or if they were very close or still days away. They remained in their ranks only having Lars and Jermys change places on occasion and Denisi to break and walk on foot; though, when she was down, usually they all rested, not wanting to travel without some support from above. They had been traveling for some time when she decided her wings could use a break. As she descended into the trees, just for a moment, she thought she saw movement. Quickly she veered that direction, but all was still. She scanned the area farther, saw nothing, and then headed back to the group.

"Greetings, Denisi," returned Maldor. "I was wondering when you would want a break." Then he saw her gaze had changed and quickly changed his tone. "What is it? Did you see something?"

"I don't know," she said, shrugging. "I saw movement, then nothing. I investigated, and there was nothing there. No creature could have moved that quickly. I was to the area in seconds."

"What do you think it was?"

"I don't know. I could not tell you if it was a bandicoot or a dragon. I just saw movement, nothing else."

Maldor waved everyone in with Jermys catching up in only moments. He explained the possible sighting and decided to hold up there and take a small group ahead first, with others at the ready to fall in behind. They all nodded in agreement, and just as they broke, they realized they were surrounded.

"What are these creatures?" asked Denisi. "I have never seen them before."

They looked upon the creatures before them. They had a covered face with two flat holes used for what appeared to be scent. Their mouths were made up of hundreds of short hairlike projections functioning as tiny arms to pull food in. However, it was the rest of their bodies that were more captivating. Their full structures were hidden under robes, but little was left to the imagination. Their bodies appeared to be large balls with approximately twelve thin sticklike legs protruding from them. There were six on each side, which extended up above their heads and then down to the rest on the ground. Maldor spun his head around the area and saw six of them equally distant apart completely enclosing their position. The maneth paused then answered the elf's question.

"I do not know, but we are not outnumbered by what we can see, and they don't appear to be looking to attack."

"They are studying us," added Fehr. "Reading our minds. Evaluating who will taste better."

Jermys lightly tapped the rat on its head just hard enough to send the message to shut his mouth. "Then I guess you will be fine as they know you will taste like sh—"

"Zhou tak moth ernest doy savy," the largest one directly in front of Maldor spoke.

"I am sorry," the maneth replied, "we don't understand." The creature seemed angered at the response, but it was not clear if it did not like the response or did not understand it. Again, the creature repeated, this time, louder. "Zhou tak moth ernest doy savy."

Denisi studied the creature's stare and noticed it was not at them. She looked at each of the creatures and followed their gaze as well. "I know what to do," she stated.

"What?" asked Maldor as the creature that spoke had taken a step closer.

"Drop your weapons."

"What! Not a chance, elf. That is the only protection we have."

The elf stepped beside the big maneth, creating a stir among the creatures. "Maldor, I believe there are hundreds behind these trees. That is what I saw. Remember, we are in their home, not the other way around." She set her bow and sword down on the ground at her feet and nodded to the creature in the process.

The creature took a step back to its previous position. "Zhou tak dopeth sai."

Maldor looked to the others, back at the creature, and then to Denisi. She nodded and softly whispered, "Do it. I do not sense they mean us harm."

As Maldor set his weapons to his feet, the others followed suit. Instantly, the trees came alive, and at least another forty-five creatures emerged around them. Maldor bent to pick up his hammer, and Denisi grabbed his shoulder, stopping him. She slowly walked up to the creature that had spoken and reached out her hand.

The creature showed no reluctance and reached out several of its tentacles. Denisi's body trembled only slightly, and in moments, they broke. The large group of creatures that had appeared after the first six immediately moved away back into the tree line. Denisi turned to the others. "I understand them now. They will help us."

"What do you mean?" asked the maneth.

"I mean they are peaceful. They live here in the forests. They protect the forest from intruders. They know Schram, his dragon mother, and Werner the red. His name is Kuen, and he is a spydig."

"A spydig? I have never heard of them." Maldor looked on questionably.

"Relax, my friend. Simply touch them, and you will see and know what I know."

The maneth stepped slowly forward and reached out one of his huge paws. As the tentacles connected, his mind was filled. It was not a probing attack but one of education. The only way to speak to a spydig was to communicate in their language. The only way to gain their language was to touch one and have it shared. The only way they would allow their touch and allow the sharing was if they felt you were not a threat. Maldor was the first maneth a spydig had ever touched. The exchange was one of amazement for both parties.

"I understand," he said softly. The others followed suit, including Fehr, who was overly excited to learn a new language. The spydig actually seemed resistant to connect with the rat due to his enjoyment and constant chatter, but the exchange took place; and immediately upon completing it, the entire spydig community regretted it.

Fehr was speaking this new language wildly, trying every word, translating everything they said from language to language. The banter even began to annoy the companions, and seeing the direction, Lars grabbed the rat and stuffed him in his pouch, sealing it tight. Mumbling was still heard through the fabric, but the reduction in volume was a pleasant change. It actually seemed to add a stronger bond with the spydigs as their agitation was also growing, and the companions did not even know what an angry spydig meant. Three of the other spydigs dispersed into the trees, leaving the companions alone with the remaining three, one of which was Kuen.

Kuen spoke, "I know Schram, Hawthorne, and Werner. They are

honorable."

Maldor seemed pleased with the start of this conversation, and although he knew the speaking of Hawthorne's name was not received well by the elves, he also knew they recognized that Kuen did not know she had passed. "How do you know them?"

"I met them many years ago. They were bearing a trek to the Realm of Darkness."

Maldor held his expression. "I am very sorry to tell you that the one known as Hawthorne has passed." He let this settle a moment and then continued, "And we too are headed to the Realm. Can you assist us as you did them so long ago?"

The spydig did not seem to like this direction, but it may also have been the news of Hawthorne that caused his tone. He turned to Denisi. "I am sorry that I spoke her name. I meant no disrespect."

Denisi was amazed at his knowledge of their custom and only nodded politely that she understood and appreciated the comment.

Kuen continued, "Why do you need to go to the Realm? A dangerous place it is. Many unknowns. Many dangers. Most who go do not return."

Maldor motioned to his hammer, which still sat on the ground by his feet. "I must return this hammer to them."

The spydig took a step back and then raised his stare to the maneth. "Your quest is honorable. I can provide you the same guidance I gave your friends so long ago." He took a short breath then continued, "A day's walk east and a mountain range will appear ahead of you. You will need to travel between the two largest peaks that rise up from the center of the chain. Beyond them, there should be a crystal pool known as Ice Lake, where you will find a path that leads directly to the Realm of Darkness."

Maldor looked to the others and then back to Kuen. "Thank you, Kuen. We would never have found it without you. As you did so long ago, you have helped us more than we can put into words." The spydig nodded slightly as Maldor continued, "How long do you think is it for us to reach the Realm?"

"Should you run into no resistance, a day to reach the mountains and another day to reach Ice Lake. From there, I cannot say, for I have never traveled beyond the lake."

"Is there anything we can provide you for your assistance?" asked Denisi.

"We do not require anything. We only seek to keep these forests free of evil. Do not prove us wrong."

The companions all nodded as they knew the message they presented was the truth, and with that, they would not disappoint. Fehr remained captive inside Lars's pouch, but he did not seem to mind as he did not stir at all. There was a little conversation left between the groups, but in truth, the companions wanted to continue their journey. They now had a direction that they carried with confidence. They had a plan and a timeline. They only hoped it would be successful. Although they were told that returning the hammer was the correct decision, none of them were present the last time at the Realm; and at this time, nothing was certain. None really knew what to expect or if there would be problems. Based on their experiences so far, they each knew the chances were high that it would not be as simple as walking into the Realm and handing over the hammer. And even if they did make it, would going to the Realm of Darkness be the safe and correct decision for any of them in the first place?

Ice City / Ice Lake

Schram rose early and made his way out of the ice city hidden away in the Arctic Circle. He walked by where many of the young troops were training, and even in just one night, he thought he saw a difference. Perhaps he was imagining it, but these creatures were indeed powerful.

Schram, are you there? A voice said telepathically. Instantly his eyes and ears drew to attention. It was faint and tough to hear. He was not even sure he had heard it. Because of the weak nature of the contact, he did not know to where or whom to respond. He stopped, watched around him, and focused.

Schram, are you there? he heard again.

Stepha, is that you? he replied. And then there was nothing. What did it mean? Was she in trouble? He tried repeatedly to contact her, even focusing on her magical bow to guide him but found nothing in return. He focused just on her, trying to feel if she was well and again felt nothing.

"I sense you are trying to communicate with those not here. I sense deception in your thoughts." The voice was not telepathic and said directly to him, as if the canok was taunting him with not using a superior form of communication.

Schram looked down to see Arston standing next to one of the larger black canoks from the other day. It was not Arston who had spoken. Schram did not know what to say but knew he had to give something. "I am trying to learn what happened at Draag. We are looking for one called Schram who betrayed the dragons. It is the point of my travel to be more precise."

The canok cringed at the use of Schram's name. "What do you know of Schram?"

Schram did not know what to say at this point, so he gave the only answer he could. "I know that he destroyed my home, and because of that, I am to bring him back to face the choices he made."

There was a pause, and Schram could feel the canok again trying to pry into his mind. He gave him only enough access to confirm the words he had just said. There was a chance the canok would recognize he was being blocked, but that was a better option than letting him learn all that was within his mind.

The canok slowly smiled. "Yes, he is not a friend of the canoks and dragons. He needs to be stopped. I hope your trek is successful."

Schram did not wish to have any additional conversations. The more he spoke, the larger the chance that he would let something slip, or that this canok would find a way into his mind. He bid them farewell and was off. He flew for several hours, always checking back to see if he was being followed. To his surprise, he was not. He had just set foot in the stronghold of the evil forces and walked out without issue. He remembered Almok. He remembered the canok simply walking out of Anbari's Dominion with Schram's blessing, and now he had just done the same thing in reverse.

Schram had gained a lot over the last night, but how he could use it was still the question. He then remembered Stepha. He focused on her again, but nothing was received back. He was worried about her. Why had she tried to contact him? What did she need? Was she in trouble? All these questions drove Schram's wings, and he cut through the wind with a speed he had never flown before. He sent small bursts of fire in his path to heat the air, both adding comfort, and more than that, making the air thinner and easier for flight. He did not know where he was going for sure, so his path was going to be straight for the Realm of Darkness. He was still days away.

***

"Maggie!" shouted Stepha.

The four dragons all swung their heads, but it was Magdalene that wore the large smile. "Stepha, so great to see you so soon." Her smile faded when she saw her expression. "What is it? Is there trouble?"

"There has been a great tragedy, one which I must get word back to my brother in Elvinott. Can you take me?"

She glanced to the other dragons, who nodded appropriately. "I can, but the travel will be long."

"I understand. Can we leave immediately?"

The dragon shook out her wings and walked to where the flyer elf had just landed. "It will take me a few moments to prepare for such a flight on my own. Use this time to rest and calm your mind."

Stepha did not like the delay, even for a short moment, but she accepted that the dragon did need some time. She shook her head and then found a place in the shade. Immediately upon sitting, she realized the rest would prove beneficial as her entire body seemed to melt into the sand. She had been flying hard, and with the pressure on her mind, she had simply remained locked in a tense state, like being chained to a wall and constantly trying to break free. She closed her eyes and thought about her brother. Then, as always happened, she thought about Schram. She prayed again for his safety. Then she remembered how they had been able to connect from so far away in the past.

She focused on her husband and his staff. She gripped her bow and said, *Schram, are you there?* She waited a moment and repeated, *Schram, are you there?*

For a moment, she thought she was beginning to feel him. Then the forest exploded around her. Her thoughts went blank, and she leaped to her feet and into the air just as the place she had been sitting exploded into flames. "Stepha, run!" shouted Maggie. The elf swung her head to see the four dragons moving to engage three other dragons coming from the north. Stepha looked closer, and her eyes dropped—the two-headed creatures from outside Elvinott. She fired her bow, and its mark hit true. The dragok screamed in pain with one arrow protruding from one of its necks. She then moved to position herself along the line of other dragons until Maggie cut over and flew right between the elf's legs, placing her directly on her back.

Phredder hollered to the group, "They want the elf. Their attack is toward the elf. Maggie, get her out of here. We will hold them off, but be mindful. They know she is here, and others will most likely follow."

Just as he spoke, a beam of magical fire shot from one of the dragoks directly at the much larger dragon. This was not dragon fire. It was a magical knife that would cut flesh on contact. Phredder dove, causing the beam to catch only his tail, severing it cleanly. Instantly, his ability to fly was lost, and he struck the sandy beach.

Maggie looked back only a moment. She was about to turn and fight when the downed dragon nodded back to her. Get out now!

Maggie turned and blew fire in her path and cut hard across the sea.

"What about the others?" Stepha said. "We can't leave them."

"We need to go now, Stepha, or we may not go at all." She paused, and her face dropped just a bit. It was probably not noticeable to most, but Stepha saw it. "Remember, a dragon knows when it is their time. They will not bring others to that time if it is not theirs."

A tear fell on her cheek. She looked back to the harbor to see a vicious display of fire and magic still commencing on the shore. They broke into the clouds and were gone.

***

Maldor pointed ahead. "There are the largest two peaks. That is our path."

The group seemed pleased that they had just reached a milestone for them. One of the markers that their path was true had appeared on the horizon. It had taken longer than anticipated, but they could see their goal ahead of them. The new day started, but they had not lost time during the night. They rested only briefly and kept their pace. They had decided that time was working against them, and finding time to rest was not at the pinnacle of their requirements. Getting to the Realm was their number one goal, and it had to take precedence.

All the companions showed a level of pleasure at the sight, but Jermys snapped to attention. He motioned to Maldor to stop the group, and then he approached from the rear. "There is something ahead. I saw movement down in the lowlands before the mountains. Our path has to go that direction, but something is there."

All studied the area and saw nothing. Denisi landed after the dwarf had spoken, and the information was relayed. "I can see nothing down there. The cover is too thick. If there is something ahead of us, we will have to engage it on the ground."

A rustling could be heard coming from Lars's pouch. He opened the large sack, and Fehr leaped out. "Quit begging. I will go."

"What?" replied Maldor.

"Who better than me to navigate through underbrush undetected? Your begging is truly embarrassing. I will be back quickly." As he darted immediately out the sack and toward the tree line ahead, he glanced back and hollered, "Get comfortable. I will need to tell you everything I see, and it might take a while for me to tell it."

They smiled, and although they wanted to protest the rodent going out on his own, they really could not argue with the reasoning. Maldor shook his head as the rat disappeared. "You know, he has been sitting in there all this time, being carried by my son. For all we knew, he was hibernating, sleeping, or doing anything but helping us. I assumed he could not even hear us. Then he just pops out and runs ahead without a question or discussion."

"Like he runs the show," added Lars, smiling.

Denisi looked appalled at the comment. "He is just lazy. He clearly does run the show. Maybe I want someone to carry me all the time also and provide me food and give me a place to sleep. He offers nothing really and gets it all."

"Sounds like a woman," Maldor whispered to Jermys. Denisi swung a stare at him like daggers. The maneth quivered. "You heard that? Stinking elven ears."

The group made a small camp and waited while the rat vanished somewhere deep in the trees. There were moments of small conversation, but most of them simply enjoyed this period of peace. After what seemed like too long, however, Maldor began to stir. He looked to the others and then to where Fehr had disappeared. "Where is Denisi?"

Fehr was large for a bandicoot. He had grown to nearly twice the normal size, but it did not take away from his agility. He was able to navigate through the trees with ease. He was not equal to an elf in ability to move quietly, but because he was so low to the ground and on four legs, in this cover, he was even better. He came to a deep thicket, and that was when he heard a language he knew all too well.

"Head to Eltak. I am told they will be there in a few days."

Dark brothers? thought Fehr. *What are they doing here?*

"Wait, what was that? I heard something." One of the dark dwarves, a particularly fat one, looked over in Fehr's direction, and the rat locked in his position, not wanting Chubby to see him. Two other dark brothers looked on.

"Knock it off. There is nothing out here but trees," a taller one said, hitting Chubby on the back.

The other one who looked jittery to Fehr asked, "What are we going to do in Eltak? The elves are not just going to let us in to wait for them."

"The Queen says it will not be a problem," Chubby answered.

"Very well, but I don't like it. We are dwarves. Why are we taking direction from someone we don't even know?" stated Jittery.

"You already know that answer," Chubby replied again, his voice and tone now showing signs of anger. Fehr had seen this often. One dark dwarf gets angry, another gets angry in return. And shortly thereafter, one or both are dead as they take arms against each other. Fehr saw the first dark dwarf begin to move his gnarly hand toward his dagger.

"Take it easy," said a deep voice from the side, a position Fehr had not even seen previously and was now in full view of the rat. "We all know the plan. We go to the position we are told to intercept this human party of rebels. We destroy them without question. Then, when the war is over, we will be given Feldschlosschen and left alone. All we have to do is stop the rebels."

The dwarves about to bear arms against each other removed their hands and took a step back. Their eyes remained locked on the other, and Fehr still felt a fight could ensue. Then the larger and broader dwarf who had just spoken took a step closer to one of them. He put a knife to Chubby's throat, and in a stern, deep voice void of any caring, said, "I said knock it off. We have eighty dwarves, and if I attack with seventy-eight or eighty does not make any difference to me. Understand?"

They broke eye contact, and the dwarf with the knife to his throat pushed himself away. Neither answered, and they both turned and left the thicket. Fehr remained motionless for several moments and then slowly began to move back. He turned and bid a direct line back toward their temporary camp. He had only gone about ten feet when a hand reached down and grabbed him by the tuft of fur behind his neck.

"Thought you could simply walk away, huh?" the voice said in perfect dwarven tongue as before. "I knew I smelled something." Fehr instantly began cursing in about three different forms of dwarven dialect, which actually brought a smile to the dark brother's face. The dark dwarf lifted the rat in the air and turned him so they were face-to-face. Fehr saw this was Chubby and could tell that he was low in command and already in an argument with another dwarf. Fehr knew that if there was just something he could do to break free and possibly even injure or kill his captor to avoid having his presence passed to the others, nobody would miss old Chubby. They would assume he was killed by one of their own.

Fehr closed his eyes and tried to summon some magical powers from somewhere deep within him. He knew all his friends had magic about them, so he believed he should as well. Almost instantly, there was a thump. He was released by the dwarf, and both bodies fell to the ground. Fehr opened his eyes to see the dark brother lying dead in front of him with an arrow piercing his chest.

Fehr wasted no time and turned and ran directly back to the camp. He did his best to remain quiet, but speed was more important than anything else. There were eighty dark brothers in the woods around them, and he had to let the others know. He would not hesitate to tell them how he conjured up an arrow with his mind later, but he had to let them know what was about to happen.

He burst through the trees to the raised weapons of his friends. "Whoa, guys, it is just me."

"Fehr," stated Maldor, "what took so long, and where is Denisi?"

"Denisi? I thought she was with you."

"No, she vanished shortly after you left."

The rat looked concerned. "There are dark dwarves ahead, lots of them. They are looking for us. Someone told them to go to Eltak to meet us. They are to kill us. If they are successful, they have been promised Feldschlosschen."

Jermys instantly grew concerned. "Dark brothers? Here? How?" He shook his head in disbelief. "Feldschlosschen? It doesn't make sense."

Fehr interjected. "It is true. I killed one with an arrow."

Now the dwarf looked a bit confused. "An arrow? You don't have any arrows. What are you talking about, Fehr?"

"I know," he replied. "The dark brother had me, and I thought I was dead. I have seen so many of you use magic and carry magical weapons I thought my only option was just that. I closed my eyes and—"

He was cut off as Denisi burst through the trees. "I shot him." She paused as she caught her breath. "Did he tell you about them? Dark brothers, shy of a hundred, I think."

Fehr looked stunned. "What do you mean, you shot him?" His voice was on the verge of anger.

Denisi looked surprised. "Yeah, the dark dwarf had you. I could not understand what you were saying, and after a quick evaluation, I thought the only answer was to shoot him before he slid his knife up your belly. I will say you sure did take off awfully fast. Good job."

Lars could see the anger in the rat growing, and if not for the last two words, he thought he was going to have to pry the rat's locked claws from the elf's face. However, the moment Fehr heard "good job," his entire face changed. He looked back toward the girl. "Yes, you are correct. I did well, as did you, I suppose." He smiled and added, "We did well."

All calmed quickly, and Maldor immediately jumped in, "The dark dwarves are being sent to intercept us and destroy us, but they are going to Eltak, which we have already passed. Somebody knows we are here but not exactly where. Think hard, everyone. Who knew where we were going? Not just Eltak, but before that. Who knew we were going all the way to the Realm?"

They looked around at each other. "Everyone at Toopek," stated Angus.

"Most at Elvinott as well," added Denisi.

"None of the dwarves," Fehr replied. He then thought more and added, "Schram did, as well as a handful of dragons."

They all froze on the last word.

"The dragons?" asked Maldor. "Do you really think they are involved, after all, even though Schram said they would not commit to this evil?"

They all looked at each other, but none had an answer. The maneth turned back to Fehr and Denisi. "We need to get around them. What path would be best?"

Fehr motioned with his eyes to Denisi. The elf said, "I don't know. They seemed to be mixed through the trees. Had we not sent Fehr out, we would have walked right into them. Perhaps head straight west and then back to the north toward the mountains."

"Does anyone disagree?" asked Maldor. All were silent, so without another word, the group headed directly west.

Maldor motioned to Denisi to take to the air, but quickly she was back on foot as she could see much easier on the ground than in the air. She moved ahead to lead the group through the trees, using her gift of moving without sound to her advantage. Twice they ran into bands of dark dwarves, and twice they skirted around them unhindered. They broke through to the outskirts of a clearing that led directly back toward the mountain range when they saw another large group of dark brothers, probably thirty in all, camped directly across the center. The group dialed back into the trees and began pointing toward different options. Jermys appeared captivated by the sight, realizing what the elf and rat had said previously was true but not actually believing it until he saw it with his own eyes. He appeared as if he was about to rush the glade all on his own before Maldor grabbed his arms.

The big maneth whispered, "One bad group does not a nation make. You have done incredible work to bring the dark brothers and mining dwarves together. Do not forget that today. We need a way around. Focus on that."

Jermys pushed his hand away and then stopped, catching his anger and holding it in check. "You are right, my friend, but should these dwarves bring arms against us, I will be first in line to end their direction."

"I understand," he replied, still whispering. "Now, what do you think we should do to get around?"

Jermys drew everyone closer so all could hear. "These dark brothers are not strategic. They simply have a direction they have been given. They will break up into different parties and then regroup at their destination—in this case, Eltak. Based on what Fehr said, they do not even know Eltak's fate. The groups we have already seen are simply the first to head that way. These will all break up throughout the rest of the day, leaving the glade empty by nightfall. It is a risk to stay as we are exposed, but if that is more of a risk than trying to go around, I do not know."

"If we are exposed, it may end this whole journey. Their mission is to destroy us. Do you see any way around? We are blocked behind them, so any path either goes right through the glade or through their path toward Eltak." Denisi pointed as she spoke, and her tone spoke of one thing: to wait.

Maldor replied, "I agree. If Jermys is correct, we can walk through without care in several hours. If he is not correct, nothing changes tomorrow with our plan. I suggest we camp, take turns on watch, and give everyone a moment to rest. If it is nightfall when we go through, it is my plan to then walk throughout the night and push to our destination. We must make Ice Lake."

Everyone agreed, and they went straight to their various roles. By the time the sun was down, not all had left the glade, but it appeared the few remaining were about to head that direction. Jermys was on watch when, out of the blue, one dark brother who appeared full of ale happened right into their camp. His dwarven tongue bit the air. "What the?" he shouted.

Jermys leaped to his feet, as did several others, but it was the dwarf who had him to the ground before any other words could be uttered. Jermys put his hatchet to his throat and motioned for him not to make another sound. The dark brother looked on in disgust, but the message was clear.

Jermys leaned closer and whispered, "What is your business here, dark brother?"

The dwarf's eyes narrowed. "Do not call me your brother. I recognize you, Jermys Ironshield. You are the one who is responsible for destroying half of our nation. Trick us in with your talk of peace then destroy us without care. I will tell you nothing. Soon your reign on the dwarves will be over, and the miners will feel what we have felt."

"What do you mean, I tricked the dark brothers?"

"Don't play dumb with me. You call us to meet. Do you know how hard we fought to even send whom we did? The majority of dark brothers did not believe you would be honorable. A few did, and they came. They brought everyone. They convinced everyone. And before we even get to the mines, you have us ambushed. You killed us all."

"I know nothing about an ambush. I had been working at peace, and I did believe we were making progress. We set up a meeting, and the dark dwarves never arrived. I assumed something happened, and we would regroup. Then I needed to come to Elvinott several moons ago, and I have not been back to regroup as planned."

"Just words, you lying miner. King of Feldschlosschen, what a joke. You are not a king. You are a murderer."

The others had moved behind Jermys, and none knew where this was going. There was no escape for the dark dwarf. He could not be released as he would bring support behind them. He could not be brought with them because they needed everyone at the ready. They could not be babysitting a dark brother. The only answer was one that nobody wanted to say but all knew would be the case. Denisi had an arrow notched and ready. Although her love for life was great and to kill in general was nearly impossible unless another life was threatened, she knew in this case, all their lives were threatened. Maybe all of Troyf as she knew it. Because of that, her arrow was notched, and if anything occurred that could at all be deemed questionable, she would place the arrow true.

The dark brother's words were tough for Jermys to hear. Maldor was about to pull Jermys from where he rested on top of the fallen dwarf when the smaller companion began to speak again, "My friend, I do not know what evil has placed these words in your mouth or destroyed your people, but I can assure you that it was not me. I can see by your actions and your words you are only acting with honor. This means you believe your words. Some evil has tried to prevent us from reuniting. That evil is strong enough to destroy races.

They have divided the elves by destroying Eltak, they have divided the dragons by destroying Draag, and now they have divided the dwarves. I am sure that my home is planned to be under siege by the dark brothers sometime soon, and I can only pray it is defended well. I do know when this is all over, the truth will be known. Whether I will be alive to see it, I do not know. But I do know that you will not. I cannot let you go, for you will not trust in what I tell you now. Therefore, may your gods forgive me."

The dark brother's eyes opened wide then closed for the last time, and Jermys plunged his axe into his throat. He turned to Denisi. "Can you assist him?"

"I can," she replied softly. Then the dwarf walked away to be alone.

REUNION

Schram continued his flight as hard as he could muster, finding every wind burst or gale to glide on when he could, and staying low to the ground when he could not. The world below him was lifeless. No more camps or outposts with which to find refuge and learn of those plans against his world. His direction was pure—straight to the Realm of Darkness. If he ran into resistance, he would decide how best to handle it at the time, but until then, he would fly.

Although he did not know exactly how far he was from the Realm, he believed he could reach the shore of Cindif by nightfall; and then, if all went his way, maybe by nightfall the next day, he could be at the Ice Lake. Both options only made his wings cut harder.

He flew through the whole day without rest. The terrain below him was still ice and snow, but patches of green and brown showed through with an occasional tree breaking the plot. Off in the northern distance, he did see something in flight. It was too far to see what it was, but it was definitely moving. He had been pleased to have remained free of interference. It meant that Arston truly did not alert anyone to his presence and his mission was still not compromised, but now that might be in jeopardy. He dove to the ground and incanted a short spell, changing his skin to white. Unless you were specifically looking for him, you would not see him as he was essentially invisible.

The dot on the horizon was actually two dots, and they grew larger and larger as they drew nearer. They were flying fast, and when they were close enough, he recognized them immediately: two dragoks. They appeared to have been flying from Cindif, but that was just their current direction of origin. It could have been anywhere. However, more curious to Schram was that they were not flying to Dragoon. They were flying straight north, a path to which there was no life as Schram understood it. Schram considered intercepting them, wondering if he could defeat them in a battle. Testing two might be better than an army the first time. He opted to wait and see if a battle was thrust upon him. At their current path, the two were going to fly within earshot should Schram decide to call to them.

As they passed, Schram did not shrink down farther into a shell. Instead, he stood tall, studying them in detail, watching their flight, their wings, and how they moved in the air. Any advantage he could gain today could possibly help him later. They flew directly above his head and then as quickly disappeared across the horizon to the north. "Where were they going?" he asked himself, actually speaking out loud, though nobody was around to hear.

He shrugged, decided he liked his new all-white color, and took to the air, a giant snowball with wings blazing a burn trail to maximize his speed. *I must make it to Cindif*, was his only thought. Schram could smell the salt air and knew he was close to the shore. He could also see a slight fog drifting high from the surface. The ground beneath him was now free of any signs of snow or ice, and he had changed his color back to his normal green-and-silver mix. The temperature had also increased, and Schram was ready for a break. He was going to make the shores of Cindif well ahead of his goal, and with that, could even start toward the Ice Lake before nightfall. He could possibly stop in Eltak if he could make the best time.

He crossed the last tree line and began to cross the plains leading to the coast when he saw it. He could not make it out at first, but there was something ahead on the shore. Schram ducked immediately down to the ground and stared ahead. He could not be sure from this distance, but what he thought he saw bit him like a knife. He surveyed the area more and then began forward on foot. If what he thought was true, coming by flight would only alert his presence for whatever caused this tragedy.

He walked for a long distance, keeping in the shadows as best he could. He wanted to get a good look at the shore and the devastation there before he went too far. Once he got to where he could confirm what stood before him, Schram lifted his head and walked with no further fear out onto the shore.

"Greetings, dragons, can you tell me what happened?"

The two blue dragons swung their heads. "Who are you?" asked one of the dragons.

"I would rather not say at this point until I know what it is that has brought you to Cindif and why one from your group has passed."

They both stared at Schram. As he looked at them, he could see they had been in a fierce battle. There was a dead dragon. That much was clear. But there was also a dead pile of something. He could not tell what, but Schram assumed it was behind whatever had happened.

The larger of the two blues stepped away from their fallen friend and answered, "I am Phredder, and with me is Stellanta. Our friend is Lorinca. Her life has left her. We were attacked by three two-headed dragons the likes of which we have never seen before. They were strong with magic, stronger than any dragon I have seen. But when we defeated one, the others fled quickly, as if they had never seen death before. When the two-headed beast hit the ground, it changed into what you see there. It wasn't even real."

Schram looked at the pile of flesh-like material, but the remains no longer took the form of the two-headed beast it was before. It more resembled a small canok than dragon, but its shape was completely gone, like all the insides had been taken out of it and it was simply a rotting shell.

"What happened with the other two? You said there were three, and how did you defeat this one? With magic?"

"When the elf escaped on Magdalene and their companion went down, they fled. They headed directly north at a very high speed. It was as if they did not know what to do and did not even understand that one of their lives could end such as this, but no, we did not defeat it with magic. Only hand-to-hand combat had any effect."

He immediately knew the two dragoks he saw were the same that had fled this battle. However, he focused on only one line. "The elf escaped? What elf?"

Stellanta saw his change at hearing the phrase and stepped forward. "The one called Stepha. She told of horrible occurrences in an elf city, and she needed to return to her home. Maggie took her on her back. They did get away."

His heart beat louder than it ever had before. *They were safe*, he thought, the relief he felt showing clearly on his face. "Do you know what she saw in the elf city?"

Stellanta's eyes now fell. "She said it had been destroyed. All the elves had passed."

Schram fell to his knees. His mind went to Eltak, and he felt the pain and destruction instantly. It was as if all he had to do was hear about it happening, and his mind was able to join the city and see the death. His form left the dragon and changed to elf before their eyes.

Phredder stepped forward beside him as he rested on all fours on the ground. Placing his foot gently on his back, he softly said, "We feel your pain, and we know who you are, Schram. We are here with you."

Schram could not even muster a smile. Having the ability to feel things through magic was a powerful tool, but also a deafening curse. He pushed himself up and stared at the two dragons. "Thank you for this information. I am sorry for my inability to accept it easily." He stopped in midthought and redirected his comment. "You said Stepha escaped. Was she alone?"

Stellanta showed the care and concern one would expect, and her voice now carried a softness. "Yes, she was alone."

"Did she say what happened to the others? Where are they?"

"They continued on their mission, their trek to the Realm of Darkness. It is why we remain to assist on their return as needed."

Schram's expression began to turn as he was breaking from the devastating lock Eltak had on his mind. "Then I must go as well. The dangers here are great, and they need my assistance."

"We understand," replied Phredder.

"Will you be okay here on your own?"

They both nodded with Phredder's being more of a bow. "We will," he said. "Go do what your destiny demands you to do."

Without another word, Schram walked over to their fallen friend and spread some elven dust across its body. There was a moment of absolute stillness, and the body vanished. All were silent with heads down. He then approached Phredder and placed his staff across his injured tail. After a moment, the damage to his tail was healed. He turned, nodded an understanding, and then he was back in dragon form and in the air. "Thank you, my friends. You saved Stepha, and I will not forget it."

Schram flew hard toward the Ice Lake. He thought previously that if all went well, the time from the shore to the Ice Lake would be one full day. Now he was starting late in the day, and flying through the blackness of night would prove difficult. He locked his mind on the Ice Lake and tried to bear the straightest path there. He was not sure if he would fly through the night without rest, but if he was able, that would be the plan. While there was still a bit of daylight left, he was going to push as hard as he had ever flown.

***

The companions had walked for several hours into the night. Once the remaining dark brothers had left the glade as Jermys had predicted, their passage through was open. Denisi was not in flight and was hanging near Jermys. Occasionally she would place her hand on his shoulder for support, but most of the time, she was just there. It was an elven choice tied to their appreciation for life. Although Maldor would have preferred she be in flight, he did not even ask. She would fly when she felt it was acceptable to fly.

They had crossed between the two peaks by daybreak and were pleased to see a very clear path to follow. They would have preferred a large sign with Ice Lake painted on it with an arrow, but this was the only path; and since they were told there would be a path, they felt pretty confident in their direction. The next question they had was what they may find in their path. Could there be more dark dwarves in their future, or perhaps whoever sent the dark dwarves had others ready should the dwarves not be successful. Maldor had all these thoughts rolling in his mind as they walked.

Fehr had been dancing in and out of the woods ahead of the group, acting like a scout of some kind. It was a new role for the small creature as typically he was content to be carried and do everything he could to not be involved. In this case and with his close relationship with Jermys, Fehr just wanted to be alone. It was about noon when Jermys raised his hands to stop their movement.

"What is it?" asked Denisi softly.

The dwarf spanned his head to each of them. "I have killed dark dwarves before. By the looks of the current state, I will kill them again. I am 275 years old. Most of my bones ache all day no matter what I do. I carry a weapon that has powers I barely understand. With all of this, I ask only one thing."

There was a long pause, too long for the rat who had made his way back. "What is it, big guy? You want us to carry your weak and decrepit body so it does not hurt as much?"

Jermys looked annoyed at first then smiled. "No, I want Denisi to return to the air. I want Fehr to return to being lazy, and I want everyone else to talk to me like we are on a mission. Nothing more."

"Done!" exclaimed Fehr. "My legs are killing me. I have been walking for hours. Hours and hours. It is crazy. How do you guys do this all day?" He trotted back and leaped into Lars's arms. Everyone was looking at him in

155

amazement. "What?" he added. "Oh, I am sorry. Yes, I agree. We can go now." With that, he vanished in Lars's pouch without another word.

There were several smiles but nothing said. Maldor slapped him on the back, and Denisi took the air, and they were back on the trail. Their steps were quick, and they felt a positive force driving them forward. Hopefully they would meet with no interference as they reached the Ice Lake and beyond. There was no reason to believe anyone would think they were already beyond the army of dark dwarves waiting for them in Eltak. With that fact and a little luck, they should be able to make it.

They did not know how long it would take to get through from the opening of the mountain range, and nobody knew what to expect when they got there either. The great Ice Lake was assumed to be just that, a large lake completely frozen over. Maldor hoped this would mean they could cross it on foot rather than walk around. Although the temperature had dropped significantly since they entered the mountains, if it reached the critical low to freeze a lake, he could not be sure. He did notice the others start digging into their packs for additional protection from the chill.

It was moments later when they finally broke through the last clump of trees, and their hearts stopped. No words could describe it. They had been caught up in the name, thinking it had meant a frozen lake environment. Probably a glacier mountain with a runoff pool that remained icy cold throughout eternity. Instead, they were greeted with a pool of shadow. All they could feel was the icy-cold loneliness of death. It was an area totally devoid of life. Yet as they drew nearer, they could see that beneath the surface of this frozen desert, there were many mysteries.

Creatures of all races furiously fought to break through the icy barrier's face while others rested at the bottom, staring sadly and palely back to those who passed. Their skin no longer held any color, and their bodies seemed to have little density. They were the condemned dead, or those who would never be granted passage, wanting throughout eternity to be released from their immortal swim of lifelessness. Denisi looked away in horror as a cold chill crept up her spine. The others stared and then turned away and stared again. It was a truly ominous and horrible sight together as one.

Maldor reached out to the elf, knowing she was most affected. "Come, Denisi. To wallow about in such a place can only bring sadness. You must accept that this is a sacred place for death to grip its evil hands, and its existence only balances that which is not here."

She noticed his gaze and then drew her bow and fired in one motion. The arrow struck the beast, but it had moved quickly, and the shot only grazed its side. Maldor swung, and the activity caused all in the group to draw to attention. Ahead of them were four dragoks. The one with an arrow protruding dove back into formation, and the weary travelers were not sure what the next move would be. It appeared from the outside as a standoff—Lars, Maldor, Denisi, Jermys, Angus, and Fehr in front of four large dragoks. Each side seemed to be sizing the other up. The companions had faced dragons before, but very rarely, if ever, in what was almost a one-to-one ratio. They each had their weapons drawn and ready.

The largest of the dragoks stepped forward. "Maldor and Jermys, I am pleased to find you here with two of the four weapons in one place." He paused when he saw Lars. "Oh, how perfect, Krirtie's scimitar as well. How pleased will the queen be when I return with three?"

Maldor gripped his hammer tighter as he heard her name. He was about to speak when the dragok continued, "And who are you?" he asked, looking toward Denisi. "You are not the one we want. Where is Stepha?"

"I am Denisi. Stepha is on a different mission, one that will bring about your destruction."

"Ah yes, fool girl." The dragok snickered. "The secret mission to move the elves from Elvinott to Toopek for protection." He narrowed his eyes on the girl. "Did you like my work in Eltak? You should have heard them beg for their lives. Perhaps they were saying, 'Denisi, Stepha, please help us.' Were you able to help them when you arrived?" The other dragoks now smiled as well, with a tuft of smoke coming from their nostrils.

In the smoothest motion ever performed, Denisi had launched another arrow toward the dragok speaking. He smiled wide and actually lowered his head into the flight of the arrow. With a crack, it hit inches from his eyes and fell harmlessly to the ground. "I will not make the same mistake twice. Your weapon is useless against me." He turned to the others. "All your weapons are useless. We have sent messages. We have shown our strength and that we are serious. Today is your day to decide. Join us and hand over your weapons, or die. There is no further discussion or negotiation."

There was a very brief exchange of glances, but none really needed to speak. In only moments, Maldor charged with Jermys and Lars in his wake. Denisi went to the air, as did three of the dragoks. The dragok who had been speaking remained directly in their path.

Fehr, although limited in ability to fight such large creatures, headed to the far side to see if any position could be gained from the side. Angus held strong and waited to see who needed his support first. The dragoks in the air began an air assault on the three attackers. One drew its attention to Denisi, who was pummeling them with arrows. They were having little effect as her bow seemed powerless against the magic created by the dragok, but it did keep one from her friends. The other two, by the companions' surprise, were having no effect on them. The same way Denisi's arrows were deflected before striking true, the magical bolts from the dragoks were doing the same. The companions' weapons hummed with power, and they each gripped them tight. Lars's almost had his body explode with the power he now felt, a power he had never felt before. As he ran toward the creature, he saw his mother standing beside him with her hand over his on the hilt. His eyes teared with both love and anger.

Weapons flew through the air. Some swings were met with rejection, and to the dragoks' surprise, some were met with flesh, but they did not actually do any damage. Maldor made first contact, plunging his hammer deep into the lead creature's throat. Though the blow did not cut through the thick skin, the force did knock one of its heads severely downward. However, with a quick reaction, its second head slammed down into the maneth's back, sending him to the ground. It turned that same head down and sent two bolts directly into his chest. As with the hammer, although the skin was not breached, the force to Maldor's chest left him nearly unconscious, gasping for any free air already thin from the cold temperature. Jermys saw Maldor go down and left the dragok he had engaged to put a barrier between the dragok's second attack and his fallen friend.

Maldor was still helpless to defend short of lifting his hammer in front of him. The dragok arched his second head again, preparing another attack, but instead reached his talon out to grab the hammer. Maldor recognized the move too late, and the creature pulled it free of his fingers. But as it came free, both dropped it when Jermys's hatchet struck right above the talon.

The dragok screeched in pain, making the other three turn their attention. Denisi used the opportunity to release numerous arrows into both necks of one of the creatures in flight, but again, the impact was negligible. The dragok turned, and instead of firing a magical barrage at the girl that she seemed easily able to maneuver around, it turned and flew full force at her. In an instant, she was struck in the air and sent down to the ground.

"Denisi!" shouted Angus as he ran to her side. The girl was not moving when he arrived. The dragok who had struck her down landed before them. Angus stood tall and hard between the creature and the fallen elf. He raised his sword and was struck at how small he was compared to this creature that approached. Its two heads moved side to side, creating a difficult, if not impossible, pattern to defend. It stepped slowly closer, almost toying with the human warrior.

Angus gripped his sword tighter, and with a silent prayer and a brief look to his fallen friend, he charged at the beast. Although Denisi's arrows did not seem to break their magical barrier, it appeared that a hand-to-hand attack could. The dragok was not prepared for the attack, thinking the human was there simply to defend, and although he was not able to swing his sword in the narrow quarters, as he was close, he plunged his knife upward cutting through the skin with ease. The creature screamed in pain, and although no blood flowed from the wound, the head fell down limp. Its second head swung down, opening its mouth, and took the human between its teeth. Swinging its head from left to right, the human flew all the way back to the outskirts of the tree line. He sat up with blood flowing from several locations where the teeth had cut, and upon moving, realized his legs were broken. The dragok looked back but left him, knowing there would be no more attacks from him.

The others were faring no better. Denisi still remained motionless. Fehr too had been struck down and appeared to not be breathing, but he was still alive. Maldor, who had recovered his hammer, had been backed up from where he had been defending a wall of magical attack the likes of which he had never seen. Jermys and Lars had paired up against one dragok, but even with their combined efforts, they were slowly retreating as their weapons simply had no effect against the creatures.

The magical attack was fierce, and all companions could feel their efforts falling short. Maldor's muscles swelled under the heat, and he recognized that their only option may be to try to escape. If not all of them, at least a few had to make it.

"There is no escape, Maldor. You and your friends are done. Take your place by our side and give us your weapons, and you will live. Claim allegiance to the queen. This is your last chance." Jermys and the maneth looked at each other. They had fought together for over twenty years. They had been on the verge of death numerous times, and both stood strong for the other. When they looked into their eyes now, they both knew. It was over.

Maldor moved next to the dwarf. "Lars," he hollered as he threw his hammer, "you must see the hammer safely to the Realm." He pulled his maneth club from his pack, lifting it into the air. "Take all who can move and run. We will defend you. You will not have long, so run hard and do not look back. The Realm must be on the other side of the lake. Go now."

The dragoks actually seemed pleased with the turn of events. Lars caught the hammer in midair and ran. Fehr had begun to stir, and when he saw what was taking place, slowly moved beside his two friends, where Jermys reached down and scratched the bandicoot's head. The four dragoks had moved in line in front of them.

Fehr glanced up. "So this is it, isn't it?"

"It is," replied the dwarf.

"Then let's take that one"—he pointed to the one with the sagging head—"with us." He leaped from the ground onto Jermys's head and then propelled himself into the air to land directly on the throat of the dragok head that had been injured. He pulled his knife from his pouch and in one motion cut from the wound all the way to its eyes. The cut sent the creature into a convulsion, which released Fehr to the ground.

Maldor and Jermys attacked instantly, driving their force directly into the creature's free head. One of the other dragoks grabbed Maldor in his teeth and tossed him aside, and the one under attack tried to free Jermys. However, the dwarf's cut had been true, and its second head was severed from its body. As if all the air had been let out from the inside, its skin evaporated into the ground.

The largest remaining motioned to the furthest one. "Go get the maneth and kill him. Take both weapons. You" —raising his eyes to the other dragok—"let's finish these three once and for all."

Just then, explosions were heard in the direction that Lars had run. The dragok smiled. "Your friend is dead. The weapons are ours. You have lost."

Jermys and Maldor were back to their feet, but both were out of breath and wounded. Blood flowed from each of them, making them too weak to even defend.

"It has been an honor, Maldor. If you can run, please do so, for I am done." He lowered his head and charged at the two dragoks. As Jermys reached the first, it arched his head in pain and fell sideways, the pain it felt clear in its echoing scream. Both its heads fell instantly limp, and its body hit the ground. Maldor raised his head to see the dwarf standing tall above the fallen dragok carcass. The other roared and turned to face what had attacked. Slowly Schram approached with Lars in his wake.

"What are you going to do, dragok? You cannot defeat me," Schram spoke directly to the beast who was slowly stepping backward.

"I can defeat anyone who stands in my way. It has been said."

"Your friends are dead, and you now must face me." Schram dropped his staff and sent two arrows directly into each head. He split both sets of eyes. It screeched in pain.

Arching its neck, it shot more of the beams toward Schram. He easily moved to the side, and the shots went harmlessly by. Schram drew closer to the creature, who had become cornered between Schram and his companions, who, although weak, had found a new strength with the change in events. "Why are you here? Why is there an army of dragoks in Dragoon? What are your plans?"

The creature seemed surprised at Schram's knowledge but also carried a confidence that simply told he did not care how much he knew. "You have learned much. The queen was right to not underestimate you. That is why we have allowed you to do so much. Every move you have made has been by the queen's doing. You have brought all your allies into one place. You have divided the dragons and the dwarves. You are the queen's puppet, and you have been your whole life. What are our plans? To destroy you. To destroy all that you know and bring a true peace to our world, one that answers to our queen."

Schram drew so close to the dragok's heads they could feel each other's breath. "Who is your queen?"

A smile slowly turned on the head that had been speaking. "Our queen"—he even chuckled a bit now—"will be the one who fulfills your destiny."

The dragok spat fire and magic back upon Schram, which he instantly answered by severing both heads from its body with one swing. "Damn, I did not mean to kill it before getting the info. Who is the queen?" he screamed.

The others looked on in disbelief, both because they could not believe he was here and secondly because he was clearly distraught over the presence of these creatures and this queen.

Fehr pulled himself back up and hollered, "What's up, brother? I sure am glad to see you. We were doing great, but the battle still could have gone either way."

Maldor and Jermys shot the rat a quick glance then moved to stand by their longtime friend. The maneth reached out his arm, locked wrists with Schram, who was now in elf form; but rather than stopping there, he pulled the man into a full hug. "I thought we were done. I thought I had failed."

Schram held the hug and then pushed him away. "You don't know how to fail, my friend." He motioned to the others who had fallen in behind. "None of you do." He paused then saw Denisi and Angus.

He walked up to Angus, who was struggling to get up. "They are broken," he said.

Schram told the young human to close his eyes and relax. He placed his staff across the human's chest, and a soft light appeared on his legs. In moments, Angus opened his eyes and smiled.

"I don't know how that works, but I sure am glad it does." Schram then walked up to Denisi, who was still motionless. In moments, she too was breaking from her sleep. The group sat in amazement.

"Where did you come from?" Maldor asked.

Schram smiled. "I hope to find that answer when I find the queen."

Maldor also smiled in return. "No, I mean now. Where did you come from now?"

He replayed the story of Draag, Dragoon, and the Cindif shore. The group was pleased to hear that Stepha had gotten away but wondered if she had met with more dangers on her journey. The sea was a very large place, and running into something would be by chance. But if they did, there truly was nowhere to run or hide. However, they seemed most questioning on these two-headed creatures that seemed to dissolve away when killed.

"Where did they come from?" Maldor asked.

Schram thought a minute and then replied, "I don't know. There is no way a person could conjure up an army the size of this in such a short time naturally. Therefore, magic has to be involved. If that is the case, however, the magic is truly great. They are alive. They carry all the traits of life, including a will to live. Further, and perhaps most importantly, they believe they are alive. I have to think about this for a while because although they appear alive and they believe they are alive, when they are killed, they look completely different."

"I agree," the maneth stated. "Something is not right."

The companions had moved off the Ice Lake back into the trees while they rested and determined their next step. All eyes had fallen to Schram, who had once again found himself the leader. Maldor even seemed eager to relinquish the role, adding additional support toward their friend. The Ice Lake was a very solemn place for Schram, and he remembered his last visit there. With that, he also remembered the short path to the guardians over the Realm of Darkness. They were on the doorstep now. If they were making a mistake to give up one of the weapons of the ring, they would find that out before the day was up. It was rare for Schram to feel fear, but today he did.

"We have had a difficult journey to finally come back together. You have all drained yourselves much. Where we are about to go will require you to be sharp and ready. I have put a small magical shell around us that should make us unable to be seen or felt. Use this time to sleep. It is important. We will only have a short time before we must move."

Although that may have been the last thing they thought they would hear, it was received with absolute gratitude. Schram looked across at his friends moments later, and all but Jermys were already asleep. It may have been the first time in longer than they could remember that they felt safe—the irony being they were on the doorstep to a place that harbored nothing but death. Jermys noticed Schram's stare and nodded to his friend. He was clearly relaxed, but not willing to sleep just yet.

Schram lifted his staff as he approached the woman. "So you are the queen?" His voice shook just a bit, which he hoped she would not notice, but he was sure she had.

"I am whom everyone has called queen."

"This place is cold, full of death. What do you claim to be a queen of?"

"I am the mother to everything you have ever known. I am the creator. They call me queen because they cannot comprehend anything else." She paused and then took a step closer to him. "Look into my eyes. You are the one who can see me."

Schram came in closer. He was captivated by this woman before him. She was a beautiful dragon, extremely large and clearly mature in age. Her eyes were a deep blue like the sea. Schram moved in front of the woman and whispered, "Are you my mother?"

As his eyes locked into hers, he felt pain from within. It was as if his stomach had just exploded and he was on fire from the inside. He saw death. He saw Toopek being destroyed. He felt a hand at his throat and his staff fall from his limp hand to the side. He saw Stepha's body on fire, and then he felt the knife protrude into his chest.

"Today is your day to die." In the corner of his eye, he saw Maldor on the ground. In his hand, he held something and he screamed.

"Wake up, Schram. Are you okay?" Schram leaped to his feet to see Maldor standing before him with weapon drawn. There was a short pause as Schram brought his friend into focus. They were still just outside the Ice Lake, and all but Maldor were resting peacefully. The big maneth looked questionably toward his friend.

His face softened, and Schram put his hand on his shoulder. "Thank you, my friend. Let's get the others together so we can go."

As Schram sat up and prepared to walk toward the others, Maldor grabbed his shoulder to stop him. "What was your dream?"

He did not answer.

The Realm

Stepha and Maggie avoided Toopek completely for fear of running into delays or resistance that they could not handle on their own. The flight across the sea had been completely free of incident, and although Maggie was extremely tired, she never showed it. Stepha could feel the enchantment of the forests growing stronger as they approached. She pointed ahead to Maggie, who lowered her head and angled her wings down. In moments, they were at the fountain in the center of the elf city.

The dragon looked around in amazement. "What a beautiful city. And the statue is truly amazing, but still does not do you justice."

Stepha smiled and placed her hand on the dragon's neck. "There is no way I can ever thank you enough for all you did to bring me here. I can promise you I will never forget it."

The dragon smiled, and they noticed that a large group of elves had started to form around them. It was truly rare for a dragon to be within Elvinott's boundaries; and usually, if one was, it was not a good thing. With their princess here as well, none showed any worry. Stepha motioned to several guards nearby to come closer. "Where is my brother?" she asked.

"To say I am behind you would be too easy," echoed Madeiris's voice from the other side of the fountain. A startled Maggie and Stepha swung around to see the smiling face of the king of Elvinott approaching. "What, a dragon lands in the city, and you don't think they will notify the king?"

Stepha ran to his arms and gave him a huge hug. "Thank Shriak you are all right."

Madeiris returned the hug but immediately realized something grave must have happened for her to return as such. He slowly pushed his sister back. "I feel it in your voice and grip. What has happened, Stepha? Is it Schram?"

She stepped back slightly but left both hands on her brother. "Magdalene"—she motioned to her friend to come closer—"this is my brother, Madeiris. He is the king of Elvinott. Madeiris, this is Maggie. It is because of her I was able to make it back here safely."

Madeiris released his sister's hand and stepped up to the large dragon before him. "Magdalene, I do not know yet what has brought my sister here in such haste, but I am very thankful you were the one to do it. You are brave and strong and always will be welcome here in Elvinott." He bowed his head in an act of the highest respect, an act rarely seen by a king in his own city. The elves in the area followed suit.

The dragon smiled broadly. "Please, raise your head to me. Your sister is the one who is fighting so hard. I just provided her the vessel to get here. Thank you for the welcome, and know that I am here to help."

The elves raised their heads, and Madeiris placed his hand briefly on the dragon's neck. Again, he whispered, "Thank you." Turning to his sister, he said, "Now, Stepha, please tell me what has happened."

Stepha led him to the Great Hall as the words she was about to speak were too grave to speak in open forum. Maggie could not fit in the hall and was fine remaining at the city center. She was intrigued with the elves whom in truth she had never spent any time with. When Stepha sat at the table before her brother, tears immediately began to flow.

"I have never felt death like that," she began. "Every elf was killed. They used the word *exterminated*. It was as if a hand had come in and wiped their lives from them. I felt things I have never felt before. Pain and suffering do not begin to explain it."

"The king was crucified and then burned with what appeared to be dragon fire. However, I do not believe it was dragon fire. I have seen it many times, and the burns were different. I can't explain it but different. I did not speak to anyone about this but Maldor, and he said he was going to keep it to himself for now. He did not know what could have done it either, but I saw the fear in his eyes. I had not seen that fear since we found him captured in Draag." She tried to continue but could not.

Madeiris placed his hand on his sister. The pain in his voice was great. "Did none escape?"

"I felt nothing in return. I felt only death. When Denisi and I aided with passage, we only knew emptiness being returned to us. I believe the entire race was destroyed."

They sat in silence for an unknown amount of time. Madeiris typically did not require much time to evaluate actions and determine direction. However, this situation left him concerned. At some point, he did look back to his sister. "What do you think we should do?"

She turned her seat to face him directly. "I believe we need to do as the maneth have done and move our entire village to Toopek. I don't believe we can defeat this enemy alone. We need to mobilize the largest force in the history of Troyf. They are going to attack Toopek. Once Toopek is gone, it will be a short trip to Elvinott."

"No force can break our enchantment. We are safe here. To expose all our elves to this evil unprotected, I don't know if I can do that."

"Eltak was protected as well. I felt it. They did not defeat the enchantment. It appeared they went through it like it wasn't there. If attacked and the barrier did not hold, then we would be destroyed as well. We cannot defeat whatever hit Eltak. We can't."

He thought in silence for a time, which made Stepha uncomfortable. She could see the pain in his face and the trouble on his mind. The decision was easy for her, but she also felt so much for the human city that, at times, it could possibly cloud her judgment. Madeiris had to be sure she was right. He stood without speaking and started to leave.

"Madeiris, what is your decision?" she asked.

"I don't know, sis, but I understand I have to make it quickly. Toopek may need us."

He left the room, and Stepha sat alone at the table. She closed her eyes and placed both hands across the great table. *Schram, are you there? Are you safe?*

***

"Did the dwarves reach Eltak?" asked the queen in a deep tone devoid of any feelings.

"They did," replied the canok.

"What did they decide?" The queen asked.

"According to our dragoks who are stationed outside the city, they believe the ones they were after are responsible. They do not seem to care that there is no motive or reason for it. They are getting very aggressive and angry, much more so than previously."

"Send the dragoks in. Surround them and confirm the companions are responsible. Tell them that mining dwarves were also present. Then get them to stand together. When they are together, I will send them back to Antaag."

"You can do that?" asked the canok.

"I brought them here, didn't I?" The queen used a tone he had not heard before, and it did not display pleasure with the probe. But the canok felt it was pertinent, so he pushed forward.

"Then why can't you just bring Schram to us now? Wouldn't that solve things for us?"

"I need the dragoks to surround the dwarves as they did before. I need that connection, and even then, if any of these dwarves had not been to Antaag before, I will not be able to move them. It is difficult and takes a great deal of energy, but a necessary requirement if we want the dwarves to become more divided. A civil war is in their future. If handled right, they will simply cancel themselves out."

"Very well," he replied. "What about the companions? If they are through Eltak, then they could be nearing the Realm."

"Do not worry. I have sent four dragoks to wait for them. Without Schram, they will not defeat them. The weapons they carry will be useless against my dragoks. If all goes as I have foreseen it, we will have two of the weapons by nightfall."

"What about Schram? He could still destroy us?" Immediately, when the canok completed the question, the queen smiled, but he did not know if this was because she felt his comment that Schram could actually win this war was so far from possible that it warranted a smile, or she simply liked hearing his name. Regardless, the answer was critical.

"He cannot destroy us." She dug her eyes into the canok, causing him to step back. "I have not felt him since he was at Draag. This could mean he was destroyed there, but all that really matters is that every vision I have has confirmed what I need to know—that Schram will not defeat me. Further, every vision I have of him confirms his failure with me. He believes so as well." She added with a smile, "He holds out hope for something, or someone that is not even there. And when he truly finds out it is not, it will be too late. He will be gone, and so will all those with him. There is nothing that can stop the hands of time. Dragons can see these things, and I believe Schram has already seen it as well."

***

The companions took their second trip across the great Ice Lake. Again, the death shown through brought each of them to various levels of sadness. Schram too remembered his first trip when Hawthorne was there for support. Now he was the support for others. He felt so many were counting on him at levels he was not used to, not in a long time. The great Ice Lake was believed to hold many mysteries, but the mysteries were minimal compared to that area beyond it, the Realm of Darkness.

Schram saw the familiar path he had walked on one time before. He felt the cold chill engulfing them from all sides. He remembered his fears from his first visit and how he was not prepared. He stopped and turned to his friends.

"This is the path that will take us to the guardians of the Realm of Darkness. From this point on, if not already, they will be aware of our presence. Do not draw on any magic in your weapons. We are entering totally in peace. Any attack upon us will have to be defended without magic, which means without your weapons. Please honor this, or we will not be able to pass."

They were on a plateau. It was a large flat circular plain that appeared to be something a large bird would use to land. Tall rocks formed a semicircle around the plateau, making the only entrance or exit being the path they had taken to arrive here. Schram remembered this place as well. This was the place they were forbidden to pass because his mother, Hawthorne, was hidden behind her human form. He learned at that moment Hawthorne was a dragon, perhaps the most beautiful green-and-gold dragon that ever walked on Troyf. The guardians refused her passage as a human, so why now had they been stopped.

The group disbanded across the clearing but again had nothing to look for. Each was staring blankly at the others, their frustrations sticking out like dented armor. Within moments, a cloud formed over Schram, Lars, Jermys, and Maldor. The others tried to approach but were kept separated by some invisible barrier that had formed as the clouds appeared. The four were drawn close, and then all vanished. Their weapons of the ring, including Schram's staff, all remained in their place. All except Maldor's hammer.

The barrier separating them vanished, and Fehr, Denisi, and Angus all ran to where they had been. Fehr kicked Schram's staff, and after confirming it was really present, turned to the others grabbing it in the process. "I should keep this. That way, we know it is safe."

The staff was nearly twice the length of his body, and its weight threw the bandicoot into a sideways stumble. Denisi reached down and grabbed it from him. "Seriously, Fehr, you think by taking it, you will be able to use it."

He looked stung. "No, I was just holding it for Schram." Neither knew Fehr well, but both stared at him questionably. The rat rolled his eyes. "Very well, maybe I was going to say a few things to see if it worked for me as well. Anbari and I were essentially father and son. I figure I know his magic as well as Schram."

She did not even show distress about hearing his name spoken after passing. She could not get past the reference. "Father and son?" inquired Denisi. "I did not know him, but what would he do if he heard that because the guardians of passage guard both evil and good, so we are in a place he is most likely listening."

Instantly Fehr's smile and confidence vanished. He choked a few words back then said, "Silly me, so often do I mess up the human tongue. I meant to say he was my mentor. I always mix up son and mentor." He chuckled softly and then added, "Wow, that's funny, isn't it?"

They did not respond. Denisi picked up the scimitar and axe and sat with all of them in the corner. "I guess we wait," she said, looking to the others for agreement. They nodded and took places beside her.

"We really don't have to mention that little mix-up to Schram, I don't suppose?" added Fehr.

Again, they did not respond, only causing the rat to fidget with nervousness, which both Angus and Denisi seemed to enjoy. That being said, moments later, the rat's snores broke the silence, and the two just smiled.

***

"Welcome, Schram, we did not know if we would truly ever see you again." The voice was loud and deep, but there was no person stating it. On his last visit, the guardians took the form of humans to help his understanding. This time, they appeared to be just entities. "Your mother is pleased to see you as well."

Schram nearly fell to his knees when the guardians referenced Hawthorne. He did not truly understand the connection of the Realm to all passages. He did know, however, that it was not just for those trapped in the Ice Lake for eternity. He thought about his mother, and then before him she stood in human form, exactly as he remembered her. She was real but somewhat transparent. She did not speak, but her smile was enough. Next to her was Krirtie. Maldor could not believe it. He knelt beside his son with a tear streaming down his face. He whispered, "Son, meet your mother." The vision of Krirtie stepped forward directly in front of Lars. She reached her hand to his cheek, and although he felt no touch, he burst into tears. She turned to Schram, Maldor, and Jermys and gave them all a huge smile of approval for how they had raised him. Moments later, they were gone.

The guardians gave them all time to absorb what they had just seen. Lars fell into his father's arms, and then the two broke to face Schram. "Whatever is needed, they may have it. That moment was worth my life."

Schram turned to the area where the voice had come. "Guardians, we are sorry for the time it has taken, but we are here to fulfill our promise. We are here to return the Anbarian Hammer." In front of them appeared two human figures. As with the others, they were partially transparent but had enough shape for the four to see. Their lips did not move as they spoke, but as intended, having that presence there did provide them comfort.

"We are grateful for the effort you have taken to return this. As time passed, we were not certain this day would come. In the Realm of Darkness, time does not hold any value. Therefore, for us, it was only moments ago you were here before. That being said, we know for you it was significant, and for continuing to honor your word and return it, we are eternally grateful."

It was then that the companions realized they did not have their weapons or Schram his staff. Maldor alone held his hammer. They did not feel any fear for the lack of weapons. This was a solemn place, safe but still dangerous. Maldor looked toward Schram, who only lowered his head. Slowly the big maneth pushed his son slightly to the side and stepped toward the figures. He reached out his hands with the hammer laid across them. "I return this hammer to you as it should have always been."

He felt a strange sensation engulf him, and then the hammer vanished. He looked down to his hands, and in its place rested a large club. It size was tremendous but weighed nearly half that which he thought it should. His eyes went to the guardians that now held the hammer.

"This club is our gift to you, Maldor. It too holds many mysteries and should serve you well." He turned to the group before continuing, "Now, we thank you all for this. We feel the urgency of your travel is at hand, and we will not delay you longer."

It appeared they were waiting for a similar statement in return, but Schram desired more. They had traveled a great distance, and at this stage in their venture, he knew he needed more information. He did not know if they would have any, but he was not going to let them go without at least asking. "Guardians, before you bid us leave, please help guide us with your knowledge. We feel great evil forming in the land. It is an evil of such great proportion that even your existence could be in jeopardy. Do you know of this?"

Even through their mystic appearance, the guardians appeared disturbed. "Schram, have you not felt the future? Do you not already know that which you need to?"

He immediately remembered his dreams, what he thought might be his visions of his own death. "I have felt things, but I do not understand them."

"You must trust in what you have felt as they cannot lie."

"Can these visions be changed?"

"Everything may be changed, young Schram, except, as the Ice Lake shows, death."

He looked confused. "I do not understand. If my vision is of death, but everything may be changed except death, then my vision cannot be changed?"

"Only you know that of your visions. What we know is that which should be. If one is or is not to fulfill their destiny below the ice layer, then that choice is within their control."

Lars turned to Schram. "He is saying that you cannot change death, but you can change your life before it."

Maldor was surprised at his son's interruption but more so by his clarity. He lightly touched Lars's shoulder to quiet him, but Schram waved him off. "I agree with you, Lars. You carry great insight." He turned back to the guardians. "Guardians, I must face that which I already know. To shy away would mean the end of the world as we know it. Therefore, I must ask because we do not know where to travel. Where can I find my mother?"

The question nearly dropped the jaw of Maldor and Jermys. The guardians did not waver. "You mother is with us."

A vision of Hawthorne again appeared before him; this time, her expression showed more concern.

Schram stepped forward. "No, I mean my human mother, Suzanne Starland."

The guardians also appeared concerned, and the vision of Hawthorne vanished. One of the guardians began to change and then, with a quick flash of light, appeared before them in a natural human form. His eyes were narrow and hair thick. He had a long face and deep-dark skin. His expression showed age, but more from stress and pain than from actual years, though Schram could not imagine if this creature even could measure his true age. He approached Schram. His voice was different, cracked and beaten. Previously they had heard their voices through telepathy, and it was so clear, it appeared as if spoken word. Schram now realized this was the real guardian. Why had he come to show himself now, he thought?

"We have no knowledge of the one known as Suzanne Starland." The statement was abrupt and cold, as if it was not the words that were important but how it was said.

Schram now stood directly in front of him. His tone was soft and concerning. "What does that mean? Is it because she has not passed that you are not aware of her?"

He continued in the same tone. "She does not exist. Not now or in the past."

"That is not possible. I knew her. She raised me. She is the one I called mother for my entire life. I can tell you for certain she does or at least did exist."

His friends were growing concerned because they could see a change in Schram, almost anger building. The guardian again continued, "The person who claimed to be Suzanne Starland was not born of that name, or we would know her. There is nothing more that I can say."

Schram's voice got deeper. "Then what you are saying is that she may have called herself Suzanne Starland but her birth name was something else."

"That would be a possibility." Schram looked almost broken. For so long, he had wanted to believe his mother was just a pawn in this evil. Now he did not even know who she really was. His eyes dropped and then slowly lifted.

The guardian was reaching out to him. He reached out his hands, and when their fingers met, Schram screamed in pain and fell to his knees. The guardian spoke softly, "Relax, my friend. I must become you to know that which you know."

He could barely hear the words. He felt as if someone was burning his blood from the inside. His head roared, and his friends saw his bones forming through his stretched skin. Jermys began to step toward the two until two hands grabbed his shoulders and held him in place. He turned to the hands, and nobody was there, but the grip held true. Schram dropped farther to the ground, and then their hands broke. His body fell limp.

"I now understand," stated the guardian.

"What does that mean?" asked Maldor, stepping toward Schram, along with Jermys, who was now free from his previous hold.

"It means when Schram awakes, tell him to travel to the northern tip of Cindif. It is there he will find what he seeks. With him, he should take this."

Before them appeared a small oval periapt. At the top was a cylinder-shaped hole as if it fit into something. Maldor knelt down and picked it up, and to his surprise, he felt as if he was holding nothing. It carried no weight. It was egg-shaped and clear, almost like glass, but etched with a magnificent design. "What is its use?"

The guardian bowed his head. "Only when times are lost and you have no other choice, use it as it is to be used." Then they vanished.

The companions were back in the original room with their friends. The hammer was gone, replaced with Maldor's new club. He also carried the strange periapt or amulet. They looked to each other, and it was clear that none understood the message. They hoped Schram would know what it meant.

Denisi and the others jumped to their side. The elf spoke first, "What happened? Is Schram all right?"

Jermys replied, "He made contact with the guardians trying to learn about his human mother. He has not moved since."

She knelt to his side and lifted his head as she knew Stepha would do if she were here. "Schram, can you hear me?"

His eyes did open, but they focused on nothing. His mind was lost, and they closed again.

Denisi felt his chest. "His beat is strong. I believe he only needs some time."

Maldor and Angus nodded agreement. Maldor responded, "We will remain here until he can travel. We are protected from the elements, and I have felt no concern from the guardians should we remain for a short time."

Fehr then broke in, "Fine, then tell us what happened."

***

"Death must come to all things at some point," stated the queen sternly.

Almok smiled. "Yes, but I would prefer mine was not in the near future."

The queen smiled and stroked his hair. "You have been a loyal servant, Almok, and your time to join your brother is not upon us yet."

"But what about Schram? If he has defeated the dragoks at the Ice Lake and has met with the guardians, could he have changed the destiny you have foreseen?"

She smiled again. "A destiny is just that—a destiny. It is unfortunate that every rift I have placed in his travel has not solved this riddle for us, but from the beginning, I have foreseen his presence here. He will arrive here with the belief he can save his mother, and that will be his undoing."

"Do you think he knows?"

She turned to look at the canok. "I do not care."

The canok used that to change the subject. "What has happened to the dwarves?"

"I have sent the dark dwarves to their home. They will spread the word that the miners are behind the deaths across the land. They will push for a war, and they will get it. They may not convince them all, but enough to storm the miners."

"Will they defeat them? The miners are much stronger."

"It does not matter. Once Toopek is ours, the dwarves will have no option but to fall in line."

"What about the elves? Even you cannot break their barrier."

The queen actually laughed. "That fool Stepha will convince her brother to bring them all to Toopek. When we destroy one, we destroy them all. Troyf will be ours."

The canok did not appear concerned, but inside, he felt something trembling. Something seemed out of balance, and he could not place it. He moved slightly away from the woman and peered into the distance. Their ice castle was built on the side of a snow-covered mountain. It was almost invisible to the naked eye, not that any creature would ever come looking for it anyway. He turned back to the queen with one simple question, "When do we attack?"

***

"What did you decide, my brother?"

Madeiris looked on. "I have battled this decision all night. I believe we will be safe behind our protection, but if others are in need, I cannot ignore that. We will take all the elves to Toopek. I believe the human city holds the secret to whether we will defeat this evil once and for all. We must assist in that protection."

Stepha appeared relieved, and she threw her arms around her brother. "Thank you, my brother. Thank you very much. When do we leave?"

He pushed her back and looked into her eyes. "This is a dangerous direction. If wrong, all the elves could pass. Our race as we know it would be over."

"I understand," she replied.

"Then gather everyone together. We will leave as soon as we are ready. Send flyers ahead now to plot our course. I do not want to engage this evil on our way. I would like to avoid it."

She nodded acceptance and disappeared immediately. He lowered his head and whispered, "Father, please guide my decision. Please watch over our elves."

The Final Walk

"He's awake," stated Denisi to the others. "Schram, can you hear me?" He nodded as he lifted his head.

"Where are we?" Maldor walked over.

"We are still on the path to the Realm of Darkness."

"How long?"

"Since we left the guardians, just one night."

Maldor was watching his friend with concern. Schram appeared disoriented and confused, a state not common with the human turned elf.

Schram pushed himself to his feet and then fell to his knees where he rested briefly. "What happened?"

"Well," started the maneth again, "you held hands with the guardians, and it did not go well for you, to say the least."

Schram pushed himself up while Angus moved in behind to secure him should he fall again. "The guardians? Wait, I remember." Schram began, almost panicked. "We have to speak to them. We have to find out where to go. I felt things when we touched. Horrible things. Death. Destruction. It was..." His voice trailed off as Maldor raised his hand.

"They spoke to us after you separated. You fell unconscious, but they told us things, and they gave us this." He held out the periapt. "Do you know what it does?"

He did begin to calm, but his heart still raced, and his voice was not fully returned to normal. He took the object in his hands. His ears started to ring, and he felt pressure, much like two magnets of equal polarity being pushed toward each other. He heard things. He saw things, and he closed his eyes, almost squinting so hard they crushed inside his head. He set it down, and his mind was clear. "Unbelievable," he stated.

"What?" asked Maldor. "What is it?"

"I don't know what it is, but it is strong with magic. It is different from anything I have ever felt before, almost as if it was a hole in space, a void, so to speak." He appeared concerned, and his tone carried the same message.

177

"What did the guardians say about it? What are we supposed to do with it?"

The maneth reached down and took the inside of Schram's arm, ensuring he was secure. He then picked up the periapt and placed it in his pack. He stared toward his friend as he spoke, "The guardians said, 'Only when times are lost and you have no other choice, use it as it is to be used,' and then they disappeared. Do you know what that means? Do you know how it is to be used or what it does?"

"It means nothing to me. We will have to see if the knowledge about it becomes known as our travels continue. That leads me to my main question. We don't know where to go?"

"We do," interrupted Jermys, with Maldor and Angus nodding. "They said that when you awake to travel to the northernmost tip of Cindif. There you will find what you seek."

They all looked at Schram for some sort of response, but he just sat stoic and staring at nothing. It was one of those pauses that simply made everyone uncomfortable, but nobody was willing to speak. Schram turned to his friends, and a smile crept over his face. "I do not know what the outcome will be. My fear in this endeavor is greater than I have felt before, but to know this is the very final end is a comfort. I do not know what to believe about my human mother, but I know that at the end of this journey, I will find out, one way or the other."

Maldor reached his hand to his friend. "I will join you. I will stand by your side to face whatever is in our future."

"Fehr and I will also be by your side," Jermys added. "We have been through everything together. I have been a part of this war for over two hundred years. I am not going to be absent at the end."

Both Denisi and Lars also were about to speak when Schram raised his hand to stop them. "I know you would all join me, but I feel only a small group will give us our best chance. Our destination is simple, and we will not be facing an army. The real support is needed in Toopek." He paused and then placed his hand on Jermys's shoulder. "Maldor, Jermys, and Lars, I believe your weapons, which have been part of this from the start, should remain. Fehr, Angus, and Denisi, I will find you passage back to Toopek. Dangers there will possibly be greater than what we face, and I believe your presence there could make a difference. I feel some hidden strength on our side in Toopek, but I don't know what it is. As for where we are about to go"—he motioned to those carrying the weapons—"I have no idea the level of evil before us."

Although their instinct was to argue, each seemed to realize the words were not open for debate. There was something different about Schram. It had happened when he joined with the guardian. Something he had seen during that time changed him. None of the companions knew what that was, but they were sure it was not about to be shared.

Denisi took Schram's hand in hers. "When Stepha learns you are going forward without her, she will insist on coming."

He smiled. "I would not prevent her even if I could. Provide her the information we have, and with luck, she will join us in time."

Fehr stepped forward. "How do you suggest we return? I am not one for swimming."

"All climb on my back. I will take you to the shores, and the dragons there can help us. They will take you back."

Schram was already in the form of a large dragon by the time his statement ended. Although carrying all of them was more than he would prefer, it did beat the alternative. They did not have the time to walk all the way back to the shore, as even by flight, it would take longer than he wished. He knew their timeline was running out. Within days, their ultimatum would be reached, and if Schram did not turn himself over to the queen before that time, the world as they knew it would be destroyed. He never believed, however, that turning himself over would prevent that destruction, and neither did his companions. All it would do was prevent Schram from taking part in its defense.

Originally, he believed he needed to be at Toopek when this time came. He could help defend it. Now he felt differently. He knew he had to defeat the one behind this whole thing. By killing the head, the rest would fall. He just did not know if he could destroy the head if the head was whom he thought it was. He glanced at his friends on his back. They were strong. They showed no fear. They would face this power together. Their combined strengths had faced every hardship dealt their direction, and this would be no different. He did not know if they could win. It was the first time he doubted their chance of success. The creature that created the dragok army and had manipulated so many things was strong, very strong. He closed his eyes and bit through the clouds at a pace that made each on his back lean forward into the small of the other's back. They gripped tightly with their legs against the wind and held firm.

Stepha, can you hear me? Schram said to himself, reaching out to the elf.

***

The flyers launched several arrows into the goblin masses. Madeiris had wanted to avoid this type of engagement, but the number of trolls and goblins in the forest was astounding. Still, the flyers had no problem punching holes through the lines, and the elves moved en masse with little effort. They were such great marksmen that when stalemates did occur, they could end it quickly and without issue.

"Toopek is ahead," shouted Stepha from the air.

"How far?" asked Madeiris.

"Once you are through the tree line, you will see it down the hill. It will be a clear path from that point. The goblins are retreating to the far side."

Madeiris signaled to the elves behind him, and they stormed through the trees. On the outside wall around Toopek, he could see humans and maneths lined up, providing any cover that was needed, but none was. Their path to the wall was clear, and in what amounted to a very short time, the entire elven village was inside the Toopekian boundary. Although they were not expected, they were very welcome.

Alan greeted Madeiris and Stepha. "Hello, my friends. I pray no fate has fallen on Elvinott to cause you to flee to our doors, but you are welcome in any case."

The elf king grabbed his hand in a tight grip. "No, just the opposite. Stepha believes that Toopek is going to be the target of a terrible attack of the highest proportion. She has seen extreme tragedy in Eltak where the entire village was destroyed. The evil is targeting our world, and Toopek is first on the list. If we can stop it here, we can end this whole thing."

Alan nodded. He understood and turned to Stepha, who had landed beside them. "Stepha, where are the others? You left to head to the Realm of Darkness, and now you are back?"

As he spoke, a large dragon slipped over the wall and landed beside them, bringing a rustling of weapons from those in the area. Stepha raised her hand and shouted, "Stop, she is with me." The elf placed her hand on Maggie's neck, and the dragon breathed fire into the air, heating the area such that several stepped back. She gave a crooked smile and a snort, showing her pleasure.

Stepha turned back to Alan. "When we saw what happened at Eltak, I feared that the evil on the land was indeed strong. Everything has told us that Toopek was the first to be targeted. I knew the maneth would be here in support but thought I should at least let my brother know so he could decide where best the elves should be."

"We decided our place was with our friends. We will fight our battle here in Toopek and end this attack once and for all." He said these words loud so all in the area could hear. They responded with a loud cheer, which brought more in the area over to join. They formed a circle around the group and began chanting in support.

Alan noticed Stepha motioning him over. The noise around them was deafening, so the elf had to pull him close and whisper directly into his ear, "Have you seen Schram?"

He shook his head and bent down slightly to answer her whisper with one of his own. "We have not seen or heard anything since he left for Draag. I had hoped he was with you."

Stepha looked as if a huge weight had just been thrust upon her. "We too have not seen him. I have tried to connect to him in my mind but feel nothing. I believe he is hiding himself from me, or us."

"Why would he do that?" asked Alan.

She shook her head slightly. "I think he is protecting us, but I don't know. I just want to find him." She rubbed her belly, but it went unnoticed by those around—except Maggie, that is.

"Night will be on us soon," stated Geoff from the side. "Let's retire to the hall to talk as I have many questions for you as well, starting with the whereabouts of my wife." He smiled slightly, but the smile was clouded by his concern. He motioned to Alan, who was busy taking steps to organize where an entire city of elves was going to live. He called several guards over and gave some direction, and in moments, the elves were being divided in groups to be moved throughout the large human city. Alan saw the maneth's gaze and followed his eyes to the large building at the city center where they continually found themselves in times of need. He nodded agreement, and they led a small party that direction.

Stepha turned to Maggie. "There are some dragons that live over on Castle Island across the bay. Can you go see if any of them know about Schram?"

Maggie smiled that she would, but before leaving, she leaned her head down. "I will do that for you, and your baby." Then she took off before Stepha could respond. The elf looked up and smiled.

In the hall sat Alan, Stepha, Madeiris, and Geoff, while a handful of guards brought information on the elves' movement into the city and ensured there was food and drink for each. They all told the information they knew and were captivated and disturbed when they learned the details about Eltak. The elves showed a deeper sadness, and they felt the loss of the elves each time it was discussed. However, as intended, it did define how powerful this force really was.

"We must assume the attack on Eltak was but the first. They will attack again, and it will be designed to eliminate." Geoff had stood when he began speaking and remained standing when Madeiris rose.

The elf king added, "We should set our defenses in the strongest areas for each. The humans are strong hand to hand and on the seas. Maneth are needed anywhere that the front could be breached by land, specifically against the goblins and trolls. You will be able to eliminate those forces without question. The elves should be the first line against anything in flight. I do not know where the dragons stand, so we should work to bring in any loyal dragons we can."

Alan stood and began pacing a bit. Geoff looked toward the leader of the human armies and saw his concern. "What is it, Alan? Do you not agree?"

"No, I believe your plan is clear and correct, but I fear it is not a physical battle we will face. This power as it has been described has been after Schram from the beginning, even targeting him in the elven forest. There have not been widespread battles anywhere except whatever took place in Eltak. By your description, Eltak did not appear to have been burned by dragon breath or the elves killed by the swords of warriors. It appeared to have been eliminated. That was the word you used. What does that mean? What does that mean to us?"

Geoff nodded. "So if I hear you correctly, you are saying we could put every man, elf, and maneth we have with sword in hand to greet whatever is coming our way, and it will make no difference?"

Alan shook his head. "No, I am saying in the past, we have had some magic behind us. Whether it was Schram building a magical barrier or weapons with powers I did not understand, something always was with us. Now, perhaps facing a power greater than anything we have or will ever experience, we have just that which we carry to protect us. It just leads to some concern."

Stepha added questionably, "What other option do we have? Should we surrender?"

Alan reacted immediately to that statement. "Absolutely not. We should never surrender. We should, however, be thinking of what we will do if swords and arrows don't have an effect."

Geoff nodded. "I agree. We must consider our options."

"What options do we have?" asked Stepha. "They are set on eliminating all life. I don't believe anyone is safe. If we can't defeat them here, is an option to run? They will find us and hunt us down. I have seen firsthand that they kill without care. They do not distinguish between an armed man or a pregnant female. They kill, destroy, and eliminate. No questions asked."

Madeiris placed his hand on his sister's back. "We understand, Stepha. All we are saying is let's make sure we put up the best defense that can make us successful. Because of all these things you said, we must not make a mistake. We won't have a second chance."

She stepped back a little with a tear forming in her eye. "I am sorry. I just don't know what has happened. It was not that long ago that I did not feel any fears for our world. It is as if life was simply snatched from us at will."

They all agreed, but nobody spoke. Geoff lifted his glass and took a long drink. Then he turned to Alan. "I agree with Madeiris. We must place our troops in the locations where they may be most effective. Let's move forward with that plan immediately. We will sleep tonight and fine-tune the effort in the morning. If any other ideas come to anyone, please share them."

Stepha lifted her hand. "I asked Maggie, the dragon who brought me back from Cindif, to see if there were other dragons that would be loyal to our effort. I know she will fight for us, but if there are others, I will not know till later."

"That is exactly what I mean," stated Geoff, very pleased with the comment. "We need all the support we can get, especially that of dragons..." His voice trailed off then returned. "I too wish your husband was here. He has a way of recruiting dragons."

They all smiled as Stepha replied, "Yes, he does." She nodded and bade them farewell as she wished to retire to her room. A guard noticed she was leaving and led her to a room that had been prepared. She was not in the room long when she sat down in a chair, rubbed her belly slightly, and then threw her head into her hands and cried.

Stepha, can you hear me? The elf raised her head immediately. "Schram," she called out. She stopped, heard and felt nothing. She placed her hands on her magical bow and closed her eyes. *Schram, I am here.*

I need you, Stepha. Can you return to Cindif?

She smiled. *I can and will. If you cannot find us at the shore, find travel to the northernmost point. We are to meet that which is behind this evil. All the weapons of the ring should be present.*

I will, my love. I will be there.

My Father

Stepha burst back into the hall, causing the others to jump and draw weapons. "Put your weapons down. Had I wanted to attack you, I would never have entered like a human. No offense," she added, looking toward Alan.

"None taken," he replied.

"I just heard from Schram. I have to go to Cindif."

"Schram," stated Geoff. "Is he here?"

She shook her head. "No, I can't explain it. I just—" She paused, looked toward the ceiling, then back to the group. She seemed confused but confident nonetheless. "I felt him," she continued. "He asked that I come to Cindif. I believe he has found the source of the evil, and I think he believes we can defeat it with all the weapons of the ring."

Madeiris looked hesitant at first then calmed. "I would never have allowed a magical message to guide our direction, but in Schram, I believe. You must go at once. Can you fly?"

Stepha answered with a nod. "No, I will call for Mags. She will take me."

Madeiris nodded in return. "Very well, then go now. If it was not critical, he would not ask."

She hugged her brother and whispered, "Stay safe and protect the elves."

"Protect yourself and your husband." He paused and then added, "And your baby." She looked up to him, surprised. He smiled and added, "I am an elf too." They hugged tightly. "Now go."

She flew to the shore and peered across the bay toward the castle. She saw several dragons, but even her elven sight could not determine if any were Magdalene. She stared and stared and then felt some warm breath on her shoulder.

"Looking for someone?" whispered the voice she knew so well.

Stepha smiled. "You are quieter than an elf, but I could not be so glad to see anyone right at this moment."

The dragon showed several teeth as she smiled. "We are connected, you know. I don't know why or how, but I can feel when you need me."

"I know," the elf replied.

The large dragon knelt down to make it easier for Stepha to climb to her back. "Do we head back across the sea?"

"We do," Stepha replied. "I know you must still be tired, but we have to try. Can you make it?"

The dragon motioned with its head for her to stop talking and climb on her back. "As soon as you get on, we will be on our way."

The elf jumped to her back and rubbed her hand on the dragon's neck. "Thank you, my friend."

"Wait!" shouted a voice from behind them.

They both turned their heads, but it was Stepha who answered, "Geoff? What is it?"

"I need to speak to you, or better said, I need to say something to you."

The elf could feel the tension in his voice and instantly grew worried. She leaped back to the ground and ran to meet him. "What, my friend? What is it?"

He stood before the woman who to anyone else appeared very powerful, but before the maneth king, she appeared as a child looking up to her father. The maneth placed his large hands on her shoulders, facing directly in front of her. His voice was serious and even sad as he spoke. "I do not know what may happen here, but everything in me is telling me we are going to face an attack the likes of which we have never seen before."

"I know," she interrupted, "but you are so well prepared."

He raised his finger before her lips asking her to just listen. She recognized he was fighting for what to say and honored his request. The maneth did not speak again for several moments before continuing. "I don't know how to say this, and I know that to speak of death is not something that either of our races feels is proper. However, in my time with Denisi, I have learned much. I have learned much about maneths, and much about being an elf. I have something." He paused then added, "Something I must give you."

A tear formed in her eye, but she remained quiet. His voice cracked and then grew in strength. "I fear for us, all of us, but if something should happen to me, I would like you to do something for me. I have three life pouches. One is for my wife, one is for Maldor, and one for Schram. Can you see that the last two are delivered properly should I not be able to do so in person?"

He reached out his hands and presented the two pouches to her. She reluctantly took the pouches in hand and placed them into her armor. She then placed her hand on his shoulder. "I do not like to hear talk of you not being present to give this to them, but I will honor your request." She fell into his arms. "I love you, my friend. Please take care of yourself."

He held her tightly. "Please take care of yourself and our friends. I love you all and will be with you."

They broke arms but did not break eye contact. Stepha moved and with a gentle lift from her wings again sat on Magdalene's back. "I will protect them, and I will see you again."

Geoff's eyes softened and he raised his hand as they lifted up across the bay. Softly he whispered, "I hope so."

***

Arston, prepare the dragoks for attack. The day is upon us.

Arston looked toward the wall and replied telepathically back, They are ready at your signal.

There was a pause that Arston assumed was Almok's discussion with the queen. After a few moments, he heard Almok's voice again, *At first light, send them all to Toopek and destroy the city. Leave no creature alive.*

Understood, my father, replied the canok.

***

"Sir, there are large groups of dark brothers forming at our boundaries."

"What?" asked Draven. "What are dark brothers doing at Feldschlosschen?"

"We are not sure, but they appear to be mounting an attack."

The acting king lowered his head. He looked at the large map on the wall and wondered where Jermys was and if he was all right. He turned back to the guard. "We must protect this city. Until we know the intentions of the dark brothers, let's assume it is hostile. Scout all the mine entrances. Enhance the magic to prevent any breach. Send heavy battle-ready support to all areas where dark brothers are currently gathering and see if we can capture one and learn what is going on." He sucked a large gulp of ale and began speaking mostly to himself, though others were still within earshot. "Something is not right. We have had no issues with the dark dwarves in some time. Something else is at work here, and we do not want to end up in a war that is not of our choosing. We need to stop this before it starts."

The dwarven guard nodded, though he was not sure if he needed to acknowledge the comment or not. Quickly and quietly, he disappeared from the chamber. Shortly thereafter, Draven heard the sounds of battle in the distance. He closed his eyes and grabbed his axe. "It has begun," he said softly. In an instant, he was out the door and headed toward the sounds.

***

Stellanta turned to Phredder and motioned that another dragon approached. "Do we move to intercept?"

"No," replied the other slightly larger blue. "It appears to be headed directly for us. We can simply wait."

They both remained on the sandy shore, staring toward the spot as it approached. They could not determine the dragon's intention, only that it was large, brown, and was traveling incredibly fast. They turned and moved toward the center of the shoreline so it would know they saw it. Dragons were not accustomed to fighting each other, but with all that had happened since they arrived, there was no telling what this meant.

The large brown landed a short distance away, shook out its wings, and proceeded to walk toward the two. It turned its head to where Lorinca had previously lain, and now the area was devoid of life. Its eyes fell briefly then rose again to face the two blues. Its voice was deep but caring. "I am Tornac. I was asked to come join you as my support may be required."

"You were asked?" replied Stellanta. "By who?"

"By a great physeter named Khaled. He said he felt my presence would be beneficial to you." He paused then added, "I do not know what that means for sure, but his tone made me believe it was pertinent."

Then Phredder and Stellanta relaxed slightly, but the situation did seem strange and left an unsettled feeling in them. Stellanta continued, "We do not know all that is happening. We are here because we feel our assistance may be warranted by a group working to find some answers to all that is occurring in our world. We have already experienced tragedy and death, and we have also split our group to assist these others. We welcome your presence but do not know what Khaled might have been feeling."

Tornac lowered his head in acknowledgement. "I understand and hold the same feelings. Can you tell me what has happened since you arrived here?"

The three exchanged information, and shortly thereafter, as the day began turning to night, they felt they should retire into the tree line for some additional safety and plan on resting for the night.

Phredder leaned over to Stellanta and whispered. "One of us needs to remain on watch at all times. I do not want Tornac looking over us as we are completely unprotected."

"I understand," she replied. "I will take first watch with him." Phredder agreed and repositioned himself in the shrubs before closing his eyes. Stellanta looked back toward the new brown dragon and nodded, but neither spoke, almost as if they both knew she would be staying up without asking.

***

The night air bit through Schram's thick scaly skin. He could tell they were no longer in Toopek. The temperature difference between Cindif and Troyf was significant, to say the least. He was sure those on his back were really feeling it, but there was nothing he could do. To stop now could seal the fate of the entire world they knew. Time was running out. Schram knew it. He believed they would arrive to the shore at first light. If they were lucky, the two blues would still be there, and one would be willing to take his friends back. If they refused, Schram believed he would have to leave them there. He could not take them with him. He was not sure why, but he was sure nonetheless. He felt the grip tighten against his back and knew his first thoughts were true. The chill air was taking its toll.

His mind drew toward Stepha. He believed he had gotten through. He hoped she was on her way but also knew that if his travel remained consistent, he and his friends would be long gone from the shoreline by the time she arrived. He only hoped she could find her way from there and find it safely. When he thought about her safety, he thought about their child. He turned his head back to Lars, whose mane was tethered straight back, pulled tight in the wind from their flight. Lars saw his gaze and nodded that he was all right. Schram thought about Krirtie, all she had gone through to save Maldor while she carried Lars. The travel had ended up taking her life.

Would that be Stepha's fate? Schram had had visions of his death, as dragons do, but he had no sense for Stepha's. She had to be all right. She and their baby had to. He closed his eyes and issued a small prayer.

***

"Why do you look at me as such?" asked Tornac.

Phredder looked down slightly then back to the large brown dragon. "Because I do not know you. Your presence, by itself, brings with it mystery."

Tornac did not smile, and his stare did not turn. "Mystery does not mean danger."

"In these times, who is to say what brings danger? I just watched my lifelong friend die on this very shore at the hands of something at least connected to dragons. I have no reason to trust any that I do not know."

Tornac acknowledged the comment but did not reply further. He simply moved from beside him to sit in the sand, his weight causing the sand to move around the sides of his belly as he sat. The blue began to say more, but because he was not comfortable with the conversation, he just ended his thoughts. He moved to rest on the sand, keeping his body facing their new visitor.

***

Stepha and Mags had flown for most of the night. Stepha could feel the dragon's wings tiring as they cut slowly through the chill night air. She had no idea how far they had traveled or more importantly, how much farther they had to go, but she believed it was still a significant distance. She used her elven ears to listen close to the dragon's breath and could tell her new friend was trying hard but believed she was not going to make it. Their first trip back had taken much out of her, and embarking on another trip so soon was simply not the right choice for the large dragon. The elf knew they had to make it, but she also knew they could not without finding some refuge.

As if presented by magic, appearing on the horizon was a small outbreak, not large enough to be called an island but still a place to land. It appeared rocky and unstable, but Stepha was sure the dragon could do it.

She leaned in close to her friend's ear. "There," she stated, pointing. "Land there, for I require a break."

Mag's smiled. "My dear, you do not require a break—that much I know for certain. However, I also know you recognize that I do."

Within moments, the two landed safely on the small rocky outbreak. It was not much, and there was no vegetation or food to be found, but it was a place the dragon could rest its huge wings. The large beast turned to the girl and sadly added, "I am sorry, Stepha. I thought I could do it. I simply cannot. I must take this break."

The elf floated down from her back and rested her hand on the dragon's neck. "Please do not say you are sorry. Without you, I would still be in Toopek, and the chance to be with those who need me would not exist. You have given me a chance."

The dragon smiled, but she could feel the elf's worry growing inside. She did not know for certain what drove the elf to head back to Cindif in such haste or, for that matter, how she knew to go. She only knew that Stepha knew what it was, and that was good enough for her.

They rested in silence for quite some time without even a movement. Mags had closed her eyes and gone into a deep meditation, calming all her aching muscles. The first light was beginning to break across the sea's surface when Stepha whispered, "Mags, what do you think that is?"

Elven sight was equal or greater than dragon sight, but in this case, the elf could not tell what she was seeing and thought maybe the dragon, with more knowledge of such sights, would be more apt to recognize it. The big blue opened her eyes and turned in the direction of Stepha's raised finger. Her eyes narrowed, and she even stretched her head out, as if the additional distance would help her see more clearly.

In a soft voice carrying the stress of what she saw, combined with the ache still radiating in her body, she answered the elf's question, "They are not dragons but similar. There are a lot of them. I would say more than one thousand." She turned to the girl. "I don't know, Stepha, but please slide under my wing and let me curl to a ball. Should they see us, then let them think it is just me nesting."

The elf did as she was told but still maneuvered her head between the dragon's wing and body so she could see the group. As time continued, the large group drew closer and closer. Their path did not take them directly over their point of safety but close enough that they could be seen. A chill grew through Stepha's veins as she could begin to hear the beat of their wings against the brisk morning breeze.

The group was now close enough to see clearly, and both the dragon and Stepha could make out their entire bodies. Mags did not react, but Stepha saw exactly what they were. "The two-headed dragon creatures Schram saw previously. An army of them." She was whispering to herself, though the dragon heard what she said. She did not reply as one of the flying creatures turned its head and saw the dragon on the rocky outbreak. It turned its flight and headed their direction. Both saw the change and froze in their place. The two-headed beast turned across the water's surface and drew within fire breath of the dragon before nodding and turning back to the sky to fall in behind its group. Both girls let out a deep breath.

"I guess dragons are not a concern for them," stated Mags.

"I guess not, my friend. Thank you for providing me protection." The dragon, still with the elf hidden under her wing and more of these flying creatures passing by in a seemingly endless band, turned her head down to the girl as if she was going to sleep with her head curled under her wing.

"Stepha, I do not want to be the bearer of sadness, but you as well as I know where they are flying."

"I do," stated the elf.

"Do you wish to return? If we take a wide path and I fly as hard as possible, I could potentially arrive slightly ahead of them. We could warn the city."

A tear formed in the elf's eye. "I know that is not the case. You could not beat them back. We cannot get around them. The city is well prepared. They will be ready."

The dragon did not add anything, but both knew they were not prepared for that attack. Stepha thought about the original warning they received. The warning that stated all their homelands would be destroyed. She now understood how. She now understood the warning was real. Much time had passed, and as the last of the flying creatures appeared, Mags turned back to the elf. "Come on. If Cindif is where you were supposed to go to stop this evil, then Cindif is where you will be." The dragon flipped the girl onto its back, using its tail for leverage, and in only moments was back to the air. Although Stepha knew the rest was good and needed, it was not long enough to make a big difference. Yet the dragon was flying with a newfound strength and determination. Their pace was quick, and they cut through the air with precision. She did not know what they were flying to, only that Schram had told her to come. She closed her eyes and prayed for their world, and for Toopek.

***

"A dragon approaches," stated Tornac.

The others turned their heads to see the spot dotting the horizon. "Do you know it?"

"Is it one of the creatures that attacked us before?" asked Stellanta.

"No," stated Phredder. "I can see it clearly. It is Schram, and he brings his companions on his back."

"What has brought them back here?" asked Stellanta, moving beside her friend.

Phredder studied the dragon approaching then turned his head toward the other two. "I do not know, but his flight seems to be very hard. His wings are cutting a tight path toward us. Worst case, he is in danger and being followed. Best case, something has happened that makes this trip urgent. Either way, we must be prepared."

They moved toward the center of the shore area and watched him draw closer. In normal flight, this would still have taken some time, but at Schram's current rate, it was only moments before his wings were kicking up the sand under his feet. As he landed, those on his back leaped to the shore and instantly took notice of the new visitor. Schram turned to the large brown dragon. "Who are you, and where did you come from?"

"Greetings to you as well," replied Tornac.

Schram, only slightly caught by the tone, repeated his words, this time a bit softer. "Pardon my abruptness, but in these times, trust is not something I give willingly. When I left, I knew whom I left behind. Upon my return, you have arrived. My question is fair."

Tornac smiled. "I understand, my friend. I am Tornac. I am here because of only one factor. I was asked to come."

"Who asked you?" Schram questioned, his tone clearly carrying his lack of trust.

"Khaled." Tornac stared at Schram, waiting to see his response to this.

He stepped closer to the dragon and used his mind to see what the creature was feeling. To Schram's surprise and furthering his concern, his search was blocked. He was about to inquire into this when the brown dragon again interrupted his thought. "You do not need to read my mind to know that I am true. Just ask Khaled yourself."

Schram could not tell if this was a bluff of some kind or if the dragon meant it. When he looked in his eyes, there was no signal that deception was part of the plan. Their stare was long and hard, and it became a battle of wills to see who would break. Schram was not even sure if he was breathing when a deep and slowly spoken voice broke the monotonous silence.

"Are you both going to stand there all morning?" Khaled coughed slightly, as water shot from his throat, breaking the speech momentarily. "I would assume we have more important items to discuss."

Schram's eyes swung toward the water, where he saw the magnificent sight. Khaled's huge eyes and head broke the surface of the water. A stream of water sprayed from the top of his head with each labored breath he took. Although Schram was thrilled to see his old companion, the creature who had helped him so long ago, he was very concerned at the sight. Khaled looked weak. His eyes were sunken, and the cough he continued to issue showed his lungs were not strong. Schram changed back to his human-elf form and walked toward his old friend.

"Khaled, I am very glad to see you, but you look ill. What can I do?"

The whale smiled slightly and then coughed again. Tornac, Phredder, and Stellanta also moved to stand before the creature, their feet all taking several steps into the water, making the broken speech that much easier to hear. Tornac nodded, but it was Khaled who spoke.

"My son, it is time that catches me, not some illness. As with dragons, the physeter can feel when our time is near. I believe all creatures can, but only a few accept it." He paused, and then his eyes softened on Schram. "I feel your concern over Tornac. I did send him. He is good and will provide support to you. This support, however, is to get those who can back to Toopek. The attack is imminent, and those who go will arrive after it has begun."

Schram's head fell, and his eyes welled up, though he would not allow a tear to fall. He turned to his friends. "Without a moment's rest, please go to Toopek. Do what you can, but if you see that you cannot win, tell everyone to run. Flee to the trees and live to fight another day."

Denisi, Angus, and Fehr were instantly on Tornac's back. The dragon did not even hesitate and was in the air. Telepathically he said, *Do not worry, my friend. I will get them there, and I will stay by their side. We will fight for our world together.*

Schram nodded, but his attention was quickly drawn back to Khaled.

The whale motioned to the two other dragons. "Phredder, Stellanta, please join them, for they will need all the support possible."

The two looked at each other and then back to Schram. He nodded that he agreed, and in moments, they were in the air in the other's wake. Schram turned back to the whale and was about to speak when he was cut off.

"Come with me, my son, for we must speak." The large creature of the sea turned parallel to the shore and began slowly moving away from the others.

Schram turned to Maldor, Jermys, and Lars and quickly said, "Build a small fire. Use the time to rest, for we will leave in short order. Eat if you can, but most of all, sleep. This break will not be long."

Khaled began a small fit of coughing again, causing Schram to give a nod and then take some quick steps to catch up to his old friend. As he approached where the whale had stopped a significant distance away from the others, concern grew across his face, which he tried to mask but clearly could not. The creature arched its back, lifting its huge head farther from the water, giving a signal for the boy to come nearer.

"Schram, there is much we need to discuss. Some may be not what you want to hear, but I fear our plan from so long ago is coming to a close, and the door will shut on our world."

"What do you mean, Khaled? What plan?"

Again, the whale coughed. "The same plan we have been following for over two hundred years. The same plan your once greatest friend, the canok, created so long ago. The only plan that would prevent this creature from taking over our world."

Schram did not know what to make of the reference to Kirven but did not interrupt to ask. It was clear Khaled had much to say.

"What is your plan now?" asked Khaled.

Schram hesitated a moment, showing he really was not sure about what he was going to do, just where he was going. "We are heading north. The guardians told us we would find those behind this there." He paused, and his voice was slightly weaker, though it was not intended as such. "We will face them."

Khaled did not respond at first, then he asked with a much softer tone, "Have you felt your death?"

"I have," he replied, his voice slightly breaking.

"So you know when you will pass?"

Schram swallowed hard as he did not know where this was going. "I do believe I know how, but it is not clear to me when."

"Do you fear it?" asked Khaled, his voice slightly stronger.

Schram moved and knelt down at the edge of the water. "Do I fear my passing or those I am about to face?"

The whale did not answer. He only closed his eyes and entered the elf-human's mind. Schram felt the whale's presence and did not defend against him. To Khaled, Schram had nothing to hide.

His eyes opened. "Tell me about your mother."

Schram instantly broke from Khaled's bond, and with the question, his demeanor changed. "Who do you mean? My dragon mother?"

Khaled did not change expression. "Yes, Hawthorne was your birth mother. She carried you in her belly, and that which you are is partially that of her. But tell me about the one you knew to be Suzanne Starland."

Schram liked hearing Hawthorne's name, though he knew it was not the way of the elves. Her name was like a song to his ears. "I do not know what to say." He paused, and he could feel himself welling up again but pushed it away. "She was the mother I knew. She was human. She was always there, and other than not being a fan of my white canok friend, she supported me completely. When I came back from the elves at age five, she never let me out of her sight. Even when I left on treks across Troyf, I could always feel her with me. When I returned, she was there with her arms wide. She loved me. So much different from my father, the king."

"Yes, tell me about your father also."

"He was the king of the largest human city on all of Troyf. He was a diplomat, leader, and carried a sword well. Until he was taken by the dragons, he was what you would want in a king."

Khaled lowered his head beneath the water and then resurfaced. "Interesting the difference. With a mother who you know was not truly your mother, you say you felt love. For a father who you believe was truly your father, you do not."

Schram appeared defensive. "My father loved me."

"Did this man try to kill you and your companions?"

Schram did not know where this was going, but he did not like it. He felt anger form inside him as if he wanted to lash out at the creature sitting before him in the water. "Yes, after he was seduced by the black dragon magic. He did not know what he was doing." He stopped his comment and narrowed his eyes on Khaled. "What is it you are asking? Why do you ask these questions? I need to know what I am facing to the north. I need to know how to defeat these attacks. I do not need to relive my heritage."

Khaled did not react to his raised voice and more aggressive tone. He simply added, "But you do need to relive your heritage. Your heritage is what this is all about."

"What do you mean?" he asked, his voice much softer.

"You know the truth. You seek a mother who loved you but was not your birth mother. You believe your father, a human, died as a result of some dragon-induced magic. You are powerful. More powerful than Hawthorne. Where did that power come from?"

Schram did not answer. He simply closed his eyes, and the area was nearly silent. Only the soft crash of waves broken by a reef a short distance out confirmed time had not stopped altogether. Almost whispering, he replied, "Twice you have said 'the man I believe to be my father.' Are you saying he was not my father?"

Khaled nodded. "There is no scenario where you could carry the power you do with a human father."

Schram looked toward the creature. "Then who?"

"Hawthorne is with us always. She may have passed in our world, but those she is closest with will always feel her. That is why I can say her name without offending the gods. She is with them, but she is also with us."

Schram smiled through his confusion. "I do love hearing her name and thinking about her. For knowing her such a short time, it was amazing how close I felt with her."

Khaled coughed again but still showed his pleasure at the comment. "Your mother was what dragons should be. Everyone saw that."

"Khaled, please do not answer with riddles. Who was my father, and is the one I knew as Suzanne Starland alive?"

The whale's peace quickly left his face. In a stern but still caring voice, he replied, "Interesting you use the past tense to describe him." He paused then added, "And as for your mother, I do not know. I have not felt her presence in over twenty years. With your father as capture or accomplice, I cannot say." He paused as another fit of coughing struck him. "The one whom you seek in the north is your birth father. I believe that though I cannot feel him any longer. His strength has grown. The same way Hawthorne took her place as your mother, he took the king's place as your father. When Hawthorne learned of this, it was too late. Her love for you would not be changed. Now you are the one thing that connects these two worlds."

The Road North

Schram knelt on the sand just out of reach of the water. Neither Khaled nor Schram spoke for a long time. Just like when he learned about Hawthorne being his birth mother, those same feelings of confusion and loss filled his mind. His confusion led to distress and distress to solitude. He simply wanted to be alone, but he knew he could not. Schram always knew he was different. He thought it was because of his time as a baby with the elves, then his time with Kirven, and then learning about his mother being a dragon. All these things did have an effect, but now it all made sense. He was not comfortable as a human because he was not human at all. He also never understood if he could only be as strong with magic as his parents, and if his parents were a dragon and human, then why was he so much more powerful? He thought it was because of his bonding with the Ring of Ku and his mastering of the Staff of Anbari. Now he understood that it was because he was not the son of a human father, but a... His mind stopped, and he turned to Khaled.

"Who is my father?"

"You father is one known as Bjork. An incredibly powerful black dragon, though he is able to alter his color at will, more commonly known as Son of Karin, brother to Slayne. I believe at the time of the conception, he understood that it was Hawthorne who was present. With the black dragon's help and understanding, he also understood how powerful you could be with a mother and father, possibly two of the most powerful dragons in the world, as parents. The full circle of the dragon oppression, the deal made by your old canok friend, and every other occurrence that has brought us to this point are all centered on you. You bring balance to the world. Should you turn, there will be nobody powerful enough to stop your family. Ruling as father and son, you could change this world to anything you wanted it to be. Not your brothers, not all the maneth, elves, or humans, or even the physeter, could stop you. Your father does not wish you destroyed. He wishes you to have nothing left but him."

"Are you saying that everyone I know, all the world I know, is going to be destroyed so I will have nothing left but this father? I will never turn to him."

Again, Khaled coughed. "Do not underestimate the draw. You share his blood. You share his strength. He is powerful. The physeter fear him. He has remained hidden for years, waiting until the moment was right. He would not do this if he had any fear of failing. He is your birth father, Schram. You cannot deny that. Many have tried to deny their heritage. All have failed."

Schram's face was saddened, but no tear was even close to falling. His sadness was replaced with anger, and his tone carried hatred. "My father died over twenty years ago. He died when a desire for power overtook his mind and changed his body. He was weak. This creature who shares my blood is not my father but a traitor who hides. Like a serpent in the deep. No true plan, just opportunity. I will not join this dragon. I will kill him. He may know his own death, and he may not see that death as now, but the guardians said the one true thing is death. It will happen, and your actions in the world control it. What he feels is one thing. My actions will change that."

"An interesting theory, young Schram, but again, he is incredibly powerful and wise. He would not show himself now if he did not feel his success was certain. You may not turn to him, but he will never turn to you."

Schram felt a weight falling on his shoulders. His whole world was again not as it should be. Things he felt were certain now again were not. He went back to his original question, "Do you feel anything for Suzanne Starland? Is she his captive?"

The large creature's eyes closed. "I do not feel she is what you believe her to be. If that means she is with him, then it may be as such. I should be able to feel her whether passed or not, and I feel nothing. It is as if I am not allowed to feel her."

Schram raised his head slightly. "Then she is blocking it?"

"She is human. She could not block me."

"Then the one known as Bjork is blocking you?"

"No, your father, I feel. He is not."

Schram looked on, clearly lost. "I am so confused. If she is alive but you cannot feel her because it is being blocked, and Bjork is not blocking it, what does that all mean?"

Khaled lowered himself slowly into the water. Telepathically he replied as he disappeared beneath the surface, *That, my friend, is the right question.*

***

Alan stared across the water. "Geoff!" he shouted. "Look across the bay, in the distance. What do you think it is?"

The large maneth ran to his side. "By all the gods. Sound every alarm. Call every fighter to the bay. Send a messenger to the dwarves. It is beginning, and there are more than we could ever have thought." He hollered toward an elf who was a short distance up the hill toward the city. "Can you make them out? Your sight is much clearer."

The elf hurried to his side and grabbed his arm. She spoke in a hushed tone so as not to create panic. "Yes, Geoff, and there are too many. We cannot defend that. The sky is so solid that even my sight cannot make out a true number, but there are at least a thousand. There may be more than we have arrows."

Alan had taken a few steps away but upon hearing these words, stayed to hear the maneth's direction. He stepped to the opposite side of the elf. "What do you think, Geoff? Is the smart option to flee while we can?"

"To stay sentences those who remain to death. Their numbers are too great, and we must assume they carry the same power or greater than that of the dragons of the past. We cannot defend them alone. But those who can fight need to buy time to help all others escape."

The elf let out a sigh in disbelief, as thinking of retreat was one thing, but hearing the king say it was another. "Are you saying we will retreat?"

He turned to the warrior elf. "No, I am saying that, right now, before it is too late, evacuate everyone you can. Those who wish to stay and fight can join me on the shoreline. We will hold them off as long as we can."

Although he saw the elf was going to protest, Alan did not spare a moment and sprinted toward the city center, barking out orders as he went. Within moments, the bell tower at the city center began to ring. This plan had been prepared just in case the worst happened. The moment the chimes were heard, organized chaos ensued. Everyone knew what to do, a full Toopekian evacuation. Two masses were immediately forming: those preparing to flee to the woods and those staying to defend the city, the latter of which was a fraction of the first.

Geoff did not speak and only stared across the water. The elf moved next to him. "Is this the end?"

"I do not know," the maneth replied. "But I can tell you for sure, I am going to make certain they know we are here to show them physically that they are not taking this city without a fight."

"You can take it from my bloodied and cold fingers," stated Madeiris from behind.

Geoff turned and placed his hand on his friend's shoulder. "I know talk of death is not something elves would ever do freely, but you too must see what is before us. I will hold no ill will if you guide the elves out of here and back to Elvinott. None of us saw these numbers."

The elf king looked across the water and then nodded to the side where a wall of flyer elves stood at the ready. He then nodded to the other side where archers sat perched, arrows already nocked into place. "The maneth guard are cutting a hole through the goblin and troll forces that appeared between Toopek and the forest. Our people will escape. Those who remain will fight to the end, but it is not the end we focus on, it is the life we are providing in the escape of the others." He looked back toward the approaching mass of flying beasts. "We may not be victorious, but I also feel we are not fighting alone. We must do what we can and pray for the others."

"I am glad Denisi is not here," the maneth said softly.

"And I, my sister." Geoff stared at the elf, who was most likely his longest-standing friend. They shared a bond that usually would only find itself between brothers or, minimally, two of the same village and race. These two had spent their whole lives a step or two below the king. Now, in the end, they stood together as leaders of their races, defending a city of a race to which neither of them belonged. However, as they looked across the sea, the maneth with his giant mitt on the shoulder of the elf, they both knew they were where they were destined to be.

"Look," stated Madeiris, pointing. "They have struck something in flight."

Geoff smiled. "Schram has always got something cooking. It won't hold them for long, but I will take any barrier to add some distance between these beasts and our people."

"Stupid human. I suppose if we get out of this, he will take credit for it." The elf was still pointing. "Look close. These are not dragons. These are those two-headed creatures, like what was in the forest."

The maneth now turned his whole body to the elf. "What do you want to do, my friend?"

The elf shook his head. "We cannot run. They would hunt us down."

"Will they chase everyone down regardless?" Madeiris's head fell downward, and his eyes closed. "The prophecy stated they would destroy all of us."

The maneth's voice lifted slightly. "Perhaps the prophecy thought we would all flee at the sight. Perhaps we need to change what we would normally do. If they intend to destroy us anyway, should they not destroy us at our strongest?"

"Are you saying we stop the retreat and put a weapon in every hand?" asked the elf.

"What do you think?"

"I think you stop that bell, and you get everyone back." As he spoke, a bright light exploded across the bay. "They are getting through," Geoff said. "It will not be long now."

***

Schram turned and walked slowly across the sand. He saw his companions sitting on the shore. A small fire did burn, but none slept. All eyes were on their friend and then quickly turned away as he approached.

Lars looked up at Schram as he drew close enough. "What's up, big ears?"

Schram smiled. "I am too worn out to do to you what I should for calling me that, but trust I will find my strength in time."

The others smiled, and then the area got deafly quiet. It was as if everybody was waiting for someone to say something, but nobody wanted to be the one. Schram sat down on the sand and appeared to be deep in thought. Maldor, Lars, and Jermys all looked at each other and then to the ground. Each thought about what their next step would be. Although each knew that they did not have time to spend waiting around, for whatever reason, they recognized that Schram needed this. It was two hours later when he rose to his feet, and speaking only two words, started the next portion of their journey.

"Let's go," he stated. The others rustled to their feet, gathering their things. Jermys extinguished their small fire, and their trek to the northern rim was on the way. Schram motioned to Jermys to join him up front, and the two maneth took spots several paces back. This seemed to please the father and son as, although they had spent nearly every waking moment of Lars's life together, there was something different about this time. Maldor recognized the danger that lay ahead, and Lars saw only adventure. The large maneth looked at his son and saw how tightly he held Krirtie's scimitar. He hoped it would protect him the way it had when he was born. He hoped they would be strong enough to defeat this evil.

Just then, Lars placed his hand on his father's shoulder. "I can feel her with me now, all the time. It is different than before. She is really with me."

Maldor just smiled and placed his arm around his son briefly. "Trust in the sword, my son, but trust in yourself more."

He nodded, and then the two continued their pace in silence. Schram leaned over to Jermys, who had just lit his pipe for a brief smoke. "You know some ahead will smell that, don't you?"

"Yep."

Schram smiled. "You really don't care, do you?"

He returned the smile. "Don't care is probably not the right set of words. More like, doesn't matter."

Schram saw the change in the dwarf's eyes. "Do you think we can win?"

Jermys stopped walking and turned to his friend. "Schram, I would follow you into a volcano if I felt it was the right thing to do, just as I follow you now. I am over 270 years old. I am tired and in pain. In all those years, I have always thought the decisions I made were for the right reasons, as I do today." He paused and sucked in deep on his pipe.

Maldor and Lars saw the changes ahead and stopped as well, so as not to disturb the two that were clearly in a deep conversation. "Do I think we can win?" Jermys continued. "I don't know. What I do know is for the first time in all those decisions, I am scared. Not scared about what we will face or the unknown, but scared that we can't win. That there is no answer that can save our world. There is great power ahead of us. Power that can do things we have never seen before. Power we do not understand. But most of all, it is a power whose source we do not understand. We do not even know whom we are going to meet."

He listened to the small man's words and felt the pain in his speech. Schram knew that Jermys had no intent of ever coming out of these woods. He believed he was at the doorstep of his destination, and nothing could change that now.

Schram looked down. "I believe we are going to meet my mother and father."

Jermys's eyes widened. "You father is dead, Schram, as well as your birth mother. I know you do not like to speak of such things, but this much we know for sure. As for your human mother, I know what you heart tells you, but she too must have passed, and there is no way she could wield this strength."

"No, my friend, the king of Toopek has passed, but not my father. And as for my 'human' mother, she too lives, and I believe she too is not the human that was portrayed. So much started so long ago in Toopek. Magic, changelings, and imposters—they all set this trek in motion, and now we have simply come to its final conclusion."

Jermys chewed on that for a few moments and replied, "Then I guess we do know whom we are about to face. I still need the smoke."

The two turned without another word and continued through the trees. The temperature had already dropped by at least fifteen degrees, and they had only been walking for an hour. Their direction was straight north, and the terrain was straight up. None of them knew how long this part of their journey would be, but all assumed they would not have a problem determining when they arrived at their destination.

***

"What in God's name are these things?" shouted Alan.

Geoff took a burst of energy off his shoulder and struck the ground before he could answer. As he pushed himself to his feet, he stated, "Do we know what will take them down?"

Madeiris heard the question as he released another arrow into one of the beasts. "Only constant physical attacks. Nothing based on any magic. When the magicians from Empor had tried anything, it was instantly turned back on them. They seemed to absorb the magic and reverse it."

Geoff regained his feet as blue blood spilled onto the sandy shore. He lifted his large club and swung as one of the creatures crossed above his head. Contact was solid, and the creature altered its flight and struck the ground hard, rolling to the side.

Madeiris released a barrage of arrows into its belly, and the creature vanished. "Did we kill it?" the elf asked.

"I don't kn—" Geoff was cut off in midsentence when a bolt of energy struck him in the center of his back. His fur was burnt and his mane on fire

204

by the time the elf could reach him. Alan drove his sword deep into the creature that stood only feet from the fallen maneth and elf king. The creature roared and took to the air before vanishing like the one before. Alan scanned the immediate area and saw at least fifty two-headed dragons coming their way.

The human leader ran to Madeiris. "We have to leave. There are too many."

The elf swung his head around and witnessed what was coming. "Help me move him."

Alan placed his hand on his shoulder. "It is too late, Madeiris." Madeiris stopped trying to lift the maneth behind the shoulders and fell to his knees. There was a moment when all sound seemed to stop. He reached behind his breastplate and removed a small pouch. Inside, he grabbed a small bit of elven dust to aid in passing. As he lifted his hand above his friend, a burst of energy from the shoreline struck Geoff's still body, throwing the maneth, Madeiris, and Alan in the air and then to the ground about twenty-five steps away.

The elf sat up to the cursing of the human leader. "Are you all right, Alan?" asked the elf.

"I think so," he replied, brushing himself off.

"I am as well," added Geoff, "though the pain in my back is great."

Both the others swung their eyes to the maneth. "You're alive!" shouted Madeiris.

"Would you think anything else?"

The two looked at each other, nodded affirmatively, and then pointed. "We have to get out of here. Can you walk?" The elf was trying to lift Geoff again as he spoke.

"Get your hands off me, Madeiris. Nothing happened to me that did not also hit you."

"I am not sure about that, but I am pleased to say we can talk about that later." The elf was now pointing as he spoke, "Quickly, we have to leave this shoreline and get some protection."

Just then, another bolt of energy struck right by their position, and again, they all fell to the ground. This seemed to jolt the three into action, and quickly they were up and running toward the city.

"Look behind us," Madeiris stated.

Geoff turned his head as he ran. The sky was black with two-headed flying beasts. "There must be thousands." He paused, stopped his run, and turned. "What are we running from? We cannot escape them." His voice grew softer. "We cannot defeat them by the current rules with which we fight."

The others also stopped and turned to the wall before them. "What do you mean, the rules with which we fight?"

"I mean, there are too many. They outnumber us, are stronger, and have magical weapons. Schram tried to create a barrier which they moved through in only moments. Further, he is not here with us. We are alone and outnumbered in power and count. If we run to the woods, they will hunt us down and destroy us all."

Madeiris placed his hand on his shoulder. "But if we stay and fight here, they may believe they have destroyed us all, and some of the others may escape. They will be weak and few, but in time, they could grow to become more and find a way to defeat this enemy."

"Aye," replied the maneth softly, his tone showing that they all understood what this meant.

Alan lifted his sword. "I will stay by your side until the end. This is my city, and I will die defending it."

"It is our city," Geoff replied. "And we all will see that fate in our lives. It is the one true thing of all on Troyf. This may be our time."

As the three men of different races all lifted their shields, swords, clubs, and bows, others who had turned to flee seemed to understand the same things. They too turned, and together they created a wall of races all standing tall to defend one last city rather than run. The line was drawn in the sand, and the final battle was forged.

***

"Schram, do you know if Stepha is coming?" Maldor asked.

He was startled by the question, but he could see in the stares of the two maneths and Jermys that the question was carried by all. The three had left Schram alone at the lead and taken a position a short distance behind for most of their walk that day.

Until this brief break, where they added cloaks and layers under their armor as the snow and cold bite of the wind was growing tougher, they had not spoken to their leader. Schram looked back to his friends and then to the ground.

In a tone similar to someone lost wanting to call for help but knowing they had to remain strong, he answered, "Why do you ask?"

Jermys stood up from the small patch he had cleared in the snow to sit. "Well, the boy"—motioning to Lars—"does not really understand everything about the weapons. One of his questions seems so simple to us now, but its answer involves the missing piece. The weapons of the ring have been part of this from the start. First, with the Ring of Ku, then searching and recovering all the weapons, then with what took place in the Realm. Lars asked a question that makes sense. If the weapons have been a part of this from the beginning—and although Maldor returned his to the guardians of the Realm, he did receive something in return—could you not argue that all the weapons need to be part of this to finish it?"

Schram's solemn stare turned a slight bit upward, and he turned mainly to the young maneth, the son of one of his closest friends. "Your wisdom is something I continue to be amazed by, Lars." Turning to the others, he added, "I agree. I do not know what we may face or even for sure whom we may face, but I do believe the weapons of the ring are a part of it. I did connect to Stepha, but I have not been able to reconnect. I do not know why. I believe she is on her way here if she is able, but I have also come to terms that we may face this evil without her and without her bow. The other part of me hopes she does not make it and remains safe. Further, however, although the weapons have been part of this from the beginning, there is something here that works against them. I believe that very deeply. Because of that, not having the hammer may be a positive for us because it will prevent whom we face from obtaining it."

The others grew silent. Jermys was still standing when he added, "Is it wiser to move forward without her, or should we wait and ensure she can join us?"

"Unfortunately, my friend, we have no option. I feel tremendous danger for Toopek, danger that will hit them in very short order. I feel if we do not find the source of this evil and destroy it now, there will be no Toopek to return to."

"How long do they have?" asked Maldor, his thoughts going to his king and others set to defend the human city.

"I cannot tell, but the attack is imminent. I erected a barrier around the city, but it will not hold against this magic. The magic I feel is different. Not necessarily stronger, but different. Almost wiser, as if it anticipates what I may do."

"Like they are anticipating our actions?" asked Maldor.

Schram nodded, but it was Lars who interjected, "Then we need to not do what is expected, like when I tricked you into moving the fallen tree outside our camp."

Maldor grimaced slightly at the memory but was caught by Schram's raised eyebrow. "What do you mean, Lars?" the human asked.

The young maneth now stood as well. "It is simple. Whatever is expected for you to do, go a different direction. It may not work, but it will definitely keep them off guard. If they are stronger with magic or more knowing or whatever you said, then you have to beat them at their own game."

Schram moved and slapped the maneth on the shoulder. "Interesting idea. I don't know if it will work, but something to chew on. Now let's head out." He paused and turned to Maldor. "And when we do, I would like to hear about the tree you moved." Lars smiled slightly but quickly let the smile fade with Maldor's muffled grunt directed his way.

Jermys slapped the older maneth on the back and said, "Don't worry, old friend. You will have hundreds of years to be humiliated by your son. It comes with the territory."

The group headed back toward the north, their trek becoming more and more difficult as the terrain and temperature required much more of their strength. Schram wondered if this was part of the reason this evil found its nest here. He wondered if turning to a dragon and flying would make more sense. He should have done that in the beginning. Now, with the cold, it would take too much out of him. Further, for some reason, he did not wish to be a dragon here. Where he was going, he needed to be the Schram he had always been.

They crossed a ridge just as the sun set, and instantly Schram felt the presence. It was foreign and strong. It wasn't that someone was watching them. It was a feeling that someone had them. His eyes batted around and came to rest on a faint light still a great distance ahead. Jermys stood by his side, trying to be tall like the human, and although his height was not the same, he still showed the same dark look Schram carried.

The dwarf broke the silence, "That is our destination." He did not say it as if asking, nor did he say it like he was unsure. He said it as if he knew.

Schram did not look toward his smaller friend. His voice was cold and direct. "It is, and they know we approach."

The other two filed in behind just in time to hear the conversation. "What do you think?" asked Maldor. "Is our plan to simply continue forward?"

Schram had not vocalized his thoughts on this yet. He had not said anything because he did not know anything. When Maldor spoke, it seemed to pull Jermys from his locked stare on the area ahead. "Right, Maldor, Schram does not have a plan. Instead, we are simply going to walk in and say, 'Hello, we are here to destroy you before you destroy our world. Sound good?' Then this ever-so-powerful evil will be struck by our tremendous strength and simply give up." He smiled and turned to his leader. "Right, Schram. That's the plan, isn't it?"

Schram's tone showed no hint of humor when he replied, "Yes, believe it or not, that is our plan."

The others froze on his words, almost pushing him to say more. When nothing came, they looked toward each other and then back to Schram. In a softer voice, Lars asked, "Do we go there tonight?"

Schram turned to the group. "No, we rest here. It would not be safe to go any closer." He stopped when he saw their faces. "Friends, I know this may not seem like a plan, but this is no enemy that we can surprise. They already know we are here. They are already well prepared for us to arrive. The victor in this battle will not be one that wins via a blindsided attack. There is no strategy. It is simple. The one who proves superior will simply be the one who is strongest."

"Any insight into who that is going to be?" asked Maldor.

"None," replied the human.

***

"How are you doing, Mags?" asked Stepha, gripping the dragon's neck tightly.

The dragon eyes were tearing as the cold wind bit against her face. "I don't know, Stepha. I am trying, but I am not sure I can make it."

"Do you know how far it is to land?" hollered the elf, her voice difficult for even her to hear in the high winds.

The dragon shook her head. "I don't know. I can't even be sure we are still on a course toward the shore."

Stepha searched her mind for any answer. They had been traveling in a fierce storm for some time. It had blown up from the sea, and the high winds had been joined with heavy rain, which now was turning to sleet. They were soaked to the bone, and even if they could ignore the cold wind, rain, and sleet, Stepha knew if they did not find shelter, they would not make it. However, they were between countries over the largest sea on Troyf. They had been lucky to find a small outcropping of rocks the day before. Even if one was below them now, they would not see it, and they were flying just above the surface of the water. Where the water's surface began and the wet, rainy air ended was completely blurred. It was as if the water from the sea had exploded, combining the two into one. A bolt of lightning struck the water's surface directly in front of the dragon, causing both Stepha and Mags to veer sideways. The sudden turn threw the elf from the dragon's back. She quickly took to flight, but her small wings were no match for the high-speed winds. In only a moment, she struck the water's surface.

"Stepha!" screamed Mags in fear. "Stepha, do you hear me?" The elf burst back through the water's surface as the dragon plunged downward. She screamed for Mags, but her voice was lost in the crashing waves around her. The dragon dove through the water and then back to the air, struggling to find her friend and calling for her constantly. Her wings were wet, and every one of her muscles ached, but her panic for Stepha drove her forward. The hard rain continued to pound the water, and the wind whipped the drops, which felt like sand blasting the elf's face.

Stepha again tried to lift herself into the air, but her wings were not strong enough. Her arms flailed in the water, and she feared she would not make it. She closed her eyes and bobbed under the surface, almost wanting to give up, but her elven heritage would not allow it. She pushed herself back up to the surface one more time and again called to her friend.

From under the water, she felt her legs get bumped; and in the next moment, she shot up from the water on the back of the dragon. Water sprayed from both their bodies as Magdalene soared upward. Lightning still bit through the air with claps of thunder all around. Stepha wanted to speak, but her exhaustion plus fear allowed her to only grip the dragon's neck. Tears formed in her eyes, but all she did was hold on. Maggie was not flying as before. She was flying scared and without any thought other than she was going to make it to the shores of Cindif no matter what. Twice the dragon's body struck the surface of the water, and twice she recovered to regain her broken flight.

Mags's flight was so low that often waves at their apex caught her feet and even worked to draw the huge beast back into its wrath. Neither knew how long they flew as time seemed to have no meaning. Stepha may have even lost consciousness, but Magdalene did not lose her drive. She was going to make it. In her mind, she knew it may be her last flight, but she was not going to have it be Stepha's. The storm had come up quickly and reached its violent level in only moments, but it was clear by the black sky ahead it was only beginning.

Magdalene had improved on cutting through the wind and rain, but the rain was again turning to sleet and the temperature dropping. She was sure she had flown too far north in the confusion, but there was no turning back now. She could use the faint light of the sun somewhere hidden well behind the clouds to guide her to the proper direction now, and with that, she was certain she would hit land.

All we need is land, she thought to herself. On land, they could find shelter, and with shelter, they would survive. If she gave up and hit the water, they would both be lost. Again a bolt of lightning struck the water directly in front of the dragon's flight, electrifying the entire area. Stepha woke from her trance and screamed while Mags tried to halt her flight in midair. The rapid stop nearly threw the elf from her back again, and if that should happen, Mags was certain Stepha would not be able to stay afloat. She recovered quickly, leveling herself in the air and hollered to her friend.

"Stepha, hold tight. We are almost through."

"I can't!" the elf cried. "I can't make it."

Mags's voice softened. "Hush now, child, and hold on. We need only one last burst forward to find land."

Mags had no idea if this was the truth, but she also did not care. The positive thought gave hope to the elf, whose tone was clearly lost and far away. She did not believe they were going to make it. She thought about her husband and what he was going to face. She believed whatever their fate was in this war, they would face it together; and should they pass, they would pass together. She had felt that since the day they had become one. Now she believed that would not be. She set her head on the dragon's back and closed her eyes, issuing a quiet prayer of passing in a soft whisper to herself. A tear rolled down her green cheek.

"Stepha, there is land ahead." The elf could not lift her head, and part of her did not even hear the comment. Mags recognized this and cut her path even harder toward the sandy shore. As she reached the edge, she instantly realized she did not recognize where she was. Snow had begun to form on the beach, bringing a pure-white, almost magical appearance to the area. She did not land on shore as the wind was still whipping up a violent front. She could see the tree line in the distance and knew that in the forest was where she would find shelter. Without missing a beat of her wings, she bit forward.

"Stepha, can you hear me?" Her voice was weak and broken, but the concern was clear. "I must tell you one thing now. When you reach your destination, don't use your magical bow..." Her voice trailed off, and she did not think the elf heard her. She wanted to speak again but could not. They crashed into the trees, breaking several trunks until finding their resting spot below a thicket, which actually worked to protect them from the elements.

The elf's eyes slowly opened. "Mags, are we okay?"

The dragon's mouth turned into an instant smile of peace. "Yes, my dear. You made it." The dragon closed her eyes and rested her head against the girl's body.

The warmth from the dragon soothed Stepha's cold body, and she reached her arm up to her friend's long nose. "Thank you, Mags. You saved me."

There was no response from the huge creature. Stepha lifted her head. "Mags!" She screamed. "No!" She threw her arms around the motionless body of the creature before her. The creature that had saved her life. The creature that had stayed alive just long enough to know Stepha was safe. The creature that had given her life to save her. Tears streamed down her face as she wrapped her arms around her lost friend. "I love you, Magdalene. I will never forget all you gave for me."

It is unclear how long Stepha sat holding her friend. Her cheeks were wrinkled due to so many tears. At some point, she lifted herself up and knelt beside the fallen creature that, in such a short time of knowing her, had done so much. She issued a long silent prayer that ended with the passing of elven dust across the dragon's body. The forest was deathly silent as the body slowly vanished.

"I will miss you, my friend. And I will not let your death be for nothing. I will find Schram, and I will help stop this evil."

A warm presence surrounded the elf. She felt it all around her. She could not place it, but it was there. She knew it was Magdalene. She knew the dragon was still with her, still watching. It may not mean anything in the real world, but it was a comfort nonetheless. She heard the word "remember."

***

The companions were stirring to the morning sun as it began to slowly rise across the horizon. Schram looked toward their destination and saw nothing had changed. He was not sure if this was good or bad, but his feelings told him that it meant nothing. Whoever or whatever they were approaching knew they were here. Schram knew they were there. And it would all come down to what happened when the two sides met. *What was the endgame?* he thought. *Why did we have to come here?*

He turned to his companions, who were also stirring. He again, as he had done the entire night, felt for the one that was missing. He felt for Stepha. *Stepha, can you hear me?* To his displeasure, he felt nothing in return.

"What do you think is our next move?" asked Maldor, breaking him from his thoughts.

"We are going to walk in," Schram replied, his voice strong but still holding some unknown uncertainty somewhere deep within it.

Maldor smiled. "Just like that? We are just going to walk right into"—he paused a moment while he thought about what to call it then just shook his head and pointed—"that place."

The large elf-human leader put his hand on his friend's shoulder, and as the others began to move in around the two, he simply added, "Yes, that is exactly what we are going to do."

They gathered their belongings in silence. Each also had a bite to eat, and as the daylight began to fire up around them, they took their first steps toward their final destination. It was not a far distance to go, but the terrain was still tough, and the cold air also seemed to be providing a barrier.

There was some light banter in the back between Maldor, Lars, and Jermys when the dwarf happened to see his friend in front change. "Schram! What is it?"

The tone of the call drew both Lars's and Maldor's attention, and all three rushed forward, the younger maneth reaching first and catching Schram before he fell. "I got you, big fellow. You okay?"

Schram appeared confused, almost lost, and he even seemed to be having trouble focusing not just on words but his whole environment. "I don't know. I feel weak. Like all my energy was just drained. Do any of you feel it?"

They looked at each other and shook their heads with the dwarf talking first. "I don't. I feel as I always have. Did something attack you?"

"I don't think so," he replied. He seemed to be regaining his strength as he spoke. "That was strange, but I am feeling better now. Let's continue." Although he spoke with a strong voice that carried confidence, Schram knew that this was no coincidence. He may not have been attacked, but something just happened.

They continued on, but the light banter that had been taking place previously was gone. They walked in silence and at full attention. Any noise or motion called all to draw toward it in defense. The tree cover was less, and they were essentially walking on a smooth snow-covered plain toward a break between two cliffs. They could see light coming from the area, light that was not emanating from the planet's sun. It was clear, even from their distance that it was not of natural origin.

Lars broke the silence in a soft, almost whispering tone, though he did not know why he was whispering. "There is something different with me as well."

Schram's attention was drawn immediately. "What, Lars? What are you feeling?"

"Nothing," he replied.

Schram appeared just slightly agitated. "It is not nothing. You would not have said it if it was nothing. What are your feelings?"

"No," he began, "that is what I mean. I feel nothing. Always before when I held my mother's sword, I could feel amazing power flowing through it, and in turn, through me. However, now I feel nothing. Like the sword is, well, just a sword."

Jermys raised his hatchet. "Now that you say that, I feel the same. My hatchet is not emanating the power I have felt in the past."

Schram turned to Maldor. "I don't carry anything to feel different. The amulet they gave us has never given me a sense of power, and it does not currently either."

Schram began nodding his head. More to himself than the others, he whispered, "Now I understand it."

"Understand what?" asked Jermys.

"Why we had to come here." He held up his hand and incanted a short spell. Nothing happened.

"What is the matter, Schram?"

"My powers are gone. Something about this place is able to defend against Anbarian magic." He shook his head. "We had to come here. We were led here because we will be powerless here. Your hatchet, Lars's sword, Maldor's previous hammer, and Stepha, should she come with her bow, would all be just weapons here, not weapons of the ring."

"Can you change into a dragon, or are you to remain as elf- human?" asked the dwarf, concern showing on his face and not knowing if Schram being a dragon would really be a benefit or not.

Without a word, Schram instantly took the form of his natural self. "Evidently, that is within me and untouched by this place. At least untouched for now," he added softly.

Lars and Maldor looked at each other and seemed to have a conversation with no words spoken, but they clearly understood the question. The older maneth asked, "Does this change our plans? Do we now not proceed forward?"

Schram, still in dragon form, tilted his head but carried a strong and determined glare in his expression. "No, our world cannot last. Now is our time. We must move forward, and by what I feel about Toopek's current state, we must move forward now."

THE END OF TOOPEK

Magical bursts of energy struck every building, every defender. Screams beat off the sides of the fallen walls and echoed all the way to the trees. When the main branch of dragoks reached the city, it was as if a wave from the sea had simply swallowed them whole. Their defense was strong, but there simply were too many. Roughly one thousand individuals, humans, maneths, and elves all fought with the strength of ten times that number, but even Geoff could see there were too many. From Castle Island, an additional thirty-five dragons joined the fight. They seemed to have better results as they could compete in the air with a combined force of fire and simply in-air fighting, but one by one, their bodies were also finding the water's surface.

The three men—Geoff, Madeiris, and Alan—had taken on injuries, but all remained in the fight. Madeiris had moved to join a large battalion of elves that had moved to hold the center of the city, providing protection and support to some of the wounded. Alan and Geoff remained near the shore. They were the first line of defense and taking the brunt of the battle. They had dug in deep into the sandy shore, creating a bunker of protection. The little protection they gained, however, really did little but give them a place to stand. Alan was decent with a bow, but even as he struck the dragoks time and time again, they had little effect. It almost appeared as if they were impervious to injury.

Geoff hollered to Alan and the men by his side, "We need a new plan. We are not taking any of them down."

"It appears they are not able to be brought down."

The maneth turned. "What do you mean?"

"I mean they are not real. Have you ever seen a creature like that naturally? I have not. They do not bleed. They do not appear to even feel any level of pain. If they were not killing our men and destroying this city, I would not believe they were even with us."

"What?" The maneth moved closer. "Do you mean they are created by magic?"

Alan lifted an eyebrow. "That was not what I was thinking specifically, but it definitely makes sense."

Without another word, Geoff turned to the maneth troops with him and shouted loud enough for Alan's men to hear, "Men, hold this city. Do whatever you can to protect yourself. Find a way to bring them down. Support the dragons as they are having the strongest effect. I need to find someone."

"You heard him," shouted Alan. "Fight like you have never fought before. Let's bring some of these beasts down." He grabbed Geoff's arm as he started to head back toward the city. "Who are you going to find?"

"Mi-Kevan."

***

Schram, Maldor, Jermys, and Lars slowly walked toward the light they saw ahead. The day was beginning to show itself more strongly, but even with the light from the sun now high in the sky, they still saw something unnatural in their path ahead. There were no trees, and the snow-covered ground seemed to lessen in thickness. The temperature was cold, though none of them could feel it bite like it had in the recent past. They did not find this any more comforting. Although Schram did not carry the same level of anxiety and fear of the unknown that his companions did, he did have an uneasiness about him. It had been a long time since he had not felt the power of the Staff of Anbari flowing within him. It had been a long time that he could not with his mind move a branch or shrub out of his way as he walked. In short, it had been a long time since he had felt human.

Although they had seen no changes as they approached, for some reason, their steps seemed to be increasing in speed, and their concentration on what was before them was lessened. It may have simply been the time it took to get there, or perhaps someone or something was making them feel more comfortable. Regardless, the feelings were welcomed by all. Lars even replaced his scimitar to his belt and left his large hands free to swing as he walked.

Then, without a word, they all stopped. "I assume since you stopped that you all saw what I just saw?" asked Schram.

"Aye," replied the dwarf, "but what was it?"

Lars again pulled his sword. "I am not sure, but it was big and fast."

"Do you sense anything, Schram?" asked Jermys.

"No, my friend. It is as if there is nothing ahead of us, though I know there is."

Maldor joined his son with club drawn. "Lars and I will go on ahead. We will verify the area is safe and then call you forward."

Schram saw the immediate response in Jermys's reaction but did not let the dwarf speak. Instead, in a soft voice, he simply stated, "No, this is a trip we will all do together. Whether you scout ahead or not, we are all going forward, so staying together is the best option."

Schram thought Maldor may protest again, but the warrior simply nodded, motioned to his son to take the rear, and he would lead. Schram, in turn, was about to protest again and then stopped and let the maneth move forward. He and Jermys took positions shortly behind, followed closely by Lars, his scimitar now drawn and at the ready.

Although there were no trees for all practical purposes, there was a clear path and area for them to go. If they went too far to the right, then they were in some treacherous rocks; and conversely, too far left, and they would fall off a cliff. They had about the width of a large dragon belly to traverse between and then into what appeared to be a large flat open area emitting some sort of unnatural light.

They stepped through the narrowest point when Schram saw the maneth stop cold in his tracks.

Every muscle appeared frozen when Maldor said, "What in the world?"

Schram was about to ask what had affected him so as he stepped through and saw what was before them all now. The human stepped in front of his friend. His voice was strong but cold. "Almok, I thought I might find you here."

The black canok with the white diamond patch turned his lips slightly upward, revealing his sharp teeth. In a voice they could all hear, the canok replied, "Yes, we assumed you would have realized your failure so long ago."

"My failure to let you go when I could have defeated you? Yes, I should have seen that long ago."

The canok laughed slightly before replying, "Had you defeated me, would I be here now?"

Schram stepped forward, showing no fear. "Almok, whether I destroyed you twenty years ago or I destroy you now makes no difference to me. I am more powerful than you, and I always will be."

He did not lose his smile, and his tone was deathly cold like the air around him. "Not here, boy."

With that, Almok shot a bolt of energy directly toward Lars. He lifted his scimitar as a reflex, but the weapon had no effect blocking the force. The young maneth was struck and thrown fifteen feet back to the edge of the cliff. Maldor ran over and grabbed his arm to secure him, but the young maneth's arm was limp. The jolt had been enough to push him unconscious, and Lars remained motionless on the ground.

Maldor turned, lifting his club in the same motion but stopping when he saw Schram moving to engage the canok. Schram lifted his hand and began to incant a spell. Although he could feel power within him, it was different. It was as if he could not quite reach the final words and thoughts. He knew them, but he could not produce them. He gripped his staff harder and tried to pull the power of Anbari through his connection. Nothing happened. Almok laughed.

"Now, boy, now you understand. My brother was a fool. You were to be the one to defeat us? You can't even stop me from killing everyone with you should I so choose." He paused, and his eyes scanned the group. "And trust that I will kill you all, in time. First, my queen and king wish to have words with you. They will be disappointed, however. My queen especially wanted that weak elf to be here as well. We will need her bow." He turned to Schram with a sinister smile and tone. "But worry not, oh great Schram. I will hunt her down and kill her as well, if she is not dead already."

Almok was about twenty steps from Schram, who had not moved, but Jermys had slowly maneuvered his way between the rocks and the cliffs and found himself at an angle from the canok, but only about half the distance that Schram was from him. Jermys had already removed his hatchet and gripped it tight. Without a word, he charged at the canok with axe drawn. He did not scream a battle cry or issue any such warning. His goal was simple. He needed the blade of his hatchet to reach the skin of the canok. He leaped into the air with a flight that would take him directly into Almok's belly. He did not care if he killed, injured, or just bounced aside, the move was to determine what they would be able to do here. It was clear that Schram could not use magic, or at least could not use it yet. They needed to find out if they had any grounds to fight and win.

Lars was still unconscious, and both Schram and Maldor were completely taken by surprise by their friend's move. Almok equally was taken by surprise, but even as close as he was to the canok, Jermys still did not have enough time to reach him unnoticed. Almok knelt down quickly moments before the dwarf reached him and issued an immediate short spell. Jermys hit a barrier around the canok as if he had struck a wall. His hatchet screeched with the contact, creating the sound of steel striking the strongest armor. Jermys followed his weapon's path and hit the invisible barrier with the full weight of his body. Upon impact, he bounced back and found himself flailing to the ground. His hatchet was dislodged, and his body hit with such an impact that he tumbled back and came to rest several steps away from the canok.

Almok leaned down and picked up the Hatchet of Claude in his teeth then flipped it with his head onto his back. "Thank you, Jermys. We needed this." Turning to the others, he added, "You may all give me your weapons and the staff now, or I will simply take them later, pulling them from the hand of your dead body if you prefer."

Schram stared back toward his best friend's brother. "You will never possess my staff. That much I am sure of." He turned back to his companions. "Are you all well?"

Jermys was pushing himself up with an angered look on his face. Schram could tell the loss of his hatchet was going to be an issue. "Jermys, don't! We will get your hatchet back."

His eyes turned to Schram, but it was the canok who spoke, "Yes, dwarf, come take it from me. I am unarmed. I have it resting on my back. You can just take it."

"Jermys," Schram again stated, "stay with me. There will be another time."

The dwarf turned his eyes to Almok then back to Schram. "I am sorry, my friend. I cannot allow this."

Schram lunged at the dwarf but was too late. He had moved quickly, more quickly than Schram would have thought possible. However, he was not so quick to reach the canok who had been expecting the move. With a short incantation, a bolt of energy shot from the four-legged creature into Jermys chest, sending him through the air to rest motionless on the thin layer of snow near the entrance.

Maldor moved quickly to the dwarf's side. Lars had begun to stir and was making it to his feet. Schram's eyes locked on the older maneth as he sat over the dwarf. Maldor looked up with a solemn expression on his face. His head shook slightly. "He lives, but his heartbeat is light."

"Of course, he lives. If I wanted him dead, he would be as such." Almok took a step closer to Schram and directed this comment to him. "Can we stop this pathetic display? You have no power here. You are helpless against us. We will not let you leave, and in time, you will join us to save your friends, or you will all die. It is your decision."

Schram took a step closer to Almok, now only a few steps away. "Who is us?"

Almok smiled. "Do you really mean you do not know? My brother was a fool. What did he think you could ever do against us?"

"Take me to my mother and father, Almok. Take me to them now."

"Oh, I will, Schram. I will."

***

Alan took another bolt from the two-headed beast. One head had been destroyed and just vanished; the other was flailing wildly in the air, firing bolts of energy in every direction. Alan stared across the shoreline and saw massive amounts of casualties, but he also saw many of the two-headed creatures being taken out. No magical weapons were having any effect, but if hand-to-hand combat was possible, a solid strike to the head basically shut that head down. Dragon fire also caused the flying beasts to head to the ground. When the creatures struck land, the elves, maneths, and humans could attack.

All that being said, they had found a way to destroy them, but there were simply too many. And with every creature they brought down, the allied fighters lost five. Alan could see it was a losing battle.

Alan turned and engaged a beast to his side and then felt a pain, as deep as any he had felt before, strike his back, sending him crashing into the sand. He rolled slowly over to face the four eyes of a two-headed dragon staring back at him. The other creature he had engaged moved over and also stood beside the first, now making eight eyes locked on the fallen human leader. Alan raised his sword vertically in front of him, holding it low by his belly and having the blade move up and split his eyesight. The dragoks seemed pleased with this, and one of the four heads arched back for a final burst of power and energy. Alan closed his eyes, and then he heard the beast explode with another burst. His arms tensed as if to brace from the impact, although

221

he knew nothing he could do would protect him from the creature's wrath. However, the impact never came. He opened his eyes to see Denisi pounding on one of the creature's remaining heads and Fehr tearing the flesh from the other. Alan leaped to his feet and swung his sword, severing all the remaining heads from the body. The creatures both vanished.

The dragon Tornac they had been riding on entered a vicious fight with some other nearby dragoks while Stellanta and Phredder did the same. Another dragon joined them, and although they were not necessarily tipping any scales, if nothing else, they were keeping those nearby busy. Angus came running up the beach as Denisi and Alan fell into each other's arms.

"Denisi," began Alan, panting slightly, "I cannot believe you are here, but I have to say, I am glad you to see you and the dragons you brought."

She smiled, and even in this time of battle against an overwhelming number of powerful creatures, Alan could not believe how beautiful she was. This, though, lasted only a second as a blast struck at their feet. Fehr leaped by and motioned to them, but with the explosions and noise, it was unclear if any words were spoken.

Without another thought, Alan leaped forward. "Come on," hollered the human, motioning to Angus and Denisi. "We have to get off this wide-open beach, or we will be cooked."

As they ran up the hill toward the city, Angus led the way with Denisi and Alan side-by-side immediately behind him. Denisi turned as she ran. "Where is Geoff? Where is my husband?"

Alan answered without changing his stare from directly forward, ensuring he did not lose a step as he moved. "Mi-Kevan. He went to find the magician."

"Why?" she asked in return.

Alan now turned and faced her as he moved. "Because in the heat of a fierce battle, when we were bordering on a full retreat with no other options, he decided he needed to go." Alan actually smiled slightly. "My only assumption is he believes the warlock can help us."

Denisi smiled slightly in return. "Where is he now?"

"I am not sure. I think—"

Alan was cut off when Angus interrupted, pointing, "There, coming through the city center with the cloaked man and one of those creatures following them."

"Hurry," shouted Alan in return. "We have to provide him some cover."

The three ran hard directly in the path of their friend. The dragok was beating a path right for them and was already arching one of its necks to fire a bolt when Denisi's arrow struck true. The one head vanished, causing the other to have just a moment of hesitation. Denisi sent another arrow flying, and it too struck its mark; but this time, the head only surged in anger. The arrow, not the head, melted away. The creature arched its neck and sent a bolt directly at the maneth. It hit him square in his back and sent him falling forward. Mi-Kevan tried to grab him, but he could not reach him in time. The magician turned to face the flying beast to see it arching its head back for another shot, this time directed at him. Mi-Kevan lifted his hands and sent a shot of his own at the creature's head, and although it struck true, the magic seemed to be absorbed or lost within the dragok.

The magician immediately turned to the others. "Now you must strike its head with some force with no magic behind it. These creatures are not of this world. They are created by magic and therefore cannot be destroyed by magic. They also learn. An arrow may work once, but fire or sword must be used to destroy the other. They are two creatures as one. Independent but together."

As he said his last statement, the magical burst previously being aligned struck him in the back. The magician vanished.

Angus had continued running and had moved in closer to the flying creature while it watched its attack on Mi-Kevan end in the wizard's vanishing. Confused by the situation, the creature hovered for just a moment, trying to determine if its attack was successful or if the magician simply had the ability to escape as such. In that moment, Angus released his dagger and struck the dragok between the eyes. His head turned for just a second before the entire beast disappeared.

"Geoff!" shouted Denisi. She ran to his fallen and motionless body.

Carefully she lifted his head and placed her arms underneath to provide some cushion and used one hand to stroke his mane.

He coughed slightly, and some blue blood spilled from his mouth. "Hey, Denisi, what are you doing here? I've got everything under control."

She smiled. "I know you do, my love. I just thought you might want some company as you win this battle."

"Alan has been sticking to me like tree sap," he replied. "To say it most simply, your company is a major improvement."

She stroked his hair again, and she could tell although he was trying to make light of the situation, his injuries were grave. "Are you okay? Should we move you to shelter?"

Geoff's face turned slightly downward. "No, my dear, there is no shelter here right now." He tried to look around. "Where is Mi-Kevan? These creatures are magic-based. I am sure of it. We need him to tell us how to defeat them."

Alan knelt down beside his friend. "He has told us, but he is also gone. We do not know if he lived or not. He was struck by the creature's magic and disappeared. Before that, he told us they cannot be killed with magic. They may only be defeated by multiple attacks from different weapons, but not magic-based."

Geoff's eyes closed for a moment then opened as if he was fighting the most painful attack he had ever felt. His voice cracked as he coughed again, causing more blood to rise. His words were choppy and difficult to understand, but their meaning was caught with all of them. "Then spread the word, Alan. This is your city. You are the leader. Lead the humans, maneth, and elves to victory. If there is a way to get word to Schram, then do it, for I am certain he faces the same."

Tears filled Denisi's eyes. "No. Please don't leave me, Geoff. Please stay with me."

The maneth stared at his wife and then felt four soft feet walking up his body. His eyes fell to Fehr. The rodent knelt on the big maneth's chest. "I will watch over her, Geoff. She will be well."

He smiled and looked back to his wife. "You see, my love, you will be fine. I will always love you." He reached underneath his breastplate and pulled out a small pouch. I told Stepha I had this. She understood."

He closed his eyes as his last breath split his lips.

Parents

Schram knelt down on one knee but only for a moment. He had felt a great pain; then it passed. Next to him were his friends, Lars, Maldor, and Jermys. Both Jermys and Lars were in pain, but neither showed it. In front of him were three creatures: two dragons and a canok. For the first time in as long as he could remember, he was in the presence of his "human" mother and birth father, neither of whom he ever knew as they truly were, or as they truly were now.

Bjork was a huge black dragon. Schram remembered Khaled said he was able to alter his color, but he believed this was his true color. His eyes sat well on top of his head, and his tail was long, longer than any dragon tail Schram had ever seen. His eyes were cold, hard, and built on fire. Drool occasionally spilled from his mouth in the form of molten ash. Schram did not know if that was simply nature or if he was doing it now for effect. Whichever the case, it did prove to be an ominous sight.

Next to him was Almok. Smug is the best word to describe the canok. Schram thought back to that day at the Black Pool, the day he let Almok walk out the door when he could have simply defeated him. Why did he do that, he wondered? Did he want Almok to take Kirven's place as his best friend? Did he simply want to believe Almok was good? Did Almok being good make Kirven good as well? All these questions rushed through Schram's mind in only moments and as quickly vanished with the telepathic message from the black canok.

Stop asking your questions. I have been one step ahead of you from the beginning. You cannot defeat me. You cannot even be in my presence without knowing that I know more than you.

The message seemed to bring Schram out of his trance, and his eyes moved to the other dragon. A huge creature as well but not as large as the black. She was blue and green, softer colors but still dark in nature. She appeared strong and determined. Her stare was different from that of the other two. She seemed inquisitive about the group before her, but her eyes were locked on just one.

She moved her head down much closer to Schram. Her eyes seemed to be staring inside him; they were so close. He could have reached out and touched her nose, but he did not flinch.

"Do you remember me, Schram? For it has been a long, long time. The last words I said to you were, 'Trust in yourself what you are about to undertake. The knowledge within you is great, and save you it can.' Those words were meant to help you reach your destiny with me today."

The dragon's voice was soft and caring—and familiar to Schram. He took a step back and replied, "I do recognize those words, but you are not my mother."

She smiled and moved her head back toward her body. "Perhaps this will help you remember."

She closed her eyes and said a few words, and in moments, she was standing before him as Queen Suzanne, queen of Toopek and mother to Schram Starland. "This is the only form I took for your entire life."

Schram's knees became weak. He knew that she had the power to shape-change, and this power gave her the ability to be his mother today, even if it was just a masquerade. However, somehow he knew she had been the mother he had always known. Despite what she truly was, the love he held for her filled his mind and clearly showed in his demeanor as he looked at her now.

When she saw this change, her eyes became soft and her voice even more gentle. "My son, I know I did not bear you as my own, but I raised you as my son. When your birth mother took my place, she did not realize I too was powerful. She did not realize I would recognize her actions. She believed I would be your mother in spirit and mind. I did not think that was possible. How could I love you when you were not truly my son? But I did. Although I did not intend to love you as only a mother could love their child, I truly did. I was always there for you. You are my only son."

Schram did not know how to respond. He had anticipated a vicious fight, a battle of immeasurable strength pitting good against evil. He did not expect to find a mother who was exactly as she had always been—a mother who did not wish to fight but wished to love him. His eyes were locked on hers until he forced them to look away. He saw his friends staring at him. He could not tell if they were disappointed that he clearly loved her or simply in shock at what they just saw. He was confused, and his mind was lost. Part of him wanted to run to her and fall into her arms. The other part wanted to just run away.

The black dragon had not spoken but seemed to be intrigued with Schram's response. "You would not know me, for until this moment, we have never laid eyes on each other."

Schram's eyes swung to the dragon who had spoken. "I have only known one black dragon, and that evil creature was killed by my hands. He had brought death and destruction to everything I value. Although I believe I know who you are, or who you claim to be, if you are the source of the same destruction and pain pushed across this world, the same fate for you I will hope to achieve."

It was interesting to all how quickly Schram's tone and words had changed. The bond with his mother was still there, regardless if she was party to this evil. The bond with the dragon who may very well be his birth father was clearly absent.

The black dragon smiled. "My son, you may deny your heritage no longer. You may feel love for Suzanne, and you may feel love for your birth mother, Hawthorne, and you may not wish to hold any such feelings for me, Bjork, the most powerful dragon on all of Troyf, but you cannot deny your blood. You breathe because of me. Your weak, power-hungry human father could not even understand his true position in all this. He was our puppet. You are all that you are because of me. Never forget it."

His companions could see the pain brewing within him. It was clear this was not the discussion he wanted to participate in, but it was also one that was now started and could not be avoided. None of them knew what the ultimate goal was. They all thought as Schram did, that they were there to battle for life in this world. However, those they met seemed to have a different plan. An unexpected plan that did not make sense.

Jermys moved closer to Schram, as did Maldor and Lars. The dwarf, in a whisper, added, "We are with you, Schram. Whatever you decide, we are here."

"Hush, dwarf!" shouted Bjork. A bolt of energy shot from his mouth and struck the dwarf hard in the chest, sending him flying into some nearby rocks. "You will not speak again."

The others turned to the dwarf, but it was Maldor who reached him first. "He is not well. He lives, but his breath is broken and whistles as he fights for air."

Another bolt shot from the black dragon, striking Maldor on the side, sending him to the ground several paces from the fallen dwarf.

"Dad!" shouted Lars.

Schram raised his hand. "Lars, do not speak and do not move. Remain by my side."

Maldor and Jermys were both motionless. Lars wanted to run to his father but heeded Schram's warning.

The black dragon tilted his head. "You are foolish. You have no strength here. You have nothing here. Bring me your staff, Schram, and, boy, bring me your scimitar. I have taken the hatchet and will take the hammer. Anbari's failure is now complete."

"As is Kirven's," stated Almok. "He put his trust in you, Schram, and you have failed him as well."

Schram turned to stare both at Almok and Bjork, though he felt a pull to look at his mother. His voice was much stronger than he would have thought possible, and its tone did seem to surprise that of those before him as well. "I told you already you will never possess my staff. As for failures, we will see what our future holds. There is much left to do this day and many questions unanswered."

Almok fired a bolt of energy at Schram who lifted his hand in defense. He felt the pain of the strike initially then something changed. There was power within him. A power he had not felt before. Power he had not drawn on before. He felt it growing. He felt it falling under his control. A whimper was heard, and the energy directed at Schram stopped.

He lifted his eyes to see Almok on the ground but quickly struggling to get to his feet. "Stepha," shouted Lars.

Schram swung his eyes up to see Stepha lifting her elven bow, not the Anbarian bow, up toward the two dragons. "Do you wish this upon you as well?"

The black dragon and Queen Suzanne both smiled while Almok climbed back to his feet; the arrow that had been lodged in his belly vanished as he moved. Bjork looked toward Suzanne and nodded, giving her the approval to act. Suzanne turned back to Stepha and without a word lifted her hand toward the elf while still in flight. No energy could be seen, but something struck the flyer elf, grabbed her like a fist, and tossed her helplessly toward the side of the cliff. She struck the ground and bounced to come to rest right on the edge. One very soft push would easily send her over.

"I never liked you, Stepha," rang Suzanne's voice. "You took my son from me. You took a part of him because your thieving father thought he was so smart as to take my son. I have waited for this day a long time."

"You will not hurt her, Mother," interrupted Schram. "She is my wife."

"Correction, my son. She was your wife. If you wish her or any of your friends to live, then you will give us your weapons now. You will denounce your allegiance to them, and you will join us. Together, we will make Troyf a place all can live, under our leadership."

"Under your dictatorship," stated Stepha. Suzanne's eyes shot back at the girl. "The next time you speak will be your last. Do not underestimate me or believe I am bluffing. I would have already killed you, but it would have delayed Schram coming to the realization he had no other option."

"No other option to do what?" interrupted Schram. "You are all out of control. I am not going to join you. I do not even want to be near you. My life is not with my mother whom I truly never knew any more than it is with the father I just learned I had. You are trying to destroy Troyf, not save it."

Suzanne was about to speak again, but the larger black dragon made a soft sound that halted her speech. Bjork stepped a little closer and lowered his head directly in front of Schram. "Listen, son, because I will say this only once. You will join us. I have foreseen it. The reason I know this is because you love your friends. In fact, it is your weakness. You will not wish them all dead. Some have already died. I am sure you have felt the state of your—I mean our—old home. You have already realized we have aligned all of your loyal races in one place. We have sent our dragoks to destroy them. It is only a matter of time now, and they will all be dead. They will all be as dead as your friend Geoff of the maneths."

He stole a quick glace toward Lars and smiled. He only paused a moment before continuing in the same point-of-fact tone, "I can stop the attack now should you swear yourself to us. I can lift Stepha over the cliff and then let her drop. I can, in one breath, end what is left of Maldor's and Jermys's life. I can make Lars's fur coat burst into flames and watch him fight for way too long in pain only to die in the end. I can even kill your unborn baby first, let you and Stepha truly understand you can do nothing to stop me, and then, for fun, kill Stepha too."

Schram's blood began to boil, but he did not want to show it. However, his feelings terrified him more than anything the dragon had said. What terrified him the most was that he thought the creature may be speaking the truth. He did not know how to stop them. He had felt the pain for Toopek as well as Geoff's voice; then it was suddenly silenced. He was not sure what direction to go. He had started to believe the only way to save his friends and to save Toopek was to join them.

"Yes, Schram. I feel your conflict. Come to your mother and me as a family."

Schram wanted his voice to be strong and defiant, but he believed the words sounded desperate. "You have no power over me. You cannot blackmail me. I will die before I join you."

"Schram?" issued a soft voice from the side.

"Yes," he paused then added with a bit of a tremor in his voice, "Mother."

She smiled at that. Her voice was still soft, and she had stepped closer to Schram just like Bjork had. "You are not thinking clearly. If you die, we kill everyone else and take the weapons. If you fight, we kill everyone and take the weapons. If you hold strong against us, we continue to blackmail you by killing your friends most violently. I do not want to kill my grandchild or the woman you love so dearly, but I will. Finally, should we kill them all and you still won't join us, then we will kill you as well. There is only one way your child lives, and that way is for you to join us. So I ask you for the last time, do you choose to have your child live or die?"

TOOPEK

"Denisi, we have to go," shouted Alan. "We can't hold them. There are too many."

"I can't," she replied, crying.

"Yes, you can," he issued again. "You have to. He is gone, but you are not."

She heard his words but did not care. She sat on the ground where Geoff's body had been. She had already prepared it, and it had been well received, but now she was simply alone.

Angus grabbed Alan's shoulder. "Those five just turned. They are coming our way. We will not be able to stop them."

Alan motioned for him to leave toward the city center and take as many of the maneth and elf warriors with him as he could. "Find a corner. Find a bunker. Find somewhere to hold up where you cannot be attacked from behind. When you have it, open fire on anything that flies by. I will tend to Denisi."

"No," stated Fehr from the side. "You all go. Leave me with Denisi. I will get her out. I promised her husband I would, and I am confident I will not fail."

Alan was about to protest, but when he saw the rat's stare, he knew Fehr would have a better chance than anyone. Further, he needed to help this stronghold. It was going to be their last.

The humans, elves, and maneth in the area led by Alan and Angus hastily ran toward the only cover they could find. It was crude and not perfect, but it served the purpose he wanted. It could only be attacked from one side. They all took positions along the front. They had a band of about thirty-five. They were all armed with bows, swords, clubs, or some combination therein.

From their position, they could see all the way through the city and a portion of the shoreline. The destruction was extensive. The wall protecting the city had been an early target. Although it appeared the goal was to allow trolls and goblins into the city, defending those creatures proved easy, and their attacks ended quickly with them fleeing back into the trees. However, it did pull the attention of those in the city away from the two-headed dragon creatures attacking, which allowed this group to penetrate further. When that happened, the tides changed quickly and Toopek took on heavy damage and casualties. As Alan spanned the foreground, he saw hundreds of bodies. His eyes fell, and for a moment, all was silent.

"Don't give up yet," stated Angus, placing his hand on his leader's shoulder. "Look, there are three bands like ours, all taking positions similar to ours. Word has spread. This is how we are going to take them down."

"I like your thoughts, but look at the sky. There are so many of them."

"More likely even you, with shall we say, your less-than-accurate shot, won't miss."

A few around chuckled, but all truly looked for guidance from Alan. He felt all eyes and ears upon him and turned to the small group. "My friends, we have fought bravely. Now is the time we must decide. Are we going to defy the tremendous odds against us and do the impossible?"

His voice got stronger with each word, and his expectation would be a resounding cheer in response. Instead, however, he received only one reply, from his old friend Denisi. "Yes, we will win this thing right here, right now."

Her response incited several others around to lift their bows and swords in the air and begin to shout. Alan lifted his sword as well and yelled, "For Toopek!"

Now the area erupted. Alan lifted his sword again and turned to the approaching creatures. "Let's go!"

They roared behind him and began running directly at the oncoming dragoks. Magic balls of energy landed at their feet, causing several to be thrown aside as they released everything from arrows to rocks toward the flying beasts. The battle was most possibly the fiercest Troyf had ever seen in its history, and certainly the deadliest. Then, without warning, the dragoks on all three fronts simply stopped for a moment and stared at those defending the city.

***

Schram stared at the three before him. "If I join you, how do I know you will still not kill my friends?"

"Schram, no," stated Lars. "You cannot join those who wish to destroy our land. They will not uphold any deals. Even if they would, I do not want to live in their world."

Suzanne tilted her head in an aggressive nature toward the maneth. "Hush your speech, boy. Trust that it is not you which brings the indecision to him. It is the unborn life of his child. His value there is not matched."

Schram was going to comment but was cut off as Suzanne turned to face him. "Your time is up, Schram. You are clearly too brainwashed to see what is best for our world. Your ignorance will be your undoing, as well as your friends." She paused and then raised her hand, causing a three-dimensional picture to appear before him. "Look, Schram. Take a good long look at Toopek. The next time you go there, if you ever get the chance, the city, as well as all your friends, will be dead."

The scene his mother showed brought Schram to his knees. He saw destroyed buildings, fire, creatures flying freely through the city, and then his eyes saw it. He knew she had done it on purpose, but he also could feel it was real. At the center of the scene he was being shown, he saw Denisi kneeling down holding the mane of Geoff in her hands. The maneth warrior was dead.

Bjork, Almok, and Suzanne all saw the reaction. Telepathically, between only the three of them, Suzanne said, *We have him.*

"No, you don't," replied a strong voice from behind Schram, which all could hear.

Bjork raised his head. "Cameron." He smiled a sinister grin. "I never thought I would see you again. And even never would not have been long enough."

Cameron did not respond to the black dragon and instead whispered a short comment to Schram. Schram then walked over to where Jermys and Maldor sat motionless. Within moments, and even a little to Schram's surprise, Maldor and Jermys began to stir. Stepha walked over to join them. Despite their absence of power with the ineffectiveness of their weapons and Schram's depleted abilities, the group of companions still appeared as a powerful force. They stood tall and showed an unbridled confidence.

Bjork saw this and roared, "What do you expect to happen here, Cameron? You are all Anbari. You have nothing here."

Cameron smiled. "It is good to see you, old friend. Do you remember so long ago, when we were young? Do you remember how close we were?"

Bjork did not smile in return. "Do not try to bring up nostalgia, Cameron. That friendship was lost long ago when you made your choice. You could have stood by my side, and instead you banished me to this life. I never dreamed you would come here. I never dreamed I would be able to watch you die."

Cameron replied telepathically. *This scene was set in motion over two hundred years ago. Nothing can stop it now, but your confidence that you control the outcome will be your undoing.*

Suzanne now lifted her eyes to meet the much larger Cameron's gaze. "Why didn't you join us, Cam? The three of us could have done it. Look at the destruction your decision caused. We had to bring the canoks into the mix. We have had to go to such drastic means to make things as they should be."

Cameron's eye's softened on the woman who was still in human form, although Schram believed that Cameron only saw her as a dragon. "Suzanne, it is truly good to see you, regardless of the situation. To lay my eyes upon you one last time means the world to me, but you know as well as I do that there was no other choice I could make. I am the first son of Anbari. My father was powerful enough to rule all of Troyf in those years, but instead he fought for peace within all kinds. That is buried within me so deep no love for you"—he turned toward Bjork—"or any for my friends would ever break that mold. My choice, as you both say it, was not a choice at all."

Bjork cut Suzanne off before she could speak again. Ignoring most of the comment, he centered on one sentence. "So you do understand that this will be the one last time you see her. You know you will never leave this place alive."

"There are many forms of life, Bjork, and I do not know for sure how any of us standing here now will leave."

Bjork turned back to Schram. "Enough of this banter. The fact that Cameron is here changes nothing other than to improve my feelings after we are done. The situation is simple. There is nothing on Troyf that can stop us except the weapons of the ring. The four of you possess those weapons. I have brought you here for one reason and one reason only. You will give me those weapons, or I will take them from your dead bodies. I will talk no longer. Schram Starland, instruct those around you to give me the weapons. If you do not, as we have the hatchet already, the dwarf will die first."

Schram stole a glance to Cameron and then to Jermys. The dwarf stood tall, without showing any fear. He was prepared to die right now. He was prepared to charge and be killed. He was prepared for whatever Schram stated, except what came out.

"Jermys, had you not already lost your hatchet, I would be telling you to drop it now."

The dwarf looked at his friend and fought with a response. Almost pleading, he replied, "Schram, no. We can't."

"Yes, Jermys, you can," echoed Bjork's voice. Turing to the others, he added, "Drop them or the dwarf dies."

Jermys turned to his friends and said one word: "No!" He stood tall in front of the dragon. "Strike me down now, dragon, for I have lived the life I was meant to."

Schram ignored the comment and motioned to the others. "Please, everyone, drop them."

Reluctantly, Stepha and Lars removed their weapons and placed them at their feet. Schram remained holding his staff, and Maldor did not move. Bjork turned his attention to the maneth. "Maldor, your king is already dead. Your village will look to you for leadership in these changed times. Do you really want to suffer the same useless fate as Geoff? There is no point to die this day. I will still take the hammer."

Maldor stared at the large black dragon, who had moved his body to face him almost directly. "I no longer possess the hammer. I returned it to the guardians as was prophesied."

"What!" shouted Bjork angrily. Schram was surprised by this immediate response, and it was definitely not expected by any of the group as their faces all showed the same. His reaction was so quick and so intense Schram needed to contemplate this. All the weapons, he thought. For some reason, he has to have them all.

"I don't believe you, Maldor, because you would never give up what provided you so much power. You must learn that to lie to me is to be punished, immediately and severely."

A bolt of energy was shot at Lars, striking him across the breastplate. The jolt sent the young maneth flying in the air even further than previously.

Maldor shouted just as Lars's limp body struck the ground motionless. "No!" he cried and started running to him.

Another bolt struck right in front of Maldor's feet. "Take another step, and he dies. Turn and face me, maneth."

Maldor stopped and turned to stare directly into the black dragon's eyes. Maldor's arms were tight and arched. His muscles bulged. Schram could tell he was going to explode. He was going to attack the dragon with his bare hands. He was going to be killed.

Bjork's voice was cold and hard. "I ask you one more time. Give me the hammer."

Maldor's voice carried nothing but hatred. "I don't have it. Use your magic to search me. The hammer is in the Realm of Darkness. If you want it, you have to go there to get it."

Cameron now spoke, "But he can't go there, Maldor, for he would never be allowed to leave." He turned to Bjork. "You will never possess all the weapons, just as the prophecy said you would not."

For the first time, Schram saw a slight loss of confidence or confusion in the black dragon's demeanor. It did not last long, but it was definitely there. He swung his eyes to Lars, who still had not moved. He then went back to Schram.

Schram glared at the dragon. "I sense your confusion. Your plans have no chance of success. You will never find true safety knowing that the hammer remains. A weapon of Anbari and Ku that can still bring about your death. You will have to hide here indefinitely. What kind of ruler has to hide? Even if you kill us all, the hammer will still be there. Our children, our grandchildren— someone someday will recover it and use it to destroy you. You will never be safe."

Cameron smiled as he saw Schram growing with confidence and understanding. Bjork roared in anger, "You fool boy, I do not need the hammer. I can rule without it. I have my power, which is greater than Anbari's. I will have all the other weapons. One hammer will not be able to destroy everything I will become."

Schram thought the dragon was probably correct, but this was the only thing that had seemed to strike the powerful creature, and letting it go was not an option. "I guess we will see." He turned to Suzanne. "Mother, I love you. I do not know why you must join in this quest for power over the land, but before we part or one of us dies, I wanted you to know that I did."

Cameron again smiled as he recognized what Schram was doing.

Suzanne's face softened. "And I love you too, Schram, but I am not the mother you believe me to be. You know my life as being the same as yours. I am not human. I had lived for hundreds of years before you were born. I raised you. I love you as my own, but my heritage is strong."

"As is mine. I am the son of Hawthorne and Bjork. Until I touched this staff, I was not Anbarian. As I throw down this staff, I no longer will be."

Stepha was about to protest, but then the elf understood. Anbari's powers are absent here, but Hawthorne's and Bjork's were not. Maldor too seemed to understand, but Jermys looked on in disgust. Cameron closed his eyes and seemed to be in a conversation with someone, though no words were being spoken. Bjork smiled. "So, boy, you do have no spine. I sensed the dwarf would have attacked me with his hands, and you throw down the only chance you had and instructed those with you to do the same. You are no enemy. I would respect an enemy."

Jermys was about to do just what the dragon implied when Maldor placed a hand on his shoulder. Softly he whispered, "Relax, my friend. Let's see how this all plays out."

The dwarf calmed slightly, but it was clear he was not completely on board.

Bjork took a step closer to Schram. "Now watch what your foolishness has brought you and your friends."

Moments later, Stepha, Jermys, and Maldor were all on the ground with sharp pains in their chests where the pulses had struck. None were dead or unconscious, but all were clearly in pain. Suzanne appeared distraught, but Schram did not feel it would ever be enough to change the direction. She was too far entwined in Bjork's wrath to ever pull free. However, he knew that he needed to see that with his own eyes to know it for sure. Almok had remained motionless for most of the recent conversation. He appeared to be smiling now, as a parent would for his child being successful. In this case, Schram believed it was seeing the failure of Kirven's plan coming to form before him. Something Schram may have always underestimated was the jealousy Almok felt for Kirven. That jealousy drove the black canok to better him somehow. Perhaps this was the only way he found.

Bjork now moved so close to Schram's face he could feel the warm breath and moisture across his nose. The area around became distorted, and then Schram was in the full shape of a dragon, as large as Bjork, still only inches apart. The black dragon smiled. "So it is time. The oppression has come full circle, and it comes down to this. I believe I will kill the young maneth first."

Schram issued a magical shot that was instantly blocked by the combined powers of Almok and Suzanne, creating a shell around Bjork. The black dragon laughed. "So you have some powers here, after all, but they are no match for the three of us." He turned toward Lars and shot a bolt that actually exploded in the air as it traveled; it was very powerful. Maldor was still on the ground and screamed again.

Just before impact, Cameron moved with incredible speed and placed his body between that of the shot of energy and Lars. The impact was enormous and sent a ripple back to everyone, even knocking Bjork and Suzanne back and putting Almok to the ground. Cameron roared in pain, and then the clearing fell silent. Schram ignored the black dragon and ran toward where Cameron had fallen. "Brother, are you well?"

Cameron lifted his head and smiled. "Schram, now is your time." His voice was choppy, and Schram could tell the injuries were deep. Cameron noticed his concern and shook his head and whispered, "Do not worry, my brother. Help is on the way to Toopek, and you hold the secret here. I do not know the answer, but our father saw this. Search out that which has happened. Find that which Bjork does not know and use it. Remember, Anbari knew this. There is an answer."

Cameron's eyes shut. The area grew still. A blue haze surrounded the dragon's body, lifted it in the air, and then it vanished.

"Yes," shouted Bjork. "I can't believe I did it. I killed that traitor. He will never bother us again." He turned to Suzanne. "A huge win for us, my dear. A huge win. I believed we would have to find a way to the Black Sea to defeat him. I can't believe he came to us."

"Why do you think he did that, Bjork? Just to die? Everything happens for a reason, and the reason my brother was here is an important one." All the time Schram was talking, he was trying to figure out the riddle. Anbari? What did Bjork not know or plan for? What was the answer? "You have not won."

Almok had made it to his feet. "You should be more respectful of your new king, Schram." He shot a bolt of energy at Schram, who had remained in dragon form. Schram reacted quickly, and the energy stopped before his face and spun there like a floating orb. Almok's eyes grew wide just before the energy shot back and threw him to the ground, burning much of his fur.

Schram turned to the fallen canok. "Almok, do not speak again. Understood?"

Suzanne may have turned a small smile up, but Schram could not be sure. The canok was clearly angry but also recognized the power Schram still carried and waited for Bjork's response, knowing it would be quick and decisive.

The black dragon leaned forward. "Well done, Schram. You have found some power I did not expect, but you are no match for me, much less me and your mother. Throwing a canok around is not the same as feeling my wrath." Another bolt shot from the dragon directly toward Schram this time. He tried to use the same magic that controlled Almok's attack, but this was much stronger. The strike hit Schram hard, causing him to roar and shoot fire to the sky. None of the companions had ever seen this from Schram. They had seen him become a dragon but never the innate, natural response to breathe fire in pain. It was an ominous sight for them to absorb. It was a painful experience for Schram. He was knocked to his side and was fighting to stand up, but something in his attack seemed to partially paralyze him. He was struggling to regain control when he saw the black dragon turn toward Stepha. A moment later, the elf was on the ground, paralyzed as well. Schram could feel the deadening in his legs beginning to fade, but not fast enough. He closed his eyes and concentrated, but he could not muster any magical thoughts. It appeared even his thoughts were affected by the magical attack.

Jermys was next in Bjork's view. Schram interjected as much to himself as anyone else, "Wait!"

His voice was so loud and strong it actually drew the dragon's attention. He looked at Schram questionably. "What, do you have something to offer before I kill all your friends?"

"Do you want the hammer? I could go recover it." Schram did not mean this and was simply trying to work through everything in his mind and needed time.

This statement caught the black dragon. "What, you would go to the Realm, convince them to give you the hammer for the purpose to then give it to me? The guardians would never allow that to happen. Do you think me a fool?"

"The hammer was stolen once. It could be stolen again," replied Schram.

Bjork smiled. "I know, let me give you your staff back"—he motioned to the staff on the ground in front of where Maldor now stood—"and perhaps I give all the weapons back and let you and your companions go? Maybe I should just trust you will all go and come back with the hammer?"

"That would be one alternative," added Schram, hearing the dragon's sarcasm. "Or you could keep my companions and send me on my own."

That did catch Bjork's attention, but again, only momentarily. "No, boy, I am not going to let my one prize leave here again. Today is your day, as well as your friends' day, to die."

"I wasn't done speaking yet," interrupted Schram, a tone similar to a parent speaking to a child, an interesting role reversal to those around. "Or you could see what the guardians gave us in return for the hammer."

Maldor swung his head to Schram questionably. Bjork, Almok, and Suzanne all opened their eyes wide. "What? What did they give you? Show me now, or the elf dies. No more games, boy. She dies by the count of three."

"You don't need to count. We will gladly show you." Schram had regained most of his motor skills now, and as he spoke, he took a few steps closer to his staff. "Maldor, please pull out the periapt and place it in the ground with the open end up."

Maldor was caught by this specific description, but again, he was letting this play out. Maldor dug into his pack and removed the amulet. Following Schram's guidance, he turned the figurine faceup, and with as much force as he could muster, he planted it on the ground at his feet.

Suzanne spoke first, "Bjork, what is it? Is it the Rift Amulet? Is this our passage?"

Bjork did not look concerned at first, but his expression slowly changed. "No, my dear. I am not sure what it is, but I sense something. It is a power I have not felt... No!"

TIME HAS COME

T hen, without warning, the dragoks on all three fronts simply stopped for a moment and stared at those defending the city. Denisi hollered, "What is happening? Why did they stop?"

"Because they see us," replied Kolkmeier. "And they see the thousand dragons behind us. My brother just told us it was time to come."

"Yeah!" shouted Alan, followed by cheers from all areas of the Toopekian forces.

Without another word, the ground forces commenced their attack forward. The dragoks seemed momentarily stunned but quickly reacted back into defense and attack formations. The dragons met the dragok forces head-on while Kolkmeier, Aizlan, and Kylscot all directed the attack and provided an energy shield. This was not a magical barrier as the dragoks were immune to Anbarian magic, but it was a physical barrier that worked like a one-way mirror. The ground forces could see the dragoks, but the dragoks could not see the forces. It made the dragok attacks useless. They were fighting blindly.

The dragon fire they were facing was taking a detrimental effect on the dragok army. Once one head was destroyed by fire, the next was attacked by bow fire from the ground or a vicious talon tearing through the free neck. With each second attack, the dragok vanished.

For the first time, the ground troops were slowly moving forward. There were still more dragoks than allied forces, dragons included, but the fighting level was about even.

Alan led his troops through the city and was nearing the shoreline where he would be able to join one of the other fronts, making a very strong barrier. The three sons of Anbari were spreading their web across the ocean as well now, reaching Castle Island. More dragons were appearing from over the sea, and those on land believed that all the dragons had turned. For the first time, Alan believed they had a chance.

***

"What is it?" shouted Suzanne. Almok too sensed the tension in the black dragon's voice.

Schram moved with incredible speed and agility despite the attack he had just faced. Bjork tried to stop him with another paralyzing energy bolt. However, Schram dove and quickly recovered the staff and slammed it into the hole in the amulet. Bjork's second blast struck Schram hard just as the staff was placed firmly in place.

The explosion was immeasurable. The sound was deafening, and ridges of waves shot out from the center as if a planet had crashed in the sea and spread its tidal wave across the land. Schram and his companions all went down immediately, placing their hands to their ears. Schram had lost all feeling in his body, but the sound emanating from the amulet and staff would have caused him paralysis even if Bjork's strike had not.

The black dragon, Almok, and Suzanne all screamed in pain and hit the ground just the same. Rocks in the area exploded, and the snow on the ground melted to water and then instantly dried. Trees in the distance were bent at the trunks, having their branches reach the ground, and the sound pushed outward. Schram nearly fell unconscious, and all his eyes could see was white light, as if he was staring directly into the sun. The sound and vibrations continued for what seemed like an eternity, and then, as quickly as they had been ignited, they were extinguished. There were a few moans in the area. Schram was disoriented and confused, and he felt different, but he was alive. He no longer felt paralyzed by Bjork's magic. Instead, he felt like he had been in the worst fight of his life, and he had suffered a significant loss. He was fighting to gain his surroundings while his main concern was for how everyone else was. He wondered what had happened and why he felt so strange. He felt as if part of him was gone. Then he heard the voice.

Bjork slowly stood. "No, it can't be."

"It is," replied Schram. Not knowing what it was, he thought it significant to claim that it really was, if for no other reason than to further confuse Bjork.

"What?" asked Suzanne. "What was that?"

"Use your magic, Suzanne, and you will see."

Suzanne tried to incant a spell, and nothing happened. She appeared scared. "What happened? I can't use magic."

"It's gone," replied Bjork. "Everything is gone. This fool boy destroyed all magic on Troyf." He turned to Schram. "Do you know what you have done? You have destroyed the world as we know it. Not just us but you as well. Your little group of companions that worked to keep balance. You have lost your powers as well. We are now just like everyone else."

Bjork was expecting Schram to be somewhere between scared and devastated. He was in dragon form, as was Suzanne, probably because that was their natural form. Instead of showing the fear that was expected, Schram just smiled. "Then we did bring balance. Everyone is actually equal."

"Yes, boy, equal. Which means I will kill you without magic for taking everything from me."

The dragon screamed in pain as one of Stepha's arrows lunged deep in his throat. Jermys was on the canok in moments. In one move, he recovered his axe and placed it to the creature's throat as well. Suzanne moved quickly and was within one talon swing of removing the dwarf and probably killing him with the contact when Schram did a similar move across the throat of Bjork, severing his head from his body.

"Mother, stop," shouted Schram. "This is your chance to stop the killing."

Almok did not move as Jermys was still on top of him. The canok's eyes were cold and lost and were locked on that of Schram's mother. "Do it, Suzanne. Do not let Bjork die for nothing. We can still escape."

"No, Almok, we can't." She turned to her son, who stood only a few paces from her. "I love you, Schram."

"No!" Schram replied as he saw her intent. She lifted her talon up to strike the dwarf a deadly blow. Schram did the same, and just as the tip of her talon reached the small dwarf, her head fell silently to the ground. Jermys was thrown clear, and although he bled from the impact, it was not life-threatening. Almok had leaped to his feet only to face the club of Maldor, taking him down for his last breath.

Schram fell to his knees with a tear running down both cheeks. "I love you too, Mother."

Stepha walked to her husband's side. "Are you all right, my love?"

"I am," he replied softly. "Today I killed my mother and father. What scares me is I believe it was the right thing to do."

Not wanting to interrupt but also not knowing what else to do, Maldor asked, "Is it over?"

A simple question yet carrying so much meaning. Schram turned to his longtime friend. "Yes, Maldor, I think it is."

"What about Toopek? Is Geoff really…" He couldn't finish because he could not say the word, as he knew if it was the case, he should not have spoken his name to Schram or Stepha, though Stepha was the only elf present now. Schram appeared to be nothing but dragon.

Schram nodded. "I do not wish to speak of death, but I did feel his loss. Toopek has been devastated, but the same power that removed all the magic from here will reach Toopek."

"So Toopek is safe?" asked Maldor.

"I don't know, but the two-headed dragons were conceived by magic. When that magic was destroyed, so should they have been. We should find travel back to Toopek as soon as possible."

"How will we get back?" asked Stepha.

"By dragon flight," Schram replied. "But first, will you join me?"

Stepha knew what he was talking about. Together they walked to the fallen bodies of those they knew as enemies. Schram sprinkled some elven dust on Almok and Bjork, and both disappeared into the ground as if being swallowed by something so bad that to never see it again would be too soon. They then moved to the motionless body of Suzanne. Schram said a few words and then sprinkled the dust across her face. There was a soft light, and then she vanished.

Stepha gripped Schram's leg, which was difficult when he was in dragon form, but she was realizing it might be something she would have to get used to. "You see, her heart was true. She was well accepted."

Schram was taken by this but did not speak further. He simply knelt down for the others to get on his back. They each picked up their weapons, knowing they would no longer hold the powers they once did but all now more confident with the weapons in their hands. Just before leaving, Schram said a few words and had his staff appear magically on his back.

Stepha pointed, "How did you do that?"

Schram smiled. "Anbari would never create magic that left Anbari powerless, would he?"

And they took off.

***

The fighting was intense, and although the tides were turning, it still was anyone's battle. Across the sea, those on land and air saw the disturbance. It was moving with incredible force, kicking up the water into a violent storm as it passed. Nobody knew what it was or what it was doing, but it looked like it would swallow the city whole. The sound coming seemed to be even more forceful than the actual storm, and it was growing in intensity as it came.

The dragons in the air turned from the fighting and flew toward land, all landing inside the boundaries of Toopek. The dragoks seemed particularly confused and no longer were fighting any on land and were trying to circle into a group. As the first edges of the storm struck the outermost dragoks, they instantly vanished. The wave continued through until it reached the Toopekian shoreline. The winds kicked up the sand into a violent storm, and all ran to find cover. Aizlan, Kylscot, and Kolkmeier all knelt down in the sand and closed their eyes in peace.

Some buildings that had been damaged fell by the force of the sound, wind, and other violent effects as it tore through. However, in the end, all was quiet. When the elves, maneth, and humans began to move from their places of hiding, all fighting ceased. All the dragoks were gone, and the sky was blue. The war was over.

Return home

"**I** miss him so much," said Denisi softly through tears.

Fehr rested his head curled up on her shoulder, and his belly lay completely across her lap. "Yeah, that big guy was a beast, wasn't he? He was a great leader, though."

She smiled and scratched his head as Alan and Angus walked in with Madeiris right in their wake. Denisi saw the elven king and jumped to her feet, tossing Fehr on the table in the process. "Madeiris! You are all right."

He held her tight. "Yes, I am fine, and I am so sorry to hear—" She put her finger to his lips. "I know. Everyone is telling me, but I know the loss is probably even greater for you. You and my husband were together much longer than he and I. You two had a bond that will never be broken."

"Thank you, Denisi. Your words are kind, and also the truth. My heart burns this day." He turned to all of them. "Have any of you heard from Schram, my sister, or any of the others?"

They all nodded, but it was Alan who spoke, "No, we have been busy with stabilizing the city. It has only been a day. If they are actually behind the storm that wiped out the dragoks as they were called, then they should be on their way back. Depending on how far they were, it could be several days before they return."

"I suppose," he replied. "Perhaps we should send out a search party?" He was asking more than suggesting.

Alan nodded sideways. "Maybe, but do you actually know where to send them?"

Just then, there was some commotion outside. They turned and left the small room to appear in the main courtyard of the city. It had been somewhat cleaned and rebuilt with scrap to become the city center once again, but it was more debris than anything else. They all smiled when they saw the three brothers. Aizlan nodded. "We will bid you leave now, my friends. We feel the city is safe."

Madeiris nodded in return. "But can you not stay to help us rebuild?"

"Not now, but trust that we will return soon. Now, however, we must rebuild Draag. We have a new bond with a great many dragons. It is time to pull all races together as one, as my father and my oldest brother once dreamed."

"Are you sure he has passed?" asked the elf, a sadness still carried in his tone.

"We are," Aizlan replied. "But I have felt my other brother, my half brother."

They all let out a collective breath of relief upon hearing this, but none as loud as Madeiris. They were not sure they would ever see their friends again, but the elf king felt the possible loss stronger than any of them. "Let me speak for everyone when we say we pray you are correct," Madeiris declared. The dragons nodded as Madeiris continued, "And above all, thank you, Aizlan, and to all of you. You saved this city." The elf king bowed in appreciation, causing everyone in the area to drop to one knee and lower their eyes.

The three dragons bowed in return. "No, my friends, you saved the world. Trust in the knowledge that you will be remembered for all you have done." He turned to Denisi. "Your husband was key from the beginning. What he did two hundred years ago in the original oppression to the battles over the last twenty years and again these days have saved our world. For him, we are thankful."

Denisi nodded, though tears still showed on her face. Kolkmeier stepped forward and stretched his wings. "The times are now changed. No longer will magic be used to destroy races. We have a chance to learn from all that has occurred. I hope that all races treat this as truly a second chance at life."

There was a smattering of cheers from the area as more arrived. Madeiris looked toward all three dragons with a concern growing across his face. "My friends, do you know the whereabouts of our other friends, those that went to the heart of the evil? Are they truly well?"

"Why don't you ask them yourselves?" replied Aizlan. "For there they are across the bay."

Flying in across the water was Schram, Maldor sitting high on his back with Stepha, Lars, and Jermys bringing up the rear. All wore large smiles, save for Jermys, who was being bounced around like tigon playing with a log. Even in this state, the dwarf was thrilled to be where he was. A crowd saw them on the shore and began following them to the city center, where the others had grouped. In a moment, Schram was on the ground, with his companions gripping arms, hugs, and sharing one of the best moments of their lives.

Schram had changed to his elven-human form and instantly was in Denisi's arms. No words were exchanged, but plenty were felt. Stepha and Madeiris did not let go. Both had assumed the worst for the other, and seeing them alive and well was nothing that could be described. Jermys received several greetings and shoulder pats, but nothing as emotional as the others, which pleased him. That was until Fehr leaped in the air and knocked the dwarf over, proceeding to lick every inch of his hairy face. Although Jermys fought to protest, inside he was very glad to see his closest friend again.

Maldor and Lars pulled Denisi aside, and the three together spent a great deal of time talking. Stepha walked up and handed Maldor the pouch she had been given by Geoff. She then did the same to Schram. Schram stood with the elf at his side and watched the group, and his heart felt sad. He remembered the first time he had met Geoff in the forest outside Lawren. Something about him then was special. He thought about that moment in his life. He, Krirtie, Kirven, and Geoff were all together in the forest. Now he was the only one left. He grew sad as he remembered his friends. Both Maldor and Schram placed the pouches carefully inside their armor to be opened when they were alone.

Just then, a shout came from the outskirts of the city toward the forest. "What was that?" asked Madeiris. "It sounded like a battle call for attack."

Schram listened closely while Denisi and Stepha instantly took to the air. Denisi returned quickly. "A huge battalion of dwarves approaches. Mostly the dark brothers, but some mining dwarves are with them."

Jermys grabbed his hatchet and began to run toward the outer barrier of the city. The walls had been mostly destroyed, but the pile of rock and debris still clearly identified the area. He looked across the glade leading to the trees.

Schram was next to him almost as quickly. "What do you think, Jermys?"

"Draven is the captain I left in charge of Feldschlosschen. He is there"— he was pointing to the front—"in the lead with those two dark brothers. I do not recognize them from here."

Schram was about to send a party out to intercept when Draven waved. "Ahoy, friends, do not fear us. We are united."

"Did I hear that right?" asked Stepha, landing next to them.

Madeiris also came by. "If you heard them say, 'Do not fear us, we are united,' then yes, you heard them correctly."

Jermys stood from his crouched position behind the rocks and asked,

"Do you think this could be a trap?"

Schram replied, "I feel no deception here. You chose a leader wisely, Jermys. He has united the dark dwarves and mining dwarves. This is truly a great time."

***

The festivities were great. The companions were all together celebrating and retelling their stories. They all agreed the best part of the reuniting of the dwarves was the fact they were able to deliver a seemingly endless supply of ale with their visit.

Draven had explained how once the truce had been made, they all agreed Toopek was in need of any support they could give. They had two garrisons headed this way. The first from Antaag were his troops, and the other from Feldschlosschen would be a few days behind. They were actually disappointed they did not arrive in time to help but also realized the city still needed all the support it could get to rebuild. Together, they would make Toopek the great city it used to be.

Many of their stories were in remembrance of Geoff. Each time they left the subject, something kept bringing them back. Schram retold the story he remembered at the city center, the time he first met the huge maneth. Upon completion, Denisi stood up and hugged him again.

"You know, Schram, I forgot to tell you, but that friendly woman in that bar in Lawren told me to tell you she was still there, and you should come see her."

There was still a lot of chatter going on, but all fell silent when they saw Schram's face. Stepha, Maldor, and Fehr all stood and looked right at Denisi. Schram touched her arm. "What woman? When?"

She was taken by the change and stuttered a bit as she spoke, "The bartender...we were not there long, but she specifically told me to tell you that."

Schram put both arms on her shoulders and kissed her cheek. "Thank you for telling me."

With that, he let the subject drop. He looked to the three standing and smiled, and they all knew they would not see him for a few days. Quietly, at a time when his city needed him the most, he ducked out and left, making a straight path to Lawren.

EPILOGUE

Schram stood outside the Minok Café in Lawren. He did not know why he was nervous about entering, but as he stood looking at the swinging doors leading into the bar, he could not make his feet take the next step. He heard a small voice from behind and nearly jumped from his skin.

"So you walking in or just going to hang out here looking good?"

"Fehr, what are you doing here?" he asked, his voice cracking slightly.

"Well, I figured this. You see, some people claim I tell too many stories. Not you, I realize, but some people do. And I got to thinking, I don't think it is my stories that cause the complaints, but I think I need some new stories, or at least that is what Maldor, Jermys, Stepha, Denisi, Lars, and Alan were saying. I think, though, that it was mostly Maldor and Jermys, and the others just followed suit. I am not sure why they would. Regardless, I thought that showing up with my half-brother"—he paused and looked up to Schram— "you do still consider me your half brother, don't you, Schram?"

"No, little buddy, we are not half brothers. We are brothers."

Fehr smiled broadly and continued, "So I figured I would swing by the Minok and see what all the fuss was about so I would have a new story to tell."

Schram now smiled. "Really, so the fact that part of me believes Hawthorne, the woman you see as your mother, will be in there is of no bearing on you being here?"

Fehr looked stunned, and his voice showed extreme surprise and amazement. "Hawthorne is possibly in there? How can that be? I was simply sitting alone in Toopek, and the idea came to me to head here. I had no idea—"

He was cut off by a soft voice from above. "Really, Fehr? You did not run off the minute Jermys told you where Schram had gone and why?"

"Stepha?" whispered Schram. "You are here, but why?"

She landed gently by his side and kissed his cheek. "Because there is no place I would rather be than with my husband." She smiled and held him

250

close. "But don't worry, I will remain out here and be nearby if you need me."

"I'm not waiting out here," interrupted Fehr.

Schram held her tight in return. "Nonsense, we are all going in, and for that matter, we have waited outside too long already." He walked up the rickety steps that led to the two swinging doors. He pushed through the doors with Fehr by his side and Stepha a step behind.

As the doors swung back behind them, a voice from behind the bar said, "Come on in, my sons." She stopped and smiled when she saw Stepha. "And daughter—and, oh my, soon-to-be grandson."

A tear immediately formed in Schram's eye. "A boy?"

She smiled. "I only have this moment, and I am so glad you came."

Schram walked to the counter and stood before the same voluptuous bartender who had been there since his first visit so long ago. She had not changed in appearance at all, but Schram knew the reason why. He looked around the bar and saw it was empty. "Mother, do you really have to keep that form?"

"Would you prefer this?" With seemingly no action, she instantly stood before them as a large female bandicoot.

"Yowza!" stated Fehr. "Now that is what I am talking about."

Stepha smiled broadly and knocked Fehr across the mouth. The large female bandicoot as quickly changed to the human woman he had first met in the canok homeland.

Hawthorne reached out her hand and touched Schram's cheek softly. "It is so good to see you, son, and I am so proud of you."

Schram grabbed her hand, but the feel was different, seemingly unnatural. "How are you here?"

"This is the place where I used my magic so long ago to give me a window back. I knew when it was going to be my time to pass, I would want one more moment with you. I knew I would not be here when this was all over, so therefore, I set up a time to return, like I have done so many times in your life."

"I remember," he replied. "You were my other friend when I was young. The only person other than Krirtie. You also sold us the scimitar in Gnome City and spoke to me telepathically to run when I first fought the black dragon. You also created that diversion that allowed us to get to Feldschlosschen, and you helped me in my battle with Kirven." His voice softened. "And you have always been here in the bar."

"Your insight serves you well, my son. I could not tell you, but it did not mean I was not with you."

"How long will you be here?"

"Not long. Just long enough to tell you good-bye. We will always be watching, but this will be my last time to return."

"I love you, Mother." Schram had a tear growing in his eyes.

"And I love you, Schram." She turned to Fehr and Stepha. To the bandicoot, she said, "You were always a fighter, Fehr. You performed better than we could have ever hoped. Thank you."

Fehr nodded, but he still wore a devious smile since seeing her as a bandicoot.

She took Stepha's hand. "Take good care of him, Stepha, and your son. He needs you more than he will ever admit."

"I will," she replied, also starting to cry. She turned back to Schram, stared at him as only a mother can look upon a son, and as their eyes met, she vanished.

There was silence in the room for a moment until a bartender Schram had never seen before suddenly appeared out of nowhere. "Can I get you folks something?"

They all smiled, and Schram replied, "No, thank you. I have everything I could ever need."

She went about her business as the three walked back out of the bar. When they were outside, Fehr said, "Our mom is hot. All this time, I thought her real form was a dragon, and to learn now she was bandicoot—I guess it explains a lot."

View other Black Rose Writing titles at www.blackrosewriting.com/books and
use promo code **PRINT** to receive a **20% discount** when purchasing.

BLACK ROSE
writing™

www.ingramcontent.com/pod-product-compliance
Lightning Source LLC
Chambersburg PA
CBHW010444100726
47904CB00008B/2477